MORWENNAN HOUSE

*Janet Tanner titles available from
Severn House Large Print*

All That Glisters
Hostage to Love
Shadows of the Past
Morwenna House

MORWENNAN HOUSE

Janet Tanner

Severn House Large Print
London & New York

This first large print edition published in Great Britain 2004 by
SEVERN HOUSE LARGE PRINT BOOKS LTD of
9-15 High Street, Sutton, Surrey, SM1 1DF.
First world regular print edition published 2002 by
Severn House Publishers, London and New York.
This first large print edition published in the USA 2004 by
SEVERN HOUSE PUBLISHERS INC., of
595 Madison Avenue, New York, NY 10022.

British Library Cataloguing in Publication Data

Tanner, Janet
    Morwennan House. - Large print ed.
    1. Smugglers - England - Cornwall - Fiction
    2. Cornwall (England) - Social life and customs - 18th century - Fiction
    3. Historical fiction
    4. Large type books
    I. Title
    823.9'14 [F]

    ISBN 0-7278-7347-4

Printed and bound in Great Britain by
MPG Books Ltd, Bodmin, Cornwall.

If you wake at midnight, and hear a horse's
feet,
Don't go drawing back the blind, or looking
in the street,
Them that asks no questions isn't told a lie.
Watch the wall, my darling, while the
Gentlemen go by!
Five and twenty ponies
Trotting through the dark –
Brandy for the Parson,
'Baccy for the Clerk;
Laces for a lady, letters for a spy,
And watch the wall, my darling, while the
Gentlemen go by!

Rudyard Kipling
A Smuggler's Song

The night was black as Hades. No stars shone through the blanket of storm cloud, no sliver of moon lit the narrow path through the gorse and bracken that grew thick but stunted and windswept on the sweep of headland. But for all that, the man strode out with confidence. He knew every inch of the cliff tops like the back of his hand, just as he knew every narrow gully that led to the hidden coves below, every rocky outcrop, every sea-sculpted cave. The gusting wind made him draw his cape tightly round him and bend low as he walked, and he could taste the salt, like sea spray, in the drizzling rain.

At the point where the headland jutted furthest into the sea he stopped and raised his head, listening. Far beneath him the sea roared like a wild and hungry beast. It slapped against the rocks, broke on the shoreline and dragged at the shingle in a ceaseless cycle. The wind moaned and whistled like a soul in torment. But above it he could hear no other sound – not the sound for which he was listening. The bell buoy was silent. Tonight there was no eerie clanging amidst the cacophony of the sea.

The man's jaw tightened. He knew all too well

what the silence of the bell-buoy meant. Mournful the sound it made might be, but to the crew of a ship looking for safe passage it could mean the difference between living and dying. The bell-buoy marked the treacherous rocks on which they could all too easily founder, the rocks that could tear the heart out of their vessel, turn it turtle, toss them like toys into the foaming sea. Even in thick fog or on a night as dark as this one it tolled a warning that every mariner understood, and it had saved many from a watery grave. But when it was silent there was a reason for that silence. A reason as black as the night and even more hellish, for whilst the storm was the dark side of nature, the silence of the bell-buoy was due to the wilful wickedness of evil men. Men corrupted by greed, who had fallen so low that their very humanity had been lost, and to describe them as animals would be to insult the animal kingdom.

His heart sank at the absence of the mournful clang of the bell-buoy, his stomach clenched, yet still he found himself hoping he might be wrong.

And then, as he watched, he saw the first lantern light appear on the rocky outcrop at the far side of the cove below him. A light that danced and flickered, a light that should have meant a friendly beacon to guide a ship to safe haven. Any mariner would aim for that light. They had no way of knowing that it was as false as the hearts of the men who had lit it, a will o' the wisp that would lead them to certain destruction on the rocks of this unforgiving coastline.

And he knew he could no longer doubt what in his heart he already knew.

They still walked the quiet lanes of Cornwall, those who plied this evil trade. They still holed up on moonlit nights and gathered with the storm cloud when a gale brewed out at sea. They hid in the thick sea mists, and danced on the watery graves of the sailors whose lives they took; they fought over the spoils of their wickedness.

The wreckers.

Fierce determination hardened within him, his only answer to the despair and outrage in his heart. If he could, he would have killed them, every last one, with his bare hands. But that was not possible, and even if it had been, it would do no good in the long run.

They had a leader, far cleverer than any of them. Without him they would have made a bad mistake long before now and in their debauched madness put a rope around their own necks. And as long as that leader was free, no matter how many of his disciples were caught and hanged, there would be others greedy enough to take their places.

It was this leader he wanted, and his mind was made up. He would see him brought to justice. A justice that would avenge the poor souls who had died already and ensure a safe passage for those who came this way in the years to come.

Looking at the false winking light, listening in vain for the mournful clang of the bell-buoy, he vowed it.

Smuggling was one thing. It was carried out the length and breadth of Cornwall and far beyond, and the worst that could be said of it was that it was illegal, and that it sometimes gave rise to the greed that spawned this other, evil business. He would never be able to eradicate smuggling, nor did he much want to. But he was determined to identify the leader of the wreckers and see him hanged.

If it cost him his own life, so be it. Whoever else was hurt in the process, so be it. The price would be worth the paying.

One

I am an old woman now. Sometimes I think how strange it is that I was young when the last century was old, and aged through the fresh, vibrant, hopeful years of the new century. In my lifetime I have seen so much change – now, for example, there is gas lighting where once it was all candles and rushlights. But though the story I shall tell you happened a long time ago, every detail is as clear in my mind as it was then. I shall never forget ... How could I?

The story is my story, but it is also Julia's story. A good deal of what happened to her was not known to me until much, much later. But I shall tell it to you as I now know it, little by little, so that you can make sense of the incredible events that took place.

Where to begin? Well, I suppose, at the beginning. And for me the beginning was the dream.

From the time of my earliest memory there was the dream, and it was always the same.

There was a house, a great house, built of Cornish granite, with creeper covering the walls between the tall narrow windows and shuttered attic rooms. It faced the sea, a rocky cove where the waves tugged ceaselessly at the shingle. But on every other side and above it the thickly wooded valley closed in so that even when the sun shone it was in deep twilight, a dark green world where no birds sang.

There were no people in my dream, just the house, and a terrible feeling of oppression. I was trapped, always trapped, and I did not know why. The door was ajar, there were no bars at the windows, no pack of snarling hounds between me and my freedom. But whenever I tried to leave the house and make for the patch of sunlight over the bay my feet seemed to be sinking into quicksand. And the feeling of oppression would close in like a thick blanket of sea mist, clammy and cold, suffocating me.

Once in the dream I found myself looking into a mirror. A large mirror, the size and shape of a portrait, hanging on the wall. I saw my familiar face looking back at me and yet strangely I felt it was not *my* face. Not me at all. And the feeling of being trapped was stronger than ever, as if it came from within those eyes that were not my eyes.

When I woke from the dream the trapped feeling would remain and I would lie wretchedly in my narrow bed, hugging myself with my arms and squeezing my eyes tight shut against the hot threatening tears. Crying would do no good. I could expect no comfort or sympathy from the Reverend John Palfrey or Mary, his wife, who were the closest thing to parents I had ever had. Nor did I want any. From the time I was quite small I somehow knew that no one could help me or take away the trapped feeling that came from the dream. It was something I had to bear alone, something that was a part of my life. My strange, mysterious life that was full of unanswered questions.

For I was a child with no family of my own. A child who might have been anyone, but belonged nowhere. A child who must count herself lucky to have been taken in and given a home by the Palfreys, who were, though dry and emotionless, good honest people.

They called me a foundling, and that covered a multitude of possibilities, for the Palfreys would never go into details of where I had come from or how I had fallen into their care.

'God sent you to us,' was all they would say. 'He has entrusted us with your keeping.'

And I would nod, not daring to ask more for fear they would think I was not grateful to them for putting a roof over my head and food in my mouth.

'Remember to thank the Lord in your prayers, for He is the Good Shepherd and He guided you to the safety of our little flock. Consider yourself fortunate, child, and contain your curiosity.'

They spoke as if curiosity was a sin, and indeed to them I think it was. Unquestioning belief and acceptance of the will of God were the tenets they lived by

And I was fortunate, I knew. Compared with a great many of the poor ragged village children I led a charmed life. We never went hungry when the harvest failed. We did not have to watch the head of our household sail away on a fishing boat and wonder if he would ever come home again, or see him exhausted and broken by long hours working in the tin mines. We lived in a good solid house, not a shack built of wattle or turf. There was always food on the table and wine in the decanter, and we ate from china plates and drank from china cups rather than the pewter or tin that so many folk used and which left a bitter taste in the mouth. But there was precious little love or even affection in the rectory. Precious little time for any of us children – small wonder, since there were seven of us, six of the Palfrey's own (and three who had not survived infancy and were buried beneath the yew trees in the churchyard) and me.

To their credit the Palfreys did not treat me so very differently to their own children. Like me they wore hand me-downs, like me they were strictly disciplined and treated with the same cool indifference. Dr John, the rector, was an imposing figure, clever and well read, but distant. Too clever, I think, to be satisfied with the living of Penwyn. He tried his best to bring succour and comfort to his parishioners, both spiritually and with the hardships of their everyday lives, but his efforts were doomed to failure because he could never quite manage to love any of them.

Mary, his wife, was a pale, earnest woman, worn down by her frequent pregnancies and childbirth as well as the constant hard work that came from having such a large family to care for, and looking back I think she was afraid to allow herself to care too deeply for any of her children in case they, like the three who lay in the churchyard, should be snatched from her. Yet, for all that they were almost as starved of affection as I was, I could never quite forget that whilst they had every right to be here I was an outsider, taken on sufferance.

The girls, Patience and Hope in particular, as they giggled and gossiped together, never let me forget. They were not really unkind but there was a bond between them that excluded me. They looked alike, with their mousy brown hair and blue eyes, whereas I had thick copper-coloured curls and hazel eyes that were almost green. They thought alike and enjoyed the same things, whilst I...

Perhaps, on reflection, the gulf was partly of my own making, for I was all too aware that whilst Palfrey blood ran in their veins and they could see the gravestones of their ancestors beneath the shadow of the church tower, I had not the faintest idea of who I was or where I hailed from, and the questions were always there, tormenting me.

Why, if I had been born hereabouts, did no one ever claim me? Why, when I was old enough to notice these things, did I never hear any whispers? No woman of about the right age to be my mother ever followed me longingly with her eyes, no man ever glared with the self-righteous anger that comes of guilty knowledge, no crones huddled in doorways put their heads together and nodded knowingly when I passed by.

I was simply Charity, named, no doubt, because that was how I must live – on the charity of the parish. I belonged to no one, I had no history. And if sometimes in the night I thought I remembered a gentle touch, a haunting perfume, a sweet voice that sang to me softly, I knew it was just wishful thinking.

I was a foundling. Mary Palfrey was the only mother I had ever known. And her tired eyes skittered over me as if they scarcely saw me and her voice when she sang – which was only in Church – was dry and tuneless.

In her own way she did her best for me though.

'Try to behave as a lady should, Charity,' she would say to me. 'It does not come easily to you, I know, but you really must try or no one will ever want you for his wife.' Then she would purse her lips and turn away and I knew what she was thinking. Who would want me for his wife when I had no dowry to bring? When he could never know what family traits might be passed on to his children?

'You are too big to be out playing with the boys in the fields,' she would say, her tight voice revealing how she despaired of me. 'You must work at your embroidery. You have not touched it for days.'

And I would frown, despairing too. I did not want to touch my embroidery. I did not care if I never touched it again. However hard I tried I could never sew neatly as Patience and Hope did. I was much happier out in the open from dawn till dusk, tagging along behind the boys as they hunted for birds' nests or caught minnows in the stream. I loved the feel of the sun and the rain on my face and the taste of salt in my throat when the wind came from the sea. I loved to see the baby lambs and the calves on the smallholdings and rub the noses of the gentle, curious cattle and feed handfuls of choice grass to the goats in their pen at the end of the lane. My knees were always scraped like the boys' and my skirts covered with grass stains and my boots thick with mud.

There were four Palfrey boys. Jeremiah – known to us children, though never to his parents, as Jem – was the oldest, then followed Bartholomew, Thomas and Joshua. And it was Joshua, closest in age to me, who was my hero. He was a tall boy for his age but whippy thin, with a shock of fair hair bleached from the family mousy-brown by the sun. Until it broke he had the voice of an angel and when he sang solo in the Church choir he looked like an angel too, his face cherubic above his ruff and that golden hair glowing in the candlelight so that it might have been a halo. I tagged along behind Joshua like a shadow and he was always kind to me, unlike Jem, who tormented me mercilessly and thought me a dreadful nuisance.

Once, I remember, when I had followed them on the long trek down to the coast, he played a particularly nasty trick on me.

It was a long hot summer day when the sea was calm and blue and the only clouds in the sky were like white feathers on a lady's sapphire silk gown. The boys had run on ahead of me, even Joshua had forgotten me in his rush to reach the sea. When I panted up to the spot where the steep path ran along the cliff edge I could see them already on the shingly beach far below me, whooping and laughing and hurling pebbles that skimmed over the waves.

There were two or three fishermen's huts along the path, old and weatherbeaten but still strong, their roofs neat with new thatch. As I passed them I noticed the door of one was ajar and, curious to see inside, I pushed it open and peeped into the dim interior. The smell of fish was strong. I wrinkled my nose but went in anyway. I could see the dark shapes of creels lined up against the walls. I ventured further, brushing the wind-swept curls off my face and lifting my skirt in case there was something unpleasant I could not see on the floor.

Suddenly there was a screech that made me jump out of my skin and a dark figure rushed past me. For a moment I saw Jem silhouetted against the bright sky. I had not noticed he was not with the others on the beach; like me he must have been investigating the fisherman's hut.

'You beast!' I cried.

Then the door slammed shut and I was in pitch darkness.

'Oh!' I ran to the door, trying to pull it open, but it was shut fast. I could not budge it by so much as a fraction.

'Jem!' I screamed. 'Jem – let me out!'

For answer there was only a laugh.

'See what you get for following us all the time, Charity!'

'Let me out! Let me out!' I was beating on

the door with my hands. But there was only silence.

Panic overtook me. The smell of the fish was making me feel nauseous, the darkness closed in on me. In that moment I thought I was living my dream. The feeling was exactly the same. Trapped. Trapped for ever. I began to shake uncontrollably, tears stung my eyes, and my voice rose hysterically as I battered wildly at the door.

'Let me out! Jeremiah! Let me out!'

My knees gave way; I crumpled to the floor, clawed myself up again, beating on the wood, still screaming to be let out.

A lifetime passed, it seemed, before I heard their voices. I was gibbering, crying with fear. My voice, when I called to them, was just a croak, scraped out through a dry throat and trembling lips. They would never hear me. They would go home without me. I tried again.

The bolt, on the outside to prevent the wind from blowing the door open I suppose, not for any reason of security, scraped back. The door opened and I fell through it, blinded by the bright sun. I must have looked a wreck, my face dirt streaked and tear-stained, my fingernails torn and bleeding from scraping uselessly at the stone and timber. I neither knew nor cared. I began to run blindly along the cliff path away from my prison, my knees gave way again, and I stumbled into a heap, grazing my hands on the scratchy gorse and shingle.

'Charity!' As if from a long way off I heard Joshua's voice. He was beside me, looking down at me, his blue eyes wide with horror. 'What is it? What's the matter?'

'He locked me in!' I sobbed. 'Jem locked me in the hut!'

Jem was hanging back, a little shamefaced now.

'I didn't hurt you,' he said defensively. 'It was just a bit of fun.'

'It wasn't fun! It was not! It was horrible. Horrible!' I could not stop crying.

Joshua turned on his brother in a fury.

'You shouldn't have done that, you idiot! You know she's scared of the dark.'

'Not the dark – the locked door!' I started to say, but I never finished. Joshua, angelic-looking Joshua, had grabbed his older brother by the neck and they were scrapping, rolling over and over on the cliff path like a couple of street urchins, perilously close to the sheer drop to the beach below.

I gazed in horror, my bleeding hands pressed to my dirty, tear-stained face, and the other boys joined in to separate them. How they all avoided going over the edge I shall never know. But somehow, in a few moments, it was all over. The boys, still arguing, dusted themselves down, and Bartholomew gave me his kerchief to wipe my face.

21

'Come on, it's time we were going home,' he said, starting out, and the rest of us followed him. This time when they noticed me getting left behind they stopped and waited for me, even Jem, who had realised, I think, that this time he had gone too far in his tormenting of me and no doubt thought he would be sent to bed without his supper if I told his father what he had done. I would not tell. I had too much loyalty and pride for that. But the brightness had gone out of the day and the terrible feeling of being incarcerated stayed with me, just like the lingering aura of my recurrent dream, a nameless fear that lurked in the shadows of my mind.

It was not only on their forays into the country or down to the coast that I shadowed the boys. I liked to sit in on their lessons, too. Their father was their tutor, setting them mathematical problems, teaching them English and Latin and a little classical Greek. At first he had smiled thinly when I expressed a desire to be present at the lessons, saying it would be better for me to practise needlework and flower arranging with the girls, or even to learn to play the piano. But when he saw how determined I was and how quick to learn, he allowed me to go with him and the boys into the study. There I would stand behind Joshua's chair following every word he wrote with avid eyes, and even sometimes whispering to him the way to solve some mathematical problem or parse some sentence. Joshua would feign impatience but I knew he was grateful to me for saving him hours of frustration for I was quicker than he to grasp the principles of the lessons and after a while Dr John allowed me to join in in my own right.

'You have a nimble brain, Charity,' he told me once and I flushed with pleasure. Whatever heritage I lacked, my parents had at least endowed me with the ability to learn.

As I grew from girl to young womanhood I began to understand why Dr John had allowed me to share the lessons with his sons.

'I believe we may make a governess of you, Charity,' he said, his pale eyes resting on me thoughtfully, and I realised that for some while he had been wondering what would become of me when I was grown.

A governess! The idea did not appeal to me in the slightest. Much as I loved learning myself, the thought of spending day after day struggling to pass on what I knew to a bunch of resentful children was almost in itself a form of being trapped. To see the sky through a casement window and not be able to run free seemed like a prison to me and I did not think I would have the patience to explain over and over again facts which I had absorbed with no effort at all. It was one thing to help Joshua, whom I adored; quite another to correct unformed writing and repeat rotes until I was heartily sick of them. But I could see that my opportunities were limited. And I could not remain at the rectory for ever, the foundling with no past and no future.

In any case I was enjoying myself less and less as the boys grew up and began to leave home, first to school, to complete the education Dr John had begun, then to make their way in the world. Jem left first, for Falmouth, where he had found clerical work, Bartholomew went far away to Bristol to become a shipping clerk, Thomas was apprenticed to an apothecary in Truro, and my beloved Joshua was set to enter holy orders like his father before him. Patience was courted by a widower from a nearby village and I knew it would not be long before both she and Hope were married women with homes of their own. And still I was left at Penwyn with no prospects, kicking my heels fretfully and living on the parish.

Dr John found me some small scraps of jobs, instructing the younger brothers and sisters of the children to whom he gave more formal lessons, but the arrangement was far from satisfactory. And then, when I was just turned twenty, Selena Trevelyan came into my life and everything changed.

Selena was visiting her old friends the Merlyns at Penwyn Hall and I first set eyes on her when she joined them in their family pew for Sunday services.

She was a striking woman with dark, grey-flecked hair pulled severely away from a strong-featured face. It was impossible to ignore that face, and her eyes, deep-set and dark, seemed to look right inside one, yet revealed nothing. Lines were etched deeply between her nose and chin and yet in spite of that, and the grey in her hair, I thought she could not be much beyond forty. She wore a gown and cape of a deep purple, so dark that in the candlelit church it looked almost black, and jewels at her throat and in her ears. She was tall for a woman, as tall as any of the Merlyn men, and throughout the service I had the strangest feeling that she was watching me. Each time I turned my head in her direction her eyes were indeed on me, and she held my gaze for discon-certingly long moments before lowering them to her prayer book with a deliberation that was almost dismissive.

When Matins was over and I filed out of the church with Patience, Hope and Mama Mary, she was already in the porch, talking to Dr John.

Mama Mary nodded and went to pass by. She was always, I think, a little in awe of the Merlyns, who were 'quality folk' or 'gentry', and very aware that it was their money which had paid for many of the fine artefacts in the church – the magnificent brass lectern in the shape of an eagle with outstretched wings, the candlesticks on the altar, the Stations of the Cross fashioned in brass, not carved from wood. But Selena Trevelyan stretched out a beringed hand and touched Mama Mary's sleeve, and those magnetic dark eyes commanded her to stop.

'You must be the rector's wife,' she said. Her voice was strong and low with only the merest hint of a Cornish burr.

Mama Mary nodded, looking a little flustered, as well she might, for though Selena was speaking to her, her eyes were once again on me.

'And these are your daughters?' she said to Dr John.

He smiled, something close to pride curving his thin lips. It was not something I had often seen in him, but I saw it now.

'Indeed. My daughters Patience and Hope.'

The dark eyes swept over me again, narrowing slightly.

'And this one is not your daughter?'

'This is Charity,' Dr John said shortly. 'We gave her a home and raised her.'

'What beautiful hair you have, my dear!' Selena said unexpectedly.

I felt a flush rising in my cheeks and

unconsciously my hand went to my thick copper curls. They marked me out, I knew, as the cuckoo in the nest, even if Dr John had not pointedly left me out of the introduction. I was proud of my hair – it was, I thought, the best thing about me. But I was embarrassed all the same that this stranger should remark on it and at the same time effectively slight Patience and Hope, with their mousy locks.

'Thank you,' I said.

'It looks so well, too, with those green eyes.'

Now I really was blushing furiously, as only those with my colouring can. One thing to remark on my hair, which was obvious for all to see – but to mention the colour of my eyes too...

I could sense Mama Mary and the girls bristling, though Mama Mary managed to keep the annoyance out of her voice as she said: 'Charity is blessed with beauty, yes. Perhaps it is the Lord's way of compensating her for having no family of her own.'

Then, with a sweep of her head, she gathered us together like a mother hen gathering her brood of chicks.

'You must excuse us,' she said coolly. 'I have a roast at home which needs my attention. Preaching always makes my husband as hungry as if he had spent his morning in the fields or the tin mines.'

27

I had never heard her speak in such a way before, so I knew she must be considerably put out by this lady's attention to me. Lips tight, chin quivering, she led us up the lane to the rectory.

When Dr John came home half an hour later he was in a state of great excitement.

'I believe I have secured a position for you, Charity,' he said, laying his Bible and the sheaf of notes for his sermon down on the table in the hallway. 'The lady who spoke to you outside the church is, it seems, looking for a governess for her young niece. I seized the opportunity to inform her that you were well qualified for such a post – I sang your praises, and fortunately she was most taken with you. You are to go to Penwyn Hall this very afternoon so that she can discuss the matter with you.'

'Oh!' I was quite taken aback; I scarcely knew what to say. But perhaps this was the explanation for the way Selena Trevelyan had watched me throughout the service – the Merlyns had already spoken of me to her and she was sizing me up before mentioning her need of a governess to Dr John.

'Well, Charity, it seems that once again the Lord has provided for you,' Mama Mary said. 'You had better change into a plain gown before you go for your interview, and at least look the part.'

There was a coldness in her tone that told

me she was still smarting from the remarks Selena Trevelyan had made about my appearance.

When we had eaten our midday meal Dr John got out the trap to drive me over to Penwyn Hall.

'Try to make a good impression, Charity,' he said as we turned into the broad gravelled drive.

I flushed a little. 'Of course I will.'

'Don't talk too much. Sometimes you are inclined to garrulousness.'

I bit my lip. I was already nervous enough about the coming interview without Dr John compounding it.

'There is no need whatever to mention your circumstances. Leave it to me to explain matters.'

I knew he was referring to the mystery of my background but since I knew nothing of it this seemed an unnecessary warning. Dr John wanted to paint as rosy a picture of me as possible, I assumed.

In the event, Selena interviewed me alone. She told me she lived with her brother, Francis, and his young daughter, Charlotte, at Morwennan House, on the south Cornish coast.

'Our father is squire at Penallack, an estate a little further inland,' she explained, 'but it is Adam, our elder brother, who will inherit. Francis's wife, Julia, died when Charlotte was born, and therefore I have made my home with him to help with Charlotte's upbringing.'

She went on to tell me that so far Charlotte had received no formal education, but she was most anxious that the little girl should be taught grammar and mathematics and perhaps a little Latin.

'I know it is not the done thing to educate girls beyond the accomplishments they will need to make good wives, but as a woman myself I feel very strongly that she should not be deprived of at least the rudiments of learning,' she said firmly, and I thought that Charlotte was fortunate indeed in having such an aunt with such forward-looking views.

Then, just as Dr John had predicted, she turned to questioning me about my own education and my background.

'How did you come into the care of the rector and his wife?' she asked, those dark, searching eyes on my face.

I held her gaze with what dignity I could muster.

'I was a foundling.'

'But where did they find you?'

'I don't know,' I admitted. 'They would never say.'

For a long moment her gaze remained on me, penetrating, inscrutable. Then she shrugged her shoulders in a quick, dismissive gesture.

'Oh well, I dare say it scarcely matters. From what I've seen of you, you are well suited to the position. I should like you to assume your duties as soon as possible.'

I was too happy to have found myself a position at last that would earn me a little money to wonder about her authority in the matter. I simply assumed that Charlotte's father left such things in her hands.

'Thank you,' I said, then added with some of that garrulity that Dr John had warned me about: 'I shall be glad not to be a burden any more on the Palfreys and the parish. I'll work hard and I won't disappoint you, I promise.'

A look that might almost have been amusement crossed her face.

'No,' she said. 'I'm sure you will not.'

I left for Morwennan a week later, and as the carriage bowled along the Cornish lanes I sat back against the soft leather seat, my hands knotted in the folds of my best cambric gown, trying desperately to prepare myself for the new life that lay ahead of me.

I could not understand the nervousness that had begun to knot my stomach. I had been so looking forward to taking up my new position. Yet now, for some reason, I was filled with foreboding. Oh, it was only natural to be a little apprehensive of the unknown, I told myself. And to know I would be responsible for a little girl's education too, with no Dr John to keep a close eye on the lessons I prepared, was rather daunting. But some deep disturbing instinct told me it was more than that.

For some distance now the lanes had been hedged with meadowsweet and cow parsley, dotted with huge clumps of white arum and vermilion day lilies. The sky was the corn-flower blue of a scorching August day, and as we neared the coast I sometimes caught sight of the sea, a rim of darker blue, smooth and inviting beyond the green-topped cliff edges. Then the carriage took a left turn and the sky and the sun disappeared with a suddenness that startled me, hidden from view by a thick tracery of foliage. The trees, lush for summer, were all around, so that it was like going into a dark green tunnel.

A nerve leaped in my throat and still I did not know the reason. I reached for the bag that lay on the seat beside me – the bag that contained all of my few worldly possessions – and hugged it tight against my side for comfort, the only familiar thing in this un-familiar world. We couldn't be far now from Morwennan.

The lane twisted again, became narrower, and began to descend a steeply sloping gully. The trees that surrounded it were thicker than ever, the overhanging branches slap-ping and catching at the windows of the carriage, the light reduced to nothing but green twilight. And my nervousness tightened another notch so that it was almost claustrophobia, almost real fear.

All I wanted then was to tear open the door of the carriage, leap out and run back up the gully, back to the sunshine and the corn-flower blue sky, back to the rolling open countryside with its sudden, surprising glimpses of darker blue sea. But of course I did nothing of the sort. For one thing I had nowhere to go. I could hardly return to the rectory at Penwyn and say I wanted their sanctuary once more. Neither circumstances nor my pride would allow it. I was simply being stupid, a silly frightened girl of the type I had never myself had any time for. Penwyn was the past – and not a very happy one at that. Morwennan was the future. But, for all that, there was a tightness in my chest that made it hard for me to breathe.

The carriage stopped, pulling into a paved area with stables and outbuildings that I imagined sheltered the carriages from the ravages of the wind off the sea, and the coachman climbed down, came round and opened the door.

'This is as far as I can go without a lot of trouble,' he said shortly. He was a typical Cornishman, soft-spoken, but not one to mince his words. 'You'll have to walk from here.'

He took my bag, giving me another of the narrow looks he had been casting in my direction throughout the drive. I climbed down and my legs felt a little shaky – because of the journey, I tried to pretend, and did not for one moment deceive myself.

And then I saw it below me in the valley – Morwennan House. Half hidden by the trees, deeply shadowed yet unmistakable. My heart came into my mouth with a great leap and all my vague apprehensions took shape, flapping about me like a flock of crows.

I had never seen the place before – never been so far from Penwyn – but I knew it at once.

Morwennan House was the house from my dream.

Two

I was afraid. In that moment as I stood staring down at the granite-grey house I was more afraid than I had ever been in my life before. More afraid even than when Jem locked me in the fisherman's hut so many years ago. I had been terrified then, yes, but at least I had understood my terror. This ... this was beyond my understanding. I clasped my bag tight with both hands and felt my knees turn to jelly beneath me. My head was spinning; I seemed to have stopped breathing. The whole world had stopped and in it I was whirling, whirling like a particle of sand in the strong wind that blew in from the sea.

How long I stood there before I began to get a grip on myself I do not know. This was foolishness. I had never seen Morwennan House before. It could not possibly be the house from my dream.

I drew a long steadying breath and then another and I forced my legs to move, first one, then the other, down the drive. With each step I could feel the sense of oppression closing in on me but also a grim determination growing. I must face this nameless fear that had haunted me all my life. I must lay it to rest once and for all.

As I approached the great front door opened. Selena herself stood there, wearing a gown of grey velvet, a half smile twisting her thin lips. It was meant to be a smile of welcome, I supposed, but at the same time I realised what it was – besides her eyes – that was so disconcerting about her face. When she smiled her mouth curved, not up, but down.

I was surprised too that she should have opened the door to me herself. In a house this size I imagined there must be servants to carry out so mundane a task. But Selena answered my unspoken question at once.

'I saw the carriage from the window. It is unfortunate that it is so difficult for it to come right down to the door but there is no space for turning. One of the disadvantages of building a house into the side of a cliff, I'm afraid. But the position suits my brother well. He likes to be within sound of the sea.'

I nodded, feeling now more shamed than anything. If Selena had seen the carriage, had she also seen me standing like a pillar of salt, staring at the house?

'Come inside and we'll have a dish of tea,' she said. 'You must be famished after your journey.' Her eyes swept the drive. 'Is Durbin bringing your trunk?'

Colour tinged my cheeks.

'I don't have a trunk. My things are here, in my bag.'

'Good heavens! I never travel without at least three trunks!' She laughed slightly. 'Well, come inside anyway.'

The hall I stepped into was square and dim. Hardly surprising, since even outside, the thick tracery of trees had shut out the light.

'Leave your bag here,' Selena said. 'Durbin can take it up to your room when he has attended to the horses.'

Reluctantly I set it down. It had become a lifeline to me and I wanted to hold on to it.

'This way.' Selena started across the hall and it was as I made to follow her that I saw the mirror, hanging over a small oak bureau that stood against one wall, and my heart came into my mouth again.

It was a large mirror in an ornate wooden frame. The very twin of the mirror from my dream – the one in which I had once seen the reflection that was my face, yet not me. The breath caught in my throat; I stared at it as if mesmerised, unable to believe what I was seeing.

'I'll have some water heated later so that you can freshen up before we eat,' Selena was saying. 'I'm sure you will want to change out of your dusty clothes.'

'Thank you.' My voice was faint.

I turned my back on the mirror, following

her across the dim hall and into the parlour. To my immense relief it was much lighter, a large square room with comfortable furnishings. Though the mantelpiece and fire surround were of Cornish granite, they did not look cold as the outside of the house had done, for they had absorbed the heat of a thousand fires, and on the hearth a brass fender and fire-irons gleamed. Pretty porcelain was aligned along the mantelpiece on either side of an ornate carriage clock and a mirror hung above it. But this one, gilt-framed, held no terrors for me. There was a large central table and a small straddle-legged one in a corner on which a vase filled with white roses had been set. The window seat was padded and covered in bright chintz; when Selena invited me to sit down I made for it instinctively and saw at once why this room was so much lighter than the hall.

It faced the sea. With no trees to block out the light the sky was clear and blue, the view of the cove uninterrupted. Directly in front of the house, well-tended lawns sloped down towards the beach and on either side the cliffs were emerald green, soft, dim brown and sharp white in the bright sunlight.

'What a beautiful view!' I exclaimed.

Selena smiled faintly. 'It is, yes. As I told you, my brother likes to be close to the sea.'

I perched on the window seat where I could see the sea and the sky as well as the room and the trapped feeling in my chest began to ease.

'I expect you are anxious to meet your charge,' Selena said.

'Yes. Yes, I am.'

'She is staying tonight with her grandparents,' Selena said. 'The squire at Penallack – you remember I told you about him? Anyway, I thought it best that you should have the opportunity to settle in before beginning your duties.'

I was surprised by this. I had thought Charlotte and her father, Francis, would be here to greet me, Charlotte perhaps a little shy and hanging back behind her father's legs, and I had even planned what I might say to put her at her ease. To learn she was not here was something of a disappointment.

'Her grandparents love to have her,' Selena went on. 'And she loves it at the Hall. Small wonder – they spoil her outrageously. My father has given her a pony and is teaching her to ride, and she enjoys the company of her cousins – my brother Adam's children. It can be very lonely for her here, as I suppose it is for all only children.'

I nodded. There had been plenty of times in the overcrowded rectory when I had wished I did not have to share a bedroom with Patience and Hope, plenty of times when I had thought that since I was an outsider it would have been nice to have some of the advantages of being alone. But I would certainly have missed the company of the boys and the adventures I had shared with them. And the trappings of wealth that were apparent in this comfortable room could never make up for the lack of company of one's peers or siblings.

'There would have been others, of course,' Selena continued. 'But, as I think I told you, Charlotte's mother died giving birth to her.'

Again I nodded. 'Yes, you did mention it.' The death of both mother and baby in childbirth was commonplace, but that did not make it any the less of a tragedy. 'And your brother never married again?' I said.

'No.' Her tone was short, clipped. Her lips tightened over it. I realised she was not going to say any more. For a moment the silence hung heavy in the room and I glanced around, expecting to see a portrait of Francis Trevelyan's dead wife, and thinking it might give me some idea of what Charlotte would look like. But there was none. A seascape – rather wild and frightening, a little alien in the cheerful room; a watercolour depicting a bowl of fruit that might, I thought, have been painted by one of the ladies of the family; a tapestry sampler, but no portrait. Perhaps Francis Trevelyan did not want to live with a constant reminder of the wife he had lost.

The door opened and a small apple-cheeked woman came in with a tray. I caught a strange, almost furtive, expression on her face when she looked at me and wondered at it. It was only natural, I supposed, that she should be curious about the newest member of the household, but somehow this was more than mere curiosity...

She set the tray down on the table with a jerk that sent the porcelain cups clattering.

'Thank you, Mrs Durbin,' Selena said sharply. 'That will be all for now. I'll pour the tea myself.'

She did so, adding a spoonful of cream to each cup and bringing one over to me.

I sipped it gratefully. It seemed a very long time since I had breakfasted at Penwyn Rectory. A lifetime ago.

'Perhaps I should warn you,' Selena said. 'My brother is not always an easy man. He guards his privacy quite jealously. I hope you will come to regard Morwennan as your home, and find the rooms we have set aside for you to your liking. But there are parts of the house that we must insist remain our domain. My brother would take exception to your invading them.'

I frowned, puzzled that she should deem such an admonition necessary.

'I'll show you around the part of the house that you are free to use,' she said, rising and smoothing down her skirts. 'And I'll show you your own room at the same time. I expect you would like to unpack so that your gowns do not become too creased in that bag of yours.'

I put down my tea cup. I had, I must admit, been hoping I might have a second cup. But at the same time it was a relief not to have to continue this rather uneasy conversation.

Selena led the way through the living rooms. Like the parlour, the dining room looked out over the sea, but to my dismay the study, where, she said, I was to give Charlotte her lessons when Francis was not using it, was off the hall, and just as dark. In the kitchen a meal was clearly under preparation, but of Mrs Durbin or any other staff there was no sign. The whole house, in fact, seemed to echo with emptiness.

Clearly Durbin had come in whilst we had been taking tea, however, for my bag was no longer where I had left it in the hall. Selena led the way upstairs, along to the far end of a narrow landing way. There she threw open a door.

'This will be your room.'

It was quite small but more than adequate for my needs – the first time in my life I had had a room to call my own. It was on the side of the house, so that although it was partly shadowed by the trees I could also glimpse the sweep of the cliffs and the bay beyond. Durbin had set my bag down in the middle of the floor and a closet door stood ajar, emptied, I could see, to make hanging space for my clothes. Far more space than I would need!

'I'll leave you to unpack your things then,' Selena said. 'And I will let you know when my brother returns home. He will be, I know, most anxious to meet you.'

'Thank you. I'm anxious to meet him too.'

But I was not. I was full of misgiving. I was wishing heartily that I was anywhere but here at Morwennan House and very afraid that this whole episode was going to be an unhappy experience. It was, I knew, too early to judge, but all my instincts were warning me. This was not a happy house. I could only hope I would not end up feeling as trapped here as I had always felt in my dream.

In the event I saw Francis Trevelyan before he saw me. I had taken my gowns out of my bag and hung them in the closet and I was stacking my undergarments neatly in a drawer when I heard voices outside.

I went to the window and looked out. A path led along the side of the house beneath my window, between it and the trees. Two gentlemen were walking along it deep in conversation. Both were tall but there the resemblance ended. While the one was athletically built, in white buckskin breeches and green cloth coat, the other was portly, his tailcoat straining over his plump chest and his knee breeches over sturdy thighs. Though they both wore pigtail wigs and cravats, the face of the one was finely chiselled and tanned from the wind and sun, whilst the other – older than his companion by around ten years, perhaps forty to the other's thirty – was jowly, and his cheeks had the high colour of a man a little too fond of his port. One of them, I felt certain, was Francis Trevelyan, and I hoped with all my heart that he was the younger of the two – for I did not care at all for the look of the other – yet my instincts were all telling me otherwise.

I stepped as far as I could behind the curtain, so that if they looked up they would be less likely to see me, and peered down curiously. Almost immediately beneath my window they stopped and their voices floated up to me.

'Five hundred pounds,' I heard the older man say. 'Take it or leave it. It's worth double that on the open market.'

I could not hear what the other replied, but a moment later the man I felt sure was Francis Trevelyan tucked his malacca cane under his arm and the two men shook hands to seal, I assumed, whatever deal it was they had been making.

They moved on then, along the side of the

house and out of my line of sight. And I was left thinking that if I was right, and the portly man was indeed Francis Trevelyan, I did not like him any more than I liked his house.

'We have a visitor dining with us this evening,' Selena said when I had freshened up, changed into a clean gown, and ventured back downstairs. 'It's unfortunate, as this is your first night with us, but there it is. Francis has been doing business with him and invited him to stay for dinner before he realised that you had arrived.'

I was a little surprised at that. Not, of course, that Francis had been doing business, since I had witnessed the deal, but that he should have been unaware that I was due to arrive this afternoon. It was, after all, his own carriage that had collected me and I would have thought that he would have been interested enough to meet the person who would have charge of his daughter's education not to have forgotten.

As if she had read my thoughts Selena gave a short laugh.

'When he is doing business everything else goes out of my brother's head,' she said. 'He is a self-made man, as I am sure you realise. As the second son he was not entitled to any consideration on the family inheritance and he has not built himself a small fortune by allowing anything to stand in his way. Charlotte's welfare is entrusted to me for the most part and I do my best to see that he is not hindered by everyday distractions.'

I nodded, but I could not help feeling it was a poor kind of father who considered his motherless daughter a distraction.

'Thomas Stanton comes here quite frequently, as you will discover,' Selena went on. 'When he and Francis are not closeted in Francis's study discussing fresh deals – and toasting the ones they have already made in the best champagne – he makes a great fuss of Charlotte. She is extremely fond of him, though I'm not at all sure I like that. I have no idea who the Stantons are or where they hail from, and I have to say I don't like strangers under my roof.'

She broke off, realising no doubt what she had said and anxious that she might have given me offence.

'Your case is different, of course,' she said. 'You can hardly be held responsible for the fact that you were a foundling. But when it comes to business ... There was a time when I never had dealings with anyone unless I knew something about them. Now ... Still, he's a handsome fellow, Tom Stanton. At least he has that to his credit.'

A faint colour rose in my cheeks as in my mind's eye I saw again rippling muscles under fine broadcloth and buckskin and a strong suntanned face beneath a pigtail wig.

'Has he a wife, this Tom Stanton?' I asked before I could stop myself, and at once felt my flush deepen. Why, it sounded as if I was mad for a man – any man – I, who had never had a suitor, nor even looked for one.

Selena, however, seemed not to notice my sudden loss of composure.

'I really couldn't say,' she replied. 'As I said, I know almost nothing of the man.'

I nodded, staring down at my hands and vowing to watch my tongue more carefully in future. And certainly not to allow myself unseemly thoughts about a man I had merely glimpsed through a casement window!

It was almost an hour before voices from the hall warned us that the men were emerging from the study. It had been an awkward hour. Selena was, I thought, a rather cold person, yet instinctively I knew that that coldness hid a darkly powerful personality that would make her a dangerous person to cross. Selena was used to ruling the roost here at Morwennan and anyone who got in her way would suffer for it. I also suspected that she had a fiercely jealous nature. From her comments it was not hard to deduce that she had disliked and resented Charlotte's mother, and she seemed to feel a certain resentment towards Charlotte too. My heart went out to the little girl and I resolved to try to bring some love and happiness into her life as well as education. I knew only too well what it was like to feel unwanted and unloved.

But for all Selena's icy self-possession there was something else, something I could not make head nor tail of but found most disturbing. Every so often I would feel her eyes on me and when I met them I thought that beneath that calculating, speculative look I could see smouldering excitement. I tried to tell myself I was imagining things – heaven alone knew my imagination had already run away with me this afternoon! – but at the sound of the footsteps and voices in the hall I was aware of it once more – a sort of anticipation that was almost tangible. Selena rose, smoothing her skirts, and her eyes were very bright. She went to the doorway and called out: 'Francis, Charlotte's new governess is here. Perhaps you would like to come and meet her before we go in for dinner.'

I rose from the window seat, trying to look demure as a governess should. I heard Francis say something to his companion and then his footsteps once more, coming closer. Selena glanced at me and that strange expression was there again on her face. She held the door wide and stepped aside. The portly figure of the man I had seen on the path outside filled the doorway.

'Good day, Miss—'

He stopped short, his voice fading away. But it was the look on his jowly face I shall never forget.

Francis Trevelyan was staring at me as if he was unable to believe his eyes.

He was staring at me as if he had seen a ghost.

Three

Startled and puzzled as I was, the silence seemed to me to go on forever. Then I heard Selena say in tones that were apparently concerned and yet somehow at the same time almost amused: 'Francis? Is something wrong?'

He recovered himself but I could not but be aware of the effort it took. The colour had blanched from his florid cheeks, now it came flooding back, higher than ever. He took a step into the room, still staring at me, and when he spoke I had the impression that the pretence at normality was for the benefit of his associate, standing unseen behind him, rather than for mine.

'Good afternoon, Miss Palfrey. I trust you had a pleasant journey.'

'Passable, I believe,' Selena said. Again I had the impression she was laughing at him.

I think I first realised in that moment that I was part of an elaborate game that I did not understand. Selena's stares at me in the church that first day I had met her, her readiness to offer me the position of governess to Charlotte after only the briefest of interviews, the fact that Charlotte had been despatched to stay with her grandparents to 'give me the chance to settle in'. Selena had known in advance what her brother's re-action to me would be and had been antici-pating it with malicious excitement. Yes, I was a part of some elaborate game she was playing. I did not understand it, and I did not like it one bit. More than ever I wanted to pack my bag and leave this gloomy house, leave the intrigue and the disturbing under-currents. I wanted to run, like the child I had once been. But I was not a child any more and for me at least this was no game. It was supposed to be the beginning of a new life and suddenly I was angry that Selena should be playing with me this way, as if I were no more than a pawn on a chessboard.

'I can't help but notice you are a little dis-mayed,' I said, meeting Francis's gaze directly. His eyes were as dark as his sister's, small sharp beads beneath fleshy lids. 'I'm sorry if I am not quite what you were expect-ing but I assure you I will not disappoint you. I may be young, but my education has been very thorough.'

'I am sure it has, Miss Palfrey. However, you are, as you say, very young. It may be that our life here will not suit you. We live very quietly and there is little opportunity for socialising. In many ways, we are quite isolated. It would not be good for Charlotte if you established a rapport with her, then decided you did not want to remain here. I am looking to instil some stability in her life, as well as learning.'

So he was trying to discourage me, politely, before I had even begun! I wondered how polite he would have been had his business associate not been standing by his shoulder.

The stubbornness with which I had been blessed – and cursed! – came to my aid then. I would not be pushed by the Trevelyans from pillar to post as a tool in whatever feud they were engaged in.

'I have not yet had the pleasure of meeting Charlotte,' I said steadily, 'but I would never treat a young girl in such a way. Perhaps I, more than anyone, know how important it is for a child not to feel abandoned. I have accepted this post in good faith and I have every intention of keeping my side of the bargain. Of course, if you are unhappy with your sister's choice of governess then I respect that. I'll leave at once, if that's what you want.'

My directness called his bluff, but I do believe he would have agreed that my leaving at once was indeed the best course if Selena had not intervened.

'For heaven's sakes, Francis, what is the matter with you? I told you Charity's age at the very outset; you did not consider it a problem then. Is it perhaps her appearance that is causing you concern?' She hesitated for just a moment, looking at him with that expression that was both challenging and amused, and the grandfather clock in the hall chimed the half hour. She let the echo fade a little and then went on lightly: 'She's a beauty, I grant you. Perhaps that is why you think she would not be content with our life here?'

Colour flamed in my cheeks that they should discuss me as if I were not here at all. And what was it about my looks that obsessed Selena so? She had described me as a beauty – well, in my opinion, at least, I certainly was not that. She had commented on my hair and my eyes. There was no doubt it was the way I looked that was behind all this. But for what reason?

'You gave me free rein to engage a governess,' Selena went on. 'Now, it seems, you are questioning my choice. I think it's a little late for that, don't you? Charity is here now and she intends to stay, isolated or not, don't you, my dear?'

To my utter astonishment she linked her arm through mine so that we stood shoulder to shoulder facing Francis Trevelyan. And she was smiling faintly.

'Let's go in to dinner, shall we, and forget all this nonsense,' she added brightly.

And drew me forward with her in the direction of the dining room.

★ ★ ★

Tom Stanton was, I thought, the most attractive man I had ever set eyes on. In spite of the strange strained atmosphere between Francis and Selena, in spite of my discomfort and anger and sheer puzzlement, I could not help but notice it.

As I had observed from the window he was tall, lean yet well muscled, his shoulders broad, his hips, under the covering of sleek white buckskin, trim. His face was angular, framed by his pigtail wig and now, at closer range, I could see that his mouth was generous with a full lower lip and his eyes a startlingly deep blue and fringed with dark lashes that any girl would have given her dowry to possess. His hands, I noticed as he handled the heavy silver cutlery, were strong and as suntanned as his face, with tapering fingers and square nails, his wrists beneath the cuffs of his green cloth coat lightly feathered with hairs that had been bleached by the same sun that had darkened his complexion.

But it was not only Tom Stanton's appearance that I found attractive. I liked his voice, deep and warm, with a hint of slow Cornish burr. And I liked his manner. There was the ease about him of a man who was comfortable in his own skin, a man who had witnessed an awkward scene and remained apparently unaffected by it.

Where many people would have preferred to ignore what they had heard and make no mention of it, he actually raised the subject over the tasty game soup, served by Mrs Durbin in a magnificent silver tureen.

'Perhaps if Miss Palfrey does find Morwennan too quiet and isolated for her tastes I could show her something of the district and introduce her to what passes for the social life in these parts,' he said, and the smile in those very blue eyes was pure mischief. 'In fact, perhaps I should begin my mission without delay before she has the chance to become bored and restless.'

In spite of myself, in spite of everything, I felt a strange twist of excitement deep inside that was like nothing I had ever experienced before.

'I think, Mr Stanton, I should remind you that Charity is in our care,' Selena said tartly. She had seen the look that passed between us, I think. 'I am not at all sure that her father would approve of her gallivanting about the country with a gentleman.'

I lowered my eyes. Doubtless she was right. But it was a most appealing prospect, all the same.

'We would not be gallivanting!' Tom protested. 'Our excursions would be educational for Miss Palfrey – and she is clearly a young lady who likes to be educated. I think such a thing would be clearly in the best interests of all concerned!'

Francis set down his soup spoon with a clatter and reached for his wine glass.

'She may not be here long enough to take advantage of your offer, Stanton.'

'Oh, don't start that again!' Selena interposed and I felt my stubborn determination stir once more.

'I shall be here as long as Charlotte needs me,' I said firmly. 'Unless of course you choose to dismiss me, Mr Trevelyan. And...' I glanced at Tom Stanton and felt a faint colour tinging my cheeks, 'with your permission I should be most happy to take up Mr Stanton's offer to show me something of the district. In whatever free time I have, of course, and provided it does not interfere with Charlotte's studies.'

Tom's generous mouth curved briefly.

'Capital! Surely you are not intending to be such a tyrannical employer that you would deny such a request, Francis? No, I can't believe it of you!'

'Oh, do what you like!' Francis growled.

And again, sneaking a glance at Selena, I saw a satisfied half-smile twist her thin lips, and my pleasure in the moment was spoiled. In spite of her earlier protest she was pleased I had agreed to go out with Tom Stanton, and I did not know why.

Unless, of course, it was simply that she

was enjoying her brother's defeat in the matter.

'I'd like to take a walk down to the cove,' I said. 'It looks most inviting and I think the sea breeze will blow some of the cobwebs of my journey away.'

Dinner was over and Tom Stanton had left. I had been sorry to see him go for a variety of reasons, not least that his easy presence had made me feel less isolated in this house of strange discordant undercurrents.

'Of course we have no objection,' Selena said. 'At least, I certainly do not.' She glanced at her brother. 'Francis?'

'As you wish,' he said, but there was still a bad-tempered set to his jowly face. 'Only watch your step on the cliff path. It's steep and covered with loose stones. You don't want to break your neck on your first day here.'

His tone was as bad-tempered as his expression. I thought wryly that Francis Trevelyan would not care much if I did break my neck.

'I'm quite used to cliff paths,' I said coolly. 'I grew up scrambling down them with my brothers. We lived within reach of the coast, remember.'

Francis's eyes were sharp. 'I thought Penwyn was inland.' He glanced at his sister.

'Nowhere in Cornwall is far from the sea,'

I said with determined lightness. 'Especially when it comes to a pair of young legs and a liking for the sound of the surf.'

'You like the sound of the surf then?' Selena asked.

'Not especially. But the boys did,' I returned. 'They were never happier than racing each other down to the beach, and where they went I followed.'

'I hope you will not influence Charlotte into wild ways,' Francis said. 'She is a young lady and I want her brought up as such.'

'I would never encourage her to be anything else,' I said with asperity. 'But I have to say it never did me any harm.'

'Oh, don't be so stuffy, Francis!' Selena grated. 'I was a tomboy too, remember. From the day Papa gave me my first pony I was in the saddle galloping on the moors whenever I could escape the house, whilst you...' Her thin lips twisted again into that disconcerting, downward-pointing smile. 'You didn't take to it half so well, as I recall.'

Francis shifted impatiently, clearly not best pleased at this reference to what I imagined to be some past failing and I had a sudden vision of a plump little boy not nearly so at home in the saddle as his fearless sister.

'That has nothing to do with anything,' he said shortly.

Selena raised an eyebrow. 'Sometimes, Francis, I think it has everything to do with everything.'

He turned to me. 'Take a walk down to the cove if you like, Miss Palfrey. But if you decide to explore the beaches, have a care. Remember the tide can come in very suddenly and there are places that become quite cut off.'

'As she has told you, she knows the coast and its ways,' Selena reminded him. 'Yes, take your walk, Charity, before the sun goes down. And come back to us safely. As you can see, my brother is most concerned about your welfare. I think already he realises how much you will come to mean to us.'

Unsure of how much irony was meant in that remark I left them – and went off on my expedition.

The hall was almost completely dark now and as yet no lamps had been lit. Francis and Selena were accustomed to the gloom, I supposed. Outside the great front door it was almost dark too in the shadow of the trees, but as I walked along the side of the house beneath the window of my room the shade became first dappled then the warm glowing light of a perfect summer's evening. As I reached the corner of the house I saw the gardens sloping down to the sea, the same view as was afforded from the parlour, and which had caused me to exclaim with pleasure. They were well tended, those gardens, a great sweep of lawn, beds of flowering shrubs and rose bushes that looked none the worse for being exposed to the wind off the sea. I paused by one bush, lifting a branch heavy with deep-pink blooms and sniffing the sweet haunting perfume that had been drawn out by the warmth of the sun.

The path sloped steeply down, interspersed by several series of steps. And ahead of me always was the sea, a darker blue now with the rippling white breakers longer and more pronounced, enclosed at either side of the cove by the jutting cliffs. They were dappled with the soft evening light and far out over the horizon the sky was decked with small pinkish clouds. I could hear the ceaseless motion of the waves and instead of the caw of the rooks I heard a seabird mew.

The feeling of space and oneness with nature was so wonderful after the horrid overbearing aura in the house that it was all I could do to stop myself from running. But I walked, as a lady should, lifting my face to the fresh salt breeze and breathing it in as if it were the very elixir of life.

At the foot of the gardens there was a little picket gate in a hedge of some wiry, wind-hardy plant whose name I did not know. I lifted the latch and went through, closing it behind me.

I was on the cliff path now and I could well see why Francis had warned me of it.

Narrow, uneven, almost worn away in places and edged with tufts of gorse and thrift, it dipped and swept its way down to the beach below.

And yet, for all that it was precarious, I could see that it was well used. Many feet had trodden this way before me. Briefly I wondered whose. Francis did not appear to be the sort of man to take solitary walks on the beach and from what he had said Charlotte was not encouraged to go there to play. Selena, then? She had admitted to being a tomboy in her time. Yet somehow I could not see it. Selena, walking on the beach with the wind disturbing her elaborate coif and the pebbles scratching her slippers?

Oh, I told myself, no doubt the path had been there for centuries, long before Morwennan House had been built. Perhaps fishermen had occupied shacks that clung to the steep cleft and over the years their feet had trodden the path so hard that new growth was reluctant to spring up.

I ran the last few feet on to the beach – I had no option for it was so steep it propelled me down – and the pebbles pinched painfully through the souls of my slippers. I gave a little gasp, then laughed at myself. This was what I had wanted – so why was I complaining?

I walked for a little while, enjoying the solitude and the sound and the smell of the sea. The tide was low; beyond the pebbles was a broad stretch of wet sand, festooned with strings of seaweed and beached shells. I walked along the edge of it, for it was easier on my feet than the pebbles, heading towards the outcrop at one end of the cove.

Now that I was closer I could see the intricacy of the rock formations on that wing of the bay, an archway, like the eye of a needle, the finger of tumbled boulders stretching towards the tide yet not quite reaching it. There might well be another cove beyond that outcrop, I knew. A cove even more secluded than this one with nothing but the sheer cliffs above it and no life but the nesting seabirds to look down upon it. There might well be caves, washed clean by the tides. There might be rock pools of sea water or even a small lagoon of fresh water. I longed to go around that headland and explore but common sense told me I must not. Not yet; not until I was more familiar with the tides on this coast. If I got myself cut off it would not be an auspicious start, particularly in view of Francis's warning, and it could be worse than that even. If the cliffs rose sheer from the beach with none of the caves and crannies I was imagining I could be drowned like a rat in a trap.

In spite of the warmth of the evening, I shivered.

I turned my back on the inviting headland,

climbed on to a boulder and sat down. It was no way to treat my good gown, but I did not care. I bunched it up above my knees like a child, loving the feel of the fresh air on my bare legs; leaning back, raising my face to the fading sun.

Here, nothing seemed so bad. I could tell myself that I had misinterpreted the dubious welcome I had received and almost believe it. Francis Trevelyan was just a father concerned for his little daughter's welfare, Selena was an eccentric, perhaps embittered at the treatment meted out to the daughter of a house who had not found a husband, forced to depend on her brother for a home. And the way Francis had looked when he first saw me – that had all been my imagination too. My fertile, foolish imagination.

I thought too of Tom Stanton. Remembered the way something strong and sweet and unfamiliar had stirred within me as I looked at him. That really was foolishness, of course. And the quirk of happiness that seemed to run through my veins at the thought of him was foolishness too. Why, I didn't even know the man! But it was welcome foolishness all the same, a spark of sunlight in what had been a rather dark day.

A figure appeared within my line of vision, moving slowly along the shoreline. The bent figure of an old woman with a creel over her arm. Her skirts, hitched up to keep them out of the softly breaking waves, stirred in the stiff breeze, her head was covered by a shawl. I saw her crouch down a few times, gathering shellfish, no doubt, from the pools left by the tide.

The sun was low now, the daylight beginning to fade. Reluctantly I decided it was time I returned to Morwennan House. I was not yet sufficiently familiar with the cliff path to negotiate its perils in darkness. I slipped down from the rock and began walking back.

As I drew nearer to the old woman I became aware that she had straightened up and was staring at me. I nodded in her direction and expected no more than a nod in return. But instead she came towards me, her mouth agape in her wrinkled, weather-beaten face, small beady eyes peering at me incredulously. Disconcerted, I stared back.

'Julia?' Her voice was little more than a dry croak. 'Julia – is it really you?'

For a moment I was speechless. This was, in its own way, the self-same reaction that I had encountered from Francis Trevelyan. Then I found my voice.

'I am not Julia, no. I am Charity Palfrey.'

The old woman continued to stare, as if she did not believe me. Then she drew a long, wheezing breath.

'Forgive me. I thought ... Oh, you are so much like her!'

My mind was whirling now and for no reason I could explain I had begun to tremble. But I knew that somehow I had to find the courage to ask the question that was burning on my lips.

'Who did you think I was?'

The old woman cackled drily. 'I'm going soft in my old age. Taking leave of whatever sense I once had. I thought for a minute ... but of course, it could not be. She's been dead for years.'

'Who?' I persisted.

But I think, even before she replied, I already knew what her answer would be.

'Why, Julia Trevelyan, of course! The maid from Morwennan House. Francis Trevelyan's wife.'

Four

Julia Trevelyan. Francis Trevelyan's wife. The old woman's words echoed and re-echoed in my head. The wind from the sea was suddenly chill and I shivered and wrapped my arms around myself.

'Am I so like her then?' I heard myself ask.

'Like her? You're the dead spit of her and no mistake. In her heyday, of course. Before...' The old woman broke off, shaking her head. 'Ah well, fate can play some strange tricks – and some cruel ones. Good day to you.'

She hitched her creel up on her arm and with one last penetrating look into my face, went on her way.

For a moment I stood motionless, staring after her bent, retreating figure, watching stupidly as she resumed her search of the rock pools. My feet seemed to have anchored themselves in the soft sand. Then, with an effort of will, I began to walk back up the beach, stumbling over the rough pebbles and not even feeling them. My mind was whirling now as the half-formed thoughts began to take shape.

I was the living image of Francis Trevelyan's dead wife – Julia, the old woman had called her. I was so like her the old crone had thought for a moment I *was* her. No wonder Francis had been so shocked when we first met! No wonder Selena had stared at me so when she had seen me in Penwyn church. But why, then, had she appointed me Charlotte's governess without telling me of the likeness? More importantly, why had she not warned Francis? She must have known it would be a terrible shock for him, coming face to face with me in his own home. Yes, undoubtedly she had known – it accounted for the strange suppressed excitement I had noticed in her as we waited for him to emerge from his study and greet me. For some reason of her own, Selena had wanted to shock him.

I felt a flash of anger that she should use me so, like a pawn in some game, but it was a fleeting anger only, for more importantly the implications of my likeness to Julia were flooding my mind now and I felt strangely elated.

All my life I had been the cuckoo in the nest. Never had I been able to look at my family and see little likenesses. Now it seemed I had come to a place where there was recognition in people's eyes. I was the living image of Julia Trevelyan, sufficiently like her to shock Francis and to convince an old woman that she had come back from the dead.

Everyone has a double, they say. But was it just coincidence, or was there another reason for the likeness? Was I related to Julia? Could it possibly be that fate – and Selena Trevelyan – had brought me home?

I reached the path and glanced up. Above me Morwennan House clung to the cliff like a giant eagle's eyrie, square and somehow menacing. Behind me the beach was still bathed in soft dying light but a dark cloud seemed to have settled over Morwennan House. There it was already night.

Taking a deep breath I hitched up my skirts for the climb and started up the cliff path.

The lamps had been lit in the house. As I drew closer I could see the glow at the windows but there was nothing welcoming about it. The windows were like hooded eyes concealing ... what?

I made my way round the side of the house and let myself in at the great front door. At once the gloom surrounded me.

The parlour door was ajar and I could hear the sound of voices coming from beyond it. Francis and Selena's voices, sounding angry.

On my way back to the house I had been preparing myself to confront them with what

I had learned, demand some answers to the questions that were seething around inside my head. Now I hesitated, unwilling to interrupt what was clearly a family quarrel, yet equally unwilling to creep away again. They owed me some sort of explanation tonight, before I spent a single night under their roof, and I was determined to have it. At this moment my resolve was high; tomorrow, maybe, my courage would desert me.

I started towards the parlour, my slippered feet making no sound on the bare floor, and the voices from within the parlour carried out clearly to me.

'You have always been a scheming, jealous, vindictive woman, Selena. But this time you have surpassed yourself!' Francis, clearly beside himself with rage. 'I don't know what you hoped to gain by bringing her here, but...'

'What would *I* gain, Francis?' Selena, her voice raised, yet clearly still in command of herself. 'I would have thought the gain would be all yours. You've been obsessed with that woman all your life. Her looks drove you to madness. Well – now you can begin all over again!'

Francis swore. 'You are beyond belief, Selena! It excites you, does it, to torture me so? But have you thought of the consequences? She can't stay. I won't have it. The whole thing is quite insupportable.'

'For heaven's sake, Francis, you are behaving like a hysterical girl. But then, you never were able to control your emotions where Julia was concerned. No, the decision is made now and you will just have to put up with it. Charlotte needs a governess, I need help in dealing with her, and I have appointed Charity, so there's an end of it.'

'But suppose she should learn the truth – have you thought of that?'

'Why should she? But now I come to think of it, it would be rather ... interesting.'

'You think so!' Francis was beside himself.

'Indeed. As this whole episode is interesting. I thought I knew you, Francis. I did not imagine you could keep secrets from me. I was wrong. But I am not wrong about who this girl is, am I? Oh no, I am not wrong. The moment I saw her, I knew.'

There was a silence, a momentary pregnant silence, which seemed to me to go on for ever. Then Selena laughed softly.

'She is Julia's daughter, brother dear. Julia's daughter, come home to us after all these years!'

I felt my knees turn weak beneath me. I grabbed at the hall table to steady myself and the pewter jug that stood on it rocked in its bowl. I thought they would hear and come to see who it was in the hall, listening to them. But they were too engrossed in their quarrel.

'You will rot in hell, Selena,' Francis said, and Selena laughed again, as if she were very pleased with herself indeed.

'Then I will surely have your company, Francis.'

I did not wait to hear more. I was too afraid they would come out and find me there. I backed away, then turned and ran to the door. I stumbled outside and closed it after me. Then I leaned against the rough stone wall, drawing the fresh night air into my lungs, feeling it cool my burning cheeks.

I could scarcely believe what I had heard, let alone comprehend it. But without intending to, Francis and Selena had given me the answer to some of the questions I had intended to ask them. They had given me the answer to the most important question of all.

If Selena had been right in her assumption about me, and this whole bizarre situation was not some terrible coincidence, I had at last discovered who I was.

I was the daughter of Francis Trevelyan's dead wife, Julia.

How long I remained outside in the pitch dark beneath the trees I do not know. I scarcely remember what I thought even. It was as if I was caught in a whirlpool of emotion, being spun around and around, sucked in and down. But I could not remain there for ever. At last I steeled myself to open the door again and step inside. All was quiet. I let the door close with a bang to warn of my return.

Francis appeared in the doorway of the parlour. His colour was higher than ever, his cravat a little askew. I tried to speak, but could find no words. What could I say to him?

'Charity,' he said. His voice was a little slurred; I could smell the brandy on his breath.

I found my voice. 'Mr Trevelyan.'

'Charity...'

I waited, wondering what he was about to say to me. Would he acknowledge me, tell me at least something of why I was here? Or would he tell me to pack my bags and go?

In the event he did neither.

'Did you have a good walk?' he asked, as if nothing had occurred at all.

'Yes ... Yes, thank you...'

'You look tired, Charity.'

'I am,' I said faintly. 'It's been a long day.'

'And a longer one tomorrow. Charlotte will be coming home in the morning. Would you care for a nightcap?'

'No ... No, thank you.' All I wanted was to be alone, to think over what had happened and try to make sense of it. 'As I said, I am very tired. If you don't mind, I think I would like to go to bed.'

He looked, I thought, relieved.

'As you wish, of course. Selena showed you your room?'

I nodded. Selena was nowhere to be seen. Perhaps she had already retired.

'Good night then.'

'Good night.'

As I left him I saw him reaching for the brandy decanter once more.

There was no hope I would sleep that night. No hope at all. I undressed in a daze, my hands performing the familiar actions automatically, and climbed into the narrow bed. Then I tossed and turned as restlessly as if it were a bed of nails, my skin crawling, my thoughts churning.

Could it be true that I really was Julia Trevelyan's daughter? But if I was, why had I been abandoned so far from Morwennan? And for what reason? I had always supposed my mother to be some poor unmarried girl who had been pushed from parish to parish when her condition became apparent. That often happened, right up to the moment of giving birth, for no parish wanted the burden of another mouth to feed, and the place of birth of an illegitimate child determined who would have the onus of responsibility for seeing it did not starve. I had assumed my mother, driven thus around the countryside, had borne me in Penwyn, perhaps in secret, left me in a box on the doorstep of the rectory and gone back to wherever it was she had come from, praying that I would be found and taken care of. I had supposed she had nothing whatever to offer me.

But if Julia Trevelyan was my mother none of those conditions would apply. Julia Trevelyan had been a lady of means, who had married into landed gentry. She must have been of good family herself. Had she, as a young girl, become pregnant with me and, mortified by the stigma, had her father forced her to give me up, place me in the care of the Palfreys? Was that the reason they had always been so reticent concerning the circumstances in which they had found me – because, in reality, they knew very well who I was and that I would be an embarrassment and shame to my natural family?

And what of my father? Who was he? Not Francis, surely! If I had been born of their union, in wedlock, then there could be no possible reason for my having been abandoned ... could there? Yet both Francis and Selena seemed to have been aware of the existence of a child.

'Julia's daughter, come home to us after all these years,' Selena had said. Oh, they had known all right! But: *Julia's* daughter. Not: *Your* daughter. No, I did not think Francis was my father – and I realised I did not want

74

him to be. I did not care for him at all. In fact there was something about him that repelled me.

As for Selena – there was, as Francis had said during their quarrel, something evil about her. To think for a moment that the same blood might run in our veins was not a pleasant notion. But why had she brought me here?

You have always been a scheming, jealous, vindictive woman, Selena, Francis had said, and I had no doubt he spoke the truth. Perhaps it was malicious spite that had motivated her. But *scheming*? In what way could I possibly figure in her schemes?

Francis had not been pleased, that much was certain. Another reason to make me think that he was not my father. But he *was* Charlotte's father ... and Julia was her mother. Which would mean – surely! – that the possibility was that Charlotte was my sister!

A thrill beyond belief ran through me. All these years without a single relative to call my own, and now perhaps I had a sister! Oh, a child as yet. And a half-sister, not full-blooded. But that scarcely mattered. My skin prickled with excitement. I couldn't wait to meet her!

A board creaked above my head, startling me. A timber settling, no doubt. Houses come alive in the quiet of the night and this

75

one was no exception. Another creak ... and another ... further away towards the door ... The house I had so long dreamed of seemed to be shifting in its sleep...

I shifted myself, puzzled still further as I remembered the dream. Had I lived here before? Was the dream a distant memory? Surely it must be so! *Julia's* daughter, come home after all these years ... And yet ... and yet...

Unable to lie in my bed a moment longer, I pushed aside the covers and swung my legs to the ground.

The bare boards felt cold beneath my feet. I reached for a wrap and slipped it on. I wished I dared explore the house, quietly and alone, but I did not dare. I was still a stranger here – a visitor almost. I could not creep about in the dead of night. Not yet. But when I felt more at home ... If Francis had not sent me on my way by then...

I crossed to the window and drew aside the curtains. Moonlight streamed in. Outside, it illuminated what I could see of the gardens so they were bright, almost, as day. I looked down at the pathway beneath my window where I had first seen Francis and Tom walking, picturing them again, the big florid man and the leaner younger one. At the thought of Tom something sharp and sweet twisted inside me and I told myself not to be foolish. There was enough on my mind already without the added complication of a crazy attraction for a man I barely knew.

I turned my head a little so that I could see the sea beyond the sheltering curve of the cliffs. A ship was there in the cove, riding, I thought, at anchor, for it seemed not to move at all. Like a ship in an oil painting the masts stood tall against the skyline; the empty sails were milky in the moonlight. For a long while I watched it sitting there and wondered idly what it was doing. Fishing, perhaps. But it did not look like a fishing boat. It looked like a cutter.

Perhaps, then, it was a ship unloading contraband. Smuggling was rife all along the coasts of Cornwall and Devon and even beyond, I knew, and this was a perfect night for such business. Though I could not see them, I could imagine the small boats that would be swarming around the cutter's elegant hull like insects, loading up with spirits and tea and tobacco and silks to ferry to some hiding place on the coast.

The excise officers and preventivemen would do their best to catch those responsible, of course, and confiscate the contraband. But they may as well sit like Canute on the beach and order back the tide for all the long-term good they would do. The smugglers were too many and too clever for them and, on the whole, communities closed in to protect them. For did not the communities benefit too from the cheap luxuries the 'Gentlemen' put their way?

At last with a sigh I turned away from the window. For all that my thoughts were racing, my emotions churning, I really must at least try to get some sleep or I would be good for nothing tomorrow. And tomorrow would be every bit as taxing as today had been. Tomorrow I would have to face Francis and Selena once more. Tomorrow I would meet Charlotte, who might be my half-sister.

I took off my robe and draped it over a chair. I climbed into bed and pulled the sheet up to my chin. I closed my eyes and tried resolutely to put all the momentous events, all the perplexing questions, out of my mind.

The house was quiet now as if it was, at last, sleeping. No creaks, no settling timbers. Gradually I became drowsy. At last I too slept.

Five

When I woke next morning the first sound I heard was the cawing of the rooks. There was something strange and disturbing about it; so close to the sea it would have been more natural to hear the mew of gulls.

As I dressed myself I wondered if I should make any mention to Selena or Francis of what I had learned last night, and decided against it. Selena's threats had clearly persuaded Francis that I should stay for the time being at least; if I began asking questions he might very well change his mind. That was the last thing I wanted. I was closer now than I had ever been to finding out who I was and why I had been abandoned. If he sent me away now I might never learn the truth. I must be patient, pretend I was no wiser than when I had arrived, and keep my ears and eyes open. Then, if my luck held, I might be able to glean the information I craved and fit it together piece by piece.

Besides, I wanted to meet Charlotte, who might be the sister I had never known I had.

As I went down the staircase Mrs Durbin

emerged from a door on the far side of the hall. She was carrying a tray laden with stacked crockery. She looked up and saw me and a strange furtive expression crossed her face.

'Good morning,' I said.

She turned and locked the door behind her before replying, then set the tray down on the spindle-legged side table and came towards me.

'Did you sleep well, Miss Charity?'

'Thank you, yes,' I replied.

'I'm glad to hear it. Sometimes it's not easy to get a good night's rest in an unfamiliar bed. I know I like my own place.'

Her hands fluttered to her mob cap, easing it over her temples, and she beamed at me.

I felt myself warming to her. Her cheeks were like polished apples, her eyes, though faded, had a twinkle in them, and her smile was the first expression of genuine welcome anyone at Morwennan had offered me.

'Yes, Durbin and me have been here with Mr Francis for more than twenty years so you might say it's home to us,' she went on. 'The only home we'll ever have, I dare say.'

It occurred to me that if Mrs Durbin had been with the Trevelyans so long she must know as well as anyone all there was to know about Francis – and Julia. But it was much too early to begin asking her questions.

'Well, I'm glad you're here, Charity,' she

said. 'More glad than you'll ever know. And what a difference it will make to Miss Charlotte! She's on her own too much, that one. A child her age needs younger company than she's used to. She's a handful, mind you! A will of her own and no mistake, even at her age. But she knows how to wind her father round her little finger for all that.' She broke off, shaking her head with another smile, then, quite suddenly her expression changed. The smile disappeared, her lips pursed slightly, her eyes were no longer on me, but looking past me.

Instinctively I turned in the direction of her gaze and saw Selena sweeping down the staircase.

'Haven't you anything better to do than chatter, Mrs Durbin?' Her tone was acerbic.

A rosy flush coloured Mrs Durbin's apple cheeks.

'Indeed I have, Miss Selena. There's always plenty to do round this house. I've told you often enough I could do with more help in the kitchen.'

'And you know perfectly well that is not possible. If you've work to do I suggest you get on with it.' Selena turned to me. 'Shall we go in to breakfast, Charity? It's all ready I hope, Mrs Durbin.'

'Indeed it is, ma'am. Mr Francis is having his already.' Mrs Durbin returned to the spindle-legged table and collected the tray she had deposited there.

I followed Selena into the dining room.

Francis looked, I thought, as though he had slept as little as I. His eyes were almost hidden beneath swollen lids and the folds of his face hung heavier than ever.

'Selena. Charity.' Even his voice sounded tired.

'Good morning, Francis,' Selena said briskly. 'No, don't trouble to get up.' She turned to me. 'We'll serve ourselves, Charity. Mrs Durbin is clearly busy.'

She swept over to the sideboard and lifted the lid of a silver chafing dish. The aroma of griddled kidneys filled the room and I realised I was hungrier than I would have believed possible. I helped myself to some and then felt shamed when Selena took a much smaller portion. Everything about her, everything she did, made me uncomfortable, it seemed.

'I have business to attend to today,' Francis said when we were seated at the table and Selena had poured hot coffee for herself and me. 'I shall be leaving as soon as I have finished breakfast.'

I found myself wondering what his business might be. Quarrying, perhaps, or tin mining. Whatever, it was clearly successful, for Morwennan House and all the artefacts in it indicated that, for a younger son, he was well off.

'Charlotte should be home by noon,' he said to me. 'Until then your time is your own, Charity.'

I nodded, thinking how strange it was that he was making no mention of the turmoil my appearance had caused him. But there was no mistaking the frostiness between him and Selena, a frostiness that even the morning sun, streaming in at the windows, could do nothing to dispel.

'I'll prepare some lessons for her,' I said, anxious to create a good impression.

Francis gave me a look that was almost surprised, as if he had forgotten my purpose for being here was to take charge of Charlotte's education.

'Oh there's plenty of time for that,' he said dismissively. 'Spend the morning relaxing. You'll have little enough time for that when Charlotte arrives. She is very like her mother in many respects.'

'Trying,' Selena interposed drily.

I froze, a forkful of kidney halfway to my mouth, and saw the warning look Francis shot at her. Immediately her lips turned down in that strange amused smile. She was still scoring points and enjoying every moment of it. But at least neither of them knew that I knew it.

Francis drained his cup, wiped his mouth, and stood up.

'I'll leave you then. Selena, you will introduce Charity to Charlotte, no doubt?'

'No doubt. Though if you remember, Francis, I have a household to run.'

'And very well you do it too,' Francis said. 'I'm sure, however, you will find the time to see Charlotte into Charity's care, since you are the one responsible for the arrangement.'

'Oh, I'm sure I shall,' Selena agreed evenly.

Selena and I finished breakfast with the same awkward atmosphere hanging between us.

'I expect as a foundling you must often wonder about your natural family,' Selena said, watching me speculatively, and I wondered if she was about to broach the subject of my likeness to Julia.

'Of course,' I replied, trying to keep my tone even.

'Have you never tried to learn the circumstances in which the Palfreys found you?' she asked.

I was determined to be non-committal until she made the first move.

'They would never tell me anything,' I said. 'I have always imagined my mother must have been some poor girl forced by circumstances to abandon me.'

'You don't blame her then?' Selena asked.

'Shame and poverty are hard masters,' I replied. 'If her family turned her out and she had no means of supporting a child, what else could she do?'

'But supposing she was not poor,' Selena said. I could feel her eyes watching me closely over the rim of her cup. 'What then? Would you still feel so kindly towards her?'

My mouth was dry suddenly; I swallowed a forkful of kidney with difficulty.

'I'm sure whatever her circumstances she must have had good reason,' I said levelly, hiding behind the reasoning I had always fallen back on for comfort. 'No, unless I was to learn something to convince me otherwise, I don't blame her. Whoever she was, she was my mother. I must think the best of her.'

Selena was silent for a moment. I wondered what was coming. Then she dabbed her mouth and stood up.

'You must excuse me, Charity. I have a great deal to do. Mrs Durbin will be expecting me to check the menus for the day and with Charlotte coming home ... As Francis said, until she arrives, your time is your own. The gardens are very pleasant at this time of day and I'm sure you would like to explore them. When Charlotte arrives I will come and find you. But I don't expect her before noon.'

So Selena was not going to take the opportunity to enlighten me as to the reason I was here. With a swish of her skirts she left the room and I was alone.

When I had finished my breakfast I found a tray on the sideboard, piled the used dishes together and took them to the kitchen. I was not sure if this was what I was expected to do or not; no one had outlined my duties beyond instructing Charlotte, but I was not used to being waited on and if Mrs Durbin was so busy it seemed the right thing to do.

The kitchen was deserted; there was no sign of Mrs Durbin or any maid. It was surprising, I thought, that the Trevelyans had so few servants. In a house this size I would have expected there to be a kitchen maid at least as well as the housekeeper. Clearly this was not the case, since Mrs Durbin had complained about the lack of help.

I unloaded the dishes into the sink but stopped short of washing them. Though I was anxious not to appear lazy, neither did I want to trespass in what was clearly Mrs Durbin's domain.

I went back to my room, made my bed and tidied away the things I had been too tired and too overwrought to attend to last night. Then I decided I would do as Selena had suggested and explore the gardens.

As I went back downstairs and through the house I saw no one. Voices coming from the parlour suggested Selena was going through the day's menus with Mrs Durbin there. I hurried past. There was a back door leading directly to the lawns, but when I tried it I found it locked, so I used the main door and followed the path around the side of the house.

The gardens were indeed pleasant, the morning sun drawing the perfume from the roses. I stopped to sniff one; it was just opening and dew lay like drops of crystal on its velvety petals. I wished I could pick it and pin it to my gown but to do so would be to kill it in all its perfection, a sacrilegious betrayal, and in any case, it was not mine to pick.

Low down in the garden, near the gate leading to the cliff path, was a sort of arbour, its high-backed frame sheltering it from the wind off the sea. I sat down on it and smelled camomile; the whole seat was covered with it and my weight had crushed it and released the perfume.

The peace was complete; far beneath me I could hear the swell of the sea but otherwise there was no sound. Even the cawing of the rooks and the cries of the seabirds wheeling overhead were muted. As I sat there pondering on all that had occurred the sun was warm on my face and I began to feel drowsy. I had, after all, slept little last night. The last thing I had intended was to sleep now but I closed my eyes anyway and felt the world going far away, this strange, unfamiliar world with its myriad of unanswered questions, at once so overbearing, so exciting, and, at the moment, so peaceful.

I slept. I must have done, because when the voice spoke to me I came to with a start, wondering for the moment where I was.

'Miss Palfrey! My apologies! I didn't mean to disturb you.'

Tom Stanton was standing before me, a small half-smile on his good-looking face. Startled, I wondered where he had come from, but since the gate leading to the cliff path was swinging open it seemed likely he had come that way.

'Oh, you are not disturbing me!' I said quickly. My heart was beating very fast – from the shock of my sudden awakening, I told myself, but knew different all the same.

'My apologies anyway,' he said lightly. 'I suppose it would be impolite of me to say I thought for a moment that you were asleep.'

'I think I might have been,' I admitted, my hands flying to my hair to make sure it had not come loose. 'But sleeping in the middle of the morning is a disgraceful thing to do. You've done me a service by waking me.'

He stood looking down at me, legs splayed, hands on hips, and that same smile that had affected me so yesterday lifting the corners of his generous mouth. Unexpectedly I felt my cheeks growing hot. That was what came of having thoughts about a man! I told myself.

'The Trevelyans are not working you too hard it seems,' he said.

I bridled a little. 'My duties don't begin until Charlotte gets home from her grandfather's,' I said. 'Until then my time is my own.'

'Ah.' Tom glanced in the direction of the house. 'I have come to see Francis. Is he busy, do you know?'

'He's out. He left on business the moment he had breakfasted,' I said. 'I don't know when he'll be back, but certainly not this morning. Charlotte is due back at noon and he asked Selena to make the introductions between us.'

'Then I have had a wasted journey.' But he did not look particularly downcast. 'Or perhaps not,' he added, lifting an eyebrow at me. 'I promised to show you something of the district and we are both at a loose end it seems. Why don't we take advantage of that?'

I felt the colour deepen in my cheeks.

'Now?' I said. 'Oh, I don't think...'

'Are you turning me down, Miss Palfrey?' The amused look seemed to have strayed into his voice.

'I ... I can't just wander off...'

'Why not?' he challenged me. 'You said your time was your own this morning. Why, if I know Selena, she'll be far too busy to even notice you've gone.'

Given Selena's especial interest in me I was not so sure about that, but I could hardly say so.

'But I must be sure to be here when Charlotte arrives,' I murmured weakly.

'Charlotte won't be here until noon, you told me,' Tom said. 'That's a good two hours off. Plenty of time for the exploration I have in mind. Live a little dangerously, Miss Palfrey, and keep me company.'

Live a little dangerously! If only he knew! And his offer was very inviting. I made up my mind.

'Very well,' I said recklessly. 'You have talked me into it. I'll come with you on one condition.'

'And what is that?'

'You must stop calling me Miss Palfrey. It makes me feel like an old spinster lady. Being a governess is bad enough!'

'So what should I call you?' he asked.

'My given name is Charity,' I said. 'It's served me well enough these twenty years.'

His eyes held mine. The smile from his mouth had reached them.

'Very well – Charity. And I am Tom. I don't much like being called Mr Stanton either.'

I stood up, tipping my head to one side and looking up into his face.

'So, where are you going to take me, Tom?' I asked pertly, and realised that for the first time in my life I was flirting.

★ ★ ★

He led me back out of the gate on to the cliff path but not down the track to the beach. In the full light of day I saw that another well-worn path followed the line of the cliff into the bay and out again towards the sentry outcrops in both directions, down, and then steeply up once more.

'How are you on rough ground?' he asked me with a doubtful glance at my slippers.

'Like a mountain goat,' I assured him. 'I grew up scrambling in the most inaccessible places after my brothers.'

'Your brothers?' he queried.

'Adopted brothers. The sons of the parson and his wife who gave me a home. There were four of them. Jem, the eldest, lives not far from here now. He's a clerk in Falmouth.'

'Falmouth!' Tom said. 'It is a small world indeed! I grew up in Falmouth.'

'Really?' Somehow the connection made it all right that I was out alone with him. 'And do you have family there?'

'No, I have no family now.' His tone was abrupt. I wished I had not asked.

'So your brothers turned you into something of a tomboy, Charity,' he said, changing the subject.

I laughed self-consciously. 'I suppose so.'

We had completed the descent now and started the steep climb up what I thought of as the left sentry cliff. Soon we had no more breath for talking – or at least I did not, for Tom was setting a fast pace and it was as much as I could do to keep up with him.

As we reached the top I stopped, pressing a hand to my heaving chest.

'Wait a moment while I get my breath!'

Tom turned, looking at me anxiously.

'I'll be fine in a moment,' I assured him. 'I'm clearly out of practice.'

'There are still a lot of ups and downs to go,' he warned me. 'Are you sure you can manage it?'

'Quite sure,' I replied. 'Only can we do the ups a bit more slowly?'

We set off again at a more leisurely pace. For the moment the path was flat across the top of the cliff but ahead I could indeed see that it wove down and up again into the coves that ran along the coast like a string of beads.

After perhaps half an hour or so of walking Tom stopped again. We were on a high plateau and the path ahead curved with the land around a narrow inlet.

'This is the place,' he said. 'We have to go down the cliff here.'

I glanced down. The ground fell steeply to a pool far below, sapphire-blue and sparkling in the sunlight. There was no clearly defined path; we would have to pick our way carefully if we were not to lose our balance and go tumbling down.

'It's not as bad as it looks,' Tom reassured me. 'And it's well worth the effort. Don't worry, I'll help you.'

He started down, picking a zigzag path, and I followed. He was right, it was not as bad as it looked and there were plenty of thick clumps of thrift to hold on to. At one point I noticed a stream trickling alongside us, roughly following the route we were taking down to the sea.

The last few feet dropped steeply between boulders to a patch of shingle.

'Wait there,' Tom said. He scrambled down to the shingle and turned, reaching up towards me. 'Give me your hand.'

I did as he said. His grip was strong enough to give me confidence, though the rocks felt slightly slippery beneath my feet. When I too was standing on the shingle he released my hand and I felt a twinge of regret. But only for a moment, for I was entranced by the tiny cove in which I found myself.

The pool I had seen from the cliff top was at my feet now, crystal clear and shimmering as the sunlight glanced off it and the little stream ran into it from the rocks above, no longer trickling but pouring like a waterfall from a height of perhaps five or six feet.

'This is a freshwater pool!' I said, surprised.

'Yes. I've rescued a frog from here before

now,' Tom said. 'They lose their way some-times and get washed down if the stream is running high.'

'Oh, poor thing! And then they drown...'

'Not if I find them first,' Tom said. 'But there's more. Provided you are prepared to get your feet wet.'

'My feet...? You mean I should paddle...?'

'If you want to see something really spec-tacular.' Tom was already taking off his shoes and placing them on a flat dry boulder.

I did. And I wanted to dabble my feet in the water which looked so inviting! I kicked off my slippers and laid them on the rock beside Tom's shoes. Then I hesitated.

'Turn around whilst I take off my stock-ings,' I ordered Tom.

'Coy, then!' he said with a grin. But he turned around anyway.

I rolled down my stockings and pushed them into my slippers. Then, throwing de-corum to the winds, I hitched up my skirts.

'Ready.'

He stepped down into the pool and reach-ed out to me.

'Take my hand.'

I did not need to be told twice. His hand had felt so good in mine. I twined my fingers with his and stepped down into the pool. The water felt icy cold to my bare feet, but sweet and soft, though the shingle was sharp and gritty beneath my toes.

'This way.' He led me back towards the cliff and I wondered what Mama Mary would say if she could see me now, wading barefoot through the water with my skirts hitched up above my knees, hand in hand with a man I scarcely knew. It was hardly the behaviour of a lady – but when had I been a lady?

There was a double cleft in the rock, a tiny narrow cave. Tom led me through it into the tiny cavern beyond, then turned me around to face the sea.

'There!' he said, and there was pride in his voice. 'Was it worth the effort?'

For a moment I could not find my voice to reply. I was too awestruck by the beauty of the vision before me.

We were immediately behind the spot where the stream cascaded over the cliff edge. It formed a moving curtain of water over the second cleft directly in front of me and the sun, shining through it, made a prism of each droplet. It made a sparkling cascade against the blue sky beyond, a magic rainbow come to earth, splashing softly, ceaselessly, into the rock pool.

'Oh!' I gasped. 'Oh – it's marvellous!'

'I thought you'd like it.' I was not looking at him – I could not take my eyes off the mesmerising cascade – but I heard the smile in his voice.

'Like it! Oh – I've never seen anything so

beautiful!'

How long I stood there entranced I do not know. Then gradually I became aware that my hand was still in Tom's and it was all part of the magic of the moment.

I looked up at him, at his face, half-shadowed and very strong-looking, and felt a twist deep inside. Instantly my defences came up.

'I suppose we had better be getting back. I must be there when Charlotte arrives.'

'We'll come again – if you'd like to that is,' he promised.

If I'd like to! I thought that never in my entire life had I been closer to paradise.

'Oh, yes!'

'Come on then,' he said.

Six

As we came through the gate that led into the garden of Morwennan House I was dismayed to see Selena on the highest stretch of lawn, her eyes shaded with her hand as she peered around, and a little girl standing beside her.

'Oh, I'm late!' I groaned. 'Charlotte has arrived and I was not here to greet her!'

I hurried up the path ahead of Tom, all too aware that my hair was coming loose from its combs and the hem of my gown was wet from where it had dragged in the water.

Even at this distance I could see that Charlotte's hair, tumbling loose over her shoulders, was the same rich chestnut as my own. My heart thudded in my chest and my breath was coming fast, both from hurrying up the steep incline and from nervous anticipation.

Suddenly the little girl came darting across the lawns towards us. I was startled – I had not expected to be greeted so enthusiastically. But Charlotte ran straight past me with scarcely a look in my direction.

'Tom! Tom!'

She hurled herself at him, her surprise and delight at seeing him obvious, and he swung her up into the air.

'Charlotte! You're home then!'

'Yes! Oh Tom, I've been at Grandfather's! I rode the pony! I rode Moonlight all by myself!'

'I don't believe you,' he teased her. 'Not all by yourself!'

'I did! I did, I tell you! I even took a little jump! Grandfather put a bar out for me and we jumped it! And I didn't even fall off once!'

'My, what a horsewoman you are going to be!' Tom said, and she flushed with pleasure.

Selena, who had followed at a more sedate pace, reached us now. Her lips were pursed, her eyes sharp.

'Charity. I was just wondering what had become of you,' she said tautly.

'Blame me,' Tom said before I could begin to apologise. 'I'm afraid I persuaded Charity to join me for a walk. We've been to Galidor. And it took longer than I expected.'

Selena's lips tightened still more.

'Galidor! It's hardly a suitable excursion for a lady, surely? Why are you here in any case? I wasn't aware arrangements had been made.'

'They had not,' Tom said. 'I called by to see Francis but Charity told me he was out and

I took the opportunity to show her one of the most beautiful sights in this part of Cornwall. My apologies if you were concerned by her absence, Selena.'

He smiled – that smile that would charm the birds from the trees – and Selena's expression softened visibly.

'Oh well, there's no harm done I dare say.' She turned to Charlotte, who was still hanging on Tom's arm. 'Charlotte – leave Tom alone, if you will, and come and meet Charity, who is to be your governess.'

Charlotte showed no inclination to let go of Tom's arm. She merely glowered at me, her smile gone, her small face set. She was not, I realised, pleased to see me.

'Charlotte!' Selena said sharply. 'Come and shake Charity's hand, if you please!'

'Go on, Charlotte,' Tom urged her with a smile. 'She won't bite, you know.'

Reluctantly Charlotte approached me and held out her hand.

'Hello, Charity. I'm Charlotte.'

I took her hand, small, soft and plump, and forced a smile to my dry lips.

'Hello, Charlotte. Tom is right. I don't bite. And I do so hope we are going to be friends.'

She nodded solemnly but there was no answering smile. Her eyes – darker than my own I noticed – were guarded. I found myself searching her face for some feature I might recognise as a childish likeness to the ones I saw each morning in my mirror as I fixed my hair, but could see none. Charlotte's face, even allowing for the fact that she was not far removed from babyhood, was much rounder than my own, her nose a broad button where mine tended to be sharp, her mouth a fat rosebud, her chin oval where mine was heart-shaped. But what had I been expecting? Though we might share a mother I was almost certain we must have different fathers and I fancied I could see something of Francis in her. His features too had in all likelihood been smooth and round – and handsome – before the years – and the drink – had turned them paunchy. I hoped with all my heart the same fate would not befall Charlotte. But for now she was a pretty child who would be prettier still when she smiled. And her hair – certainly her hair was the same colour as mine.

'If it was Francis you came to see, then I am afraid he is unlikely to return before late afternoon,' Selena said to Tom. There was a coolness in her tone. 'I would think it would scarcely be worth your while to wait.'

'Perhaps you're right,' Tom returned equably. 'I'll come back tomorrow or the next day.'

'Shall I tell Francis you called?' Selena asked in the same acerbic tone.

'By all means.'

'Can I pass on some message that might

save you having to return?'

'No. My business with him is not urgent. And I shall be glad of the excuse to return.' He glanced at me, his eyes holding mine teasingly, and I felt the colour flooding into my cheeks again.

Selena, I think, could hardly have failed to notice, but she ignored the innuendo anyway.

'Then we will bid you good day,' she said briskly. 'It's time for Charlotte's midday meal and I think the sooner she and Charity get acquainted the better.'

'You don't have to go, Tom, do you?' Charlotte pleaded.

'I'm afraid I must, sweeting.' He chucked her chin affectionately. 'But I'll see you soon...' Over her head his eyes met mine again. 'And Charity too, I hope. Perhaps we can go exploring again – if Selena will permit it. There are plenty of exquisite places to visit.'

'Oh, can I come too?' Charlotte was bouncing up and down with anticipation.

He rumpled her hair. 'We'll see.'

'I would prefer,' Selena said icily, 'that Charlotte should learn to behave like a young lady. Come along, miss. Say goodbye to Tom.'

'Goodbye, Tom,' she said reluctantly.

'Farewell, Charlotte. Selena. And Charity...'

'Tom,' I said demurely. But my cheeks were still hot.

He turned to go back across the lawns to the cliff-path gate, and Selena, Charlotte and I went towards the house.

I spent the afternoon trying to strike up some sort of rapport with Charlotte, but with limited success. By the time we took tea she seemed to have accepted me a little more but she was still very reserved and that, I thought, was hardly surprising. I was, after all, a stranger to her still. And perhaps not an entirely welcome addition to her life. I hoped with all my heart that before long I could break down the barriers and see some of the ease with which she had greeted Tom, but that, I thought, would take time. I could not expect instant acceptance. She had no idea that I might be her sister and nor should she have. Not yet. Not until I was sure. And even then only if it was in her best interests.

'Charity,' she said as she ate her tea – and I sat opposite her. 'That's a funny name. Why are you called Charity?'

'Why are you called Charlotte?' I countered.

'Because my mama chose it,' she replied promptly.

My heartbeat quickened its pace.

'Your mama?' I repeated, gently questioning.

'Yes. My mama. She's dead though. She died when I was born.' She said it matter-of-factly, taking another bite of cake. 'Anyway, Charlotte is a proper name. Lots of people are called Charlotte. But not *Charity*.'

'I can't see that there's a great deal of difference,' I said, determined neither to apologise or explain. 'They both begin with *Char* after all.' She frowned. '*Char* lotte and *Char* ity. Perhaps we should make spelling one of your first lessons, then you'd be able to see it.'

'Oh, I can spell!' she returned impatiently, then, after thinking for a moment. '*Char* lotte. *Char* ity. Perhaps you're right.'

'I'm sure I am,' I said with a little smile. 'Not all the time, as you will find out. But this time certainly.'

'Mm.' She took another bite of cake. 'Charity,' she said, and her tone was guarded, 'how do you know Tom?'

'I didn't until today,' I told her.

'Then why did you go for a walk with him?' She was watching me narrowly and suddenly I understood her hostility towards me. Just a little girl she might be, but in her own childish way she was in love with Tom, just as I had once been in love with Joshua.

Tom was handsome and fun and he made a great fuss of her. Perhaps she even harboured a secret hope, as in my turn I had done, that one day he would marry her. The

103

fact that at least Joshua had been close to me in age whilst Tom was a grown man would have nothing to do with it. The first time she had set eyes on me I had been with her beloved Tom; no wonder she resented me.

'He took me to see a beautiful cave where the sun shines through the water,' I said. 'Have you been there?'

She shook her head.

'The next time, I promise you shall come too,' I said.

'Really?' Her face lit up. 'But Aunt Selena said...'

'I am sure we can get around your Aunt Selena,' I said, and I winked at her.

From that moment it seemed at least some of the reserve melted into thin air and I felt jubilant that I had found some common ground on which to build. And if it meant I had to sacrifice the pleasure of being alone with Tom, then so be it. The most important thing in the world to me at this moment was that I should begin to form some sort of bond with the little girl I felt sure was my sister.

I had no trouble falling asleep that night. I was so tired that not even thinking of all that had happened could keep me awake. My eyes were drooping over dinner; by the time I was undressed and my hair braided ready for bed I felt as heavy-limbed as I had once felt when, as a child, I had had a bad tooth-ache and Mama Mary had dosed me with laudanum. As I made my way from dressing table to bed I was almost staggering with tiredness. I pulled aside the covers, collapsed gratefully on to the bed, and was asleep the moment I settled my head on the pillow without being aware of drifting through any of the usual stages of drowsiness.

How long I slept, heavily, dreamlessly, I do not know. Then some unfamiliar repeated sound began to impose itself on me. I stirred, drowsed, stirred again, feeling a little bad-tempered at being dragged from the depths of my slumber.

The sounds continued, heavy, dragging sounds that seemed to come from outside my bedroom window. At first I tried to ignore them and return to that pleasant limbo where I had recently been but they nagged at the corners of my mind, bringing me more and more awake.

What was it I could hear? What could possibly be making those scraping sounds? And I thought I heard voices too. Intermittent, low and indistinct, but unmistakably men's voices for all that. Puzzled and a little frightened, I dragged myself out of bed and over to the window. My limbs and my eyes still felt unnaturally heavy so that every movement was an effort.

I pulled aside the curtains. The moon was

less bright than it had been last night, with banks of cloud scudding across it, but as I leaned forward, pressing my face against the glass, there was enough light to show me that I had been right.

There *were* men on the path beneath my window. Two were dragging something heavy – a large container from what I could make out. The grate of it on the stone path had been the sound that disturbed me. But there were other men too, moving more quickly because the bundles they carried were small and lighter; they stepped on to the lawn that bordered the path to overtake the two who manhandled the large container and disappeared out of my view around the corner of the house. One carried an armful of small packages, another a long roll wrapped in what looked to me like paper and straw. And still the two with the heavy container struggled with it along the path, stopping only to wipe the sweat from their faces.

'Get a move on, for the love of God!' The voice was low but authoritative. I could not see the speaker but I recognised the voice at once as belonging to Francis.

One of the two men swore roughly – and loudly.

'Do it yourself if you're not satisfied.'

'Keep quiet can't you! Do you want to wake the whole district?' Francis hissed. 'Get on with it and silently, or you'll not work for me again.'

The man muttered a reply I could not catch and resumed his efforts. After a while he and his companion also rounded the corner of the house and were lost to my view, but the dragging sound continued for some while, growing fainter as they got further away. I could only assume they were going up the gully away from the house. Judging by the length of time that elapsed before the man who had carried the smaller packages and the one who had balanced the straw-wrapped roll reappeared empty-handed, they were not going very far, perhaps to the top of the rise where the carriage had deposited me on the day I arrived.

Though my brain was thick as porridge, I was in no doubt as to what was going on. I had seen the cutter riding at anchor in the bay last night and thought of smugglers – with a feeling of sick certainty I knew I had been right. Whatever contraband had been brought ashore then was now being retrieved from its hiding place and sent on its way through the grounds of Morwennan House.

Perhaps there was a cart waiting at the top of the rise – or even a whole string of carts. That was what it would take to transport away all the items that were being carried along the path beneath my window, for, as I stood there watching, the steady procession went on and on.

There were perhaps ten or a dozen men in all, some distinctive enough for me to recognise when I saw them pass by for the second or third time, others more run of the mill so I could not be sure if they were the same ones I had seen before or not. But I was able to mark the progress of the ones who stood out and it seemed they took much longer from the time they returned empty-handed until I saw them come back, laden once more, than it had to deliver their burdens to their destination after passing beneath my window. If they were dropping the packages off at the top of the rise then it therefore followed they were going at least as far as the cliff path in the other direction and perhaps further, but of course that, too, was outside my line of vision.

After a while the constant quiet industry on the path below began to have an almost mesmeric effect on me. Drowsiness was overtaking me again, my eyes so heavy that, resting my head against the window frame, I almost fell asleep where I stood. And still they came with their bundles and packages, a never-ending procession.

My eyes were drooping, my legs felt as if they would support me no longer, my mouth was parched and I had the beginnings of a headache throbbing dully in one temple. Drawing the curtains against the scene outside I stumbled back to the bed and collapsed on to it.

I could still hear the sounds from outside but they were muted now, as if coming from another world. I was already in the murky hinterland that borders unconsciousness; everything had become unreal and I could no longer grasp at my thoughts.

But at least I knew that one question that had puzzled me had been answered.

I had wondered what Francis's business was, how he had made enough money to build Morwennan House and maintain it, and to afford the lifestyle he, Selena and Charlotte enjoyed. I was no longer in any doubt.

Francis was a smuggler on a grand scale. He was, no doubt, the mastermind behind a huge, well-organised ring.

And Morwennan House was its head-quarters.

When I woke next morning my head felt thick and my mouth furred. What had occur-red during the night felt like a dream to me, a highly coloured figment of my imagina-tion. I got up, drew the curtains to the morn-ing sunshine, and looked out. The path was deserted now and there was no sound but the interminable cawing of the rooks. But the grass, trampled at the edge of the path and scored where the corner of the heavy crate had caught it, told its own story.

So – Francis was the organiser of a smuggling operation. Yes, it was all quite feasible. No wonder he had chosen to build Morwennan House here! The bay, sheltered and secluded, was a perfect dropping-off point for contraband, the caves sealed off from prying eyes at high tide provided a first staging post, the cliff path and possibly tunnels I had not noticed provided access to the gardens and thence to the secluded gully road. Carts could be driven down it under cover of darkness and no one would see or ask questions when they were loaded and driven away again.

Had the carts been waiting last night, or had the contraband been concealed in the myriad of buildings that comprised the stable blocks to wait for another night, perhaps at the dark of the moon? I had not heard wheels or hooves so perhaps that was how it was done.

And what then? The consignment I had seen being moved was far more than could be disposed of locally, I felt sure. Given that almost every community along these coasts dabbled in the free trade to a greater or lesser degree, supply on this scale would certainly outstrip demand. Almost certainly the contraband was bound for markets much further afield and the success of the enterprise must depend on the efficient organisation of a transportation route out of Cornwall, into Devon, and maybe beyond. Was that why Francis had been absent most of yesterday? Had he been finalising arrangements for the next stage in the dispersal of the brandy, tobacco, silks and laces I had seen carried past my window?

I pressed my fingers to my forehead where a dull ache still lingered. I did not like the thought that I was living in a household built on illegal gain. It was one thing for poor fisherfolk to bring in boatloads of merchandise under cover of darkness to avoid paying duty and earn themselves something extra to make their harsh lives a little more comfortable. But this ... this, I felt sure, was in a different league altogether and must have been going on for many years or Francis would never have had the wherewithal to build Morwennan House in the first place.

How had he got away with it for so long? These days revenue vessels patrolled the seas and there were far more excise and preventivemen than there had used to be, for the government were trying their best to crack down on smuggling. Even in the sheltered inland town of Penwyn I had heard of running battles when shots were fired. But from the number of men involved in last night's operation it seemed likely that much of the community hereabouts was involved. Perhaps even those employed to wipe out the free trade were in Francis's pay and the local magistrate was in his pocket.

Another even less welcome thought struck me and I wondered why it had taken so long to occur to me.

Tom.

Tom had been here discussing 'business' with Francis on the day I had arrived. He had turned up again yesterday for further discussion. And that could mean only one thing.

Tom was involved in the smuggling ring. Heavily involved, since he had direct contact with Francis.

I bit my lip. I did not want Tom to be a criminal. Honesty was important to me; I could not contemplate becoming involved with someone who cared nothing for the laws of the land and made their living from crime.

Then I pulled myself up with a jolt. Good heavens, I had only just met Tom – we had been for one walk together – how could I even think for a moment that I might become involved with him, whatever his profession! It was utter madness and I would do well to put it right out of my mind.

As for Francis, how he made his money was really none of my business. I had enough on my mind without worrying about that. Establishing a rapport with Charlotte, for one thing. And discovering the truth about myself for another.

I pressed my fingertips to my aching head, thinking again about the quarrel I had over-heard between Francis and Selena on my first night here. They had spoken, both of them, as though it was an accepted fact that I was the daughter of Francis's dead wife, Julia, but there had been not a single word to indicate why she might have abandoned me.

The one thing that had come out, referred to more than once, if I was not mistaken, was Francis's deep love for Julia. More than that. Obsession, Selena had called it. And said that Francis had no control over himself where Julia was concerned, or something of the sort. It seemed a strange attitude, to pour scorn on him for loving his wife – something I would have thought should be considered a virtue!

Would I ever know the truth? I wondered. Would I ever know for certain whether I was Julia's child? Perhaps, if I was lucky. But as to the rest ... her life, her relationship with Francis, her death ... All that, I felt, was some jealously guarded secret.

Little did I know then how right I was. Little did I know then that it was Francis's obsession that was behind the whole sad story. Little did I know then that one day I would indeed discover all I so longed to know ... and things that I would wish had remained hidden from me...

Seven

Julia

From the very first moment he set eyes on Julia Stacey, Francis Trevelyan's mind was made up. He had to have her.

It was a sweet day in early spring and Francis was driving the gig across his father's land on his way back to his house at Morwennan when he saw a great grey horse heading at full gallop across the open ground. His first reaction was one of annoyance; this rider was trespassing, and Francis determined to tell him so.

As he drew closer, however, he realised with a sense of shock that the rider was not a man, but a woman. She wore a scarlet riding habit but no hat. Her hair, rich copper, had come loose from its pins; it tumbled in tangles and curls about her shoulders, and her face was flecked with speckles of mud. But what a face! Heart-shaped, with a tip-tilted nose, flawless skin flushed rosy by the wind, grey-green eyes sparkling behind a

114

dark fringe of lashes.

All the angry words died in Francis's throat. For a moment he was, for the first – and perhaps the last – time in his life, literally dumbstruck.

The girl reined in her horse, raised one hand and brushed a long copper curl behind her ear.

'Good morning,' she said. 'You must be Francis Trevelyan.'

At the age of just twenty-five Francis ran one of the most successful smuggling rings in Cornwall with the help and connivance of his sister Selena. The proceeds had netted him all the benefits that would never be his by inheritance – all his father's estate would pass to his elder brother, Adam – but thanks to the illicit trade he had a fine house of his own and more than enough income to keep him and Selena in comfort, not to say luxury.

Now, however, he found himself reacting to this beautiful woman like a callow youth. To his eternal annoyance, he could only stutter: 'How do you know who I am?'

'This is Trevelyan land, isn't it? I expect I'm trespassing. I tend to get a bit carried away when I let Rascal have his head. Anyway, I know you're not Adam Trevelyan, and you're too young to be Samuel, so you must be Francis.'

She smiled at him, giving no indication of the fact that she knew all about him and did not much like what she knew. Breath constricted in his chest.

'I'm Julia Stacey,' she said. 'My father farms Porthcreer. I've always lived in Falmouth with my aunt – my mother died when I was just a little girl – but now I've come to live here with my father.'

'Why?' Francis heard himself ask; again he cursed himself for his stupidity.

A shadow crossed her face. 'I wanted to get away from Falmouth for personal reasons.' Then, as if determined not to think about them – whatever they were – she forced another smile. 'In any case, Papa needs a woman to look after him. He behaves very badly left to his own devices.'

Francis returned her smile. Certainly Harry Stacey's reputation in the locality bore that out. He was known as a hard drinker and a gambler who would place a wager on anything that moved, or risk everything he possessed on the turn of a card.

'Well, Miss Stacey,' he said, managing to sound a little more like his usual self, 'if you are living at Porthcreer perhaps we shall see something of one another.'

'Perhaps we shall,' she said, but there was nothing of the coquette in her tone, nothing to give him hope. Simply the open friendliness that seemed to come as naturally to her as breathing.

'Good morning, Mr Trevelyan,' she said, touching her horse's flanks with her booted feet. 'I'll try not to stray on to your land again. But I can't make any promises.'

And: 'As far as I am concerned you can ride on our land whenever you like,' Francis heard himself say.

He watched as she galloped away. He had forgotten all the business matters that had been occupying his mind; all the resentment that always filled him when he rode across his father's land and knew it would never be his; all about his sister Selena's dominating ways, which had also been irking him.

Long after she had disappeared behind a patch of woodland and on to Stacey land he was seeing copper hair streaming in the wind and grey-green eyes and a face that would haunt him for the rest of his life.

For her part, Julia forgot all about Francis Trevelyan the moment she bid him good day.

She rode Rascal hard until they were both exhausted but when she slowed him to a walk the shadow Francis had seen when she had mentioned her life in Falmouth was back on her face and the weight was still there on her heart. A good gallop helped for a little while, but when it was over, the grief was always there, waiting.

'Oh, John,' Julia whispered and his name echoed through her like the wind in the gorse on a stormy winter night. 'Oh John, my love. Where are you? Why did you have to leave me when I love you so?'

As ever, there was no answer to that question, only the certain knowledge that he must be dead, drowned in some foreign ocean. If he were not, he would have come home to her long ago.

She thought of the last time she had seen him, standing on the quay at Falmouth and watching his boat, the *Silver Star*, sail out for the long voyage to the New World with its cargo of copper. John had promised her that when he returned they would be wed but his words were of no comfort to her that day. There had been a heaviness in her heart that was a thousand times worse than any other farewell had ever been, and the tears had blinded her. It was as if she had somehow known that it was not to be; that she would never stand beside him and take her marriage vows.

The foreboding had remained with her throughout the long months, growing more overpowering as the time approached when he should have returned. And then the fear for the future had become the present reality. Day after day, week after week, she had waited, hope fading.

Aunt Prudence, with whom she lived, had

tried to keep her cheerful.

'Just because he hasn't come home does not mean he is lost,' she had said, brisk as ever. 'Why, there could be many reasons why he has been delayed.'

But Julia could see in Aunt Prudence's eyes that she did not even believe the words of comfort herself. Too many men sailed away never to return. Too many ships were lost on the perilous oceans, and much nearer to home than the New World with all its unknown dangers.

Day by day Julia's despair grew, day by day something within herself died. The thought of never again holding John in her arms, never again feeling his lips on hers or looking into his laughing eyes was a pain too sharp to bear. And all the places where they had loved and laughed and planned for their future together were a constant reminder of her loss.

On a visit to her father at Porthcreer Julia realised that he too was no longer the man he had once been. The drinking and gambling that he had indulged himself in since her mother's death had begun to take their toll. Once, Julia had blamed him for the way of life he had fallen into. Now, however, she found she could understand the pain that had driven him to seek solace in the bottle. If Papa had suffered one quarter as much over Mama's death as she was suffering over

John's then he deserved only sympathy – and all the loving care she could offer him. She made up her mind to leave Falmouth with all its memories and come home.

Except of course that the memories came with her. And the longing. And the grief. When they became unbearable she would take Rascal and ride out, galloping wildly as if she could somehow leave it all behind her. Not that she wanted to leave John behind. She wanted to carry him in her heart to the day she died, her only love. But the pain. Yes, she wanted to leave the pain. And for a little while the wind in her hair and the pounding of Rascal's hooves and the rhythmic movement of his muscles beneath her did help. But not for long. Never for long.

Julia made her way back to Porthcreer more sedately and the weight of her loss went with her.

Francis could not get Julia out of his mind. He thought about her constantly, so much so that it affected every area of his life.

He began calling at Porthcreer. To his dismay he found that although she was pleasant enough, as she had been on that first day, she was also just as distant. For all his efforts he could make no progress with her.

Harry, her father, however, was quite a different matter. He was flattered by the attention of a gentleman of Francis's standing in the community whose father was, after all, squire of a fine estate and a magistrate into the bargain – and Francis, who liked to gamble and drink himself, found it a simple enough matter to cultivate him. It wasn't what he wanted of course but at least it was a start. He often stayed at the farm late into the evening, and though his heart always sank when Julia retired to bed he gained a curious pleasure from knowing that under the same roof she was undressed and in her nightgown with only the creaky floor of her bedroom separating them.

For her part, Julia became increasingly uncomfortable with Francis's frequent visits. She was under no illusion as to his motives and she realised that he was quite prepared to form a friendship with her father in order to get close to her. A friendship – what was more – which was far from good for Harry.

'I wish you wouldn't encourage him, Papa,' she chided Harry when Francis had spent another long evening in their parlour. 'He's a very bad influence on you.'

Harry widened his eyes into a look of childlike innocence.

'A bad influence? Whatever can you mean?'

'You know very well, Papa,' Julia told him. 'Don't think I don't know that you were rolling dice with him after I went to bed the other night. I heard you. And you would do well to remember Francis Trevelyan can afford to lose a great deal more than you can.'

A guilty flush spread up Harry's neck. When Julia took that tone she reminded him very much of Catherine, her dead mother. Catherine had not approved of him gambling either. But a man had to have some pleasure in life...

'Where's the harm in a game of dice?' he pleaded.

'None – if you know where to stop,' Julia said tartly. 'I'm not sure you do know, Papa.'

'I wish you wouldn't treat me like a child, Julia,' he complained. 'In any case, don't you know it's not me Francis comes to see. He has his eye on you, if I'm not much mistaken.'

'I know it,' Julia said tersely. 'It's another reason I don't want him here.'

Harry frowned. 'You shouldn't dismiss him so readily. A Trevelyan would be quite a catch, even if he is the younger son. He's done well for himself. That's a fine house he has over at Morwennan – solid as the cliffs it's built on, and furnished like a palace so they say.'

'Papa!' Julia closed her eyes briefly. 'I don't want to marry anyone. Especially not Francis Trevelyan.'

Harry shook his head sadly. 'Oh, my little

one. You can't grieve for ever. The last thing I want is to see you a sad old spinster. And I've nothing to leave you. This house will go to your cousin William when I'm gone, as well you know. You'd have a fine home at Morwennan – and someone to keep you warm in bed at night. It's no good to be so choosy...'

'I don't want anyone but John – and certainly not Francis Trevelyan,' Julia said firmly. 'I don't like him and I don't like what he does. You know as well as I do how he has made his money. It's no secret in these parts. He's a smuggler.'

'What if he is?' Harry raised his eyebrows in exasperation. 'Half Cornwall is involved in smuggling one way and another. If it's making him rich where's the harm?'

'It's easy to say that,' Julia argued. 'But I wouldn't want to live in a house built on the proceeds of running contraband, even if I liked Francis, which I most certainly do not. It's one thing sinking a few casks of spirits in the bay and bringing them in with the lobster pots, but smuggling on the scale Francis Trevelyan does it is something else entirely. If the authorities catch up with him he'll end up in gaol and his fine house and everything in it will be confiscated.'

'With his father a magistrate? I doubt it!' Harry scoffed. 'Their sort always look after their own. A blind eye will be turned, mark my words. No, if Francis has done so well already, he'll do even better with experience. You could look forward to a life of luxury if you were his wife.'

'Well I won't be!' Julia returned sharply. 'I have no intention of marrying anyone, least of all Francis Trevelyan. So will you please listen to what I say and tell him he is not welcome here?'

Harry sighed. And from the mulish look on his face, Julia knew he would do nothing of the kind.

Julia was not the only one who was displeased at the attention Francis Trevelyan was showering on her. His sister Selena was equally annoyed, though for quite different reasons.

For as long as she could remember, Selena had dominated Francis. As a small child she had bullied him mercilessly, taking full advantage of her two years' seniority. Then, as he grew to be as big as she, she changed to more subtle tactics.

As the second son with no hope of inheriting as long as his elder brother Adam lived, Francis suffered from severe feelings of inferiority. Whilst Adam was constantly at their father's side, being groomed for his future role, Francis was left alone in the nursery with Selena.

She took full advantage of the chance to

mould his will to hers. On the one hand she showered him with praise, bolstering his fragile ego and making him feel vastly important. On the other she would withdraw her approval on a whim, leaving him floundering wretchedly, a small boy with no real future to look forward to and no place in the family hierarchy. The approach was seductive; Francis grew to depend on Selena without even realising that she was equally dependent on him.

Selena was, in her own way, even more resentful of the laws of inheritance than Francis. As a woman she had no hope of ever owning anything in her own right. Whilst Francis would become heir should Adam break his neck riding or fall victim to the pox, both Adam and Francis could die and she would still be the loser, for the estate would pass to the next male in line. The unfairness of it ate into her like a cancer and she assuaged the pain of it by asserting her power over her younger brother. It was like a drug to her, that power, to have him do her bidding or to see his eyes follow her, hungry as a starving puppy, for a crumb of praise.

In adolescence Selena had become aware of yet another avenue of power: her sexuality. As her body developed the curves of womanhood she noticed Francis's interest and took a dark delight in displaying herself, tempting him with first a glimpse of her breasts or her long shapely legs, then a forbidden touch. She led him on whilst always remaining in control, quick to slap him down and then tempt again until she could bend him ever more readily to her will by promises of delights to come.

By the time they were fifteen they were lovers in the fullest sense and Selena's power over her brother was almost complete.

It was she who suggested smuggling as a means of making a fortune of his own, it was she, the stronger and the cleverer, who plotted and planned while he did her bidding. When, with the proceeds of his illicit dealings and a loan from his father, he built Morwennan House she moved into it with him. A mere woman in a man's world Selena might be, but the power she wielded was enormous.

Just as in childhood, Francis was the puppet and Selena pulled the strings. In every aspect of their lives he danced to her tune.

Now, for the first time, a situation had arisen over which Selena had no control. Francis had become obsessed with Julia Stacey and day by day Selena felt her power over him slipping away.

She did not like it one little bit, but for the moment it seemed she was powerless to do anything about it.

In the weeks that followed, as Francis's visits

to the farm continued, Julia found herself hopelessly torn between what she thought of as two evils. If she stayed downstairs in the long evenings she had to endure Francis's company and his clumsy attempts at courting her; if she retired to her room she knew the two men were likely to embark upon some game of chance.

On balance, she decided, less harm was likely if she stayed. Unwelcome as Francis's attention was it was preferable to her father gambling – and in all likelihood losing – what they could ill afford.

One evening, however, Francis was even more unbearable than usual. Julia found it impossible to avoid his gaze; even when she was not looking at him she could feel his eyes on her, devouring her. She bent over her needlework, her skin prickling with irritation, yet still his eyes bored into her, magnetising her, until she felt compelled to look up. Then he would smile, that rather soft, slow smile that she was beginning to find distinctly repellent.

Worse was to come. When her father left the room, Francis rose and crossed to her chair. He stood for a moment gazing down at her embroidery admiringly.

'You are a very talented needlewoman, my dear.'

'No, I'm not,' Julia disagreed. 'I make an awful botch of it most of the time.'

'You do yourself a disservice.' His voice was silky. 'Your talents are limitless. I never met a woman like you before, Julia.'

His hand was on her shoulder, just a light touch at first, so light that she told herself she was imagining it. Then, growing bolder, he slid his fingers up to stroke her neck. She twisted her head away; he caught a ringlet and held it fast.

'Oh, Julia – Julia!' he moaned.

For a moment she was pinioned like a butterfly, then, as he raised his head, she brought her hand up hard, striking him full in the face. He released her, his fingers flying to his stinging cheek, the look of a whipped dog, hurt and puzzled, in his eyes.

'You forget yourself, sir!' she blazed.

A half-smile lifted one corner of his fleshy mouth.

'Oh, I like a woman with spirit! And you have that in abundance, Julia. What a pair we would make, you and I...'

Julia drew herself up. 'I think it is only fair to tell you I have no feelings for you at all and I find your constant attention wearing, to say the least of it. I am sorry if I am being harsh and cruel, inconsiderate of your feelings, but it's better to be honest about these things than to allow you to nurture false hopes.'

There was a curious light in his eyes; later Julia would learn to recognise it as a stubborn streak which rose to the fore whenever the route to getting his own way was obscured. The self-indulgent side of his nature could not bear to be thwarted.

'We shall see,' he said. 'I don't give up so easily, my dear.'

Julia felt a twinge of misgiving. The light in Francis's eyes was the light of obsession.

'Then I can say no more,' she said. 'I think it's best you don't come here again.'

Gathering her skirts and what was left of her dignity she pushed past him and out of the room. Behind her, she heard her father return.

'Is something wrong?'

And Francis's forced laugh. 'Women! What delightfully unpredictable creatures they are! Well, since it seems Julia is not going to grace us with her company this evening, shall we play a game of loo?'

Julia's hands tightened into fists but she continued climbing the stairs. Tonight her father would have to take care of himself. Nothing on earth would induce her to return to the parlour and play nursemaid to save him from the despicable Francis Trevelyan.

An hour or so later, however, when she opened her bedroom door and saw the chink of light still spilling out from the parlour, her temper had cooled sufficiently to give way to concern once more. So – they were still down there playing. Well, enough was enough. It had to be stopped.

Julia pulled on her wrap and started down the stairs ready to fly at her father as well as at Mr Francis Trevelyan. She pushed the parlour door wide.

'Papa...' She broke off, horrified at the scene before her.

The two men were, as she had expected, still seated at the table. But it was the pile of chips at Francis's elbow that shocked her so – that and the look on her father's face. She had seen that look before – the look of a man losing heavily, far more heavily than he can afford, and it chilled her to the marrow.

'Papa!' she said sharply. 'What are you doing?'

He glanced up, guilt making him snappy. 'Oh, be quiet, Julia. It has nothing to do with you.'

'How much have you lost, Papa?' she demanded.

He could not answer her; it was Francis who spoke.

'Rather a lot, I'm afraid. Shall we play one last game, Harry? Come on, I'll give you another chance to recoup your losses.' He glanced at the pool of chips. 'Double or quits. What do you say?'

'No!' Julia flashed. 'You must not! I won't let you, Papa!'

He looked at her like a naughty child. 'I have to, Julia. I cannot afford not to.'

'What do you mean?' she whispered, frightened.

'I can't afford to pay him out...'

'Oh, Papa – you fool!' she cried. 'How could you play for money we don't have?'

'But I was winning...'

'That's what you always say, Papa. Haven't you learned yet that you always end up *losing*? I can't believe you could do this...'

'But he has, I'm afraid,' Francis said in mock sympathy, but there was no disguising the look of triumph in his eyes.

'And you!' she cried. 'How could you lead him on so? You know we're not rich like you. We can't afford to lose fortunes on the turn of a card. Why, you'll cost us the roof over our heads!'

Francis smiled thinly. 'Which is why your father cannot refuse my offer to play double or quits. I can't say fairer, can I?'

'He's right, Julia. Don't you see?' Harry's voice was a little slurred; Julia realised he had not only been gambling with what they did not have but drinking too, encouraged, no doubt, by Francis Trevelyan. 'Double or quits and we might yet be saved.'

'And if you lose – what then?' she demanded.

'I won't. It's time my luck turned once more.'

'If you lose,' she repeated, 'how are you to pay your debts? Have you thought of that?'

'I can't pay them now...'

'If he wins,' Francis said smoothly, 'all will be well and there'll be enough to buy you a wardrobe of new gowns. If he loses...' His lip curled slightly.

'Yes?' Julia grated at him. 'If he loses – what then?'

'Then I will decide how my dues should be paid.'

'I have no choice but to try, Julia,' Harry said. And to Francis: 'Double or quits it is.'

Julia wrapped her arms around herself in despair. But if her father had already lost more than he could afford to pay she could see he had little choice. Perhaps this time fortune would smile on him. Loo was a game of chance, depending entirely on the hand dealt, but it was also a game of judgement where the decision as to whether or not to throw a hand in or play could be vital. In his state of high anxiety Julia doubted whether Harry's judgement could be relied upon and the liquor he had consumed would make things worse. Julia closed her eyes briefly and prayed.

Francis shuffled and dealt the cards – three each to Harry, himself, and three into the extra hand – the 'miss'. There was a slight smile on his face but his eyes were hard and shrewd. He was playing to win, she knew, and felt a rush of dislike. How could he do this to them?

The card was turned for trumps – hearts – and as the two men examined their hands Julia examined their faces. Francis's was inscrutable but she fancied she sensed his smug satisfaction and her stomach lurched. As for her father ... Indecision was written all over his face. Without seeing the cards, Julia could guess that what he had been dealt was not a good hand, but not a bad one either. The very worst sort, for the decision now had to be made – play with the cards he held or throw them away and take the 'miss'. She saw his hand hover, withdraw, hover again. The 'miss' could contain three unbeatable cards – or three useless ones. There was no way of knowing. But once taken that would be the hand with which Harry would be left, the hand he would have to play.

Julia's nails bit into her palms. Oh, let him make the right choice, whatever that might be! For seemingly endless minutes Harry deliberated, then, with a sharp, almost desperate flick of the wrist he threw his hand down on to the table and reached for the 'miss'.

She knew at once that he had made the wrong choice. It was written all over his face and he seemed to slump in his chair.

'Are you ready to play?' Francis asked. By contrast he looked eager, buoyed up by anticipation.

Harry led – an eight of clubs. Francis

topped it with a jack. The first trick was his. Harry laid a five of diamonds. Francis, smiling, placed a king with great deliberation on the table. The game was now virtually over, but Harry had one last chance to win at least a third of the pool and so remain in the game. White-faced he played his best card – the ten of clubs. Francis had already played the jack and Julia found herself praying it had been the highest he had – and that he had no trumps. But a moment later hope died as Francis nonchalantly tossed the queen of hearts on to the table-top.

'I win, I think,' he drawled.

Julia bowed her head. Anger with her father had now given way to despair; she could not bear to look at his defeat.

Slowly Harry pulled himself upright; he even attempted a small mirthless laugh.

'Well, Trevelyan, I won this place on the turn of a card – it's fitting, I dare say, that I should lose it the same way. Though what Julia and I will do now – where we will go – I have not the first idea.'

Francis lounged easily in his chair, every inch the winner. He was a man in control now – and he knew it.

'I don't want your property, Stacey. I've no interest in farming a few paltry acres that sit on the rump of my father's land like a fly on a cow in calf. And I wouldn't take the roof from over your head. I am not that much of a bastard.'

Harry's brow furrowed. 'But you said...'

'I said if I won I would decide how my dues should be paid.' His glance slid to Julia. The curious light was there again in his eyes and he passed the tip of his tongue over his fleshy lips.

A chill hand seemed to grip Julia's stomach. But Harry still looked puzzled and anxious.

'What then, man? What is it you want? The horse – the grey? You admire him, I know...'

Francis chuckled. 'Oh, a little more than just the horse, I think – though now you come to mention it, I'll ask you to throw Rascal in for good measure. And Julia loves to ride him, I know, so perhaps it will keep her happily occupied whilst I am occupied with making enough money to keep us both in luxury.'

'What are you talking about?' Harry demanded.

Francis's lip curled. He was playing with them now and enjoying every moment of it.

'I think you know very well what I want, my friend. And if you don't, Julia certainly does. I can see it in her face – and if she is not overjoyed at the present time, I sincerely hope I can change her feelings before long. She will come to realise, I'm sure, that I am not such a bad bargain. And I shall certainly do everything in my power to make her happy.'

Realisation began to dawn on Harry, yet he shook his head, unable to believe that he was reading Francis's intentions aright.

'I don't follow...'

'Oh, come!' Francis laughed softly. 'You know how I feel about your daughter. Surely you can't think I ride over here night after night for the sake of your company alone? Dear me no!' He paused, then said in an almost throwaway tone: 'You can pay your dues to me, Harry, by giving me the hand of your daughter in marriage. Now that's not such a bad deal, is it?'

She was icy cold, shivering from head to toe. Oh the ignominy of it! To be taken as the prize in a game of loo! To have the whole of her future determined on the turn of a card! To be put into this impossible position by her father's reckless folly!

'I won't do it!' She pressed her balled fists into her breasts, her arms forming a barrier between her and the two men. 'You can't make me wed where I don't want to, either of you! I won't do it, I tell you!'

'Julia – the wager was made!' Harry protested. 'My honour...'

'And what about *my* honour?' she cried passionately. 'And my happiness? My whole life? You know I swore—'

'I will make you happy,' Francis interrupted. 'You will have a good life. You will have fine clothes and want for nothing, that I promise you...'

'No!'

'Think of the alternative,' Francis said. His eyes were glittering. Though his patience was wearing a little thin, Julia's fury had excited him still more. The prospect of mastering all that spirit was causing his groin to harden and his palms to grow damp. 'Do you really want to see your father thrown out of his home and you along with him? Living on the parish is no joke, I assure you. If he is unable to settle his debt in the way I choose then I shall be forced to take the alternative.'

His tone was silky but there was no mistaking the ruthless determination beneath it.

Julia felt tears of helpless despair pricking at her eyes; furiously she blinked them away. She may have to capitulate to this monster, but he would not see her cry.

'In that case, sir,' she said with all the dignity she could muster, 'I dare say I have no choice.'

Francis relaxed; his smile became one of triumph.

'I am very glad, my dear, that you have come to your senses. I shall make arrangements for the marriage to take place as soon as possible.'

★ ★ ★

But it was Selena who took charge of the arrangements for the marriage. Shocked as she was by the news she quickly realised there was nothing she could do to stop it. Moreover, Julia had no mother to help her choose a wedding gown, her father had neither the wherewithal nor the breeding to play host at what would certainly be an important wedding in Cornish society, and his farm was not a suitable setting for the wedding breakfast.

When Julia walked down the aisle on the arm of her father, pale yet still beautiful in a gown of ivory watered silk made by Selena's dressmaker, Selena herself followed as her self-appointed attendant. During the wedding breakfast, held at Morwennan House, she was the perfect hostess, hiding her seething rage behind a tight smile that curved her lips downward. But when the newly wed couple left for a month's wedding tour in France, which she had helped to arrange, the bitter jealousy was so intense Selena thought she would faint with it.

When at last she was alone she went to her darkened room, threw herself down on her bed, and, for the first time in years, cried until she had no tears left.

'So, my dear, alone at last!'

As the carriage pulled away from Morwennan House and began the steep ascent beneath the overhanging trees Francis reached for Julia's hand, placing it on his plump, silk-covered thigh.

A nerve jumped in her throat and she wanted nothing more than to pull her hand away and move to the farthest corner of the carriage so that no part of her was touching him. But she knew to do so would be useless. She was his wife now and trapped as surely as her small hand was beneath his. He could do with her as he would; the only thing left to her was her dignity and that, Julia vowed, she would cling to as she had clung to it throughout this long, nightmarish day.

She closed her eyes briefly, reliving again against her will the long walk up the aisle on her father's arm to where Francis stood before the altar. He had turned to look at her, his eyes narrowed with desire, his lips moist with anticipation. Her breath had been constricted in her chest but she met his gaze full on, head held high, glaring at him proudly. A slight satisfied smile twisted his mouth and the trapped feeling swelled in her until she thought she would choke with it. Then he turned back to face the minister and the marriage service had begun.

The familiar words had sounded to her a long way off, the priest intoning with suitable solemnity, Francis making his vows in firm clear tones which echoed to the rafters, her own voice seeming not to belong to her as she repeated the phrases the priest fed to her. And then the ring was on her finger, the priest pronounced them man and wife and the last of her futile hope was gone.

She could feel the ring now, biting into her flesh as Francis pressed her hand against his thigh, a symbol of the servitude she must endure for the rest of her life. Tears pricked suddenly at her eyes; she jerked her head round sharply, staring out of the carriage window so that he should not see and blinking furiously.

'Julia?' There was concern in Francis's voice. He released her hand, slipping his arm instead about her waist, pulling her closer to him. He bent his head towards her; even with her face turned away she could smell the powder in his wig and the cigar smoke and whisky on his breath. 'Don't turn away from me, my dear. You are my wife now.'

She snapped her head back, her eyes bright with hatred and the unshed tears.

'Yes, I'm your wife, Francis – heaven preserve me.'

He drew back a little, shocked by the venom in her tone.

'Oh, Julia, I had hoped you were becoming used to the idea. These last weeks you have said nothing—'

'Because there was nothing I could say. And if I had, what difference would it have made? You won me, Francis, in a game of cards. Between you, you and my father used me for a pot of chips. I had no choice in the matter at all.'

'Julia, you are far more than a pot of chips to me,' he cajoled. 'I could have taken the roof from over your father's head if I had wanted to – ruined him – and you too. But it could have gone the other way – if he had won he could have ruined me. The reason I played for such high stakes was because I wanted you so much. And I still do.'

'And now you have me!' she flashed angrily. 'But don't think the marriage vows and a blessing from the reverend gentleman will make any difference to the way I feel about it.'

Francis's eyes narrowed. Something about her spirited rejection of him was stirring the fire that was there in his belly whenever he looked at her. From the first moment he had set eyes on her he had never stopped wanting her; every waking moment he thought of her and at night she came to him in dreams so that he woke bathed in sweat with the need to have her in his arms. He wanted her with every fibre of his being, body and soul, and now she was his. Whether she liked it or not.

He moved his hand up a little so that it brushed the swell of her breast beneath her cloak; he felt her stiffen, but beneath his fingers her breast was soft and yielding. He squeezed it gently and heard the sharp intake of her breath. He moved closer, the blood pounding in his ears, slid his hand upwards until it encountered bare flesh, then down again beneath the silk of her bodice, squeezing and stroking.

She tried to pull away then.

'Can't you wait?' Her voice was sharp; it only served to excite him more.

'No,' he grunted breathily. 'I have waited long enough.'

With one hasty movement he lifted her bodily, so that she was half lying on the seat of the rolling carriage, and bunched her skirts up to her thighs. Julia gasped, struggling briefly to sit up as he towered over her, pulling down his breeches, and then his weight came down on her, pinning her there as helpless as a speared butterfly. His hands were on her shoulders, his wet mouth stifling the scream that rose to her lips. And then his aroused manhood was between her legs, unerringly seeking the softest, most vulnerable part of her.

Pain so sharp that she thought it would tear her in two brought another scream to Julia's throat. She scrabbled at him with her hands, fighting him though she had promised herself she would not. Her nails drew blood from his cheek, his wig fell askew, revealing dark springy hair beneath the powdered white, and still Francis drove into her like a man possessed.

Would it never end? The rocking carriage, the painful thrusting between her legs, his fingers biting into her shoulders, his breathing ragged against her throat, punctuated with guttural groans. Julia squeezed her eyes tight shut, her head thrown back into the corner of the carriage, her soundless sobs keeping time with the working of his body. Then, with a loud cry, he thrust himself still deeper into her and was still, and she knew that for now, at least, it was over.

The carriage swayed around a bend in the road, Francis toppled on to his knees and looked up at her, his face soft with satiated lust.

'So, my dear,' he said, half laughing, 'now we really are man and wife.'

For a moment Julia remained motionless, then, as he pulled up his breeches and regained his seat, she moved slowly and painfully, raising her cricked neck and pulling her skirts down over her sticky thighs.

'I hope you are satisfied,' she whispered.

He smiled. 'For the moment.' Then, as the triumph of passion satiated began to subside, a look of something like shame crossed his fleshy features. 'I didn't mean it to be like this,' he said, almost apologetically. 'You goaded me.'

'I am sorry, I'm sure.' Her voice was trembling yet defiant.

'I meant to woo you – to show you how it can be between us. And I will show you, my dear.'

'I have no doubt you will try,' Julia replied bitterly.

As the coach reached the high road and gathered speed she sat ramrod straight, staring out of the window, and seeing the familiar countryside through eyes that sparkled with tears of pain and humiliation. If she had disliked Francis before, now she despised him, and the knowledge that she was trapped, tied to him for as long as they both lived, was like a physical weight around her heart.

Yet a fierce determination was hardening inside her. She might be forced to live in Francis's horrible dark house, share his bed and do his bidding. But her response to him was still her own. He could insist she sat opposite him at breakfast, luncheon and dinner, but he could not make her amuse him with her chatter. He could use her body as often as the fancy took him – and no doubt he would – but he could not take her heart.

Her one weapon was to withhold from him the thing he wanted most – her love. And though she was his wife she would ensure that she never truly belonged to him.

★ ★ ★

Throughout the month-long honeymoon tour Julia clung to her resolve. She did not dare allow herself to think of the long years that lay ahead of her with this man but lived each day and night as it came, refusing to be impressed by the sights and sounds of the places they visited, submitting to his embraces but remaining coldly aloof. She drew satisfaction from Francis's growing frustration and wept only when she was alone with no one to see.

'For the love of God, Julia, this is no pleasure for either of us,' he exploded one night as he rolled from her unresponsive body.

And: 'I am glad we agree about something,' she replied coldly, though his efforts to arouse her had left her nauseous and so desperate to escape from him that she could feel the beginnings of panic.

He sighed deeply.

'Can we not at least try to begin again? I'm not such a bad man, and I am trying my best to please you and make you happy. Could you not make some effort to meet me half-way?'

She said nothing, staring stonily into the shadows thrown by the candelabra while the tears pricked at her eyes.

He threw aside the covers and got out of bed, padding across the floor in his night-shirt to find a cigar and light it from the candle with a taper.

'Are we to live our lives like this? Is that what you want?'

She gave a low, bitter laugh. 'Does what I want matter?'

'Goddam it, of course it matters!' he grated. 'I love you, Julia.'

'But I don't love you,' she said. 'You knew that my heart still belongs to the man I lost and I don't even like you very much. Yet you insisted on marrying me. It's scarcely a recipe for happiness.'

He paced the floor.

'Plenty of women go into marriage without love. They learn to make the best of it. In time, with a shared life, bonds are formed. They know how to be grateful for the comforts provided for them in a harsh world. Some even come to enjoy the physical pleasures that you seem to find so repellent.'

'I will do my wifely duty by you, Francis,' Julia said with the same chilly hauteur. 'I've not refused you or fought with you since that first demeaning episode in the carriage. But please don't expect anything more, for I am quite unable to give it.'

He sank into a chair, burying his head in his hands. Had she not despised him so, Julia might have felt a modicum of pity. This was a man who had been so determined to have his way he had given no thought to the consequences. This was a man so obsessed that nothing in the world mattered beyond his hopeless, all-consuming love for a woman who would never love him.

This, undoubtedly, was a man in torment.

By the time they returned from the honeymoon tour Julia had begun to suspect she was pregnant. A month later and she was sure. The absence of her usually regular courses, the constant vague nausea, the changes in her body, slight as yet but still unmistakable, all told her it was so.

A new despair filled Julia. Bad enough to have to live with a man she despised, but to bear his child ... The thought of his seed taking root and flourishing like a cancer within her was anathema to her. Worse still, it was yet another fetter, tying her to Francis for ever.

Julia's mind was made up. She would not give birth to this monstrosity. Like every country child, she knew there were ways and means and she began to employ them.

To his credit, Francis still allowed her to visit her father and ride her beloved Rascal. He would drive her over to her father's farm and sit yarning with him while she took the horse out alone, and her flushed cheeks and bright eyes when she returned pleased him.

Now, however, it was not the freedom that riding afforded her that made Julia beg a visit to the farm. She was hoping desperately that a good hard gallop and even a jump or two would dislodge the weed that had taken root in her and shake it free.

'Are you sure you are feeling well, my dear?' Francis asked anxiously as he installed her in the curricle. 'You are very pale this morning.'

'I'm perfectly fine,' Julia retorted, though she did indeed feel horribly queasy.

'We could always delay the trip until another day...'

'No, I'm fine I tell you!' She couldn't wait another hour to be in the saddle and losing this burden she carried, let alone another day.

But though she rode Rascal like a madwoman, urging him to the wildest gallop and recklessly urging him over hedges and ditches she would normally have considered too dangerous, both she and Rascal came home unscathed. No welcome blood came to tell her the nightmare was ending. Francis's child clung as tenaciously to her womb as she clung to Rascal's sleek muscled back.

In desperation Julia next paid a visit to an old woman in the village. She had heard tales of other unfortunates who had been helped out of their predicament by a concoction of herbs and poison.

The old woman, more used to seeing frightened servant girls or the women of easy virtue who plied their trade on the harbour or in inns of ill repute, was startled to see Francis Trevelyan's beautiful and well-dressed wife on her doorstep. Julia fed her the story she had decided upon – that she needed the potion for a friend in a delicate situation with a married man, but the old woman's sharp eyes told her she did not believe her. At first, wary of inviting the wrath of a man who was not only gentry but also one of the 'Gentlemen', as the smugglers were known, she refused to help. But the silver coins Julia pressed on her changed her mind. Reluctantly she parted with a stone flagon containing the evil brew, telling Julia that 'her friend' must drink all of it if it was to do its work.

Julia carried it home with her and that night, whilst Francis remained in the parlour talking with Selena, she poured the contents into her night flask and managed to swallow it, though the smell and the taste of it made her retch.

The sickness started a few hours later and went on for another day and night, and the pain in her stomach was so bad Julia feared she was dying. But when at last it subsided, leaving her weak and ill, she still carried Francis's child within her.

Nothing, it seemed, would dislodge it. Not the scaldingly hot baths she subjected herself to, not Francis's love-making, not even the terrible jarring of her body when she resorted to throwing herself down the stairs in a last desperate attempt to rid herself of the hated burden she carried.

It was Selena who finally put an end to her vain attempts to miscarry.

'Are you with child?' she asked baldly one morning when Francis had left the house on business.

Julia, who was attempting to force some breakfast down her protesting throat, looked up sharply, the truth written all over her face.

'You are, are you not?' Selena pressed her. There was little point in denying it. Already her breasts were fuller and her waist thicker; soon her belly would be rounding out too.

'Yes, I am with child,' she said steadily. 'Given your brother's ravenous appetite, that is hardly surprising.'

She was startled by the look that crossed Selena's face at her words. The slate-hard eyes narrowed, the thin lips worked for a moment, there was a hollowness suddenly about her cheeks. With a sense of shock Julia realised the truth.

Selena was jealous. And somehow, instinctively, Julia knew it was not simply the jealousy of a middle-aged spinster who would now never bear children of her own. With a flash of insight she knew it was a jealousy of the act that had begotten the child, and also that it had to do with the fact that it was Francis who had impregnated her.

From the very outset Julia had been aware of Selena's coldness and animosity towards her. But until this moment it had never occurred to her that there might be something unnatural and unhealthy about the relationship between the two of them. She had thought Selena's attention to her brother's needs and whims was simply sisterly solicitude. Now, in a moment of clarity, she saw that it was more. Much more.

And the knowledge exhilarated her. For the first time she was actually glad that she was carrying Francis's child. In some strange way it empowered her. And she saw that it gave her power not only over Selena, but over Francis too.

'Does Francis know?' Selena asked. The look of jealousy had gone now, hidden by her usual hard-faced mask. But the tightness of her tone confirmed that she was seething inwardly.

Julia set down her knife and fork and stood up. For the first time in weeks she held herself proudly, as if to display her swelling body rather than trying to conceal it.

'Not yet,' she said levelly. 'But I intend to tell him this very evening. I hope you won't spoil the surprise by mentioning it to him

151

yourself first. I think he is going to be proud and pleased, don't you?'

Then, with a small satisfied smile, she left the room.

With her pregnancy an acknowledged fact, Julia's life at Morwennan began to change for the better.

Francis was delighted to learn he was to become a father and he redoubled his efforts to please Julia. She had only to express a desire for something and he ensured it was hers, and he treated her with gentleness and consideration, as if she were a delicate piece of porcelain.

To Julia's enormous relief he no longer forced her to perform her wifely duties, moving to a cot in his dressing room and leaving her to enjoy the luxury of their big feather bed free from the fear of being woken in the night to submit to his demands. The love and pride were there in his face whenever he looked at her, his touch was no longer lustful but tender.

To her own surprise Julia found that her animosity towards him was lessening. She still recoiled inwardly when he touched her intimately, she still preferred him to kiss her on the cheek rather than the lips, but she found a certain comfort in the strength of his feelings for her now that she was no longer threatened by the physical bonding she found so distasteful and humiliating.

Selena remained cold and aloof but on occasion Julia glimpsed the same look of jealousy Selena had been unable to hide when she had first learned of Julia's pregnancy, and the knowledge that she could arouse such powerful emotion in the older woman was a secret satisfaction, whilst the evidence of Selena's weakness made her seem less threatening.

As for her feelings for her unborn child, Julia could scarcely believe the change they underwent. How could she ever have thought of the precious new life she carried as a cancer to be ripped out? With the first flutter high under her ribs Julia experienced a feeling of excitement and anticipation; she stood with her hands pressed to her waist, waiting for it to come again. When it did she laughed aloud with pleasure. As her body swelled so did her desire to protect her unborn child and she passed her hands lovingly over her bulging belly trying to communicate the love and tenderness she felt. When she bathed she rubbed oils into the full breasts that would suckle her child and imagined how it would feel to have a small eager mouth fasten on to her nipples.

It was now very much *her* child; it was as if Francis had nothing to do with it at all.

And yet, she thought, he might well make a good father. His pride would only increase when he held his little son in his arms; the new tenderness he was showing her would extend to the child. And certainly the baby would want for nothing. Francis's 'business' was thriving; though she asked no questions about it, that much was clear from the way no expense was spared about the house, in the preparation of the nursery, and in the presents he bought for her – a whole new wardrobe of new gowns to accommodate her changing shape, exotic perfumes, jewels that must have cost a king's ransom.

Julia had never cared over much for such fripperies but they gave her a feeling of being cherished nevertheless and added something extra to the feeling of contentment that pregnancy had brought with it and which never failed to surprise her.

Another benefit came in the shape of the new staff Francis was able to employ at Morwennan – a married couple. Durbin, the husband, was coachman and groom, his wife maid to Julia. Julia had never before had a maid of her own and found the prospect a little daunting, but Francis was insistent. A maid would ensure Julia did not overtax herself and Mrs Durbin came with all the credentials to ensure she could help Julia through the last difficult months, attend with the doctor at her confinement, and oversee the nursing of the child. In any case, it was only right and proper for a lady of

Julia's standing to have her own personal maid.

The moment Mrs Durbin was installed all Julia's doubts fell away. The two women established an almost immediate rapport and before long Mrs Durbin was confessing to friends that she had come to look on Julia as the daughter she had never had. For her part, Julia at long last had a friend and confidante in the Trevelyan household and a replacement figure for the mother she had lost at nine years old.

For the first time since her enforced marriage to Francis, Julia had a purpose in life, a friend, and hope for the future. For the first time she felt, if not ecstatic happiness, then at least peace.

It was not to last.

The baby was born on a blustery March day when the waves dashed violently against the cliffs, the wind howled around the house, and the branches of the overhanging trees creaked threateningly.

Julia had laboured all the previous day and all night, while Mrs Durbin hovered anxiously, sponging the sweat from her face with a cloth wrung out in warm water and securing a towel to the bedhead, on which she could hang when the pains became too great to bear. The doctor was sent for; he strutted and tutted but his face betrayed the extent of his anxiety. Both Julia and the baby were weakening before his eyes; if it did not come soon he would lose them both.

Outside the bedroom door Francis paced helplessly, each and every one of Julia's moans and cries a knife thrust in his heart. Only Selena remained unperturbed, a faint smile twisting her mouth downward as she went about her business.

At last – at last! – the doctor managed a difficult manipulation.

'Thank God!' he muttered, and to Mrs Durbin: 'He's turned at last! He'll come now, I think.'

Mrs Durbin bent over Julia, holding her hands and encouraging her to push with her last remaining strength, and with a sudden rush the baby came into the world.

For a moment Julia lay back exhausted, feeling nothing but relief that the hours of pain were over, too weak even to raise her head to look at her baby. Then she felt the first twinge of alarm. Something was wrong. There was no joyous bustle in the room, no healthy protesting cry from her new-born baby, only an ominous silence. She struggled to find the strength to sit up.

'What is it...?'

'It's all right, my lamb. Lie still now...' Mrs Durbin was beside her in an instant, easing her back against the pillows, blocking her view of the room, but not before she had caught a glimpse of her poor child, blood-stained and blue, in the arms of the doctor.

'He's dead, isn't he?' she sobbed. 'Oh – he can't be dead! He can't be!'

'Oh, hush, my lamb, hush!' Mrs Durbin's rosy apple face was crumpled with distress. 'Maybe it's for the best...'

'No ... No!' Julia scarcely heard her, let alone understood. She beat weakly at Mrs Durbin with her hands, desperate only to get to her child. 'Let me ... please! Let me!'

And then at last the baby cried, a thin protesting wail that was music to Julia's ears.

'Oh, thank God! Thank God!' she whispered.

The doctor's broad shirt-sleeved back was towards her as he worked on the baby but when she glanced at Mrs Durbin Julia was puzzled not to see her own joy and relief reflected in the older woman's face. Mrs Durbin still looked as if she was about to burst into tears.

The baby wailed again and Julia felt a rush of impatience.

'Let me have him! Oh, please let me have him!'

Mrs Durbin's lip wobbled and the tears began to run down her crumpled apple cheeks. 'Oh my lamb, it's best you don't see him...' She looked imploringly towards the doctor.

He lay the infant in the crib and crossed to

157

the bed. His face was grave, he held his bloodstained hands, as yet unwashed, stiffly in front of him.

'There's no easy way to say this, Mrs Trevelyan. Your baby is malformed. It's a miracle he's alive now, all things considered, but I don't think he will live long. And that you must look on as a blessing.'

She stared at him uncomprehending, yet feeling the panic, the horror, the grief, all gathering within her in a great flood tide.

'But he's alive! I want him!'

'He's not a pretty sight, my lamb.' Mrs Durbin's voice was full of tears.

And: 'I don't care!' Julia cried. 'I don't care what he looks like! He's my baby! He needs me! Bring him to me! Bring him to me now!'

They exchanged a glance, the doctor and Mrs Durbin, as if to share the responsibility of deciding what was for the best. Then the doctor nodded.

'Very well, Mrs Trevelyan, if that is what you want. But please prepare yourself...'

Mrs Durbin wiped her eyes on her sleeve, squeezed Julia's hand, and crossed to the crib. She wrapped the baby gently in a linen sheet and brought him to the bed. Julia raised herself painfully and held out her arms.

He was tiny – so tiny. How could such a scrap have caused her so much pain? She gazed with love and awe at the little screwed-up face peeping out from the swaddling sheet, still blue-tinged, with a deep indentation around the forehead, but perfect. Button nose, little pursed-up mouth, long eyelashes lying in a dark sweep across his cheek.

'There's nothing wrong with him!' she cried indignantly.

Then she pulled aside the enfolding sheet and, with a rush of utter, paralysing horror, knew what they had meant.

The baby lived only a few hours.

Julia was distraught. She lay with her face turned to the wall, too weak and wretched even to cry, while her aching body trembled ceaselessly with bouts of dry sobs. Though she had not eaten for two days she refused all food. It was all Mrs Durbin could do to get her to take sips of posset.

Francis, his face grey and heavy with distress, came to sit with her, and when he took her hand between his she did not even trouble to pull it away. For the moment she felt no distaste for his touch; it was almost as if he were not there at all. Nothing was real but her grief for her poor malformed baby. And the guilt that washed over her in waves.

It was her fault – hers alone. She must have damaged the child with her efforts to be rid of it. And she could tell no one. It was a burden she must bear alone.

Julia thought she would die of remorse and hoped that it would be so. To live with this weight on her heart was truly unbearable.

Eight

I did not, I must confess, feel at all well that morning after I witnessed Francis's smuggling activities. In fact, I felt decidedly peculiar. My mouth was furred, my head throbbed dully and my eyes burned. And the memory of what I had seen weighed heavily upon me too. But the Trevelyans were not paying me to take to my bed sick, and I was anxious to be with Charlotte again and continue building the bridges I had begun yesterday.

As I went down the stairs I noticed that the door on the other side of the hall – the door from which Mrs Durbin had emerged yesterday – stood slightly ajar and I wondered where it led. To the Durbins' quarters, perhaps? But I rather thought their rooms were at the rear of the house, reached by the back stairs from the kitchen.

Charlotte and Selena were already at breakfast and I was gratified when Charlotte greeted me with a shy smile. She was looking very pretty this morning in a gown of sprigged muslin and there were ribbons in

161

her hair. I smiled back at her, remembering the days when I had been young enough for my hair to flow loose in a shining chestnut curtain over my shoulders; remembered too when Mama Mary had helped me to put it up for the first time on my sixteenth birthday, and how grown-up it had made me look. Would I be here to help Charlotte put her hair up for the first time? It was as yet a long time in the future, of course, but I hoped with all my heart that it would be so.

'Charity. You slept well?' Selena enquired, pouring me coffee.

'Like a log,' I agreed.

'You certainly look a little bleary still,' she commented. 'You didn't wake at all?' Her eyes on my face were narrowed, watchful, and I realised she was trying to ascertain if I had heard anything of the night's activities.

'I scarcely even remember my head touching the pillow,' I said.

Selena relaxed visibly and her lips turned down into that odd smile of hers.

'It's the sea air, I expect. Bracing and soporific, especially when you are not used to it. That and the wine at dinner. Put together they no doubt acted like a drug. Oh – do help yourself to eggs. They are in the chafing dish.'

I froze momentarily as something clicked into place in my aching head, something so shocking I could scarcely believe I was even thinking it.

I moved automatically to the sideboard but my mind was not on what I was doing. I could hear nothing but what Selena had said about how heavily I had slept.

A drug. It described all too well the way I had felt. Heavy-eyed, heavy-limbed, dry-mouthed, uncoordinated. Why, hadn't I even compared it myself to the way I had felt when I had been given laudanum for a toothache as a child?

Could it be that either Francis or Selena had slipped something into my wine last night to make me sleep heavily so that I would not hear the activity beneath my window?

My hand trembled a little as I lifted the lid of the chafing dish. I felt very vulnerable suddenly. If they had drugged me so easily once, they could do it again and again. It was a monstrously disturbing thought.

'What plans have you for Charlotte today?' Selena asked when I was seated at the table.

I looked across at the fresh innocent young face and felt determination harden within me. I would not let these people and their wicked scheming deter me.

'I think Charlotte and I will spend today getting to know one another better,' I said, smiling at her. 'Then the lessons will come easier, won't they, Charlotte?'

She nodded, looking relieved. Lessons

were something she was a little apprehensive about, I guessed.

We finished our breakfast and when we left the dining room Francis had still not put in an appearance. Unsurprising, really, I supposed, considering that he must have been up for much of the night.

'Shall we go for a little walk, Charlotte?' I suggested.

'Is Tom coming?' she asked, her face brightening.

'Oh, I don't expect so,' I said, thinking that, like Francis, Tom would be catching up on some much-needed sleep – and thinking too that it really was just as well.

Even if he had not been a smuggler, this really was not the time for the sort of distraction that Tom offered. And if I were to form some sort of bond with Charlotte, it would be best done by spending time alone together, not with the man who seemed to have the power to excite both of us!

That day and the days that followed, were, I think, the strangest, the most disturbing and at the same time the most exciting I had ever lived through. My mind was in a constant whirl, my emotions so close to the surface that it was all I could do to keep them hidden. My once-simple life had been turned topsy-turvy and nothing would ever be the same again.

For the most part my days were spent with Charlotte, and slowly but surely the understanding I so longed for began to develop between us. As she became more used to me her first reserve began to fall away and I was able to glimpse the impishness Mrs Durbin had spoken of and the bubbling enthusiasm I had witnessed that first day when she had greeted Tom with such excitement.

She was, I discovered, a child who could be as exasperating as she was charming. Sometimes she was a wily little coquette with an instinctive knowledge of how to get her own way – especially with her father; sometimes as much a tomboy as I had been, with no care for scraped knees and grass-stained skirts. Sometimes I took her down to the beach, where she took off her shoes and stockings and waded in rock pools to find limpets and interesting strings of seaweed; sometimes we sat in the gardens, making daisy chains and trying to capture fluffy dandelion seeds that floated by and which Charlotte insisted were fairies.

'If you catch one you can make a wish!' she told me, and promptly managed to trap one between her cupped hands. Then she sat holding it in solemn silence for a long moment, lips pursed in concentration, eyes squeezed shut.

'What did you wish for?' I asked when she opened her eyes again.

'Oh, I can't tell you that! If you tell, your wish won't come true!' she admonished me.

I laughed. 'You wished for a day without a single lesson tomorrow,' I challenged her.

'Not exactly. Lessons with you are not so bad,' she conceded. 'No, I wished for something very special.'

No amount of questioning from me would persuade her to tell, but next morning when Tom turned up unexpectedly and she threw me a smug look whilst hanging on to his arm I thought that I could hazard a guess as to what her wish had been and wondered if perhaps there might be something in the silly superstition after all!

'Tom, Tom – are you going to take us to Galidor like you promised?' she begged, eyes shining.

'No – I've come to talk to your father. Just tedious old business.'

'But afterwards,' she pressed him. 'After you've talked to Papa – what about then?' She looked at me, enlisting my support. 'You'd like to go to Galidor again, wouldn't you, Charity?'

I felt the colour begin to rise in my cheeks. All very well to have told myself Tom was not the sort of man I wanted to become involved with – the moment I had set eyes on him again my heart had begun to beat a little too fast and my stomach tied itself in knots.

'I'm sure Tom is far too busy to spend time

with us,' I said coolly.

'Charity is quite right.' Tom's eyes found mine over the top of her head and I felt my cheeks grow hot. 'I don't have time to take you all the way to Galidor today and in any case it's too far for you, and too steep for your little legs.'

'Oh!' Her face fell. 'You promised!'

'I did nothing of the sort,' he replied, grinning. 'But if I finish talking to your father in time we'll go for a little walk in the other direction – to Dead Man's Cove. How would that be?'

'Oh, yes! Yes! Say you'll be finished in time! Please, Tom! He must, mustn't he, Charity?'

'I'm saying nothing about it,' I said firmly. 'It's very bad of you to bother Tom so.'

'It's no bother, sweeting. The pleasure is all mine.' Again his eyes sought mine, again something sharp and sweet twisted deep within me and I turned away in case it showed on my face and gave me away.

Tom *was* finished in time and I could think of no good reason to refuse to accompany him and Charlotte on the outing. It was better to go along with them and remain cool and collected, as if it really made no difference to me one way or the other, I decided.

The walk to Dead Man's Cove, as Tom had called it, was less onerous than the one to Galidor; there were no bits of cliff path that required him to give me his hand to assist me and, whilst I was grateful for that, I was also treacherously disappointed. In any case, for the most part Charlotte was claiming his attention and that was as it should be.

'Why is it called Dead Man's Cove?' she asked curiously as we stood on the path high above the sparkling blue water and the rocks with the sea spray breaking over them in frothy curls.

'Because a ship ran aground here once and was lost,' he told her. 'Every soul on board was drowned before help could reach them.'

'Oh!' She stared intently down. Then, after a moment, she asked: 'Does that mean there are ghosts here?'

Tom smiled. 'I shouldn't think so. I'm not sure I believe in ghosts anyway, Charlotte. I've certainly never seen one. Have you, Charity?'

'No.' I shook my head firmly. 'I've never seen a ghost either.'

'I have!' Charlotte said importantly. 'We have a ghost at Morwennan House.'

'I don't think so, Charlotte,' Tom said gently.

'We have! I've seen it!' she protested in-dignantly.

Tom decided to indulge her. 'So when have you seen it? And where?'

'When I've been in the garden playing. I've seen it at the attic window.'

She said it with enormous conviction and though the corners of Tom's mouth twitched he managed to restrain himself from laughing.

'Ghosts only walk at night, Charlotte. Not in broad daylight. What you saw was sun and shadow on the window pane.'

'It was a ghost! Truly it was! It was watching me!'

'Very well, have it your way. It was a very unusual ghost.' Tom's mouth quirked again with amusement. 'Now, do you want to go down to Dead Man's Cove or not? Because if we don't make haste there won't be time.'

'Yes, I want to go down,' Charlotte said promptly and the talk of ghosts was forgotten.

By the time the excursion was over and we were back at Morwennan I had forgotten my resolve to be cool with Tom too. His easy company made it impossible to remain aloof for long and it was only when he left us at the cliff gate and Charlotte asked him eagerly: 'When will you be coming again, Tom?' and I found myself inwardly echoing the sentiment that I remembered and caught myself up sharply.

'You really must stop plaguing Tom,' I reprimanded her. 'If you don't you can be sure he'll tire of you and not come at all.'

'Oh!' Her small face fell.

'How could I tire of such enjoyable

company, imp?' he teased her, but it was my eyes he was teasing. 'I'll come again soon, I promise.'

And in spite of all my good intentions I felt my treacherous heart leap. Whatever he might be, it was not going to be easy to resist Tom.

That afternoon, like the others, Charlotte and I spent on her lessons. To my relief Francis was busy in his study – that dark little room in the shadow of the trees that I so disliked – and we worked in the sunny parlour.

Though she had received little formal education she was quick to learn, so that teaching her was quite a pleasure and not the onerous task I had expected. I set her some simple sums, and when they were completed we did some reading. We then played a game I had devised to help her with her spelling, which was, I had discovered, very weak. I would come up with a word and she had to think of others which rhymed but were spelled differently, each one counting as a point. Ten points were worth a sweet-meat or an apple.

Already, though, Charlotte had become so good at my game that I had decided the rules would have to be changed.

'You're too clever, Charlotte,' I told her. 'If we go on at this rate you will be getting fat and I shall have to take the blame.'

'Oh!' she groaned. 'You can't change the rules!'

'Indeed I can!' I assured her. 'I'm the tutor, remember. From now on it's twenty points, not ten, and the reward is an excursion down to the beach.'

'With Tom?' she came back, quick as a flash.

'No, with me. But you like the beach, don't you?'

Indeed she did. Until I had arrived she had spent remarkably little time there, it seemed, for although it was within easy walking distance she had not been allowed to go alone and neither Selena nor Francis were ones for scrambling up and down the cliff path.

They left us mostly to our own devices and I was glad of that, for I was not comfortable with either of them.

What a strange pair they were, so cold and distant! I thought it a miracle that Charlotte had turned out so well when she had been raised exclusively by them. But Francis at least seemed genuinely fond of her, as did Mrs Durbin, who, I presume, had acted as her nurse when she was younger. But Selena ... Selena never unbent by so much as a fraction. To my mind she always gave the impression that Charlotte was more of an inconvenience than anything else.

As for the relationship between Selena and Francis, I couldn't make head nor tail of it. On the one hand the animosity between them was almost tangible, on the other there was clearly some kind of unspoken bond between them. It came from shared secrets, no doubt, for I felt sure there were plenty of those in this dark house.

High though my curiosity ran I shrank from raising the subject of Julia with any of them. I was afraid of arousing Francis and Selena's suspicions if I began asking questions, since almost anything I could say would demonstrate that I had some knowledge of the situation, and it seemed unfair to question Charlotte about her mother. It could very well upset her, and besides, I did not imagine she knew very much, since Julia had died when Charlotte was born.

One day, however, when Charlotte and I were in the garden, she mentioned her mother of her own accord.

We were sitting in the arbour on the seat of camomile and around us the roses were blooming in their full glory, their heavy heads open to the warm summer sun.

'Do you think we might cut some roses, Charity?' Charlotte asked suddenly.

'I don't know,' I replied. 'Why do you want to? Would you like some in your room?'

She shook her head. Her small face was serious.

'No, I want to take them to Mama's grave.'

I was startled, I admit it. My heart began to beat very fast and for a moment I did not know what to say.

'Where is she buried then?' I asked at last.

'Why, in the family tomb in the church-yard, of course,' Charlotte replied as if it were a stupid question, which, I suppose, it was. 'Papa used to take me there sometimes but I haven't been now for ages and ages. And I'm afraid Mama will think I've forgotten her.'

'She wouldn't think that I'm sure,' I said. 'But we could go if you'd like to, Charlotte. Is it very far?'

'It's in the village.'

I did not remember passing through a village when the carriage had brought me here.

'Do we have to go back up the gully road?' I asked.

'No. That's one way. But we can walk along the cliff the way we went with Tom the other day,' she told me. 'That's far nicer.'

'Ah.' So it was the village Tom came from when he came to Morwennan by way of the cliff path. 'Very well, Charlotte, we'll cut some roses and you can show me the way. Which ones would you like to take?'

'Pink.' Charlotte said at once. 'Pink was Mama's favourite colour.'

'How do you know that?' I asked.

'I just know,' she replied confidently.

We cut the roses and set out through the gate. As we picked our way along the cliff path with the sun warm on our faces Charlotte was very quiet, very solemn, and I guessed she was thinking about the mother she had never known. I was glad of the silence, for I was thinking of her too.

Just before we reached Dead Man's Cove Charlotte pointed out a track that forked inland from the cliff path.

'This way.'

I had not noticed the other path on our excursion – perhaps I had had eyes only for Tom! – but now I saw that, though narrow, it was well worn, snaking through the knee-high thrift and gorse. Perhaps the men who had carried the contraband up to Morwennan House had come this way, I thought. Certainly the old woman I had met on the beach on my first evening would use it to get to the beach with her creel for collecting shellfish. And Tom...

My heart skipped a beat. *Oh, Tom, how you have me in your thrall!*

We walked for perhaps a mile with the breeze from the sea at our backs before I saw the village ahead of us, a cluster of low stone cottages and daub-and-wattle shacks in a shallow basin that would afford some protection from the gales of winter. The church was on the seaward side, its tower rising

174

square against the periwinkle-blue of the sky. The churchyard was reached by way of a lychgate. I unfastened it and we went through. At once I felt the sense of peace that always comes to me in a graveyard. Even the little tic of nerves that had begun to throb in my throat as we neared Julia's resting place was stilled. I had been brought up by a minister, remember, and the churchyard had been as familiar to me as our own garden.

The churchyard here at Morwennan was not as well kept as the one at Penwyn had been; the grass grew up tall and waving around the old tombstones, some of which had crumbled and toppled over, and a tree which had grown up leaning from the wind had heavy boughs drooping so far they almost touched the ground. But none of that seemed to matter. Bumblebees droned lazily in the patches of nettles and a bird carolled from the branches of the stunted tree. All was peace and tranquillity and oneness with nature for the souls who slept here.

Charlotte led the way along the path towards the church door, then stopped beside a box-like structure of granite, a little larger than grave size and perhaps three feet high.

'This is it,' she said in a hushed voice. 'This is where our family lie.'

I nodded. The proximity to the church door was evidence of the importance of the

Trevelyan family in the parish. I would have expected nothing less, but it still gave me a slight shock to see their name engraved in the granite, generations of Trevelyans. The tic throbbed in my throat again.

Charlotte stepped on to the grass and went to the foot of the tomb. Then she stood quite still, the bunch of pink roses still clutched between her small hands, staring intently at the stone.

I followed her gaze and saw the inscription.

JULIA
Beloved wife of Francis Trevelyan
1747–1782
Resting with the Lord

In that moment time stood still and I stood still with it. My heart seemed not to beat, nor my pulses; I was not even aware of breathing. I had become, it seemed, as inanimate as the grey granite, as lifeless as those who lay in the soft earth beneath it. My eyes were fixed on the name of the woman I felt sure was my mother and it was the first contact I had ever had with her within my living memory.

Then my skin began to prickle and my heart to flutter and the breath I drew was long and shaky. Yet still I stared at the stone and the letters cut into it and I felt I would never be able to tear my eyes away.

After a little while Charlotte laid the roses in the grass immediately below her mother's name then turned to me quite matter-of-factly.

'We can go home now, Charity.'

I did not answer, and I heard her tone become puzzled.

'Charity? What's wrong?'

With an enormous effort I recovered myself.

'Nothing, of course. Very well, Charlotte, if you are ready we will go back.'

Charlotte chattered now as we picked our way back along the cliff path. She had visited her mother's grave, laid her flowers, and now, satisfied, her mood had returned to normal. But my replies to her seemed to me to come from someone else. My mind and my heart were still back in the peaceful churchyard with the birdsong and the hum of the bees and the waving grass.

And my mother.

'Where have you been? I've been looking for you everywhere!'

Selena was at the cliff gate waiting for us; her tone was sharp.

Charlotte replied for me. 'We've been to Mama's grave. I wanted to take her some roses.'

'I'm sorry if you were anxious...' I began, but Selena ignored me.

'What nonsense!' she said sharply to Charlotte. 'I don't know why you find it so difficult to put your mother out of your head. It's not as if you ever knew her. And going to the graveyard is a complete waste of time. I've told you before. She's not there.'

Charlotte stared at her aunt for a moment, still as a statue. Then her face crumpled, she burst into tears and ran as fast as her legs would carry her up the path towards the house.

I stared at Selena too, shocked by her callousness.

'That is the cruellest tirade I ever heard in my life!' I said angrily before I could stop myself. 'How could you say such a terrible thing to a child?'

Without bothering to wait for her reply, I hurried off up the path after Charlotte.

I found her in her room, sobbing bitterly.

'Oh, Charlotte, you mustn't take notice of what your Aunt Selena said,' I told her, putting my arms round her shaking shoulders. 'She was worried because she didn't know where we had gone. She didn't mean it.'

'She did so,' Charlotte managed between sobs.

'No, she did not. People sometimes say things they shouldn't because they are upset.'

'But she's said it before.' Charlotte looked up at me with tear-filled eyes. 'I don't understand, Charity. If Mama isn't there, where is she? She has to be somewhere! If she's not, I just can't bear it!'

My heart bled for her.

'Your mama is everywhere, Charlotte,' I said gently. 'When someone dies their spirit is not confined to a body any more. She is in the sea breeze, in the sunshine, in the roses. She is with you always. Why, even now I expect she is looking down, watching you. And she will be sad if you cry. Please, sweeting, don't cry! For, truly, there is nothing to cry about.'

I held her, feeling her hair soft against my cheek and her small body firm and warm in my arms. At last her sobs subsided a little and she looked up at me.

'You really think she's with me, Charity?'

'I'm sure of it,' I said softly but earnestly. 'Though you never knew her, your mama loved you very much. Love like that can never die.'

She nodded slowly and I only wished that I could believe the same was true of me, and Julia had loved me too. But if she had loved me, why had she abandoned me? My throat closed. I felt very alone suddenly, the deserted child with nothing to cling to.

I tried to push the mood aside. I was a grown woman who had survived twenty years of aching loss. Charlotte was just a little girl who needed love and understanding, not the cold cruel words of a woman with a heart like stone. Why, there was more giving in the granite of Julia's tomb than there was in that one!

I smoothed Charlotte's hair away from her tear-wet face and smiled at her gently.

'You have so much to be glad of, Charlotte,' I said gently. 'You have a nice home, a father who loves you ... why, you even have your own pony to ride when you go to your grandfather's house, don't you? What was his name?'

'Moonlight,' she said, rubbing her little snub nose with the back of her hand.

'Moonlight. That's such a lovely name. Is he a lovely pony?'

'Yes ... yes, he is. Do you think I'll be able to go and see him again soon?'

'I'm sure you will,' I said, relieved to see she was brightening. 'We'll ask your papa the moment he comes home, shall we?'

'Yes – oh yes!' She looked up at me and the look in her eyes made my heart turn over. 'I'm really glad you came to live with us, Charity,' she said.

Nine

I was still furiously angry with Selena when I went back downstairs, leaving Charlotte playing with her dolls. I simply could not understand how Selena could have spoken so and I was determined to confront her over her disgraceful outburst. But I think Selena realised what my feelings were and before I could say anything she pre-empted me.

'I gather you think I was too harsh with Charlotte,' she said bluntly.

'Yes,' I replied, echoing her bluntness. 'What you said upset her dreadfully.'

'There are worse things than being upset,' Selena said, her voice hard. 'It's better that she should forget all about Julia.'

'I can't agree,' I argued, angry enough to throw caution to the winds for the first time since I had come to Morwennan. 'She's just a child and she needs her mother even if she has never known her. I never knew my mother at all but I thought about her constantly and still do. It's a bond that nothing can break – not desertion and not death.'

Selena speared me coldly with those sharp

grey eyes.

'That is your opinion, Charity. But then you know nothing, do you? Nothing of Julia and nothing of my reasons for considering it best that Charlotte should not be encouraged in this foolish sentimentality. Charlotte's mother was not a woman to be admired. I would not wish Charlotte to grow up to be like her.'

I frowned. She was, after all, talking about the woman I believed to be my mother too.

'Julia was flighty and faithless,' Selena went on. 'She caused my brother a great deal of heartache over the years, almost from the day he met her. I advised him against marrying her but he would not listen. And he paid the price over and over again.'

'Are you saying their marriage was not a happy one?' I asked. I was trembling deep inside. This had gone much further now than an argument about Selena's treatment of Charlotte. For the first time I was on the brink of discovering something about Julia.

Selena laughed shortly. 'They shared little happiness, certainly, though through no fault of Francis's. He was besotted with her. She had everything she could possibly wish for. But she could never be satisfied. Finally she left him and ran away with a sea captain.'

My chest felt tight; I could scarcely breathe.

'She ran away?' I repeated faintly. 'When?'

'Long before Charlotte was born. She was gone for two or three years. The shame of it almost killed Francis – that and the pain of losing her, though I tried my best to make him see he was better off without her. And then, when she finally came running home with her tail between her legs, he was fool enough to take her back and it all started again.'

'What started again?' I asked.

'Her attitude towards Francis – she would not have him near her. Her moods – heavy and black with sulks that lasted for days on end. And then she began drinking. Francis had to lock away every bottle of spirits in the house. He even stopped serving wine with meals in an effort to wean her from the habit but she still managed to get liquor from somewhere. Bribed the servants, no doubt. She became a wreck and a liability as I had always known she would. Francis did his best – everything a man could do – but it was never going to be enough. She came close to destroying my brother with her wild and wilful ways and she would have destroyed Charlotte too. That is the reason I don't want the child worshipping her like some plaster saint.'

She paused. Her eyes, dark with hatred, never left mine.

'When I told Charlotte her mother was not in the churchyard I was speaking the truth.

Wherever she is, be assured Julia is in a hell of her own making.'

I scarcely remember leaving Selena and going back upstairs. My mind was awhirl, my senses reeling. I know I looked in on Charlotte to make certain she was still happily occupied with her dolls and then I went to my own room.

At first I paced, then I sat down on the bed, my head in my hands. About me in the silence the house settled as it did at night, this house that seemed to have absorbed into its walls and floors something of Julia's torment so that the boards creaked as if her ghost still walked them and the plaster gave back her misery as an atmosphere of oppression.

How unhappy she must have been when she had lived here! Though Selena's version of events had been coloured with her own brand of venom, I did not doubt that it had contained elements of the truth. Julia had not loved Francis and theirs had been a marriage of convenience, on her part at least. She had tried in every way she knew to escape from him – first by running away with another man and later by trying to lose herself in the oblivion that comes from a bottle. Perhaps she had been flighty and fickle as Selena would have me believe, but I could not help but feel that any indiscretions

184

had come about because she was desperately lonely.

And at last – at last! – I had uncovered a window in her life when she might have given birth to me. She had been gone for two or three years, Selena had said – plenty of time for her to have become pregnant and bear a child. Was that what had happened? Was my father the man Selena had described as a 'sea captain'? Or some other man she had fallen in with in the missing years?

But why had she abandoned me? Had she really been shallow and selfish, a baby an unwanted burden that would hinder her pursuance of her search for pleasures? Or had she been alone and desperate, unable to raise a child by herself? Had she cared that she had lost me? Was that the reason for her black moods and depressions and the fact that she had turned to the bottle – that she was pining, longing for the baby she would never again hold in her arms?

So many questions, so few answers.

Why, I did not even know for certain that Julia *was* my mother. But on one thing I was more determined than ever. Somehow I would find out the truth, no matter what it cost me. And when I did I would make both Selena and Francis very sorry indeed for all the misery they had inflicted.

A tap at the door interrupted my reverie. I

pulled myself together, smoothed my hair away from my face and, expecting it to be Charlotte, called out: 'Come in, sweeting!'

The door remained firmly closed, the only response another tap. Puzzled, I crossed the room and opened the door to find Mrs Durbin standing there.

'I'm sorry to disturb you, Charity,' she said in her soft Cornish burr. 'Only Mr Francis wants to speak to you – right away. You'll find him in his study.'

I frowned. Apart from the evening meals we had shared I had seen little of Francis during my time at Morwennan. He had been out a good deal on business – running a smuggling ring as complex as this one must involve a good deal of liaison with contacts further down the line, I imagined – and when he was at home he was mostly closeted in his study, where, presumably, he worked on a mass of accounts and records. It had also occurred to me to wonder if he might be avoiding me. It must be disturbing for him to have someone who looked so like his wife in her prime living under his roof, and even more disturbing if he believed that I was her daughter.

Now, however, he was actually asking for me, and in a rather formal way. Did his reason for wanting to see me have any connection with my conversation with Selena? Had he decided he no longer wanted me here and was about to dismiss me? If so it would be a blow indeed.

'Thank you, Mrs Durbin,' I said. 'Please tell Mr Francis I will be with him in just a moment.'

She nodded and once again I noticed the warmth and sympathy in her faded eyes. As yet no opportunity had arisen to further the friendship I had hoped might blossom between us but Mrs Durbin was the one person in Morwennan House who was not hostile to me, and I thought that in all likelihood that meant she had not been hostile to Julia either. For that I was grateful to her.

I checked my appearance in the mirror over the dressing stand and went downstairs. The door to the study was ajar. I knocked on it firmly, determined not to begin this interview at a disadvantage.

Francis was standing by the window, his back to the door. When I entered the room he turned around and I knew at once from his high colour and from the faint smell of liquor that, early in the day though it was, he had already been drinking.

'You wanted to see me,' I said.

'Yes.' He moved away from the window, pulled a high backed chair away from the wall and set it nearby and facing his own captain's chair. 'Sit down, Charity.'

I sat, warily, and folded my hands in my lap to keep them from trembling and betraying

187

my nervousness. Francis, however, remained standing, pacing a little before he spoke as if choosing his words with care.

'I believe you had something of an altercation with my sister,' he began.

'Yes, that's true,' I agreed. 'She said some rather harsh things to Charlotte about her mother, which upset her a good deal. I'm afraid I made my feelings on the subject known to Selena.'

I must have spoken with acerbity for he responded quickly.

'Please don't think I am criticising you. My sister sometimes says things she should not. She means well but her approach is not always wise and I can understand that you might disagree with her from time to time, especially where Charlotte is concerned. I am very pleased with the way things have turned out between you and Charlotte. She seems very fond of you. I must thank you for that.' He paused, then went on: 'Indeed, it is the reason I felt I must speak to you now.'

I said nothing, waiting and wondering what he meant.

'Selena has intimated to me that as a result of your concern for Charlotte's welfare she mentioned other, rather private, matters,' he continued uncomfortably. 'She told you of the problems Charlotte's mother caused me.'

'Yes,' I said.

Francis lowered his head so that his fleshy chin made a deep frill like an old-fashioned ruffle about his neck. I could see this was painful for him.

'In truth,' he said, 'these are things I don't care to talk about. They were not happy times, nor anything to be proud of. But since the subject has been broached I think there is something else I should tell you. For if you are here long enough you will hear it from someone else and I think it best it should come from me.'

Breath caught in my throat. The whole world seemed to be standing still.

'You look very like my wife,' he said.

This, of course, was no surprise to me. I wondered if perhaps I should pretend that it was. But Francis seemed lost in a world of his own, another time and another place far from this darkly shadowed study.

'Selena saw it the first time she set eyes on you,' he went on. 'It was the reason, I think, why she offered you the position here as Charlotte's governess. She thought it would please me.'

I said nothing. I certainly did not believe for one moment that Selena's motives had been so altruistic. Even if I had not over-heard something of the furious quarrel between her and Francis on that first night, her remarks today would have left me in no doubt of her feelings where Julia was

189

concerned.

'And you *are* very like her,' he said. His voice was low, and in it I could hear undertones of emotion, something I had never before associated with bombastic Francis, though Selena had intimated that his emotions were never far from the surface where Julia was concerned. He was looking at me too in a way I did not care for, very intently, his eyes narrow in his fleshy face and reflecting some of the emotion I could hear in his voice. 'To look at you, Charity, is like looking at Julia when she was your age. Your hair ... your eyes ... your chin...'

He reached out his hand, heavy with rings, and I thought for a moment he was going to touch me. Instinctively I recoiled and he must have felt it because his hand dropped back to his side.

'Yes, the likeness is uncanny,' he said. 'And not just your appearance, either. You have her spirit, too. Her spirit as it was before it was broken.'

My mouth felt parched. 'What broke her spirit?' I asked.

He moved impatiently then, and I knew I had asked the wrong question. Francis had deemed it necessary to tell me so much, but there was a great deal more he was not going to tell me.

'She destroyed herself,' he snapped. 'I thought Selena had explained that to you.'

'She said Julia turned to the bottle,' I said boldly. 'But surely there must have been a reason for that? Was it something she was trying to forget? Something she regretted?'

'Certainly she had a good deal to regret.' He picked up a paperweight from his desk, rolling it between his hands. Then his mood changed again. 'Frankly, Charity, it is not something I wish to discuss with you. I simply felt that I should appraise you of the fact that you are very like her, for the fact will undoubtedly cause talk once you have been seen and noticed.'

He moved toward the door; clearly he had decided the interview was at an end. But I had seen my opportunity and I was not about to let it slip away.

'Why would it cause talk?' I demanded, remaining firmly in my chair.

Francis frowned. 'I would have thought that was obvious.'

I drew a deep breath. 'Because Julia left you for a time and because I am a foundling,' I said. 'Because you think that they will say the reason I am like Julia is because—'

'Enough!' he snapped sharply.

'But it is the obvious conclusion,' I said steadily. 'And Selena thinks so too, doesn't she? It's the real reason she brought me here. Not just because I look like Julia, but because she suspected that Julia was my mother, born to her, perhaps, in the years when she had left you.'

There. It was said. I was trembling but I faced him out boldly and saw the flash of fury.

'You go too far!' he shot at me. 'I hoped that by talking to you I could ... But I see I was wrong. I think, Charity, it would be best if you were to leave Morwennan House...'

I rose then, not because I had the slightest intention of departing the study but because I did not want to be disadvantaged by him towering over me.

'Very well,' I said haughtily. 'If that's what you want. But I think I should warn you I have no intention of leaving it there. I have spent the whole of my life wondering who I am. For the first time I have a starting point and I shall not rest until I have learned the truth about what happened to Julia in the time she left you. I think you will find the questions I ask in the district and beyond a good deal more embarrassing than the mere fact of my appearance.'

Francis looked very old and tired suddenly. If he had been a more likeable man I might even have felt sorry for him.

'I hope you won't feel the need to do that, Charity,' he said. 'It would, as you say, cause a great deal of upset and I don't think you would find anyone to tell you what you want to know. When she left me, Julia left the parish too. No one hereabouts would be able to say with any certainty whether you are her child or not. Any more than I can. You look like her, so I suppose we must assume it is a possibility. But there is no way to go beyond that without tracing her movements of more than twenty years ago – which would be difficult to say the least of it. As to the other matter...' He paused, giving himself a little breathing space. 'As to the other matter ... I spoke in haste. You have worked wonders with Charlotte and for that I am grateful. It would be a great pity if you were to leave now and I think it would make Charlotte unhappy.'

I stood my ground, determined to clear the air once and for all.

'Are you saying you do not want me to go, then?'

He nodded his agreement. 'I do not want you to go, Charity. And not only for Charlotte's sake either.' His eyes were on me and I glimpsed in them that same look I had seen earlier. A look of intensity and longing. A look meant not for me but for Julia as she had been.

A pulse jumped uncomfortably in my throat.

'You are so like her,' he said softly.

I knew in that moment that the sensible thing to do would be to go now, whatever he said. This house with all its secrets and undercurrents was no place to be. I knew, with a deep sense of foreboding, that by remaining here I was flirting with danger – and in ways that had not occurred to me before.

But at the same time I knew I would not go. I could not leave Charlotte, who had, as Francis said, grown fond of me and who might very well be my sister. And I could not leave without learning more. For there was more to learn, I was certain. Francis had not told me everything there was to tell. It was there in his eyes, along with that frightening desire for me.

'I can't promise not to ask questions,' I said. 'You must understand how important it is to me to try to find out for certain who I am and why my mother abandoned me, whoever she might be.'

His eyes held mine, but the desire had gone now, replaced by a guarded look.

'I would counsel against that, Charity. Sometimes it is better to remain in ignorance. You are very young; you still have your dreams, and they may be preferable to the truth. In this life there are things we are better off not knowing.'

'You may be right,' I said steadfastly. 'But still I want to know.'

'Then you will have only yourself to blame if you don't like what you learn,' he said, and I fancied there was something of a threat in his words.

'It is time for Charlotte's tea,' I said abruptly. 'If there is nothing else...?'

'Nothing else.'

He opened the door for me; as I walked past him I was very aware of him, a strange, mysterious, brooding man in whom passions ran very deep.

I rather fancied that Julia had broken his heart.

Ten

Julia

Spring came, and summer, and Julia gradually regained her strength. But the bursting buds and the bright sky only served to increase her misery. Not a day passed but she thought of her baby, counting how old he would have been by now, first in weeks, then in months, imagining how he would have grown, picturing him lying in his crib or baby carriage, looking up at her with those dark-fringed eyes. In her visions she saw only that perfect little face, never the hideously deformed body. That came to her only in nightmares, from which she would wake to find her pillow drenched with her tears.

On rainy days the darkness closed in around her, when the sun shone it was still there, a heavy cloud that followed her wherever she went. And that was not far. She had no interest in anything or anyone; when spoken to she could scarcely bring herself to answer. She grew thin, her once-full breasts now as small as a boy's; her face lost its bloom. Francis saw her fading before his eyes and it tore his heart in two.

He talked to Selena about it, pacing the floor while she sat unmoved, uncaring, secretly triumphant.

'She's in a bad way, Selena. Dr Fletcher says she's pining for the child and needs a long trip away to take her mind off things. But I can't get away just now. This is the busiest time of year for the free trade, as you know.'

'Then send her alone,' Selena said bluntly.

'Alone?' Francis was shocked. 'I hardly think that would benefit her. And it would be highly improper.'

'Perhaps her father would accompany her,' Selena suggested.

'I doubt it. The farm needs all his attention.' Francis paused in his pacing, a thought striking him. 'She was with relatives in Falmouth before she came home to live. Perhaps she could go to them for a few weeks. Yes, now I come to think of it, I believe I have the answer. I'll speak to her about it right away.'

He blustered out of the room, not even noticing the smirk of satisfaction that twisted Selena's thin lips.

She rather thought that in her lethargic state Julia would agree to anything and it would be good – so good! – to have her out of the way, so good to have Francis to herself again, even if it was only for a few weeks. And once Julia had gone, who knew? She may never come back.

The arrangements for the visit were made. Francis had asked Selena if Mrs Durbin could be spared to accompany Julia, but the house where Julia's aunt and uncle lived was a modest one and could not accommodate a servant, so in the event Julia travelled alone.

As the carriage topped the steep rise out of the heavy shadow of the overhanging trees and into the bright clear sunshine, Julia thought dully that she should be feeling like a bird set free from a cage. This, after all, was what she had wanted for so long – to leave Morwennan House, and Francis. But she could feel nothing. It was as if the weight of grief and guilt had squeezed dry every other emotion. She watched the burgeoning hedgerows flash past the windows of the carriage, saw a kestrel hovering in the clear air, heard the birdsong, the clopping of the horses' hooves and the swish of the carriage wheels as if through a dense fog, muted, joyless, colourless.

It was only as the carriage approached Falmouth and she saw the wooded hillsides rolling down to the sea and the impressive Pendennis Castle silhouetted against the skyline that a stab of emotion pierced her and then it was not pleasure but bittersweet nostalgia, an ache of longing for days gone by and a future lost.

Aunt Prudence was shocked by the sight of her. She knew Julia had suffered and had known that all that had happened would have left its mark on her, but she was quite unprepared for this sad wraith that was but a shadow of the lively, beautiful girl Julia had been. She hustled her into the little house, fussing around her like a mother hen.

'Whatever has become of you, my cherub? You're in need of some loving care, that I can see. Well, you've come to the right place. We'll get the roses back in your cheeks, just see if we don't. Now, what do you fancy?'

Julia looked back at her with dull eyes.

'Oh, nothing, Aunt Prudence. I'm not hungry.'

'Of course you are! Now, what about a nice piece of poached chicken? That'll go down a treat!'

Julia shook her head.

'A posset then. You shall have the chicken tomorrow when you've recovered from the journey. You have to have something, and your Aunt Prudence is going to make sure you do.'

She was as good as her word. Little by little she tempted Julia with the dishes she had made when Julia was ill as a child – egg custards, warm and soft, that slid down her throat with no effort at all, apple stewed with spices, rabbit braised to tender flakiness and washed down with fresh lemonade. There was junket with wild strawberries, fresh caught fish, floury bread warm from the oven. Under her gentle insistence Julia began to eat again, and found as she did so that her appetite was returning.

It was good, too, to sleep in her old room, surrounded by the familiar furniture and the cheap little ornaments she had loved as a child. The room had been a haven to her after the death of her mother and it became a haven once again. After a week or so Julia found she was sleeping better, not waking at two or three in the morning to lie restless whilst the relentless thoughts churned around and around in her head, and the terrible dreams when she saw again her tiny son's deformed body came less often.

Uncle Silas played his part too, taking her down to the harbour to watch the boats, or persuading her to take a walk with him on soft summer evenings. Though she was still painfully thin, a little colour began to return to Julia's cheeks and, to her joy, she found that the dark clouds were receding a little, sometimes for hours at a time, then a whole day, and she was able to think more clearly.

They still hovered on the horizon, however, ready to close in again at the slightest provocation. One such trigger was a visit from Francis.

'You are looking much better, my dear,' he said, taking her hand. 'Soon you will be fit enough to come home to me.'

Julia no longer recoiled from his touch; it was as if in some unconscious part of her mind she knew she must accept it. But the mention of going back to Morwennan brought the dark clouds rushing in and her whole body began to tremble.

Yet somehow she could not find the words to protest. It was as if the depression had made her dumb. She knew deep down that the time would come when she would have to resume her old life, but she thrust it far to the back of her mind, living each day as it came and pretending that this welcome hiatus could go on for ever.

Now the shadow was back, dark and threatening. She felt the tentacles of fate closing in around her, trapping her. Home! Morwennan would never be home to her. It was a prison where Selena, the black widow spider, waited, where she would have to submit once more to Francis's unwelcome attentions, where her poor deformed baby had been born and died. The shadow was back and it would not let her go, not even when Francis had departed once more and the little house was empty but for Aunt Prudence bustling comfortably as she prepared the evening meal.

The walls of her haven seemed to be closing in on her; she had to get out, though she knew that even in the open air the feeling of being trapped would go with her.

'I'm going for a walk,' she said, and her voice seemed to come not from her own lips but from somewhere outside herself.

Aunt Prudence nodded. She could see that Francis's visit had upset Julia.

'Don't be too long though,' she said. 'There's fresh mullet for supper, landed this morning.'

And: 'I'm not hungry,' Julia replied in an echo of the words she had used so often when first she came.

Aunt Prudence sighed. 'Well, don't be too long anyway.'

Julia took a shawl and left the house. She walked without direction in a haze of despair until she found herself in the harbour.

It was a fine clear evening. The sun, already low in the sky, cast a pinkish light on the grey stone harbour wall, lazy waves lapped at it gently and ran in white-frilled sorties on to the shoreline. Julia stood with her shawl drawn about her shoulders, watching them, mesmerised. And suddenly it came to her that if she were to walk into the sea and keep on walking there would be no need for her to return to Morwennan – ever.

The water looked inviting to her, a deep grey-green that, further out, became aquamarine and then deep sapphire. She imagined it closing over her head, cool, salty and sweet, taking away the pain in her past and her dread of the future. She would be a part of it, swirling with the strings of seaweed on the tide.

Julia took a step forward. The shawl fell from her shoulders. Oh, it would be so easy! One more step and then another...

'Julia!'

She frowned. The sea was calling her name. She took another step.

'Julia!'

She paused, confused. The voice seemed to be coming from behind her, not from the waves at all. She turned, the light breeze lifting a loose strand of hair and blowing it across her face.

A man was standing there, a tall, well-made young man whose shirt ruffled in the same breeze that teased her hair. A young man she recognised, a young man from another life.

He has come to say goodbye to me, Julia thought. Or to lead me to the other side...

And then he began to run towards her and she realised this was no ghost.

'John!' she whispered, the first stab of disbelieving joy breaking through the wall of foggy despair, then rushing through her like the pent-up wall of water breaching a crack in the sea wall. 'Oh, my dearest love! John!'

He reached her, took her in his arms, held her so tightly the breath was squeezed from her body. Her face was pressed into his shoulder, the tears she could not stop were soaking his shirt. She clung to him, lost in the sheer wonder of the moment. Then, as he smoothed her hair away from her tear-wet face, she raised her head, looking at him, drinking in the sight of his lean, weather-tanned features.

'I don't believe it! I thought you were dead!'

'Not me.' He smiled into her eyes, a smile that stopped her heart just as it always had. 'I thought *you* were dead – to me, at least. I heard you were wed.'

She caught her lip between her teeth.

'I am.' She saw the shadow come into his eyes and rushed on: 'But not willingly! I would never have wed willingly! No one but you!'

'You thought I was dead. You just told me so.'

'But I'd have waited for ever in the hope ... Where were you? What happened?'

'Well, I was at sea, of course. The voyage took much longer than I expected.'

'They said you were lost.'

'And so we were – to all intents and purposes. We ran aground on the Spanish coast.' He held her away, looking down at her critically. 'What has happened to you, Julia?

204

I scarcely knew you! Have you been ill?'

Her eyes filled with tears again.

'Oh, John ... I can't tell you...'

'You must.' He took her hands in his. 'I think we should find somewhere we can talk. There's a great deal we have to say to each other.'

She nodded wordlessly. Hand in hand they walked away from the sea.

The sun had gone down in a ball of red fire before they finished talking.

Julia learned of the voyage that had so nearly ended in the disaster she had feared, and how, when he had returned to Falmouth, he had found her gone.

'You went to see Aunt Prudence?' she said in astonishment.

'Well of course! I thought to find you there. Instead she told me not only that you had gone to your father's but that you were betrothed – to a gentleman with a fine house.'

'I don't understand,' Julia said. 'Aunt Prudence never said a word to me about it – not then nor now. Why did she not tell me?'

'I dare say she thought you were lost to me. And no doubt she reasoned that to tell you now would cause only trouble.'

'I dare say. But still...' She pushed her puzzlement aside. There was so much she wanted to know that was of far greater interest than Aunt Prudence's omission.

'What do you do now? Have you given up the sea?'

He laughed. 'Me? Never! I'm master of my own packet now. We sail next week with the mail and a cargo of bullion to Brazil.' There was pride in his voice, but Julia's heart sank.

'All the way to Brazil? Next week? Oh, John, I can't bear it!'

He looked at her narrowly.

'You have a husband now, Julia. How can it matter to you how soon I leave – or how distant my destination? It's for the best, no doubt.'

Julia bit her lip, tears pricking her eyes. The thought of returning to Morwennan – and Francis – had cast a dark enough shadow before. Now, knowing that the love of her life was not dead as she had thought, but alive, it was insupportable.

'Take me with you.' The words escaped with no thought at all, but the moment they were spoken she knew she meant them with all her heart. 'Oh please, John – take me with you!'

'But your husband...' The love, the longing – and the indecision – were written all over his face.

'I hate him,' she whispered. 'I loathe and despise him. He won me, John, in a game of loo with my father. Won me like a bag of chips. I married him because he gave me no choice, but I believe I have repaid my father's debt to him many times over. Oh please, my love, don't leave me again! I can't bear it. Do you know what I was planning to do when you called my name? I was about to drown myself rather than go back to my old life. And I'll do it. I can't go back to him – I can't! If you love me, John, if you ever loved me – take me with you, I beg you!'

He looked into her lovely tormented face and felt a tide of anger against the man who had done this to her rise in him. Love her? Oh dear God, yes, he loved her with all his heart. He remembered the nights lying in his narrow cot on board the tossing vessel when he had ached for her, body and soul, the overpowering desire to return to England and make her his, his despair when he had thought he had lost her to another man. He had been torn apart by the vision of her in the arms of another, living, loving, laughing, sharing the days and nights, bearing his children. But he had tried to tell himself that she had so much more than he could ever offer her and if she was happy that was all that mattered.

Now he could see all too clearly that she was not happy.

What in heaven's name had this man done to her that she had become in such a short time this pale despairing echo of her former self? As yet he did not know. It would take time to learn the secrets of her disastrous marriage. But one thing he did know. He could not – would not – fail her again.

'I can't promise you an easy life, my love,' he said. 'I can't give you all the things your husband can. But if it's what you want, then I will take you with me.'

'Oh, John!' she whispered. 'It's what I want more than anything else in the world.'

And the tears that gathered in her eyes now and ran down her cheeks were tears of relief and happiness.

When John sailed from Falmouth the following week Julia was with him.

Only Aunt Prudence knew of her plan – an Aunt Prudence who was filled with remorse for not telling Julia that John had come looking for her.

'I thought it would just upset you and make things worse my dear,' she said anxiously. 'I thought it was best to let it lie in the past since you are bound to Francis Trevelyan. I see now I was wrong. I'll help you now and I'll keep your secret. But I think it's best your uncle knows nothing of your plans. Since you are in our care he might feel obliged to warn Francis.'

And so when Julia left the little house at the crack of dawn, taking with her only those few things she could carry, there was only Aunt Prudence, who had crept out of the bed where her husband snored, to hug Julia and wish her well.

John's packet, the *Guinevere*, rocked gently in the harbour; despite his preoccupation with making ready to leave, John was watching for her, and he hugged her close before leading her up the gangplank.

'Julia – you came!'

'Well of course I came!' she retorted. 'Did you not want me to?'

'I want you beside me more than anything,' he replied. 'But this voyage will not be easy for you, my love.'

'I don't care,' she said fiercely. 'As long as we are together and I never have to go back to Morwennan I don't care about anything.'

They sailed with the morning tide and before long Julia understood John's apprehension. As the boat pitched and tossed she became violently seasick and was forced to retire to the small cabin, where she lay for days on the narrow bunk, thinking dizzily that her wish for death was about to be granted. She could keep nothing down, not even a cup of broth or a dish of tea; even a sip of water churned in her protesting stomach. She slept fitfully in the heaving bunk and was only dimly aware of John sponging her face and changing her stained and crumpled bodice when he spared himself from the duties of captaining his ship towards calmer waters. Never in her life had Julia been so ill, but though she longed desperately to be back on dry land, never for one moment did she regret leaving with John. This sickness would pass. Life with Francis had been a hell she had thought she would be forced to endure for ever.

Then one morning she awoke feeling better. When she raised her head the cabin no longer swam around her and she realised to her amazement she was ravenously hungry. John counselled that it was best for the moment to content herself with a cup of soup, but when it was finished she begged for a slice of salt pork and some ship's biscuit. When she rose from her bunk she felt a little dizzy and weak and her legs wobbled like milk jelly, but the sickness had gone.

Julia went on deck, looked with pleasure at the billowing sails, stood at the rail and scanned the endless horizon with eyes filled with wonder, and watched with interest as the mariners went about their work.

This was John's world, now she was a part of it. Julia felt as free as the seabirds that followed the fishing boats into harbour, or the porpoises she glimpsed among the froth-topped waves in the wake of the ship.

Life settled into an easy routine; she be-friended the little cabin boy, on his first voyage and homesick for his mother; she mended the rents and tears that appeared in the clothing of the officers; she nursed the bosun when he fell ill. And whenever John could spare the time they sat together talking and talking, hungry for every detail of the other's life in the time they had been apart.

The one thing Julia was quite unable to bring herself to mention was the brutal way in which Francis had taken her virginity, but it scarcely mattered now; it was something that had occurred in another life. The girl who had held herself so stiff during his subsequent love-making was gone now; as she gave herself gladly to John Julia found herself wondering at how something which was so utterly repellent with one man could be such heady joy with another.

John was a sweet and tender lover and, mindful of the unpleasant experiences he felt sure she had endured, he led her gently and without demands until one night Julia, frustrated rather than comforted by his reticence, took the lead. She crawled astride him as he caressed her, straddling his body with an instinct as old as time and stopping his surprised response with her mouth.

'Lie still,' she whispered urgently. 'My darling, lie still.'

Startled, he did as she bid. Slowly, deliberately, she lowered her wet softness on to his hard body, raised, lowered, again and again until she took him inside her, deeper, more fully than ever before. A groan, half pain, half delight, escaped her lips and he rolled her over on the bunk so that he was once again in control. But this time there was no holding back, no restrained gentleness. He drove into her with every atom of his need, taking her with a great shout of triumph and then assisting her to reach the same dizzy heights of delight.

'Oh, my love,' he murmured as they lay naked and damp with sweat in one another's arms. 'Oh, my love – I did not hurt you, did I?'

And she murmured back, drowsy and gloriously replete: 'If that is hurting me, John, you can hurt me as often as you like.'

In all her life Julia thought she had never known such bliss, and though she could never quite forget her poor baby, the pain faded to a dull ache and whole days passed when she did not think of him at all. As for Francis, she tried very hard not to think of him either. He must know by now that she had left him, but she thought it would be his pride that was hurt the most. She had, after all, brought him little pleasure. She thought that in all likelihood he would be glad to be rid of her.

Eleven

No further mention was made that day by either Francis or Selena of anything that had passed. I did notice, however, that Mrs Durbin looked at me oddly when she brought in Charlotte's tea and I wondered if she knew something of what had been said.

It would not surprise me. Very little escaped Mrs Durbin. And if anyone knew the whole story of Julia and what it was Francis and Selena were keeping from me, it was her, I felt sure. She had been here so long and she was so much a part of the family.

I made up my mind that at the first opportunity I would sound her out, but as it happened she raised the subject herself when I carried the dirty china back to the kitchen. Though she was busy preparing vegetables for the evening meal she turned to me with a determination that suggested she had been stewing things over in her mind and could keep silent no longer.

'Don't believe everything you're told about Miss Julia, Charity. She was a lamb and don't you let Miss Selena tell you anything different.'

So – she had overheard Selena talking to me and I had been right in thinking she had been fond of Julia.

'Will you talk to me about her, Mrs Durbin?' I asked urgently.

Mrs Durbin lopped the green fronds from the top of a carrot.

'It's more than my job's worth. You'll hear nothing from me. Just don't believe all you're told,' she repeated darkly. 'There's things they don't want you to know, that's all I'm saying.'

And I could get no more from her.

That evening after dinner Tom came to the house. The atmosphere over the meal had been strained and his appearance was doubly welcome to me.

All very well to tell myself Tom was not the sort of man I should be taking an interest in; it made not one bit of difference to the way I felt whenever I saw him. My pulses raced and my tummy flipped and, whatever problems had been concerning me, I experienced a sudden inexplicable surge of happiness. It was silly and irresponsible, I knew; it was courting trouble, I knew, and yet I could not help myself.

Francis seemed less pleased to see Tom. 'There's no problem is there?' he asked shortly.

'Not at all.' Tom was smiling, seemingly oblivious to the tension that hung heavy in the air. 'For once I have not come to talk business, Francis. I've come to ask when you next intend to give Charity a day away from her duties, and I hope I can persuade you to make it next Wednesday.'

I quickly averted my eyes. I could feel the colour rushing to my cheeks and those treacherous pulses hammering.

'Next Wednesday?' Francis said. 'What significance does next Wednesday have in the scheme of things?'

'Why, it's the fair in the village. Surely you cannot have forgotten? I was hoping to take Charity – if she'll consent to come with me, that is,' he added with a smile in my direction.

'Oh, if there's a fair I'm sure Charlotte would like to go to it!' I said quickly.

'I'm sure she would,' Tom said drily, and I knew that he had been hoping to have me to himself. 'What about it, Francis?'

'Whatever you like,' Francis said. He looked tired and bad tempered.

'Good! And since it's a lovely evening, perhaps I could persuade Charity to take a stroll with me now. With your permission, of course.'

'Whatever you like,' Francis said again. 'Charlotte is in bed now – Charity's duties are finished for the day.'

I knew I should refuse his offer. But oh, I did not want to refuse!

'Thank you,' I said. 'That would be very nice.'

And tried to tell myself that it was because I was anxious to escape the claustrophobic atmosphere in the dining room, and nothing to do with the way I felt about Tom at all, that made me accept his invitation so eagerly.

We went to the beach. We walked along the firm sand just above the low-tide line and I found myself wishing desperately that I could unburden myself to Tom. But of course I could not. I did not know him well enough, and in any case it would have been a shame to impose on the respite from my turmoil that his easy company afforded me.

There was a little chill in the air this evening, a sure sign that summer was drawing to a close, and I was glad I had thought to pick up a light shawl. The sun was lower in the sky too and sinking fast without the brilliance of the glorious sunsets of the last weeks. Further along the beach I could see the old woman I had met on my first evening crouched down on the tide line.

It was a peaceful scene. It calmed my ragged nerves and after a while I began to be very aware of Tom walking beside me. We were not touching, yet the skin of my arm, bare beneath my shawl, seemed to prickle and reach out to his as if some sort of energy filled the space between us. For a little while it seemed more real than any of the problems that tormented me. I forgot even that Tom was one of *them* – a smuggler and common criminal, someone I should have more sense and more integrity than to become involved with. I simply savoured the feelings he was arousing in me, tasting them tentatively and liking them.

We talked a little, but not of anything of great consequence. Then Tom said suddenly: 'How do you find Francis?'

The surface of the magic bruised a little; I did not want to think about Francis, much less talk about him, and I could not understand why Tom should mention him now.

'I really have very little to do with him,' I said evasively.

'And Selena?'

This time I was more frank. 'I don't like her,' I said.

Tom laughed. 'You are not going to become friends, then?'

'I don't think that's likely.'

'She's a strange woman,' he agreed. 'I fancy though that her bark is worse than her bite.'

'Perhaps – but she's a terribly cold person. I would like to see her show more kindness and affection towards Charlotte,' I said –

and immediately felt guilty for discussing my employer with him. Dr John had been right to warn me that I talked too much! 'It's not my business, of course,' I added.

'Oh, I don't know,' Tom said. 'You *are* Charlotte's governess, after all. It's only right you should be concerned about her welfare, especially since she's such a lovely little girl.'

'Oh yes, she is,' I said, relieved to be able to change the subject. 'She's enormous fun, and very quick to learn too. But then, you know that without me having to tell you.'

He nodded but there was a thoughtful look on his face and it occurred to me suddenly to wonder why he had raised the subject of the Trevelyans. It was as if he had wanted to draw me out concerning them for reasons of his own. Why I should think this I did not know – he had, after all, said nothing whatever out of the way – but over the years I had learned to trust my instincts and just now my instincts were all whispering to me that Tom had a hidden agenda.

Oh, perhaps I was being overly suspicious, I told myself. Such an idea would never have occurred to me if I had not discovered that Francis was in the business of free trade and Tom was an associate of his. As it was, I could not help feeling that he was trying to gain an advantage in some way – and making use of me to do so.

'Do you know, Charity, your hair is the

exact same colour as Charlotte's?' Tom said suddenly, as if he had only just noticed.

'Is it?' I laughed a small embarrassed laugh.

'Yes. And such an unusual colour too.' He stopped walking, reached out and pulled a strand free from my combs, twisting it around between his fingers. Breath caught in my throat, a tiny sharp shard of excitement twisting deep inside me, and all my doubts were momentarily forgotten.

'But very pretty,' he said. And tugged on it lightly, pulling me towards him.

To my shame I made no effort to resist. His lips grazed mine; they tasted of the salt in the wind. His hand moved to the nape of my neck, holding me there, my lips against his, for a long moment. Such a gentle kiss and yet it seemed to draw the very heart out of me and I wanted it to go on for ever. Then, just as gently, he released me, drawing back and smiling at me crookedly.

'Now I suppose you are angry with me.'

I shook my head. My pulses were fluttering, my senses spinning. I had never been kissed by a man before.

'Why should I be angry?'

'For taking advantage of you.'

'No. You can kiss me again if you like,' I said before I could stop myself.

His grin widened. 'If I kissed you again, Charity, I surely would take advantage of you. I think it's time we were getting back.'

But he took my hand, his fingers curling round mine with a firmness that set the sharp sensation in my stomach leaping once more. And he held it as we walked back across the sand.

'I shall see you next week. Take you and Charlotte to the fair,' he said when he left me at the cliff gate.

I nodded. There was a joy in me that felt a little like the anticipation that fills me each year at the coming of spring, when the first buds begin to burst on the trees, the first spears of the snowdrops push through the hard earth and there is warmth at last in the sunshine.

Next week. I could scarcely wait.

'Mrs Durbin, did Julia have any family?' I asked.

I had found her in the parlour, dusting the mantel ornaments with vigour – it seemed to me sometimes that Mrs Durbin carried out every task on the run. Hardly surprising, since she had no help whatever in the house.

Ever since the cryptic conversation I had had with her when she had spoken in defence of Julia, I had been wondering how I could persuade her to tell me what she knew. And on one of my sleepless nights, when the boards above me creaked like ghostly footsteps, it had occurred to me for the first time that Julia must have a natural family somewhere.

With the realisation had come a pang of excitement and I could scarcely believe that I had not thought of it before. If I could discover who they were and go and see them I might find them less reticent than the Trevelyans. And perhaps Mrs Durbin would see no harm in telling me what I wanted to know.

I had waited patiently for my opportunity. No, I had waited *impatiently* – but I was anxious neither Francis nor Selena should come upon me discussing Julia with the old housekeeper.

Now, though I wanted my enquiry to sound sufficiently casual so as not to set Mrs Durbin on her guard, I could scarcely keep the eagerness out of my voice, and Mrs Durbin's duster paused in its energetic work. She looked at me over her shoulder, head cocked to one side like a bird, her faded eyes screwed up warily in the ripe-apple face.

'What are you asking that for?'

'Oh, I'm just curious,' I said. 'Charlotte goes to see her Grandfather Trevelyan and her uncles and cousins. I wondered if she had any relatives on her mother's side.'

Thankfully my explanation seemed to satisfy her.

'Her father used to live nearby, but he lost

his farm long ago and moved to Launceston.' She picked up a china dog, rubbing it energetically with her cloth. 'It's too far for the little maid to travel alone, and Mr Francis and Miss Selena would never take her. There's bad blood nowadays between them and Harry Stacey.'

A pulse jumped in my throat. Harry Stacey. Stacey. For the first time I had a name for the family who might be my kinfolk by blood, not just by marriage!

Just then the clock on the mantel struck the hour and Mrs Durbin looked at it sharply.

'Lawks, is that the time! I've a fowl in the kitchen waiting to stew. It'll never make good strong stock if I don't get it on. And here I am gossiping!'

She bustled out and I was left alone, frustrated that the conversation had ended so suddenly, but excited too with the new shreds of information I had gleaned.

As Mrs Durbin had said, Launceston was a good distance away, with the wide, wild expanse of Bodmin Moor separating it from any place I had ever been. But at least Julia's father was still in Cornwall – unless, of course, he had died, or moved on again...

But even that possibility failed to dampen the exhilaration I was feeling. I could not believe that fate had brought me so far only to lead me up a blind alley. At last I had a name to go on; somehow I would find a way to follow it up. And then, perhaps, I would discover a whole family I had never known I had.

Wednesday, the day of the fair, dawned cloudier than of late and distinctly cooler. Tom arrived after breakfast, just as he had promised.

I had expected we would walk to the village by way of the cliff path but to my surprise Francis offered to drive us. He wanted to view the livestock, he said. But since I knew livestock – apart from horses – played no part in Francis' life, I thought a more likely explanation was that he did not want his daughter to be seen arriving on foot and perhaps a little dishevelled. He was, I think, very jealous of his position in the community, even if some of the villagers, at least, must know that his wealth came from smuggling.

As we left the house by way of the main door the storm clouds were casting a dim grey light and I decided it would be sensible for Charlotte and myself to take cloaks in case rain set in. Whilst the others walked on up the rise I ran back into the house to fetch them.

The door that led from the hall to I knew not where was standing ajar and I glanced at it curiously. Apart from the time I had seen

223

Mrs Durbin emerging from it with a tray, I had never seen it open. As the front door banged after me I heard footsteps on the staircase that I could glimpse behind that open door and Mrs Durbin emerged. Her face was a little more flushed than usual and she seemed surprised to see me.

'Oh – I thought you'd all gone!' she said, sounding flustered.

'I've come back to fetch our cloaks,' I said. 'I thought it might be going to rain.'

She nodded, standing stolidly in the doorway as if to protect whatever lay beyond. Her stance and the expression on her face, sheer discomfiture, puzzled me. I ran upstairs, collected the cloaks, and when I came down again there was no sign of Mrs Durbin. The door was firmly closed.

Francis and Charlotte were already in the carriage when I made my way back up the rise. Tom stood in the drive, waiting. He handed me in and I thrilled to the light but firm touch of his fingers on mine. Durbin flicked the reins and we moved off slowly up the steep drive under the heavy trees.

Apart from the visit with Charlotte to the churchyard I had never been into Morwennan village. Today it was a hive of activity. As we drove along the narrow street, villagers touched their forelocks and I had to suppress the urge to giggle.

Tom noticed.

'You must get used to that sort of thing when you are with the gentry,' he whispered in my ear.

'Are you used to it?' I whispered back.

'Oh no, but I can carry it off,' he replied, smiling.

And so he could. I realised I still knew next to nothing about Tom's background apart from the fact that he was from Falmouth, and I found myself wondering about it. I wanted to know everything there was to know about Tom.

In spite of the lowering sky Morwennan village was a hive of festivity.

Stalls and booths with gaily coloured awnings had been set out along the streets, which were crowded by people dressed up in their Sunday best. As we mingled with them Charlotte darted between us, holding first on to Tom's hand, then her father's, then tugging excitedly at my sleeve. We watched tumblers performing the most amazing acrobatic feats and mummers entertaining, and the usually quiet village was noisy with the scrape of fiddles and the cries of pedlars selling their wares.

'Oh, look – look!' Charlotte cried as we made our way to the village green and we saw that, though it was autumn, the May pole had been erected and a dozen or so little girls were dancing round it, threading the gaily coloured ribbons into an intricate pattern. As we watched, Charlotte bobbed up and down excitedly, and I knew that she was itching to join in.

Privileged she might be, compared to these children, but living in comfort at Morwennan House meant she was missing such a lot of fun and companionship, I thought regretfully.

As the dance came to an end a great wave of excitement rippled through the crowd and, following the craning necks and pointing fingers, I saw a strange sight bobbing its way along the street – a long boat-shaped structure covered in a tent of tarpaulin and hung with painted panels.

'It's the Hobby Horse,' Tom said.

I laughed aloud in delight. Almost every village in Cornwall had its own version of the Hobby Horse, and this one was no exception. There was, of course, a man inside the structure, balancing it on his shoulders, and though he was completely hidden he could clearly see out well enough, for every so often he made a dash for a pretty girl in the teasing crowd, enveloping her in his flowing cloak.

'I've never seen a Hobby Horse do that before!' I exclaimed – each village Hobby Horse had its own customs.

'He's giving them a pinch,' Tom explained. 'It's supposed to bring good luck.'

As the Hobby Horse drew nearer I inched closer to Tom, not wanting to be singled out. But just as it came level with us a young village lad shouted a bawdy comment and the unwieldy horse turned in our direction, hesitated for a moment, then made a dive at me.

'Tom!' I squealed, but he only stood by laughing as the Hobby Horse grabbed me, pulled me momentarily into the folds of fabric, and gave me a sharp pinch.

I laughed too. It was just so silly! But the laughter died in my throat as I saw Francis's face.

His expression was one of outrage and fury. To my utter disbelief he raised his cane and brought it down sharply on the Hobby Horse as he might do on an aggressive dog. The man inside the horse was not hurt, of course – he was far too well padded for that – but he nudged Francis playfully two or three times, making sport of him. Villagers were staring, open-mouthed, at his sudden display of fury, a child laughed loudly, pointing, and his mother clapped a hand over his mouth and drew him away as if she was afraid he might be the next to feel the sting of Francis's cane. Charlotte stared at her father in puzzled dismay. Tom frowned. Even Francis himself was startled by his own reaction, I think, and a little ashamed, for he turned red and began to bluster.

'Impertinent lout! They go too far, these country clods. He would never have dared lay a finger on you, Charity, if his identity was not concealed by that ridiculous get-up! I'll find out who he is and have him horse-whipped!'

'He meant no harm. It was only a bit of fun,' I protested.

'And she'll have good luck too, Papa!' Charlotte put in. 'Did you not say a pinch from the Hobby Horse brings good luck, Tom?'

'Indeed I did.' But Tom still looked serious. No sign now of his ready smile. And for me too some of the spirit of fun had gone out of the day, for I knew instinctively why Francis had reacted so angrily.

It was not just that he was offended that it was our little group that had been singled out for attention. It was because *I* was the one who was pinched. I, who looked so much like his beloved Julia. For a crazy moment it had seemed to Francis that it was not me, Charity, who was the subject of the Hobby Horse's attention, but Julia herself, and he had struck out unthinkingly at the man he believed to be violating her.

I shivered, frightened by the violent and unreasoning emotions my similarity to his dead wife awakened in this man.

'I am going to the field where the livestock market is being held,' Francis said, blustering still. 'It's the reason I came today. And I would like Charlotte to accompany me. Look after Charity, Tom – see she is not bothered again by some drunken hobble-dehoy – and I'll meet you outside the ale house in an hour, or as soon after that as my business is completed.'

'Oh, Papa, can't I stay with Tom and Charity?' Charlotte pleaded.

Francis smiled at her suddenly, his loss of composure forgotten.

'Well you can,' he said teasingly, 'but I thought you might like to look at the ponies and see if there's one that takes your fancy.'

'Oh!' Charlotte skipped excitedly into the air like a spring lamb. 'A pony! Papa, you don't mean...? You are not going to buy me a pony?'

'No promises. I said we would look at them. But if there's a suitable one, and at the right price ... It's too far for you to go to your grandfather's to ride Moonlight as often as you'd like, and the meadow beyond the Hollow would make a home for him and a practice ring for you ... Well, what do you say? Are you coming with me – or do you still want to stay here with Charity and Tom?'

Charlotte caught at Francis's arm, her face alight.

'A pony of my very own! Oh – a pony!'

Her pleasure was infectious; I felt my own

mood lightening again. What a surprising man Francis was! Clearly it had been in his mind all along that he might buy Charlotte a pony at the fair, yet he had made no mention of it until this moment. He had kept it a secret, as he kept so many things secret. But for all his faults there was no doubting he loved his daughter very much and took pleasure in her happiness.

'Well,' I said as the two of them headed off in the direction of the horse fair, 'I hope Francis doesn't expect me to teach Charlotte to ride as well as to spell and do sums! I've never been on a horse in my life!'

'Then you should!' Tom said. 'There's no greater pleasure than galloping across the moors with the wind in your hair.'

He took my hand; as the warmth spread through my veins from where his fingers touched I thought that I would be able to dispute with him which things in life brought the greatest pleasure!

'You ride?' I asked to cover the flush of happiness I was feeling.

'Well of course! My brother and I were brought up on our own grandfather's farm. We rode all the time. I remember straddling a cart horse that was bringing in the harvest when I was scarcely big enough for my legs to reach across the breadth of his back,' Tom said, smiling.

'Oh!' I said. For one thing, Tom had once told me he had no family. For another, he had said he came from Falmouth, which I associated more with the sea than with farming. Again I realised just how little I knew about Tom.

'You didn't follow the family tradition and farm yourself, then?' I probed gently.

'Hardly family tradition,' Tom said. 'My father was a sailor.' He paused, and his face grew hard suddenly, his eyes narrowed, tight lines appearing round his mouth. 'My brother did put to use the horsemanship we learned, though,' he went on, his tone matching the expression on his face. 'He became a riding officer.'

'Oh!' This revelation surprised me still more. Riding officers were employed by the authorities to patrol the coasts and watch out for evidence of smuggling – the very trade from which I felt sure Tom made his living. No wonder Tom was not best pleased at his brother's profession. 'Is this his district?'

'He has no district. He is dead,' Tom said shortly.

'Oh – I'm sorry...' I murmured foolishly.

'Unless they are corrupt, riding officers tend not to live long and healthy lives,' Tom went on in the same cold hard tone.

I stared at him, shocked. I had heard, of course, of the unfortunate 'accidents' that often befell riding officers. The laming of their horses was the least of it, a fatal fall over a convenient cliff the worst. Smugglers hated riding officers – unless, of course, they were in their pay – and from what Tom had said his brother had not been one of those.

The different paths they had followed must have set brother against brother. The one had died. And judging by the way he had related the tale, Tom, the smuggler, was not in the least sorry.

Suddenly I no longer wanted my hand in his. I tore it away. Tom glanced at me.

'Is something wrong, Charity?'

'Nothing!' I forced lightness into my voice. I did not want to even think about the unpleasant thoughts that were occurring to me, much less put them into words. 'Look – there are some mummers performing! Let's go and watch!'

And though we did, and although I laughed as they danced, handkerchiefs waving, bells jingling on their hats and at their ankles, I felt that the heavy storm clouds that still darkened the sky had somehow got inside me and lay darkly about my heart.

An hour later, as we neared the ale house, the strangest thing happened. Francis and Charlotte were already there waiting, and Francis was talking to a man whose back was towards us but whose whole stance and appearance reminded me of Jem. It couldn't be, of course – what would Jem be doing here in Morwennan village, and talking to Francis at that? But he was sufficiently like him to give me quite a start.

By the time we fought our way through the crowds to where Francis was waiting, the man had gone.

I could tell from Charlotte's downcast face that she had no new pony to take home with her.

'There was nothing suitable,' Francis explained. 'No pony I could trust with an inexperienced child. And the prices that were being asked were outrageous for such poor specimens.'

'I did so want one though, Papa,' Charlotte said miserably.

'I know you did, sweeting, and you shall have one. I'm sorry you have been disappointed – I should not have told you what I intended until I'd seen what was on offer today. But I will begin making enquiries amongst the local farmers without delay to find the very pony for you. Now, does that make up a little for your disappointment?'

Francis spoke to her tenderly; once again I marvelled at the opposing sides of his character.

Charlotte brightened at once.

'Oh yes, Papa! And you aren't going to talk business with any strange men again today, are you? It's so tedious when you talk business!'

'No, not today,' he promised her, smiling.

So – the man who had reminded me of Jem was another of their number, I thought, and hated the way my mind was continually being drawn back to this free trade by which both Francis and Tom made their livings, and the unpalatable fact that where the law was broken other, worse, crimes followed as night follows day.

If Tom associated with smugglers, he associated with murderers too, I thought. And there was no escaping the feeling of unease which pervaded me.

Twelve

In the early afternoon the rain that had been threatening all day began. A light misting in the air soon became a steady drizzle and there was little doubt that it had set in for the day. There was nothing for it but to return to the carriage and set out for home, but I could not be sorry about that, for all my pleasure in the day had gone with those cold words of Tom's for his brother who had died whilst attempting to put a stop to the illicit free trade.

I had thought we might leave Tom in the village or drop him off where he lived – wherever that might be. But instead he rode back with us to Morwennan House. Perhaps he and Francis had more illicit business to discuss, I thought darkly.

As the carriage descended the gully road the rain fell from the trees upon it with heavy plops. A small gig I had not seen before was drawn up at the point by the coach houses where the gully became steep and narrow.

'It seems we have visitors,' Francis said, frowning. 'I was not expecting anyone to call today.'

I fastened my cloak at the neck and pulled the hood up to cover my hair. Tom handed me down from the carriage and I shrank from his touch. It was then that I saw someone coming towards us up the rise from the house.

I stared, disbelieving. It couldn't be, surely! First to think I had seen Jem in the village, and now ... Oh, I must be imagining things again...!

But at the same time I knew that this time, at least, I was not.

My heart gave a great leap of pleasure, and forgetting all propriety I ran eagerly down the gully towards the advancing figure.

It was my beloved Joshua!

Never, in all my life, I think, had I been so pleased to see anyone. Joshua had always been my friend and protector as well as my hero; today, upset and vulnerable, I felt desperately in need of friendship and protection. I threw myself into his arms, hugging him, and he hugged me back warmly.

'Charity!'

'Joshua! What are you doing here?'

'Well, come to see you, of course! But I thought I had missed you. I was about to leave again.'

'Thank goodness we got home when we did! Oh, Joshua, it's so good to see you!'

It was; though it was also a little strange, for he was, of course, clad in the attire of a curate. But it suited him – the black coat and hat favoured his fairness and above the dog collar his face was as angelic as ever.

The others had reached us now and were looking at Joshua curiously, puzzled, no doubt, by the enthusiasm with which we had greeted one another. Francis looked stern, Tom a little put out, I thought. Well, it would do him no harm.

'This is Joshua Palfrey,' I said to Francis. 'His parents raised me. We were brought up as brother and sister.'

Francis nodded. 'A man of the cloth, I see.'

Joshua smiled, that open cherubic smile that might have come straight from a painting of the heavenly throng.

'Trying to be, sir. Though there are times when I wonder if I was mistaken to believe I was called to follow my father into the ministry.'

'This is my employer, Francis Trevelyan,' I said to Joshua. 'This is Charlotte, my charge. And Thomas Stanton. A friend of the family.'

'We had better go inside,' Francis said. 'We are getting wet standing here. Though you, Mr Palfrey, look as if you have had a soaking already.'

'I am a little damp, yes,' Joshua agreed.

That was an understatement if ever I heard one! Rain water had collected in the brim of Joshua's hat and was dripping down his neck, his cloak looked dark and heavy and sodden.

'You're wet through!' I said. 'Have you been waiting here long?'

'Only a little while. A drop of God's good rain won't do me any harm,' Joshua said.

'Is there no one in?' Francis asked, opening the door. 'Did no one answer your knock?'

'No – but perhaps I did not knock loudly enough,' Joshua replied, trying as always to attribute to himself any blame that might be construed. 'I confess I was concerned at disturbing the household when you do not know me from Adam. But I was passing through the neighbourhood and I took the opportunity to call by and catch up with Charity. Since I have taken holy orders and moved to my new parish I have missed my family. And Charity most of all.'

He turned his smile on me; I warmed beneath it. Oh, it was so good to see a friendly face – especially Joshua's!

'I am sure the two of you must have a great deal to catch up on,' Francis said. 'Why don't you take your brother into the parlour, Charity? I'll have Mrs Durbin bring you a dish of tea – if she can be found. Where the devil is everyone?'

As if on cue Mrs Durbin appeared from the door in the hallway. She looked a little flustered.

'My – are you all home already? I didn't

expect you until dinner time.'

She patted her hair; I wondered if she had been taking a nap. It would explain why she had not heard Joshua knocking. But surely she would have taken a nap in her own quarters?

'Where is Selena?' Francis demanded.

'Gone out. I don't know where. She didn't say.' Mrs Durbin still looked flustered.

'Take our visitor's hat and cloak if you will, and see about that tea,' Francis ordered, a trifle impatiently.

I took Joshua into the parlour.

'So how are you, Charity?' he asked, taking my hands in his the moment we were alone. 'Are you happy here? Are they treating you well?'

I hesitated. I so longed to tell Joshua everything – but where to begin?

'Oh, Joshua, there's so much...'

'And is Mr Thomas Stanton part of it?' he asked shrewdly.

I coloured. 'What makes you think that?'

'The way he was looking at you – especially when you were greeting me.' He smiled. 'I think if I had not been wearing priest's garb he might have given me a bloody nose.'

'Oh!' Even given the doubts I had been entertaining about Tom today, Joshua's words still pleased me.

'I *am* fond of him,' I admitted. With my face as pink as the roses in the garden it was useless to pretend otherwise! 'But, Joshua, I have much more important things to tell you. I think I might be on the verge of learning who I really am...'

I told him of my likeness to Julia, and as much of the story as I knew. He listened as patiently as he might listen to a parishioner's confession but his face was clouded and serious.

'Are you sure it's wise, Charity, to hold out such hope?' he asked when I paused for breath. 'Francis may be right; sometimes there are things we are better off not knowing. And you could be on the wrong track, anyway.'

'What makes you say that?' I demanded.

'I once heard Mama and Papa talking,' he said carefully. 'I didn't understand much of what they said – I was only a child at the time – but there was something about you being rescued from a terrible fate. That you had almost died *"at the hands of those evil people"*. I'll never forget those words. "At the hands of those evil people." ' He paused. 'That does not sound as though you were abandoned by some poor woman who simply did not have the means to look after you, does it? You must, I think, have been ill-treated at the very least, and perhaps removed from the care of your family.'

I bit my lip. This was an unwelcome revelation indeed. I so wanted to believe that

I was Julia's daughter and the reason she had given me up was because her lover had left her alone with no means to support herself, let alone me. But if there was some darker side to the story it would explain why Mama Mary and Dr John had always been so reluctant to talk about the circumstances in which I had come into their care.

'Oh, Joshua, I don't understand any of it!' I confessed. 'But whatever the truth, however unwelcome, I have to know. I have spent my whole life wondering, and now...'

'Yes,' he said slowly. 'Yes, I can see that. I would feel the same in your position, I expect.'

'When I can, I am going to try to make contact with Julia's family,' I said. 'I seem to have run up against a dead end here. Francis and Selena know no more about what happened in the years Julia was missing than I do – or that's what they say, at least. But maybe she turned to her parents. That's possible, is it not?'

'And they live in Launceston now, you say?' he asked thoughtfully. 'It's a long way, Charity. And how do we know they are not the "evil people" Papa referred to?'

'We don't,' I agreed. 'Though, as you say, it's a long way off. It's hardly likely your mama and papa would have taken me from such a distance away. Surely I would have been cared for much closer to where I was rescued from. But if I don't speak to them, or at least try to find out something about them, we'll never know, will we?' I hesitated. 'Would *you* help me, Joshua? Could you not question your mama and papa when next you see them?'

'I could, I suppose,' he agreed doubtfully.

'And the Staceys – Julia's parents ... You never go as far afield as Launceston, do you...?'

'I have my own transport, it's true,' Joshua said, 'and a certain amount of time to myself. But I've been away from my parish now for the best part of a week. I have been visiting Jem in Falmouth.'

'Oh!' I exclaimed. 'Have you really? It's most odd, because I thought I saw him today in Morwennan – and then I came home and you were here...'

'I think it's unlikely he was in Morwennan,' Joshua said with a smile. 'I left him at his own home around eleven, and he told me he had a busy day ahead of him.'

'Oh – I know it couldn't have been him,' I said. 'It was just ... odd. And then to come home and see you waiting at the door ... How is Jem, anyway? Is he well?'

'Yes – and prospering too from what I could see. But then he would, would he not? Jem was always the clever one.' He grinned ruefully. 'But as I was saying, it will be a few weeks before I am allowed free time again. In

242

the meantime I will certainly see if I can learn anything about these Staceys. If they lived in this part of the world at one time they may still have connections here. And when I can I'll try to get to Launceston and speak to them myself,' he promised. 'They may be more prepared to talk to me than to you. This does have certain advantages.' He tapped his dog collar. 'But I only hope I am not doing you a disservice in this. What we learn may not be what you would like to hear.'

'Whatever you discover, I'll accept it,' I said earnestly. 'But I have to know. Good or bad, I have to know.'

We talked some more over the tea that Mrs Durbin brought in, of the family, of the old days, of Joshua's new life. Then he rose regretfully.

'I am going to have to take my leave of you, Charity, if I am to get back before nightfall. I should prefer not to be driving on unfamiliar roads after dark.'

Unexpectedly tears welled in my eyes. Joshua couldn't stay for ever, of course, and it made sense for him to make the journey in daylight. But oh – I didn't want him to go!

'Charity?' He looked at me anxiously. 'Is something wrong?'

'No ... no...' I tried to assure him, swallowing hard, but the tears made my voice choky and unconvincing.

243

'There's something else you haven't told me, isn't there?' he said perceptively. 'I've sensed it all the time we've been talking. What is it, Charity?'

I hesitated, wondering if I should tell him about Tom and Francis and the smuggling. It would be such a relief to share it. But it would also be a mistake. If I burdened Joshua with what I knew he would, in all likelihood, feel he had no option but to go to the authorities. Joshua had always had principles; now he was a man of the cloth those principles were likely to be even more finely honed. And though I too felt strongly that Francis's operation was very wrong and should be stopped, the last thing I wanted was for a magistrate to turn up now, seize any contraband that might still be on the premises, and arrest Francis. If that happened then almost certainly I would be sent away and I would lose contact with Charlotte, along with any chance of learning more from the Trevelyans.

With an enormous effort I swallowed my tears and rubbed my eyes with my fingertips.

'I'm just being foolish,' I said. 'It was so good to see you, and now you're leaving again. Don't take any notice of me.'

Joshua's eyes searched my face. 'Are you sure?'

'Of course.' I forced a smile. 'Go on, Joshua, it's high time you were going. I don't want to be responsible for you running off the road in the dark, or colliding with some stray animal.'

'Very well, Charity. But promise me...' His voice tailed off. 'Look – if you are worried about anything or in need of help or advice, Jem is not so far away. Promise me you'll go to him should the need arise.'

'I promise.'

Jem and I had never been close as Joshua and I were but, for all that, he was as near to being family as was possible without the link of blood. If the need arose, I felt sure he would not fail me. But nevertheless, as I watched Joshua walk up the rise to the coach house, I thought I had never felt more alone in my entire life.

The wet weather that day marked, it seemed, the end of summer. Rain fell almost ceaselessly for the best part of a week and with it the colour began to fade from the sodden leaves. The first ones came tumbling down, as yet no more than a sparse scattering, but a clear warning of the deluge to come, when, I imagined, the ground would be covered by a thick brown carpet and drifts would build up in the banks and hedgerows.

Francis persuaded Charlotte it would make a great deal more sense to wait until spring to acquire a pony and, to make up for her disappointment, arranged for her to go to her grandfather's, where she could ride her beloved Moonlight. I was to go with her.

I was a little apprehensive as the carriage set off the first dry day after the downpour. This was, after all, Grandpapa Trevelyan, father of both Francis and Selena, and I imagined an older, crustier version of them, with an amalgam of all their faults.

I was in for a pleasant surprise. Samuel Trevelyan was the epitome of a country squire, bluff, red-faced and genial – and obviously delighted to see Charlotte.

'Fancy coming all this way just to visit your old grandfather!' he teased, and I could not mistake the twinkle in his eye. 'Shall we have a game this afternoon? Chequers, perhaps?'

Charlotte bit her lip, bravely trying not to hurt his feelings.

'If you like, Grandpapa. But ... I did think ... If the rain holds off...'

'The rain? What has the rain to do with it?'

He relented then, pinching her cheek between finger and thumb and smiling.

'It's all right, my little maid. I know it was Moonlight you came to see and not your old grandpapa.' He turned to me. 'Do you ride, Miss?'

I shook my head. 'I'm afraid not.'

'Oh well, I suppose it will fall to me to put the lass through her paces,' he grumbled, but I had the impression he was far from displeased at the prospect.

The rest of the family were just as easy to like. Adam, the elder son, who would inherit the estate, was a younger version of his father, his wife Anne was a gentle, kindly woman with a ready smile, a good deal younger than him, and Charlotte's cousins, Harry and Richard, seemed as genuinely pleased to see her as her grandfather had been. They whisked her off to reacquaint her with Moonlight and I was left with Anne, who sat serenely sewing as we chatted.

'How do you find Francis and Selena?' she asked, threading her needle with a new length of silk.

'I see very little of them,' I replied truthfully. 'Most of my time is spent with Charlotte.'

'It must be lonely for you,' she said, glancing at me.

I had no intention of being drawn into a discussion on my situation and certainly not on my employers.

'Charlotte is very good company. She's quite grown-up for her age,' I said.

Anne sighed. 'That is what happens to children who spend most of their time in adult company, I am afraid. Though she can be wilful, I'm told.'

Like her mother. The unspoken words hung in the air and I guessed who it was who had done the telling – Selena, with her bitter resentment.

But Anne must have known Julia as her sister-in-law, I realised, and I thought it strange she had not shown any signs of surprise at my likeness to her. Unless, of course, Francis or Selena had warned her in advance. Yes, that must be it. But certainly there must be a good deal she could tell me about Julia if she chose to do so. I wished desperately I could ask but I knew that a first meeting was not the time for such questions.

'I certainly haven't found Charlotte in the least difficult,' I said. 'We get along very well together.'

'Good.' Anne buried her needle in the fine sampler she was stitching. 'I wish she could come to visit us more often. She so enjoys herself with the boys – and the pony, of course! It's not good for her, stuck in that dark house with no siblings of her own. I've mentioned it often enough, but Francis and Selena always seem to be too busy to bring her over. Now that you are here, though, there's no reason at all why you should not make regular visits.'

'I'd like that,' I said, genuinely pleased. 'And I do agree with you, company closer to her own age is just what Charlotte needs.'

The day passed pleasantly, the evening meal was a good deal more convivial than it ever was at Morwennan, and the room they had allocated to me was light, airy and comfortably furnished.

From the chit-chat over dinner, as well as the remarks Anne had made to me earlier, I formed the distinct impression that this branch of the family were not overly fond of Francis and Selena, and *that* was scarcely surprising. They really had very little in common and it was almost impossible to believe they could be so closely related.

But then, I thought, perhaps Francis and Selena had been adversely affected by the fact that they were the younger son and the daughter, and, where landed gentry was concerned, did not count in the scheme of things.

They would never inherit their lovely home, or indeed any part of it. They had to watch whilst their elder brother was favoured, and whilst his children roamed the sweeping grounds they had once roamed. The people in the portraits hanging on the walls were their ancestors too, the same blood ran in their veins as in Adam's, and yet every stick and stone, every artefact, would pass to him when their father died. They would get nothing, for an estate was an estate, and could not be divided. It must be passed intact from eldest son to eldest son so that the wherewithal for its survival was not dissipated. Sensible, perhaps – practical, perhaps – but at the same time rather cruel to those who were the losers.

Could it be, I wondered, that Francis and

Selena would be more like their brother if they were not eaten up by the jealousy and resentment that came from knowing that everything would go to him? Perhaps that was it. For the first time I felt a little sympathy for my employers.

I was genuinely sorry when it was time for Charlotte and me to leave Penallack. I had been truly relaxed for the first time in weeks, and I had slept better too. Though this house must be much older than Morwennan there were no creaks overhead here to disturb me, and the morning sun, when I drew back the curtains, streamed into the room from a lovely open aspect instead of filtering fitfully between overhanging branches.

Almost the first thing I noticed on returning to Morwennan was that there were deep score lines and footprints in the soft ground alongside the path beneath my window. Clearly fresh, they had eaten into the rain-softened ground. I knew at once what it meant. There had been illicit activity here last night. Another load of contraband had been transferred from the cove to the next staging post on its journey inland.

Immediately it occurred to me that perhaps Francis had had an ulterior motive in despatching me and Charlotte to his father's house for the night. It must be of concern to him that my window was directly above the path; clearly he did not want me to know

250

what was going on. The first time goods had been moved when I was in occupation they had slipped a sleeping draught into my wine, I felt sure; this time my absence had been engineered.

I must confess the realisation disturbed me. What would they do next time to try to ensure I did not discover what was going on? More than ever I felt the menace of Morwennan closing in around me, and the sympathy I had felt briefly for Francis evaporated.

He was a ruthless man, I had no doubt – and Selena was not much better. She could scarcely be unaware of Francis's activities. Had Julia been aware too? Was it possible that the reason she had run away had more to do with her distaste for Francis's 'business' than it did with her flighty nature, as Selena would have had me believe? Perhaps she had grown tired of having to pretend she was blind and deaf where those nocturnal comings and goings were concerned.

I simply could not believe that my mother would have been any more in favour of 'the Gentlemen' than I was. And I hoped with all my heart that soon I would find someone prepared to tell me the truth.

Thirteen

Tom came to the house next day to see Francis and when they had completed their business he came to seek me out. Charlotte and I were working quietly in the parlour and the moment he put his head around the door my heart skipped a beat. No matter what I thought of Tom, it seemed, my senses refused to listen and my inability to control the racing of my pulses whenever he was near disturbed me.

Did I really want to become involved with a man whose colleague was prepared to drug me or get me out of the way whenever it suited him? A man who had spoken so coldly of the death of his own brother? Of course I did not! With an effort I drew myself tight and refused to meet his eyes.

As always Charlotte had no such inhibitions. She bounced out of her chair, knocking her books to the floor in her haste, and ran to greet him.

'Tom! Tom! Guess where we went yesterday!'

He rumpled her hair. 'I know where you

went. To ride Moonlight. And now you have to catch up with your lessons. It's Charity I've come to see.'

'Oh – Tom!' she wailed.

'If you are very good I might find a bonbon in my pocket...'

Her eyes widened. 'One of the special French ones?'

'One of the special French ones – if it's not squashed to a pulp...'

He pulled a twist from his pocket and passed it to her, and I tightened my lips. A French bonbon. Just a small item from the booty brought ashore last night, no doubt.

'Now – get on with your sums while I talk to Charity and maybe there will be another one for you,' he said with a smile.

I turned away. He came up behind me, slipping a hand beneath my elbow and steering me towards the window.

'Why are you avoiding me?' he asked in my ear.

The directness of the question took me by surprise. I held myself stiff, though the touch of his fingers seemed to be burning into my skin, and my flesh tingled in response to it.

'Why should I be avoiding you?'

'I don't know. But you are, Charity. Ever since the day of the fair. Is it because of the man who came to see you – Joshua? Are you and he...?'

'Of course not!' I replied sharply. 'Joshua is

my brother! At least, that's how I think of him.'

'Yes. You were treating me with coldness even before he came, of course. But why, Charity? I thought that we...'

'Very well.' I glanced over my shoulder. 'Charlotte, go on with your work for a few moments. I shall be back very soon.'

I moved to the door. Tom followed me. As we went into the hall I saw Mrs Durbin emerging from the mysterious door on the far side. As she caught sight of us she drew back, then, seeming to think better of it, came out again, locked the door behind her and disappeared in the direction of the kitchen.

'So,' Tom said. 'What have you to say to me that can't be said in front of Charlotte?'

I faced him squarely, taking my courage in both hands.

'There are things going on in this house that I don't like.'

'You've noticed,' he murmured wryly.

'And you are involved in them. Well, I want no part of it.'

'Oh, Charity!' He was silent for a moment; the tick of the grandfather clock sounded very loud in the hush. Then: 'I thought it might be something of the sort. But you don't understand—'

'I understand all too well!' I interrupted sharply. 'I realise I may be placing myself at risk by admitting it, but I feel I must speak out or place myself at even greater risk. I know that Francis is running a smuggling ring, and I know that you are one of their number. Please don't bother to deny it.'

A look of alarm crossed his handsome features. 'Is Francis aware you know this?'

'No,' I said. 'He has been at pains to keep me in the dark. But I am not a fool, Tom, whatever you might think.'

'I certainly don't think that. But if you know what is going on here and don't like it, why do you stay?'

'I've reasons of my own,' I said. 'But I won't be drawn into it, Tom. And I don't want to involve myself with those who are.'

'Charity.' He spoke urgently, looking around as if to be sure we were alone. 'You must believe me when I say I don't like what is going on any more than you do.'

'So why do you do it?' I asked with asperity.

'I too have reasons of my own. But I am not like Francis, believe me. He is a dangerous man, and if you have learned the truth about him, then I would urge you to leave this house now, for your own safety. If he thinks you might be a danger to him, Francis would stop at nothing.'

My heart was beating very fast. Tom was echoing my own thoughts. But I could not leave now, with so many secrets yet to be

255

uncovered. And I could not abandon Charlotte.

'I'm sure I'm not in any immediate danger,' I said with more confidence than I was feeling. 'Unless of course you intend telling him I know the truth.'

'Of course not! I would protect you with my life,' Tom said, and I found my treacherous heart wanting to believe him.

'Oh, Tom.'

'Listen to me, Charity. I am not in Francis's pocket, nor for him in any way,' Tom said urgently. He took my hands in his.

Oh, it was easy, so easy, with his hands holding mine, to believe what he said when it was what I so desperately wanted to believe! I couldn't pretend I understood; like so much else in my life this was beyond my understanding. But when has comprehension had anything to do with it? I only knew that my heart was crying out for him, my body responding to his touch, and everything in me needed so much to trust this man who stirred me so.

'Do you believe me?' he asked.

I nodded dumbly.

'Then you can do something for me. Something that may put an end to this whole dreadful business that you hate so.' He looked around again, then leaned close so that his lips almost brushed my ear. 'I need to take a look in the storerooms.'

I frowned.

'The storerooms,' he repeated, impatient that I had not instantly understood. 'The rooms at the top of the rise, behind the coach house. That's where the contraband is taken when it is brought up from the caves before it goes on its journey inland.'

'Ah!' I nodded as the pieces of the puzzle fitted together. 'But why...?'

'Never mind. It's better that you don't know. But it's important. You must trust me on that. There's something I'm looking for which I think might be there. To get in I need the key. Francis always carries one set on his person, but there's another set in his study. Do you think you could get them for me?'

A little shock ran through me. Was this the man who only a moment ago had said he would protect me with his life?

'I don't know,' I said. 'Why can't you get them yourself?'

'I am never in Francis's study except when he is there. You are. When he's out you give Charlotte her lessons there. You could easily slip them into your pocket and pass them to me.'

'But if he found them gone,' I objected. 'He'd know it must be me who had taken them.'

'He'll never miss them,' Tom said confidently. 'Why would he when he has his own set on his belt? And I would need them for a

257

little while only. I would give them back to you, you could return them to their hook, and no one need be any the wiser.'

'Oh I don't know, Tom...'

But his hands holding mine were persuasive, his mouth, close to my ear, even more so. I was lost and I knew it.

'Very well. I'll see what I can do.'

He kissed me then, hard on the lips, his arm circling my waist and drawing me close so that my breasts were squeezed against his broad chest and my hips fitted snugly with his. A wave of desire so strong it made me dizzy rushed through my veins and sensations I had never before experienced set me trembling with anticipation and sharp sweet delight.

'I knew I could count on you, Charity,' he murmured.

When he had gone and I was alone all the doubts came rushing in. Why did Tom want to get into the storerooms? How could I know that his reason was any more honourable than Francis's? Was this a falling-out among thieves – Tom taking his opportunity to help himself to more of the spoils than was his due? For hadn't he on the one hand told me to leave for my own safety and then, almost in the same breath, asked me to do something which would undoubtedly put me at serious risk should Francis discover what I had done? Was he just using me for some dishonest purpose of his own?

No. I could not allow myself to think it. Maybe I was the biggest fool alive, but with all my heart I wanted to believe that Tom was better than some greedy smuggler. I couldn't lose my heart to someone like that – and I had lost my heart to Tom without doubt.

For better or for worse I knew that I could not refuse him anything. Without meaning to, I had fallen in love.

My chance came next day.

Francis and Selena were both out – Francis on business, Selena visiting friends – or so she told me. As always when the study was free Charlotte and I went there to work on her lessons.

Some of Francis's heavy ledgers lay on the desk. I pushed them to one side, surprised, in view of the fact that he was so anxious in other ways to keep me in the dark about his activities, that he should have left them there where I could so easily see them. But then, what would I find if I opened one? Nothing, probably, but a list of items that could just as easily have been an inventory of honest trading, the books of a merchant. I was not, in any case, much interested. I could think of nothing but the bunch of keys which hung on a hook in a small alcove behind the door.

Dare I take them? How long would it be

before I saw Tom again and could pass them to him? Would Francis miss them and guess I was the culprit? And why did Tom want them in any case? My head spun as I set Charlotte some simple Latin grammar. And all the while my eyes kept returning to that bunch of keys hanging there in full view on the study wall.

In the end I took them, just as I had always known I would. Whilst Charlotte's head was bent over her books I slipped them off the hook and into the deep pocket of my apron. They jangled a little as I moved and my heart seemed to stop beating. Suppose Charlotte heard? If she asked me why I sounded like a chatelaine I would die on the spot!

I do not know how I got through the morning's lessons. Certainly Charlotte glanced at me oddly once or twice. Then, like a mirage in the desert, I saw Tom on the path outside the window.

'Finish translating that verse,' I said to Charlotte, grateful that she had been too engrossed in her work to notice Tom. 'I won't be a moment.'

I slipped outside.

'He's out, isn't he?' Tom said abruptly by way of greeting. 'I saw him in the village. Did you manage to get them?'

'Yes.' I was a little hurt that he had no kiss or even a smile for me. 'To be truthful, Tom, you could have got them yourself and not involved me in this deception at all.'

'Can I have them then?' He held out his hand. 'Durbin is with Francis – the place is deserted. If I'm quick I can do what I intended now, and with daylight to help me.'

My fingers fastened round the bunch of keys, holding it tightly.

'Tom, I'm not sure about this. You are not going to rob Francis, are you?'

'Of course not!' he snapped. 'There's something I'm looking for. Something very important.'

'Very well.' I handed him the keys. 'Only bring them back quickly, won't you?'

Perhaps half an hour or so passed before Tom returned – to me it seemed like a lifetime. I was jumpy as a kitten, terrified Francis or Selena would come home and discover him in the buildings behind the coach house. Then, just as I was wondering how I could possibly make Charlotte's lesson last any longer without a break, he walked past the window and signalled to me.

I made an excuse to Charlotte and slipped out. Tom's face was grim; even before I asked I knew he had not found what he was looking for.

'It wasn't there,' he said, confirming what I already knew.

He handed me the keys. I took them and

turned back to the house, anxious only to replace them on their hook before Francis returned. Tom arrested me with a hand on my arm.

'Charity – listen to me. What I am looking for is a ship's bell. Have you ever seen anything like that anywhere in the house?'

I shook my head, puzzled. 'No, I don't think so.'

'Are you sure?' His tone was urgent.

I ran a quick mental inventory of the rooms to which I had access then shook my head again.

'I've never seen a ship's bell. I'm sure I'd remember if I had.'

'What about upstairs?' he pressed me.

'I've never been into Francis or Selena's rooms, of course,' I admitted. 'But surely no one would keep a ship's bell in their bedroom?'

His hand tightened on my arm. 'Could you look for me when the coast is clear? Just in case? It's very important, Charity.'

I hesitated. 'I don't know ... I suppose so...'

'Could you look now? If Francis happened to return I would keep him talking until you got back downstairs and he would assume you had been up to your own room.'

I bit my lip. I did not like it one bit, but Tom could be very persuasive. And I had to admit my curiosity was aroused now.

'Very well. But I must return the keys first.'

Leaving Tom outside, I did so, ensured Charlotte was still fully occupied, then, heart thumping, started up the stairs.

The door to Francis's room was firmly closed. My nervous hands were so slippery on the knob that at first I could not turn it and I thought it must be locked. Then it gave and the door flew open.

It was a large room but sparsely furnished, very much the domain of a single man, with no trace of feminine influence. I could see at a glance there were no ornaments whatever and certainly no ship's bell. Relieved, I closed the door and retreated. If it had been there – what then? Would Tom have expected me to keep watch while he crept upstairs to steal it?

Simply to satisfy myself – and Tom – I looked into Selena's room too, though I could not imagine for one moment that it would be there, and I was right. There was a rather grand Chinese screen and the dressing table was set with the various accoutrements a lady needs, but in other respects the room was almost as bare as Francis's. Only one thing struck me as strange and out of keeping with Selena's austere nature – an ornate powdered wig on its stand gracing a small bureau. It was a little dusty now, and past its glory days when it had been the height of fashion, but I supposed that once, in her youth, Selena must have worn it on grand occasions with pride, and could not bear to part with it and the memories it evoked for her. Strangely this little act of vanity made her more human in my eyes; I closed the door quickly and went back downstairs.

Tom was pacing restlessly. 'Well?' he demanded.

I shook my head. 'There's no ship's bell in either Francis's room or Selena's as far as I can see.'

He cursed softly. 'Is there nowhere else you can think of where it might be? The cellars? The attics?'

'Oh Tom, I don't know!' I said helplessly, growing a little tired of his obsession with this bell. 'I don't think there are cellars – I should think the rock beneath the house would make them an impossibility. And the door to the attics is always kept locked.'

His eyes narrowed; I could see that far from discouraging him I had given him fresh hope.

'The key to the door is likely on the same ring you borrowed for me,' he said. 'Will you see if you can locate it and have a look for me?'

'Not now!' I said crossly. 'It's far too dangerous. Francis or Selena could return at any moment and I don't know where Mrs Durbin is. She goes up there sometimes. I think they must be used as storerooms for household items that aren't in regular use.'

'Are they indeed?' Tom looked thoughtful. 'Well – not now then, but when the coast is clear?'

'And if I should find it, what then? Surely you don't expect me to lug it down and hide it for you?' I said a trifle sarcastically.

'Of course not. All I need at the moment is to know its whereabouts,' Tom said.

Then and only then his hand slipped about my waist, pulling me to him.

'You're a good girl, Charity.'

His breath was warm and teasing on my neck, his lips as they touched mine sent such a rush of delight through my veins that the whole unpleasant business of the morning suddenly seemed worthwhile.

It was only later, when he had gone and my heartbeat and pulses had returned to normal, that I found myself wondering again if Tom was using me, tweaking my emotions to make me dance to his will.

But my capacity for pushing unwelcome thoughts to the back of my mind seemed to have grown like a field mushroom on a summer morning since I had met Tom. Once again I put my doubts aside and dwelt only on the memory of what his touch could do to me – the memory that all by itself could send delicious little spirals of excitement licking through the deepest parts of me.

Perhaps I was being a fool, but surely every girl has the right to be a fool once in her life? And the way Tom made me feel was certainly a welcome distraction from all the other matters that troubled me so.

Fourteen

Francis was in a foul mood when he returned. A wheel had come off the carriage and he had been badly delayed whilst it was repaired. I heard him ranting about it to Selena, who had joined him in his study; I was lurking in the hall because my sense of guilt over borrowing his keys was so great I needed to reassure myself that he had not noticed they had been touched.

'The man's an idiot!' he raved, referring, of course, to Durbin. 'Why hasn't he kept a regular check on these things? The horses could have been injured – we could both have been killed!'

'But you weren't,' Selena said reasonably. 'So there's no harm done.'

'No thanks to Durbin! He's too old to do his job properly, that's the trouble. And so is that wife of his. They should have been put out to grass years ago, the pair of them!'

'I have no complaints about Mrs Durbin's work,' Selena replied briskly. 'And in any case, it's no good complaining. With the situation as it is you know we have no choice but to keep them on. If you were to do something about it then perhaps we could take on other, younger staff, but as things are you know very well that we cannot take the risk.'

I frowned, wondering what Selena meant. She had said something of the kind before, about there being a reason Mrs Durbin had to manage alone. With all the men involved in the smuggling operation I couldn't imagine that was enough of a secret in the village to prevent them employing more staff.

Then I heard Francis mention my name! 'You took the risk when you brought Charity here,' he thundered at her. 'I don't know what you were thinking of – I still don't. I should have insisted on her leaving that first night.'

Selena laughed softly.

'But you couldn't bring yourself to, could you, Francis? Not when she's the living image of Julia as she was when you fell in love with her. Do you think I haven't noticed the way you look at her? It's all you can do to keep your hands off her, is it not?'

Francis swore. 'You are an evil woman, Selena. I don't know why I put up with you in my life.'

'Because you could not manage without me, my dear.' I could hear the smirk in her voice. 'You may not have wanted me after you met your precious Julia, but by God you needed me – and you still do. As for your anxiety about little Charity learning the truth – it scarcely matters where she is concerned, does it? She is, after all, family.'

I was trembling now, my whole body taut. So they really did believe that I was Julia's daughter!

'And that is what you have planned all along, Selena, is it not?' Francis said, cutting in on my whirling thoughts. His voice was low and full of bitterness. 'I think you intend Charity to find out. What I don't understand is why.'

Selena chortled unpleasantly. 'Then, Francis, you are an even bigger fool than I took you for,' she said.

The study door was flung open; there was no time for me to dive for the sanctuary of the kitchen. I stood transfixed like a rabbit caught in the glare of a poacher's torch. For a moment I thought she would be angry; after all, she could be in no doubt but that I had overheard their quarrel. I thought she would chastise me for lurking there. But she did not. After her initial surprise a smirk crept across her face and she raised an eyebrow.

'Why – Charity!' she said.

Then, without another word, she turned and swept up the stairs.

★ ★ ★

So Francis had been right when he had accused Selena of intending that I should learn the truth. The moment I saw her smug face I was sure of it. I had overheard every word they had said; she knew it and she was secretly pleased.

But why ... why? What was the secret they both knew I would be bound to find out sooner or later? The secret Selena wanted me to know and Francis was so anxious to keep from me – and from the rest of the world?

I stood there motionless, one hand pressed to my hot face, the other tightly clutching at my skirts as Selena flounced triumphantly up the staircase. Should I confront Francis, tell him what I had overheard and demand to know the truth? If I was indeed Julia's daughter, surely it was no more than my right? But I shrank all the same from the encounter. 'There are some things it is better not to know,' he had said to me once before, and Joshua had echoed those sentiments. Was I strong enough to face whatever it might be?

As I stood there, trying to gather my courage to confront him, Charlotte came running into the hall.

'Oh, there you are, Charity! I've finished my lessons. Isn't it time for a game?'

I stared at her for a second or two, unseeing, and she tugged at my hand.

'Charity? What's the matter?'

I gave myself a small shake.

'Nothing,' I said.

For the present, I knew the moment had gone.

The tension was heavy in the house that night. It lay in the air between Francis and Selena, and as for me, I was tight as a drum, wondering whether I should speak out but unable to find the words.

As soon as I reasonably could I excused myself and went upstairs. I needed to be alone, to think. But as I reached the landing I heard footsteps behind me on the stairs and turned to see Francis following me.

'Charity,' he said. 'Is something wrong? You've been very quiet this evening.'

I drew a deep breath. This was my opportunity.

'You talked to me once before about your wife,' I said.

'Julia.'

'Yes, Julia. You told me I was very like her. You even admitted the possibility that I might be her daughter.'

'Yes, it's true. I did.'

'I think it is more than that,' I said as levelly as I could. 'I think there is something you know which I do not that makes you believe without doubt that I am. And I want to know what it is.'

He was silent for a moment. Then: 'Very well,' he said heavily. 'I don't know for certain – no one could. But I do know that Julia had a child in the time she was lost to me. A little daughter.'

My heart seemed to have stopped beating. The whole world around me seemed to have stopped too.

'And this would be about twenty years ago?' I heard myself ask.

'Yes.'

The moonlight shining in through the casement window showed more clearly than daylight the ravages that pain had etched into his face. Every sagging line was evidence of it.

Julia had hurt him very much, I thought. Talking of her and the other man's child she had borne was agony for him. No doubt it desecrated his memory of her, marred any happiness they may have shared before – and after – that time when she had left him. But no – there could not have been many happy times, for Julia at any rate. If there *had* been she would never have run away. Never have turned to the bottle and virtually pined away when she had returned to him.

And what about me? All my loveless years – all the agonies of wondering – surely they deserved an explanation. I licked my dry lips.

'Why did she abandon me?' I asked.

For a moment he did not answer and, just when I thought he was not going to, he spoke.

'She thought you were dead,' he said.

His words shocked me to the core. Whatever I had expected it was not this.

'She thought I was *dead*?' I repeated in a whisper. 'But why ... why would she think that?'

'Oh, Charity ... Don't ask, I beg you.'

'But I must,' I said firmly. 'What you are telling me makes no sense at all.'

He seemed not to hear me. He was looking at me intently, yet there was a haziness about his eyes.

'You are so very like her,' he said softly. 'It's uncanny. So like her...'

I shifted uncomfortably beneath that intent gaze. 'Please...'

'Oh, Charity, Charity...' he murmured, and seemed to sway on his feet. I thought for a moment that he was ill, that the stress of all this had brought on a stroke. Then I smelled the liquor on his breath and knew I was being too kind in my assessment of his condition.

He swayed again and reached out for me as if to steady himself. But there was something horrible in the way he clutched at me, not as a support but in a way that might have been lecherous had I not realised it was not me he was seeing in that moment but the reincarnation of the young Julia standing there in the moonlight.

I tried to step away but my feet seemed anchored to the floor.

One podgy and moist hand grasped mine, the other went about my shoulders, pulling me close to him. A little cry broke from my lips before his mouth covered mine, stifling it.

It was wet, that mouth, and flabby, and I tasted the liquor I had smelled earlier on his breath. Again I tried to pull away and could not; I thought I was suffocating beneath its relentless pressure, and panic rose in me along with nausea. Somehow I dragged my hand free, pushing at his brocaded waistcoat, and kicked at his stockinged legs with my slippered feet. Yet still he held me fast, his breathing laboured, his body heaving close to mine. And it was not my name on his lips now, but hers.

'Julia ... Oh Julia...'

My flailing hand found his face. I gouged at it with my fingernails. I must have taken him by surprise, hurt him even, for he gasped and relinquished his hold on me a little.

It was the chance I needed. I hit out again and again, screaming and sobbing.

'How dare you! How dare you!'

I might have woken Charlotte, alerted Selena and Mrs Durbin, but I was beyond caring. Nothing in the world mattered but that I should escape from this monster that Francis had become.

And my cries sobered him. He released me so suddenly I stumbled and almost fell.

'Forgive me...' His voice was a broken whisper. 'I thought...oh Charity, I thought...'

'I know what you thought!' I hissed, scrubbing my fist across my mouth to wipe away the hateful taste of him. 'You thought I was my mother. Well I'm not! And if you ever lay a finger on me again I'll...'

'You must understand, Charity! I loved her so...' he interrupted me, his voice thick as if he were crying. But I could feel no pity for him now, only revulsion.

'Get out of my way!'

'Charity...!'

The moonlight shining in through the window was full on him; he no longer looked like a monster but a shambling broken man. For all that, I did not care to be alone with him a moment longer, no, not even though I had never been closer to learning the secrets of my birth.

'Get out of my way!' I said again, very low, but very clearly and decisively.

And to my immense relief he did so. I pushed past him and ran along the corridor to my own room. There I closed the door and turned the key in the lock. I leaned my back against it, felt the use going out of my knees and sank down so that I was sitting on the bare board floor with my arms wrapped around myself. It was a long while before I began to stop trembling and even longer before I had any thoughts that so much as bordered on the coherent.

The first was – why had Julia thought me to be dead? No mother would think such a thing of her child without good reason and then, surely, she would want to hold the little lifeless body, see it laid to rest?

I pondered for a long while without making much progress – except that ideas I did not care for at all suggested themselves to me. Then I found myself wondering why Selena had not come to my assistance when Francis had tried to kiss me. She must have known he had followed me upstairs, and what he was capable of. She must have heard my cries. Yet she had ignored them.

There were more evils in this house than I had realised; for the first time I was truly afraid of what it was I would uncover if I persisted. But my fear did nothing to weaken my resolve.

Julia had suffered at the hands of both Francis and Selena, I felt sure. As a consequence I had suffered too. If I did nothing, how long would it be before Charlotte too fell victim to their scheming? She was as yet a child, they protected her and were, I felt sure, honestly fond of her. But Selena was pure wickedness and Francis ... where Francis loved, disaster followed, for the only love he was capable of was selfish and destructive. I could not abandon Charlotte to such a fate as would surely be her lot. Julia would not have wanted that and neither did I.

From somewhere I would find the strength and the resourcefulness to finish what I had begun.

That much I owed to my sister – and to my mother.

How I managed to sleep that night I do not know. But I must have done so, for I woke once to hear what sounded like an unearthly wailing.

At first I thought it was the cry of a wild animal being tortured by a predator, but as I lay tense and shaking from my sudden awakening it came again and again, and it seemed to me that it came from inside the house, for it was all around me. It was, I thought, as if the house itself were wailing.

When it stopped and there were only the usual heavy creaks, I thought of the recurrent dream I used to have and the feeling of being trapped. I had not thought of it lately, for reality had replaced fancy, but now I wondered if it had been prophetic in some way. I *was* trapped here now – trapped by my curiosity and my sense of duty towards Charlotte. Yet, for all that I was frightened and upset, the feeling of claustrophobia was not as strong as it had always been in the dream. Was that because there was yet more to come, I wondered, along with the discoveries I still had to make?

The thought, in the stillness of the night, chilled me. I drew the covers tight around me and still I shivered.

At last I slept again, but it was a restless, troubled sleep, disturbed by dreams that verged on nightmare. And always the questions were there, haunting me.

What had happened to Julia? Why had she thought that I was dead? Who were the 'evil people' of whom Mama Mary and Dr John had spoken so long ago? And what would I do when I finally learned the truth?

Fifteen

Francis did his best to avoid me next day. He looked shamed and there were angry scratch marks on his face where my nails had gouged into the flesh. Selena, though, appeared smug and pleased with herself. I felt sure she knew what had occurred and in some perverse way was revelling in it.

I longed to face her out and demand an explanation but shrank from making another scene. If Charlotte were to overhear, she was bound to be upset by it. I would ask Mrs Durbin, I decided. She knew the truth, I felt sure, and being a little removed from it she was less threatening than either Francis or Selena.

When I had set Charlotte some lessons I went in search of her.

I found her in the kitchen preparing vegetables. She looked a little flustered, pale for her, and her knife jerked agitatedly as she cut off chunks of potato peel. Perhaps she too had heard something of the commotion last night, I thought. If so, what had she made of it?

I pushed the door almost closed behind me and crossed to stand beside her.

'Mrs Durbin, I must talk to you.'

She glanced up at me, her beady little eyes troubled.

'You have been here a long time,' I began. 'You must have known Julia well.'

She huffed a little, her eyes skittering away from mine again.

'Why do you keep asking about Miss Julia?'

'I think you know the answer to that very well, Mrs Durbin,' I said levelly. 'Everyone says how like her I am.'

'Yes ... well ... What's that to do with anything?'

'Please, Mrs Durbin!' I said urgently. 'There are things I have to know and I think you can tell me. You liked Julia, didn't you?'

Mrs Durbin's mouth worked convulsively. Then she said: 'Liked her? I *loved* her!'

'So please – please talk to me!' I begged. 'She was my mother, wasn't she? Francis and Selena think so, I know. I was born to her in the time she left Francis, but for some reason I was raised as a foundling. Francis said she thought her child was dead. Why did she think that, Mrs Durbin?'

'Oh lawks, lawks!' Mrs Durbin slammed down the potato knife and wiped her apron across her face. 'Don't ask me these questions, Charity. It's not for me to say. And anyway, I don't know everything...' She paused. 'One thing I do know, though. I've only stayed in this house for Julia's sake. If it weren't for her I'd have gone long ago and Durbin with me. And, if you've any sense, that's what you'll do. It's an evil place. Oh, if it weren't for Miss Julia...'

'You mean you stay because she would want you to look after Charlotte?' I asked.

'Never mind what I mean,' Mrs Durbin said darkly. 'You'll learn nothing from me. It's for Mr Francis to tell you – if he chooses. Or else...' She broke off, her mouth working still.

'What?' I pressed her.

'Maybe there's things you'll learn by accident, given time. And when you do...' She was becoming more and more agitated. 'When you do he'll have to tell you. Or she will. But it's not for me. I haven't kept silent all these years to break it now.'

And try as I might I could get nothing more from her.

'Charity, do you think we could take some more roses to Mama's grave?' Charlotte asked. 'There aren't many left now. I'd like to do it before they all die.'

I frowned. It was true, the recent bad weather had spoiled the rose bushes. They were looking sad and bedraggled, some of the leaves turning brown and what flowers there were faded. Soon there would be none worth the picking and I knew how much it meant to Charlotte to take flowers to Julia's last resting place, for now it also meant a great deal to me too.

But Selena had been so angry that we had been to the churchyard before and I did not want her upsetting Charlotte again with her cruel remarks about Julia 'not being there'.

'You know your aunt does not approve,' I said reluctantly.

'She won't know if we don't tell her.' Charlotte gave me a sly look. 'We can say we've been to the village.'

'It's not right to tell lies, Charlotte,' I reprimanded her.

'But it wouldn't be a lie!' Charlotte argued. 'The churchyard is in the village, so we would have been there!'

I had to smile. There was no denying the childish logic, though if I had not so thoroughly disliked Selena I might have pointed out that a distortion of the truth was equally dishonest. As it was, the prospect of deceiving the horrible woman was rather a satisfying one. I succumbed to the temptation. After all, why should I allow her to prevent us from visiting our mother's grave?

'Very well,' I agreed. 'But I will tell Selena myself that we are going to the village. Better my sin than yours, Charlotte.'

To my surprise I found Selena in Francis's

study. They appeared to be going over the ledgers together, Selena's finger running down a column of figures whilst Francis made notes with a quill pen. They were so engrossed they barely seemed to notice what I was saying.

Charlotte and I cut the best of the roses and set out. It was an overcast day, the sun from behind a blanket of cloud looking more silver than golden. The grass in the church-yard was wet to our feet, the ground soft and yielding from the recent rain. We removed the husks of the roses we had laid before and replaced them with the fresh ones, then stood for a moment looking at the tomb. Once again it gave me a strange prickle down my spine to see Julia's name etched into the stone, yet I was struck by a feeling of emptiness. Perhaps Selena's words to Charlotte had affected me more deeply than I had realised, for truly I did not feel close to her at all. Today it felt to me as if Selena had been right. Julia was not there.

I took Charlotte's hand, anxious to feel close to her at least. Then, when she was ready, we turned back to the path.

I saw him at once, standing by the lych-gate, and my pulses began to hammer. Tom! At the same moment Charlotte saw him too, dropped my hand and ran towards him.

'Tom! What are you doing here?'

He swung her into the air. 'I was passing

and saw you. What are *you* doing here?'

'Bringing roses for Mama. Aunt Selena doesn't like me to, but Charity told her we were going to the village,' she said, throwing the blame entirely on me.

'You're not above a little deceit then, Charity!' Tom's eyes held mine with a long, amused look. 'I hope it's not me that's a bad influence on you!'

I flushed. He certainly was a bad influence on me and he knew it.

Tom had set Charlotte down. Now he pointed to a tangle of bramble bushes close by the lychgate.

'There are blackberries there, Charlotte, plump and ripe for the picking. Why don't you find some?' He pulled a kerchief from his pocket, unfolded it and gave it to her. 'Get some for me too. I've a fancy for blackberries for my tea.'

She smiled at him, pert and adoring, then scampered off, only too delighted by the opportunity to be of service to her hero. The moment she was out of earshot he caught my arm and asked the question that was clearly burning on his lips.

'Well? Have you found it?'

Disappointment and resentment welled in me. All Tom seemed to think about these days was the ship's bell.

'There's been no chance,' I said shortly.

'But you will search as soon as you can? It's

284

important, Charity.'

'I've said I will, haven't I?' I retorted crossly and Tom's fingers became more gentle on my arm, moving in a little stroking motion.

'Charity – I don't want you to think...'

He was pulling me closer. I tried to resist the shivers of desire that were spiralling within me. Oh, in spite of everything, I wanted so much to be in his arms!

'I don't think anything,' I said.

His mouth was close to my ear. I could feel his breath warm on my neck.

'Afterwards – when this is all over – I'll take you away from this place.'

The desire for him spiralled again more sharply. Again I tried to resist it.

'Don't make promises you can't keep, Tom.'

And: 'I always keep my promises, Charity,' he said.

I let myself lean against him for a moment, my heart thudding, treacherous warmth spreading through my veins. Oh, if only ... If only ... Then Charlotte came running back, Tom's kerchief laden with blackberries. Her fingers – and her mouth – were stained purple.

'There you are, Tom – blackberries for your tea! And they're so sweet and juicy! Why don't you come home with us and share them with us?'

Tom smiled at her.

'Not today, sweeting. I have things to do. But you can have them if you like and return my kerchief when next I see you.'

'Oh, but I picked them for you!' she objected.

'You'd like them though, wouldn't you? Go on, take them, Charlotte. Your palate is less jaded than mine. You'll enjoy them more.' He glanced at me. 'Share them with Charity.'

We left him at the lychgate.

'Tom is wonderful, isn't he?' Charlotte said dreamily as we headed back towards the cliff path. 'He's so kind and generous and such fun!'

And he is also manipulative, I thought wryly. Manipulative and secretive and rather ruthless. But somehow it made no difference.

Charlotte and I were both under Tom's spell and not even knowing it made it less potent.

When we returned to Morwennan House there was a letter waiting for me. I was surprised – and puzzled. Who could be writing to me? But the moment I saw the handwriting on the envelope I recognised it as Joshua's. I settled Charlotte down with a book and tore it open eagerly.

Joshua had written,

Dearest Charity,

It was so good to see you again! I had not realised just how much I missed you! We must keep in touch more closely. It would make me so sad if we should drift apart.

I write now, however, to tell you I have made some progress in the enquiries I promised to undertake on your behalf.

Firstly, I pressed Papa for more details of how you came into the care of him and Mama. Perhaps because I am now grown – and a minister like him! – he opened up somewhat on the subject which he has always avoided, and I have to say I can now understand the reason for his reticence. I can scarcely believe the story he told me, and I have to say it is not something I feel able to set down in a letter. I will try to come and see you again soon, Charity, and tell you face to face what I have learned. However, one thing I will mention, as it may help you to confirm or otherwise whether you are indeed who you think you may be. You were found at Porthcreor.

My eyes flicked up momentarily from the parchment. Porthcreor! It was on the coast, a hamlet perched on the cliffs, where the sea pounded the rocks beneath and rushed over a pebble beach into crannies and caves.

I could not imagine why Mama Mary and Dr John should have been given care of me if I had been found in Porthcreor, for it was not in Dr John's parish. But it *was* by the sea, so, in a way, that formed a link with Julia. She had run away with the captain of a ship, I had been told. Had he left her in Porthcreor, alone and with child? Was it perhaps his home port? But surely not! Porthcreor was a most inhospitable bay.

And what of the circumstances in which I had been found – circumstances that my dear Joshua found too distressing to set out in a letter? I could not begin to imagine what they might be. I returned to the parchment. Joshua continued,

As to the other matter, I have made some enquiries and it seems the Stacey family are still in the Launceston area. At present I do not have an address for them but I am pursuing their where-abouts with all diligence and will be in touch again when I have some news.

Do not be downcast, Charity, and remember Jeremiah is close at hand if you need a friend.

For the present, I remain
Your loving brother,
Joshua.

Momentarily a great rush of warmth filled me – warmth that came from knowing that at least there was one person in my life who truly cared for me. Joshua had never let me down or abandoned me, never used me or hurt me. I wished with all my heart that he was here beside me now. I touched my fingers to his name on the letter, drawing comfort from it.

But all too soon the other emotions came rushing in, and the questions. Always the questions. Frustration gnawed at me. Once again I was close, so close, to the truth. And once again an impregnable wall separated me from it.

My chance to do as Tom had asked and search the attic room for the bell that was so important to him came the next day.

Selena informed me that she, Francis and Charlotte were to drive over to her father's home to visit. I was surprised she did not suggest I should go with them, but Selena said it was high time I had another day to myself. Since I would be left all alone at Morwennan I failed to see how she thought this would benefit me, but then, consideration of my interests had never been high amongst Selena's priorities.

As I watched the carriage pull away up the steep rise I could not help feeling a little annoyed that they had not told me sooner that I would be free today. Perhaps I could have made some arrangement to spend some time with Tom. For all my doubts about him, I could not seem to stop thinking about him and wanting to be in his company. As it was...

If I searched the attic rooms now, without delay, I thought, I would at least have the perfect excuse to go into the village to seek him out and give him whatever news I might have. Then, perhaps, I would find out whether he was interested in me for myself, or whether he was simply using me to gain his own ends. If that was the case I would be terribly hurt, I knew, and deeply upset, but at least I would be no longer under any illusion.

The great house echoed with emptiness and the cawing of the rooks. Durbin, of course, had gone with Francis and Selena to drive the carriage, and Mrs Durbin was occupied in the kitchen.

I went to Francis's study. For some reason I had almost convinced myself he would have taken the bunch of keys with him, though why he should have done so I could not imagine, unless it was that he did not trust me, and I knew that was my guilty conscience worrying at me. But the keys hung where they always hung, on a hook in the alcove behind the door.

My breath was constricted in my chest as I took them down – already I felt like a thief, though it was not my intention to steal anything. I was merely to investigate a part of the house not usually open to me, and doubtless the search would prove as fruitless as the earlier ones had done. If by some chance I should find the bell, I would merely report to Tom. What he did about it would be up to him.

I must confess to a certain curiosity of my own. Since the household was so small, I could not imagine why there was need for any locked doors, especially one that led only to storerooms. But I supposed that if one is engaged in an illicit business, one is likely to become secretive.

I went into the hall. The sound of Mrs Durbin singing tunelessly, as she often did when she was engrossed in her cooking, reassured me, but even so my hands were shaking so much it took me several attempts to find the right key and fit it into the lock.

It turned easily, proof, if any were needed, that the door was opened frequently, and there was not the slightest creak of the hinges as I pulled it open. Neither were there cobwebs to brush my face. The flight of stairs beyond the door led straight up, narrow, clean-swept, and, to my surprise, carpeted. Why would anyone carpet attic stairs? Except perhaps to muffle the sound f footsteps.

I pulled the door closed behind me in case Mrs Durbin should emerge from the kitchen and notice it open, then stood for a moment waiting whilst my eyes accustomed themselves to the pitch darkness. Then, feeling my way, step by rickety step, I began to climb.

It was a long flight of stairs, understandably so, since it reached beyond the upper storey of the house. At one point it widened out with a step on the left; I explored this but found only a small landing with a carved wooden chest stored upon it. I lifted the lid, feeling inside in case Tom's bell should be hidden there, but it contained only cloth. Blankets, stored for the summer perhaps, or winter cloaks – in the dark I could not tell, nor was I much interested. I returned to the main staircase, creeping on upward.

There was still no chink of light and I wished I had thought to bring a candle. But, knowing there were attic windows, I had not thought it necessary. Suddenly my searching hands encountered solid wood. Another door! This explained why the stairs were so dark, but it was another setback. If this one was also locked I would have no hope of being able to see to find the right key. I ran my hands over it until I found a handle, and turned. It gave and the door opened a crack. Relieved, I pushed it wide.

And stopped short, my knees almost giving

way beneath me with shock.

I was looking into a low room that spread over a large part of the top of the house. But it was not the dusty attic storeroom I had expected.

It was furnished – a chaise, a table and a couple of chairs, a bureau, a bed.

And there was someone there.

A woman, sitting in one of the chairs, a needlework frame balanced on her knees. A woman whose snow-white hair and grey gown gave her the appearance of a ghost. But I knew this was no ghost, knew instantly too that in spite of her ravaged face and wasted frame she was much younger than she at first appeared.

When she saw me she shrank back into her chair as if afraid; in truth, she must have been as startled as I.

'Who are you?' Her voice was cultured, but a little croaky as if from disuse.

I stared into that pale, ravaged face that was as familiar to me as the one I saw each morning when I looked into my mirror – only older, much older – and knew that I had no need to ask her the same question.

All my life I had sought my mother.

In that moment I knew I had found her.

I could not speak. I thought I was going to faint clean away. It could not be! I must be imagining things! And yet ... and yet...

Suddenly so many inexplicable things were explained. The creaking of the boards above my head in the stillness of the night, which I had thought was the house itself settling. The wailing I had once heard. The 'ghost' Charlotte said she had sometimes glimpsed at the attic windows. Mrs Durbin emerging from the door into the hall with a tray. Her reluctance to tell me anything. The reason the door was kept locked. Selena's remarks to Charlotte that her mother was 'not there' in the churchyard. All these things and more came to me in a flash as my head reeled and I clung to the door for support.

Only the biggest questions of all remained, and another barrage added to them.

Why did Francis and Selena pretend that Julia was dead? How long had she been locked up here – and for what reason?

'Who are you?' she asked again. 'I've seen you in the garden – with Charlotte. You haven't come to take her away, have you...?' Her voice rose to a frightened wail.

Somehow I found my own voice, trying to reassure her.

'Of course not! I'm here to look after her. I'm Charity.'

'Charity?' Of course, the name meant nothing to her. But I was surprised she could not see the likeness that was so apparent to everyone else – the likeness to herself as a young girl.

'Yes, Charity,' I repeated.

I was beginning to regain some control of myself, though my head was still spinning. I must not say or do anything to frighten her any more, for clearly she was already terrified and very confused.

I moved towards her slowly and felt I was moving in a dream.

'Don't be afraid,' I said gently. 'I mean you no harm.'

She shrank away again, her eyes, huge in her wasted face, never leaving mine, and I thought I saw a glimmer of recognition in them.

'Charity. I never heard that name before. But you are...?' It was almost a question – one which I dared not, for the moment, answer. Instead I asked one of my own.

'Why are you here? Locked in the attic?'

She laughed without humour, a small breathy sound.

'I live here.'

'But why? Why not downstairs with your family?'

She swallowed. 'I'm ill. I've been ill for a long time. Ever since Charlotte was born. They say it's best I should be here. It's for my own good.'

Anger rose in me in a white-hot tide.

'Well you won't be here for much longer! I shall see to that!'

She sobbed aloud, pressing her hands to

her mouth.

'No! No – I'm safe here...'

I knelt beside her.

'You'll be safe with me. Don't worry, I'll find a way. They can't keep you here, Julia. I won't let them. Only, you must tell me everything.'

'I can't ... I don't remember ... Oh, please, just go away and leave me alone, whoever you are!'

'I can't do that,' I said. 'I'll never do that.'

But what was I to do? I needed time to think, to plan. And to come to terms with the realisation that the mother I had thought was dead was not dead at all. But in the meantime...

What would Francis and Selena do if they knew I had found Julia? They would stop at nothing, I feared, to keep their secret. I was vulnerable, she more so, and heaven only knew how Charlotte would be affected if she learned the truth in some shocking manner. For her sake if nothing else I must not act hastily but work out a plan that would cause her the least distress possible.

'Listen,' I said urgently. 'You must not tell anyone I have been here. Even Mrs Durbin.'

'Dear Mrs Durbin.' Her face softened. At least, I thought, Mrs Durbin had been kind to her.

'This is to be our secret,' I went on. 'But I will be your friend. I'll come and see you whenever I can. You must be so lonely.'

Her face clouded, her eyes going far away.

'Lonely? Oh no, not any more. I can watch from the window. I can see Charlotte playing...'

'Winter is coming,' I said. 'Charlotte won't be able to play in the garden much longer. And the days will be short and dark.'

'I'm safe here,' she repeated. 'It's for the best. When Charlotte was born...'

'What?' I pressed her. 'What happened when Charlotte was born?'

She lowered her head, knotting her hands in her lap.

'I don't remember.' Her voice was shaking, yet stubborn. 'I don't want to think about it.'

This I knew was not the moment to press her. First I had to gain her confidence.

'Is there something you would like?' I asked. 'Something I could bring you?'

She shook her head, then hesitated. For the first time a little light came into her eyes.

'Roses!' she whispered. 'I should like to have some roses.'

My throat tightened. How ironic that Charlotte and I should have taken roses to the place we thought she lay. But now the roses were so nearly over and, in any case, bringing them to her would be a great risk. They would scent the attic room; even if I found an out-of-the-way corner to put them in, Mrs Durbin would be sure to notice.

'I'll do my best,' I said.

And I had no way of knowing then the reason she had asked for them. No way of knowing that though she had closed her mind to what had happened to cause Francis to incarcerate her, she cherished memories of the happiest years of her life. Roses, for her, signified those years. The years she had spent with John. The years when she had given birth to another baby – a little girl. Me.

Sixteen

Julia

There were roses around the door of the little house John bought for her in Flushing, the settlement opposite Falmouth where many of the packet captains lived and which had got its name from the Dutch engineers who had come to build the quays and sea-walls a century earlier.

By the time they had returned from Brazil Julia was pregnant. Clearly she could not sail with John in such a condition and, in any case, horribly mindful of what had happened before, she was determined to cosset her unborn child and give it every chance of healthy survival.

She adored the little house, which was as different from Morwennan as could be, and soon she had turned it into a home. John managed to arrange shorter trips – to Spain and Portugal instead of the Americas and the West Indies – and while he was away Julia sought the company of other captain's wives, who understood one another and lent mutual support in the lonely times. If any of them suspected Julia and John were not properly husband and wife, it was never mentioned.

She visited Aunt Prudence, too. The old woman told her of Francis's fury and distress when he had learned she had run away, but seemed to think he had washed his hands of her.

'He's never been back but the once,' she told Julia.

'And if he ever comes again you won't tell him I am living in Flushing, will you?' Julia begged.

'Be sure I will not – though even if he turned up at your door he could hardly carry you off bodily – especially in your condition,' Aunt Prudence assured her.

Julia worried about it all the same, just as she worried that it was some inherent weakness in her and not the terrible attempts at abortion that had caused the malformation of her little son. If such a thing should happen again – if this baby should suffer the same fate – she did not think she could bear it.

She need not have worried. Her baby – a little girl – was born on a beautiful day in early summer.

The confinement this time was short, the birth so easy Julia could scarcely believe it.

When the baby was placed in her arms love and joy filled her, but she could not feel completely satisfied until she had unwrapped the length of flannel that swaddled her and seen for herself the perfect smooth body and the small, gently waving arms and legs, and counted every finger and toe, each capped with a tiny shell-pink nail. Then and only then did she bury her face in her baby, drinking in the fresh sweet smell of her, rubbing her cheek against the thatch of silky soft hair, lost in wonder and gratitude.

'What shall we name her?' John asked when he was allowed into the room, and stood proudly beside the bed looking lovingly at his wife and admiring his child.

'Nancy,' Julia said. 'I'd like to call her Nancy.'

John smiled. 'Why Nancy?'

'It has a joyous sound to it, don't you think? Nancy.'

'That's fitting then,' he said, satisfied. 'For this child will surely bring us much joy.'

The two years that followed Nancy's birth were undoubtedly the happiest of Julia's life.

Nancy thrived, growing from a contented baby to a sturdy happy toddler, adored by both her parents and perhaps even spoiled a little, for Julia could scarcely bear to chastise her. Not that she needed to. Nancy followed her around the house as soon as she could toddle, helping with the chores or playing with her favourite toys, a rag doll Julia had made for her and a tambourine which John brought back for her from a voyage to Spain.

His frequent absences were the only blot on an otherwise idyllic landscape, for Julia missed him sorely when he was away. When Nancy took her first faltering steps she longed for him to be there to share the moment with her; Nancy's first word was 'Papa' and he was not there to hear it.

But the separations kept their love fresh and new. Each time he returned home and they fell eagerly into each other's arms it was like the first time but even better, for now there was the ever-growing bond between them, their shared life and dreams for the future, the certainty of their love for one another. Julia learned almost to treasure the pain of parting when she stood in the harbour, Nancy in her arms, to watch his ship set sail, for she knew that her joy would be the greater when he returned.

Sometimes the wives of the captains or first officers sailed with their husbands. Since that first voyage when she had run away with him, Julia had not done so, for she felt it was unfair to a baby to subject her to life on board a packet. But in the summer when Nancy was two the *Guinevere* was detailed to sail to Madeira and John suggested they should accompany him.

Remembering her own terrible seasickness on her first voyage, Julia hesitated. Suppose Nancy should be as ill as she had been? Suppose she should be ill again herself and unable to care for the little girl? But John laughed off her fears. Nancy was his daughter through and through – she would take to the water just as he had. And if Julia was ill it would be for only a few days and he was certain there would be plenty of willing nursemaids amongst the crew, all of whom adored Nancy and loved to play with her, tease her, or jog her on their knee whilst they sang rousing sea shanties to her.

At last Julia agreed. The temptation to be with John was too great. It was to prove to be the most fateful – and tragic – decision she had ever made.

The outward voyage passed pleasantly enough. Nancy showed not the slightest sign of sea sickness. She played happily in the cabin and was thoroughly spoiled by the officers and crew. Julia herself, after a day or two of queasiness, found her sea legs. She loved watching John go about his work by day and when he was not needed on deck she revelled in the luxury of falling asleep in his arms at night.

They were approaching Madeira when disaster struck – a mast snapped, badly injuring a crewman, and the *Guinevere* was forced to limp into port. But as John made arrangements for the repair of the mast and the crewman began a slow but sure recovery from his injuries, Julia had no premonition that a chain of events that would change her life for ever had been set in motion.

She fell in love with Madeira, the soft warm air, the towering green mountains, the exotic perfumes on the gentle breeze.

'Oh, John, I could stay here for ever!' she said one night when Nancy was asleep and they sat on the verandah of their lodgings sharing a drink and watching the sun set over the sea.

'At present it looks as if you might get your wish,' John said seriously. 'The repairs are taking a good deal longer than I had hoped. Men here work more slowly than they do at home – it's the warm sunshine, I suppose. It makes them lazy.'

Julia stretched luxuriously.

'Well they can be as lazy as they like so far as I am concerned. Truth to tell, I feel lazy myself!'

His gut stirred. 'Too lazy to make love to your husband?' he teased her, and when he reached for her, drawing her close, it was easy to forget his nagging concern over the continual delays with the repair work.

But next day he was fretting about it once more. With the *Guinevere* in dry dock he was losing money he could ill afford – the crew's wages still had to be paid. Worse, the delay would mean that the calm summer weather would be at an end before they reached home. John knew all too well the storms that could blow up; he did not like the idea of Julia and Nancy having to endure such uncertain conditions. But complaining to the native workers seemed only to make matters worse.

There was nothing for it but to make the most of these stolen weeks, enjoy the opportunity to spend time with his beloved wife and child, and pray the storms they would almost certainly encounter would not be too severe.

Seventeen

I was in turmoil. To whom could I turn? I could trust no one in this dark house, not even, I thought, Mrs Durbin, for although I had no doubt but that she cared for Julia, she and her husband depended on Francis and Selena for their livelihood, the very roof over their heads. And with so many years in their service, the Durbins must surely feel a sense of loyalty to their employers. If one or other of them should mention that I knew this terrible secret, I feared the consequences.

By the same token I did not feel able to confide in Tom. He was too close to Francis. And however much I might try to make excuses for him I could not avoid the unpleasant suspicion that he was out for his own ends. I did not understand his reasons for snooping and searching for a ship's bell, but the fact that he was prepared to do it said things about his character that I did not like and could not deny in spite of the attraction he held for me. There was a hard edge to Tom that disturbed and even frightened me a little. He could be ruthless, I scnsed, and I was not sure enough of his feelings for me to trust him.

There was only one person in the world I felt truly sure of. My dear Joshua. But Joshua was not here. He was far away on the north coast, in St Agnes. I turned the problem over in my mind and finally came to a decision. I must arrange to go and see him. Joshua would know what to do. Joshua would help me.

'I would like to visit my brother,' I said to Francis.

Francis looked puzzled – almost momentarily alarmed, I thought.

'Joshua Palfrey,' I explained. 'You remember he came to call on the day of the fair? I miss him greatly and I was hoping I might be entitled to a few days off. I have had precious few in the months I have been here.'

Francis considered. 'I dare say it could be arranged. I will speak to Selena.'

My heart sank. That one was likely to say she could not spare me, I thought. But in the event she agreed. I wrote to Joshua to make the arrangements and eagerly awaited his reply.

In the meantime I visited the attic room as often as I dared. It was not so difficult; Selena and Francis were often out and when the coast was clear I would set Charlotte some work to do, palm the key and slip up the stairs, locking the door behind me. My greatest fear was that Mrs Durbin would discover me and my heart was always pounding as I emerged into the hall once more. But if she did suspect, or if Julia made mention of her secret visitor, she said nothing. In any case it was a chance I had to take if I was ever to gain Julia's confidence and get to know her.

Gradually she became used to me and, I think, came to look forward to my visits. Gradually, as she became less wary, she began to respond to me. But I knew I must tread carefully indeed. And though there were so many questions I was impatient to ask her and so much I could tell her, I knew I must wait for the right moment.

It came one afternoon when Francis and Selena took Charlotte visiting, leaving me alone in the house. Mrs Durbin was, I knew, having her afternoon nap; I had peeped into the kitchen and seen her snoozing in the chair beside the range. Taking care to make no sound that might disturb her, I unlocked the door and crept up the stairs.

It was a dark, overcast day and the attic room was unpleasantly dim. Julia was sitting in her chair, unable to see well enough to work at her embroidery.

'Charity!' Her face lit up when she saw me; the sight of it lifted my heart.

'Julia.' I wished I dared call her 'Mama'. 'How are you today?'

'Oh, quite well, thank you,' she replied politely as if this were a perfectly normal social visit. And then, to remind me it was not: 'The house is very quiet. Is everyone out?'

'Everyone but me and Mrs Durbin, and she's fast asleep by the fire,' I said.

Julia smiled, a sad little smile. 'She's getting old, is she not? I remember when she was quite a young woman.' Her face clouded. 'Oh, what will I do when she gets ill and dies? I shall have no one! No one!'

'You have me now,' I said firmly.

'Yes,' she said, nodding. 'I have you.'

I set about lighting the lamp, reminding myself I must put it out again when I left so as not to arouse suspicion. When I turned back to her, I saw that she was looking at me closely.

'You remind me of someone, Charity,' she said in a puzzled tone. 'I keep trying to remember who. And the closest I can come is ... I think you look as I used to look, long ago when I was young. But I'm being foolish, am I not?'

My heart had begun to pound very loudly, so loudly that I thought she must hear it. I crossed the room to her and dropped on to my knees beside her.

'No,' I said gently. 'No, you are not being foolish.'

'But...'

You once had a little daughter, did you
t?' I could scarcely breathe for the tight-
s in my chest.

ie nodded. 'Charlotte. Yes.'

o – longer ago than that. Ten years and
more before Charlotte was born. Another
little baby girl.'

Her eyes went far away. I saw the pain
etched clearly on her face. Then she shook
her head.

'No, there's only Charlotte. The others are
dead.'

The others. *Others?* Had I more siblings I
did not know about? But I could not concern myself with that now.

'There was another daughter was there
not?' I pressed her.

'I don't remember...'

'You do remember, Julia,' I said insistently.
'You try to forget because it hurts you so to
remember. Isn't that true?'

'I ... I suppose so...' The haunted look in
her eyes tore at my heart. I wondered if it
was wrong of me to pursue this path,
whether I was in danger of upsetting the
fragile balance of her sanity. But surely my
revelation could bring her only happiness?
And in any case, I knew that nothing on
earth would stop me now.

'Suppose, Julia, that the baby girl you gave
birth to twenty years ago was not dead as

310

you believe, but alive?' I said urgently.

That lovely smile that came so rarely transformed her features suddenly.

'Oh!' she cried, clapping her hands together. 'That would be wonderful!' Then her brow furrowed. 'But she is dead,' she said. A tear escaped and rolled down her cheek. 'I lost her. I saw her die.'

She covered her face with her hands then, drawing in on herself, and I felt a moment's doubt. Was I wrong? Were Francis and Selena wrong? Was it just an enormous coincidence that I was a foundling who looked as she had once looked? Fragile though Julia was in both mind and body from her years of incarceration, strange and distant and frightened, I did not think she was mad. Though she seemed to have closed her mind to a past she did not want to remember, she could talk quite lucidly about the present and particularly about Charlotte. Why, then, should she say she had seen her child die if it were not so?

I took her hands in mine, easing them gently away from her face.

'Are you sure, Julia?' I pressed her. 'Are you quite sure she died?'

More tears rolled down her pale cheeks. 'She must have done,' she whispered. 'She could not have lived. And I never saw her again.'

My heart leaped. I longed to press her to

311

explain but dared not. For the moment it was enough that she had never seen the body of her child.

'She did not die,' I said with certainty. 'I don't know what happened to her, but she did not die. They lied to you when they told you she did. Look at me, Julia. The reason I remind you of yourself when you were young is because I look just as you did. Everyone thinks so. *Everyone*,' I emphasised.

She blinked away the tears, looking at me intently. She freed one of her hands from mine and tentatively touched my hair, her fingers hovering nervously before stroking a bright strand.

'My hair,' she said wonderingly. 'My hair was just that colour.'

Then she touched my face, just as hesitantly, and explored like a blind man the contours of my cheek and chin.

'It is like seeing myself as I was,' she murmured. 'But she was just a baby. You are a woman.'

'Every baby grows up,' I said gently. 'Every little girl becomes a woman.'

'Yes – yes, it's true. And it was so long ago. Long before Charlotte...'

She broke off and I could read in her transparent face her struggle to understand. Then, quite suddenly, the tears began to flow once more. Her whole body was rigid.

'Julia!' I said, alarmed.

And she threw her arms around me.

'Nancy!' she whispered through her tears. 'Oh, Nancy, is it really you?'

Nancy. So that was the name she had given me. My real name. It sounded strange to me but I rather liked it. Not Charity – child of the parish. Nancy.

I held her. I was in my mother's arms for the first time for many long years and I was weeping too.

'You have come back to me,' she said when she could speak again. 'I can't believe you've come back to me. But it is you, I know it. Oh, Nancy, you won't ever leave me again, will you?'

'No,' I vowed. 'I won't ever leave you again. I'm going to take you away from this place – you and Charlotte too. We'll all be together. When the summer comes you can sit in the sun and smell the roses. And the sea...'

'No!' She stiffened suddenly and there was panic in her voice. 'Not the sea!'

'Hush!' I calmed her. 'Not the sea then, I promise. The countryside. The rolling moors. Would you like that better?'

'Will there be horses?' She spoke now like a child looking forward to a special treat. 'I love horses!'

I smiled. 'There will be horses, I'm sure, if you want them. But you must say nothing of this to anyone yet. It is our secret, remember?'

She nodded.

'And now,' I said, 'I must put out the lamp and go back downstairs.

'Nancy, don't leave me...'

'I must for the moment,' I said firmly. 'But I'll be back soon, I promise. And we'll leave this place forever.'

I turned out the lamp and went back downstairs. Then, before I could go back to Charlotte, I found a quiet corner where I could cry out all the emotions that were seething within me.

At last I dried my eyes and washed my face. Julia's features looked back at me from the mirror, the familiar features we shared. I tidied my hair; pulled myself together.

I did not yet know how I was going to achieve my promise to Julia but I was more determined than ever. Somehow I would take her and Charlotte away from this dark house. Somehow I would ensure that the years that were left to her would be good ones. Somehow, at last, I would give Julia the happiness that had eluded her for so long and which she so richly deserved.

The letter I was awaiting from Joshua arrived at last. Carefully I explained to Julia that I had to go away for a few days but that I would soon be back.

It seemed she had accepted completely that I was indeed her little lost daughter

314

grown up, and my belief that she was not mad but perfectly sane was vindicated by the questions she asked me about my upbringing and the lost years. Yet I could never prise from her any detail of how she had come to lose me or why she had been so convinced that I was dead. Whenever I tried gently to probe the circumstances I saw the shutters come up in her face, she would become distressed and murmur: 'I don't remember. Please, Nancy, don't ask me. I simply don't remember.'

Whatever it was, I thought, it must have been so terrible that she had blotted it out. But soon now I would know the truth, for Joshua had said much the same in his earlier letter – that my past, as he had discovered, held some secret so dark he would only tell me to my face when he was there to comfort me.

I saw nothing of Tom in the week before I left. He made no calls to Morwennan House and when I casually mentioned his absence, Selena told me that he was away. She said it with an amused half-smile, and I thought she gained pleasure from the fact that nothing seemed to have come of his interest in me. It was the kind of vindictiveness I had come to expect of her, but although when I thought of Tom it was with an ache of yearning, I have to confess I did not think of him that often. I had too much else to occupy my mind.

The following week I left for St Agnes. As the coach bowled along the lanes, muddy now and bare for winter, I sat deep in thought, wondering what it was Joshua could tell me about my past, and how he could help me plan for the future.

I arrived in St Agnes at nightfall. The coach set me down at the vicarage and when I rapped on the door Joshua himself answered it.

'Charity!' He hugged me. 'Oh, it's so good to see you! Come in, my dear!'

I could see at once that Joshua was living in some style. St Agnes was a parish rich from the proceeds of tin, and the vicarage, where Joshua lived with the vicar and his wife, was a far cry from our old home at Penwyn.

It was comfortably furnished and full of artefacts almost as fine as those at Morwennan House. The vicar and his wife extended me a warm welcome, sitting me down before the fire, providing me with a good meal, and fussing around me as if I were a long-lost relative of their own, not the foundling sister of their young curate.

At long last they retired to bed and Joshua and I were alone.

'What has happened since I last saw you, Charity?' he asked me at once. 'Something has, I know. I could tell it from the tone of your letter, and now ... I can see it in your face.'

I swallowed hard at the tears that suddenly threatened me. I so needed to share the burden I had borne alone since finding Julia in the attic room. But I could hardly bring myself to tell the terrible story to anyone, even my beloved Joshua.

'You will treat everything I tell you in the strictest confidence, won't you?' I said anxiously. 'You won't tell another living soul?'

'Oh, Charity!' He took my hand. 'Do you need to ask such a question? Of course I won't repeat a word to anyone if you don't want me to.'

I nodded. 'I scarcely know where to begin,' I said.

Joshua smiled, that angelic smile that looked so well with the clerical collar he now wore.

'At the beginning, perhaps?'

I told him everything and saw his face grow dark.

'Oh, Charity, you must get away from that terrible place!' he said when at last I finished. 'Those people are pure evil. You cannot stay there.'

'I will never leave without my mother,' I said with determination. 'She has suffered enough. I have to rescue her, try to give her some sort of life that is worth living. And I won't leave Charlotte either. But what am I to do, Joshua? Did you manage to trace Julia's family in Launceston?'

He shook his head, looking guilty. 'I've been kept very busy with my parish duties.'

My heart sank. 'I was hoping her family might provide a haven to which I could take her,' I said.

'But her father will be an old man now, Charity – if he's still living,' Joshua pointed out. 'In any case, I really don't know when I'll be able to make the trip to Launceston. Have you thought of going to the local magistrate?'

I gave a hollow laugh. 'The local magistrate is Francis and Selena's father.'

'But he's not in on this, surely?' Joshua said.

'No, I don't think he is,' I agreed. 'And he seems a decent man. But I could hardly count on him to support me by going against his own children. It would be a terrible scandal – imagine what it would do to the family reputation if this were to get out! He would do everything in his power to keep it quiet, I'm sure.'

'Well, I don't know what else to suggest,' Joshua said, looking perplexed, and it shocked me to see he was at as much of a loss as I was.

'Perhaps it would be best to leave things as they are,' he went on.

'Leave my mother locked up in an attic?' I

318

cried, shocked. 'How could that be for the best?'

Joshua shifted uncomfortably. 'Sometimes when people have been incarcerated for so long the things they want from life change,' he said uneasily. 'Julia may well be frightened by the outside world. She may not want to have to meet other people.'

I bit my lip, remembering her reaction when I had first found her. Certainly she had seemed frightened. Certainly she had begged me to go away and leave her alone. But she had soon grown used to me and to look forward to my visits. If only I could rescue her I could help her to adjust to society once more and that would be for the best, not leaving her locked away until her dying day. In any case, I could never leave the house knowing she was there, and I did not want to remain an hour longer than was necessary.

'I'll never abandon her,' I said hotly. 'There has to be a way and I'll find it. Supposing I was to go to the authorities about Francis's smuggling ring? I need say nothing about Julia – if I intimated that contraband was stored in the attics, they would search there – and discover her. Francis would be under arrest and unable to do anything to harm her – or me...'

'Smuggling ring?' Joshua said. 'What smuggling ring? I knew nothing of this, Charity.'

'Oh – he heads an organisation that covers half of Cornwall and beyond,' I said. 'I've seen boxes and bundles carried up from the bay by night and closed my eyes to it. But perhaps I could turn what I know to my advantage.'

Joshua looked concerned. 'That's a dangerous route to take, Charity. Smugglers can be ruthless indeed if they feel themselves threatened. And how could you be sure that the very official you speak to is not in Francis's pay? So many are corrupt.'

'I know it,' I said. 'But a desperate situation calls for desperate measures.'

'I don't want you putting yourself in the way of danger, Charity,' Joshua said decisively. 'Promise me you'll do nothing rash and I will try to see what I can do. I'll talk to Papa – he may have some suggestion to make. He's a wise man, and a good one. And he loves you as his own child.'

'Does he?' I smiled wryly, remembering my loveless childhood.

'Indeed he does, Charity, though he has never been good at showing his feelings – for any of us. He took you in, did he not? He gave you a home and raised you.'

'He did, it's true...' I broke off, reminded by his words of what, in my anxiety over Julia, I had forgotten. 'You said in your letter that you had learned the circumstances in which I was found,' I said. 'What were they,

Joshua?'

'You still don't know?' he said. 'Julia has not told you what happened?'

I shook my head. 'She has closed her mind to it. She thought I was dead. That's all I know.'

'Very well, Charity, I'll tell you what Papa told me. It's not the full story, of course. It can't be, but...'

'Never mind that,' I said impatiently. 'Tell me what you know.'

'Prepare yourself then,' Joshua said. 'It is not a pretty story.'

Eighteen

Julia

At last the repairs were effected and the *Guinevere* made ready to leave Madeira for the return voyage to Falmouth. At first it seemed John's prayers had been answered, for the seas were calm. But by the same token the winds were light and the currents less favourable and the *Guinevere* did not make the speed he might have hoped for.

Then, when they were within striking distance of home, the weather changed for the worse. A storm blew up that tossed the *Guinevere* like a toy boat in its relentless hold. For two days the crew never slept as they battled the mountainous waves.

Julia and Nancy were confined to their cabin, and though she was sick and weak again from the tossing, Julia did her best to keep Nancy from becoming too alarmed. The child, on the other hand, did indeed seem to have inherited her father's sea legs. The bucking of the ship affected her not at all.

They sighted the Cornish coast at nightfall on the second day, before it was lost to them in the murky darkness. It was John's intention to ride out the storm until daylight came, for he was well aware of the treacherous rocks that studded the peninsula. But with nightfall the storm gathered force once more, driving them willy-nilly towards the coast.

'Stay below!' John ordered a frightened Julia. One of his crew had already been washed overboard and lost; a woman and child on deck in these conditions would stand no chance at all.

He left them in the cabin huddled together on the narrow bunk, Julia trying to sing to Nancy to keep her spirits up, though her voice was barely audible over the creaking of the timbers and the moaning of the wind in the rigging.

The wild wind whipped around him in a frenzy as he yelled orders to his exhausted crew; the deck heaved, awash with water, beneath his feet. John cursed himself for having persuaded Julia to make this voyage with him. Bad enough to have to fight to save his ship and crew; knowing the lives of his wife and child lay in his hands was an added weight of responsibility. If the ship should founder...

He pushed the thought aside, concentrating on the battle in hand. But for all his efforts the relentless winds and currents drove the *Guinevere* closer to land – and the unseen dangers of the rocky coastline. Bone tired, drenched to the skin, John feared the worst.

And then by some miracle the wind dropped for a moment and he saw it. A light shining out into the darkness. And another … and another. Harbour lights! Praise be to God! Salvation was at hand.

With renewed vigour he issued orders to direct the storm tossed *Guinevere* towards the lights. Closer they came, closer and closer.

Suddenly, with a terrifying crash, the prow hit solid rock. For a moment, as the boat shuddered violently, he was so startled he could not imagine what had happened. Then, in a flash, he knew.

The bobbing lights were not the lights of a harbour or safe haven. They were the sirens of the Cornish coast, luring the unwary mariner straight on to the rocks. These lights were the work of evil men.

The wreckers.

The ship bucked violently and John knew there was nothing more he could do to save her. All he could do now was try to save his wife and child. He rushed below, slipping on the sea-drenched companionway and landing in a heap before the cabin door. He pulled himself to his feet and wrenched it open. The first impact with the rocks had put out most of the lamps; by the one remaining he saw Julia clinging to the bunk, Nancy in her arms.

'Come with me!' he yelled.

He took Nancy from her mother and somehow got the pair of them on to the sloping deck. Above them in the rigging men screamed and swore. Another gigantic wave slammed into the ship, she thudded once more against the jagged rocks and he heard the sickening sound of splintering wood. The *Guinevere* was breaking her back. Soon she would be torn apart. He had to get Julia and Nancy into a boat and pray they could reach land without being overturned.

And then, by some miracle, the moon emerged from the thick bank of cloud and a shout went up.

'The water's shallow here! We can wade to land!'

John's heart leapt. Perhaps there was a chance for them after all! One of the crew was indeed out of the ship and seemed to be standing waist deep in the water. There must be a sand bar beneath the rocks! With luck it would stretch to the beach!

The men swarming in the rigging clambered down, shouting their relief and throwing themselves into the water. John put Nancy in Julia's arms, helped her along the sloping deck to the point closest to the shallows.

'You can make it to shore here, my love. Just follow the others.'

'John – come with us!' she begged, shrinking back from the icy water.

'I have to make sure none of my crew are trapped. I'll see you on shore. Take care, my love.'

He helped her over the side, his heart contracting as the sea seemed to swallow her momentarily. Then she found her footing and began to wade towards the shore, Nancy held high in her arms.

And then the shouts began, and the first rocks came screaming through the air. In all the tumult he had scarcely noticed the lanterns that now bobbed on the shoreline; it had not occurred to him for a moment that the wreckers would attack the defenceless survivors of the ship they had lured on to the rocks. Now he watched in helpless horror as the deadly missiles struck them down and the air was filled with their screams and cries. The wreckers were stoning the survivors to ensure that none of them reached the shore alive and able to testify to the evil work that had been wrought here this night.

John threw himself into the water in an attempt to reach Julia and protect her. He floundered through the hail of missiles and saw that some of the wreckers were themselves waist deep in the water and beating those who had survived the missiles about the head and face with rocks and stones. Men fell about him, screaming for help, but he ignored them, his only care for his wife and child.

He had almost reached them when a rock caught him full in the face. He fell back, his eye gushing blood, his gaping mouth filling with sea water. For a moment he threshed helplessly, then found his footing again, stunned but unaware of any pain, so intent was he on reaching Julia and little Nancy.

Julia had stopped, frozen with fear, torn between braving the hail of rocks and being driven back into the icy waves. He managed a step towards her, calling out her name. Then a rock caught her, she stumbled, and he saw Nancy slip from her arms.

'No-oh!' he screamed, redoubling his efforts to reach them.

Another rock hit him, and another. John's head swam, blinded by blood he struggled on, his legs useless beneath him. And then the wreckers were upon him. He had no weapons with which to fight them, no remaining strength. He fought for his life and the chance to save his wife and child there in the foaming surf and knew he had no chance of winning.

'Julia!' he gasped as the salt water filled his mouth once more. It was the last word he would ever speak.

★ ★ ★

Every last member of the crew of the *Guinevere* died that night, stoned to death before they could reach land or driven back into the water to drown. The wreck was stripped to the bone; by the time the alarm was raised and soldiers and customs officers reached her, everything of value had gone, even the sails and the rigging. The wreckers had not gained the haul they had anticipated, for they had thought it was a cargo vessel they had lured on to the rocks, but they swooped on it greedily anyway, knowing that packets sometimes carried bullion and hoping perhaps for valuables amongst the mail.

The pickings were thin. The entire crew of the *Guinevere* were lost for a few baubles, a length or two of torn canvas and a brass bell.

But Julia did not die that night. And though Julia was to spend twenty years mourning her, neither did little Nancy.

Nineteen

'You were found wandering on the beach the morning after the wrecking,' Joshua said. 'God alone knows how you survived. Everyone else on board the ship that night died, stoned to death in the shallows or held under the water until they drowned. The cove was littered with bodies for days, Papa said, for more were washed up with every tide. The wreckers had made certain there was no one left to tell the tale – no one to identify them as the perpetrators of such wickedness.'

For long moments I was silent, my hands pressed over my mouth, trembling, shocked to the core. I had heard of wrecking, of course, but thought the stories to be exaggerated.

'It's beyond belief that any human being could behave so towards others,' I said at last.

'It goes against every tenet of my ministry to say it, but I truly believe they are beyond redemption,' Joshua agreed. 'To lure ships on to the rocks for the sake of robbing their cargos is wickedness enough, but worse, I think they actually enjoy the suffering of their victims.'

'Yet somehow I survived,' I mused. 'And Julia too. If I was on board the ship then surely so was she. How did we both escape when everyone else died? It makes no sense.'

'Perhaps you had gone alone on the voyage with your father, the sea captain,' Joshua suggested. 'When the ship was lost Julia would naturally assume you had been drowned.'

'I can't believe she would have not been with me,' I argued. 'And in any case, she said she saw me die.'

'Maybe she is confused about that,' Joshua said gently. 'You say she claims not to be able to remember her past. Maybe that's because she feels guilty about letting you go alone. And maybe she has imposed false memories too to help her cope with that guilt.'

'Maybe.' I could not argue with the logic of it, yet for some reason it did not sit easily with me.

'I have to say Papa doubted the whole story,' Joshua went on. 'He found it hard to believe that a tiny child could have survived not only the waves but also a night on the beach, drenched through and exposed to the elements, and be found alive next morning. I think it crossed his mind to wonder if you were ever really on the *Guinevere* at all. He thought it possible that someone had wanted to abandon you and seen their opportunity when the ship was wrecked.'

My hand flew to my throat. 'Did he not try to find out then if anyone in the village knew me?' I asked.

'He did, of course. And when he had established that no one recognised you and no one missed a little girl, he went on to try to discover if you had any living relatives in Falmouth, the wrecked ship's home port.'

Falmouth. How often, it seemed, I had heard mention of Falmouth in the last months.

'And what did he learn?' I asked.

'That the master of the *Guinevere*, a John Fletcher, did indeed have a little girl of about your age, and since his house was locked up and empty, it was assumed that his wife and child must have sailed with him. But no relatives of either the captain or his wife could be traced. There seemed to be a web of mystery surrounding them and they kept very much to themselves. Even the wives of the other sea captains who were your mother's neighbours knew nothing of her background or where she came from.'

Given the circumstances, that was understandable, I thought. Julia and John must have lived in fear of Francis coming after her if he had discovered her whereabouts. But there were still so many unanswered questions...

'Is it possible that Julia was waiting with me on the beach and when she saw the wrecking she was so distressed that she lost her mind and ran away, leaving me there?' I pondered, returning to the puzzle of how the two of us had managed to escape with our lives when everyone else on board the doomed ship had drowned.

Joshua shook his head. 'Why would she have been on that very beach? John would not have intended to make land there with all the dangerous rocks, and so far from Falmouth.'

The irony of it struck me again.

'It's such a coincidence,' I said thoughtfully. 'Tom comes from Falmouth.'

'Tom?'

'The young man you met when you came to visit me at Morwennan.'

'Ah.' Joshua's expression became petulant. For a moment he looked like a spoiled child who has seen his favourite toy snatched by a playmate. 'I think you should be wary of him, Charity.'

I frowned. 'Wary? Why?'

'How much do you know of him?' Joshua asked.

'Not a great deal,' I admitted. 'Well – next to nothing, to tell the truth.'

'Exactly.' Joshua nodded sagely. 'You are very vulnerable at the moment, Charity, and I don't want to see you hurt.'

I bowed my head, not wanting to admit to Joshua just how involved with Tom I already was.

'How do you know he is not one of Francis's gang?' Joshua persisted.

'No – he's not!' I said quickly. 'I thought the same at first, and confronted him with it, but he assured me he was not. He says he has his own reasons for associating with Francis...'

'Ah-ha! And you don't know what those reasons are?'

I shook my head.

'Then you must be doubly careful, Charity. Perhaps it is no coincidence he comes from Falmouth. Perhaps there is a very real connection – through John Fletcher.' He broke off, reddening, and I knew in an instant what he was implying.

Sailors were well known for their lack of fidelity. John Fletcher could have fathered other children by other women – or even by Julia herself. With a jolt I found myself remembering what Julia had said – that she had lost not one child but two or more. Had there been others, left behind for some reason when she had sailed on that fateful last voyage? Had Tom come to Morwennan searching for her? Certainly there was something about him that was very mysterious. Could it be that he was my brother? No! It was too ridiculous to contemplate.

Joshua had only made the suggestion because he was unbelievably jealous of my feelings for Tom, and I ... my imagination was working overtime. Hardly surprising given all the unlikely things I had discovered in the past months and was still learning, even today. I would not give such a possibility a second thought, for there was not the slightest scrap of evidence to suggest it might be so.

But, for all that, I remembered the instant attraction I had felt for Tom and shivered.

'What I don't understand,' I said, changing the subject, 'is why your mama and papa never told me any of this. Why did they keep it a secret?'

'They thought it would upset you,' Joshua said.

I laughed, a small hollow sound. 'It upset me to think that I was a foundling, abandoned by a mother who did not want me! Surely it would have been better to tell the truth as they knew it – that my parents were drowned.'

'But wrecking is such a terrible thing,' Joshua said – trying to make excuses for the incredible omission, I knew.

'My parents were the victims, not the perpetrators,' I responded tartly. 'And what could be more terrible than believing your mother left you in a bundle on a doorstep?'

Joshua flushed uncomfortably, and I

rushed on: 'And why did they call me Charity? If Dr John spoke to people at Falmouth who knew me, he must have learned that my real name was Nancy. Why did they take even that away from me?'

'Nancy?' Joshua repeated, looking at me quizzically. 'It's a pretty enough name. I don't know if I could get used to it though. You will always be Charity to me.'

'Exactly!' I fumed. 'They called me Charity so that I would never be able to forget that I was a burden on the parish. That is so very like them.'

'They were good to you,' Joshua said. 'I won't let you talk about them so, Charity.'

'Nancy!' I corrected him furiously. 'My name is Nancy!'

'Very well ... *Nancy*,' he said, looking so crestfallen that my anger died as quickly as it had come.

'Oh, Joshua, I'm sorry,' I said. 'Of course you can still call me Charity. It's what I still think of myself as anyway. I couldn't get used to a change of name either – not after so long.'

An impish smile lit his eyes.

'You do look like a Nancy.'

'And how do Nancys look?'

'Oh – happy, pretty, the way you always looked when we were children, skipping along, your hair loose over your shoulders ... And the way you look now.'

He broke off, his flush deepening. He had said more than he meant to, I knew; revealed more of his feelings than he was comfortable with. Dear, dear Joshua.

'Do you really have to go back to Morwennan?' he asked.

'I do.'

'Then promise me you'll be careful, Charity ... Nancy! Don't take the slightest risk with those people, and do nothing until you hear from me.'

'What are you going to do?' I asked.

'I don't know yet.' Joshua's face was very serious, very determined. 'But I'll think of something. I can see how important this is to you, and that makes it important to me.'

I took his hands in mine and kissed him on the cheek.

'Thank you. Oh, thank you. I knew I could rely on you, Joshua.'

He coloured again – from pleasure this time, I thought.

'I'll do my best, really I will. And Charity – if you are at all worried, go to Jem. I'm so far away, damn it, but he's within striking distance. He would help you, I know.'

'He's not you,' I said.

'No, but you were brought up as his sister too, even if you didn't really get along the way we did. And he's quite an influential man these days – certainly doing well for himself from what I could see of it. Promise me you'll go to him if you think you are in the slightest danger.'

'I promise,' I said, to satisfy him.

But I was thinking I would have to be at my wits' end to turn to Jem, brother or not. And in any case, I would never turn my back on Julia and Charlotte.

I returned to Morwennan with mixed feelings indeed.

I had learned a great deal but not enough. I had enlisted Joshua's help but I did not know how long it would be in coming. As for the house itself, I dreaded being once more under its dark oppressive spell, but longed to see Julia and Charlotte again and assure myself that they were safe and well. Not, of course, that any physical harm was likely to befall Charlotte. Her father adored her and would defend her, I felt sure, with his life. But, with so many secrets under that roof, I feared for the effect they might have on her should she stumble across them, and as she grew up and became more and more independent and aware, the likelihood of such a thing happening grew ever stronger.

As for Julia ... she was, I felt, in constant danger. Why they had kept her there for so long, alive but incarcerated, I could only guess at. But if she became a danger to them, then they had nothing whatever to lose by disposing of her as ruthlessly as they had kept her prisoner all these years.

As the carriage descended the steep incline beneath the trees the sense of being trapped myself closed in on me once more. The trees were bare now for winter, no heavy foliage blotted out the sun, and yet the darkness and the sense of oppression remained.

I found myself remembering the recurrent dream that had plagued me for so long before I ever came to Morwennan. Not once since I had been here had I dreamed that dream. It had been eclipsed by the reality. But it was strange, was it not, that it had happened at all when I had never set eyes on the place, never in waking life ever experienced such a feeling. It was, I thought, as if Julia had somehow been reaching out to me, relaying her own despair on some esoteric level. It was as if in those dreams I had become my mother.

And it did not stop with the house either. I recalled how once I had dreamed I was looking into a mirror, the very twin of the one that hung in the hall, and seeing a face that was so like my own, yet was not me. There had been some force at work that was beyond understanding. I only hoped it had the power to offer me – and those I loved – some protection in the dark days that lay ahead.

Charlotte came running to greet me and my heart lifted as she threw her arms around me.

'Oh, Charity, I'm so glad you're home! I've missed you so!'

Home. The word jarred on me. Morwennan would never be home to me. And, I suspected, had never been home to Julia either, for all the years she had lived here. But for Charlotte it was different. This truly was the only home she had ever known, Francis and Selena her family. And I was planning to tear her world apart.

Charlotte was tugging at my sleeve.

'Come with me, Charity! I've something to show you!'

She led me into Francis's study. There, laid out on the desk, was an enormous collage of autumn leaves. It was artistically done, and the vibrant oranges, reds and yellows amongst the inevitable brown stood out strikingly against the white background.

'Why, Charlotte, that is beautiful!' I praised her.

She smiled proudly. 'I collected them from the drive and stuck them on with flour-and-water paste. Mrs Durbin made it for me.'

'Well, I do believe you are going to be an artist!' I said. 'You must try your hand at something else. Sketching, perhaps.'

'Oh, I'd like that!' she cried eagerly. 'Could you teach me, Charity?'

'Me?' I laughed. 'Oh no, I barely know one end of a chalk from another. Can your father draw?'

'I don't think so.' Her fine brows drew together thoughtfully.

'Well, you certainly inherited your talent from somewhere,' I said. 'I think we must find someone to encourage you and give you some tuition. This is quite fine enough to be framed and hung on the wall.'

'Do you really think so? Oh, I'll find Papa and ask him if it can be done!'

She ran off, happy and eager, and I was left alone in the study, looking longingly at the attic key on its hook and wishing I could take it now, this minute, and go up to see Julia right away. But I knew I dared not. As before, I must wait my chance and I had no idea how long that would be.

In the event it came sooner than I expected – thanks to Mrs Durbin.

I was in my room unpacking my things when there was a tap at the door and Mrs Durbin's head popped round. Her face was a little flushed and she looked anxious.

'Can I have a word, Charity?'

'Of course. Come in,' I said.

She did, closing the door behind her. Then she stood uncertainly, her hands twisting in the folds of her apron.

'What is it?' I asked, curious and a little disturbed.

'You know, don't you?' she said. 'You've found her. Miss Julia.'

My heart gave a great frightened thud.

'She told me,' Mrs Durbin went on. 'She said you had told her not to say anything, but she couldn't keep it to herself, poor lamb. She was asking for you, wondering why you had not been to see her.'

Plainly there was no point denying what Mrs Durbin knew to be the truth.

'I explained to her that I had to go away for a few days,' I said.

'I'm sure you did, but she forgets. Some days her mind is clear as a bell, others...' Mrs Durbin broke off, shaking her head. 'Anyways,' she went on, 'she's longing to see you, I know that for a fact.'

'And I'm longing to see her!' I said fervently. 'But I have to wait my chance...' A sudden awful thought struck me. 'Francis and Selena are not aware of this, are they? You haven't told them I know?'

'As if!' She pursed her lips together. 'If they knew you knew, I don't know what they would do. But, my, you've taken some chances, Charity!'

'And so have they!' I retorted hotly. 'How could they think I could live under the same roof and not discover the truth?'

She gave a small shake of her head, not even attempting to answer my question.

'All I know is you've made her happier than she's been for years,' she said. 'And I just wanted you to know from now on I'll help you all I can. You've no need to steal the key any more and sneak up to the attic behind my back. When the coast is clear I'll open the door for you myself, aye, and keep watch for you, too. She needs all the company she can get, poor sweeting, and who better than the child she thought she'd lost all those years ago.'

'Thank you, Mrs Durbin,' I said gratefully, and wondered for a moment if I should confide in her my plans to free Julia and take her away from this house for ever.

But I decided it was safest to keep that to myself for the moment at least. I wasn't sure enough yet of where Mrs Durbin's loyalties lay. That she loved Julia dearly was not in doubt, but Francis and Selena were the employers and had been for a very long time. She may not even want to lose Julia herself. No, I couldn't take the risk of my plans being scuppered before they had even been formulated.

But at least for the first time since I had come to Morwennan I had an ally. And perhaps a friend.

Julia clung to me as if she would never let me go.

'Oh, Nancy, I thought I'd lost you again! I couldn't bear it if I was to lose you again now!'

'I told you I had to go away for a few days,'

I said gently.

'I thought Francis had taken you. He's a ruthless man, Charity. He has no heart at all.'

'I don't think that is quite true,' I said. 'I think *you* hold his heart, and that is the root of the trouble.'

'I don't want his heart!' she cried passionately. 'I never wanted it – never! He forced me into marriage, he forced me to have his child – I hated him! Hated him! And I still do!'

It was the first time she had ever spoken of the past.

'Why did you marry him?' I asked softly. And she told me.

When she had finished I understood just why she loathed this man with such vehemence. But I felt too a stab of sympathy for him which surprised me. To be as obsessed with a woman as Francis was with Julia, to love her to distraction – to madness – and never to have that love returned...

That, I thought, was the measure of Francis's tragedy.

I was living on the edge of my nerves. How I had managed before to visit Julia with no assistance at all I could not imagine. Now every creak of the boards made me start. As for Francis and Selena, I was convinced a hundred times that they knew that I knew –

I could read it into the most innocent remark or expression. Yet nothing untoward occurred at all. Life continued just as it always had at Morwennan.

A few days after my return Tom came to the house. When he had finished his business with Francis he sought me out.

'Fancy going off for days on end and not even telling me you were going!' he chided me.

'Why on earth should she tell you?' Selena, busy with her embroidery as usual, asked.

And Charlotte, making a tea party for her doll before the roaring fire, chirped up: 'I missed her too, Tom. Tell her she must not go away again!'

'You must not go away again, Charity,' Tom repeated obediently, his eyes holding and teasing mine.

In spite of my preoccupation with all my worries, my heart fluttered wildly. Tom had lost none of his attraction for me, it seemed.

'Why, surely I'm entitled to visit my family sometimes!' I said, striving to keep my voice level.

'Not if it means you deserting us,' Tom said, mock sternly. 'As a penance I think you should accompany me tomorrow evening.'

My eyes widened. 'Accompany you...? Where?'

'To the village. Where else? A group of strolling players are performing there. You would enjoy it, I think.' He turned to Selena. 'You have no objection, have you?'

'I suppose not,' Selena said, but she looked disapproving, as though she did not think such entertainment quite proper.

Charlotte jumped up, scattering the small china cups and saucers she had set out in her haste.

'I'd enjoy it too! Oh, can I come with you to see the strolling players, Tom?'

'Certainly not!' Selena said sternly. 'It will be well past your bedtime, miss, before it is over. And the night air might well give you a chill in any case.'

'It would not! I can wear my new cloak and fasten it right around my neck! Around my mouth if you like, so I couldn't breathe in *any* of that night air!' she added for good measure.

'I think it would be a good idea to fasten it around your mouth right this minute,' Selena said acidly. 'Then we might hear a little less of your nonsense.'

Charlotte subsided, crestfallen.

'Don't worry, I'll tell you all about it,' I promised her.

'Then you'll come?' Tom asked.

'Yes – if Selena will allow it...'

'You are not a prisoner in this house, Charity,' Selena said coldly. 'So long as you fulfil the duties for which you were employed you may come and go as you please.'

My cheeks burned suddenly, my nervous mind latching on to her words. Did they have hidden meaning? Oh, perhaps not. I was simply reading into them something which was not there.

But I could not escape the irony of them all the same.

Twenty

The barn where the performance was to be given was brightly lit with lanterns swinging from the rafters and, by the time Tom and I arrived, crowded with excited village folk. Some wooden blocks had been erected at one end to form a small stage and a corner was curtained off with some lengths of heavy plum-coloured chenille.

Tom led me through the crowd, nodding a greeting or exchanging a friendly word with many of them, but I felt very conspicuous as their eyes followed me, frankly curious.

We found a seat on a wooden bench and Tom took my hand, threading it through his crooked arm.

'So, I have you to myself at last, Charity!'

'Hardly to yourself!' I retorted. We were squashed between a plump elderly village woman and a gangly youth whose bony elbows dug into my ribs each time he moved.

'But afterwards...' Tom's mouth was very close to my ear, his warm breath tickling my cheek, and I felt a little twinge of excitement spiral deep within me.

For all my doubts about Tom, for all the anxiety for Julia which made me want to be near enough to know all was well with her even if I could not actually be with her, yet I could not help but be glad I was here, squashed up close to Tom and breathing in the heady anticipation of the villagers and the smell of the burning lamps.

Very soon the performance began. I had never seen strolling players before and had no idea what to expect. The first half took the form of a short play, an extract, Tom told me, from William Shakespeare's *A Midsummer Night's Dream*, and entitled, aptly enough, *The Fairies*. I found myself admiring the beautiful shimmery costumes and laughing heartily at the antics of poor Bottom in his grotesque ass's head, and enjoying the lyricism of the words I had so far only read in books.

Then, when the cast had taken their final bow, a motley crew of entertainers followed. There was a girl who sang folk songs so sweetly to the accompaniment of a mournful fiddle that tears sprang to my eyes; a so-called 'mathematical dog' who barked out the answers to simple sums, and a contortionist who twisted his body into the most amazing shapes. I have to confess it made me feel quite ill to see a head poking through a pair of spindly legs, for all the world as if it

348

had been chopped off and was resting there between the knees. I shuddered and turned my head away. Tom's warm fingers squeezed mine and he laughed softly.

'It's only a trick. You can look again now.'

I did. The man was standing to take his bow, rubbery, as if he did not have a single bone in his body.

When at last the entertainment came to an end we filed out of the barn with the rest of the audience.

It was a bright clear night as cold as if it were Christmas already, the stars very bright in a sky of ebony velvet, a dusting of frost sparkling on the ground and the bare branches of the trees. There was no wind at all; the air was crisp and still. A good night for smugglers, I thought. A perfect night to unload a cargo of contraband. Would there be a privateer at anchor in the bay when I returned to Morwennan? Had Tom been detailed to take me to the entertainment to get me out of the way? I shivered.

Tom, who had been turning up the collar of his cloak around his ears, turned to fasten the ties of mine for me.

'It's bitter enough to freeze a brass monkey! But at least it's good and clear. No ships will founder on the rocks tonight,' he said, as if he had somehow read my thoughts. And then, when we had left the crowd of villagers behind and were alone:

'Charity, I have to ask you this. Have you had any opportunity to search further for the ship's bell I spoke of?'

All my pleasure in the shared evening melted away, as the frost on the trees would melt in the morning sunshine, while all my doubts about Tom's motives came flooding back.

'No,' I said, a little stiffly. 'I've been away, if you remember. And in any case I have other, more important, matters on my mind.'

Tom did not ask what it was that concerned me so. He stopped walking, turned and gripped my forearms with his hands so that I was facing him.

'Nothing could be more important than this, Charity.'

I was angry suddenly – angry and hurt. In that moment I truly believed the whole reason for Tom's interest in me was this bell he was so anxious to find. He was using me, I felt sure, and had been from the very outset. Why, he had in all likelihood only asked me to the entertainment tonight in order to get me on my own and pursue the matter further! Joshua had been right to tell me to be careful of him.

'Why?' I asked harshly. 'What is it about this bell that makes it so important? Is it solid gold? Is something valuable hidden inside it? Is that it?'

'No – it's nothing like that.'

'Then what?' I asked impatiently. 'You can't expect me to look for it unless I know the reason why.'

In the moonlight Tom's face was all planes and shadows.

'There are some things it's better you don't know.'

'Oh fiddle!' I exclaimed. 'I've had enough of being fobbed off with that one. Whenever I ask awkward questions of anyone, I am told it's better for me that I don't know. Well, I'm sorry, but that's not good enough. I'm not a child and I'm not a fool, and I can only assume that it's for your good, not mine, that I am being kept in the dark.'

'That is not true,' Tom said vehemently. 'I'm trying to protect you, that's all.'

'Well, you have a strange way of doing it – asking me to snoop around my employer's house!' I retorted. 'It seems to me as if a falling-out between thieves is behind this. You are one of 'the Gentlemen', whatever you may say to the contrary. You help Francis in some way with his business enterprises. He's cheated you, I suppose, failed to give you what you consider to be your dues in some shady deal, and you intend robbing him of what is hidden in this bell to set matters right. Well, I've no intention of helping you. Settle your scores with him yourself or not at all. I won't be a party to it. I have enough problems of my own.'

Tom sighed. 'You have it all wrong, Charity. But I can understand your reasoning. I can see I shall have to tell you the truth.'

'I should warn you I am not given to believing in fairy tales,' I said tartly.

Tom ignored this. Though we were quite alone he looked round as if afraid of being overheard.

'If I tell you this I put my life and the lives of many others into your hands. I am trusting you to keep what I tell you to yourself, and to breathe a word to no one. Have I your word on that?'

'How can I promise anything of the sort when I don't know what it is you are going to tell me?' I asked, still hurt and annoyed, but his expression was so serious I could not ignore it. 'I'm sorry,' I said. 'Of course you have my word.'

Tom nodded, unsmiling. 'Very well. Firstly, I told the truth when I said I am not one of Francis's gang. Not one of 'the Gentlemen' as you call them – though such a term is flattery indeed for this unsavoury crew. I am not, and never have been, a smuggler, though I have gone out of my way to make Francis think I am. Evil lurks on this coast, Charity, and I am determined to put a stop to it and bring the perpetrators to justice.'

A chill shivered over my skin. 'You're talking in riddles, Tom.'

He faced me urgently and the look on his face made me shiver again.

'Have you ever heard of wreckers, Charity?'

Tom's words stopped me in my tracks. It was almost beyond belief that he should be raising the subject of wreckers after what I had learned in the last few days from Joshua.

'Indeed I have,' I whispered. 'But...'

'There is a gang of wreckers who operate along this coast when conditions favour their evil intent,' Tom went on. 'They have been active here for many years. On foggy nights they silence the bell-buoy and show false lights to lure unsuspecting ships on to the rocks. I believe that Francis and his cronies may well be the ones behind it. But before I can act I need to be sure – and to have the necessary evidence in my possession too. The bell is the evidence I need – and I must locate it quickly, before the fogs of winter close in. Time is short if more lives are not to be lost to this devilish crew.'

'You work for the authorities, then?' I asked.

'I work for myself.' Tom's voice was hard. 'I have my own personal reasons for wanting to bring the wreckers to justice.'

A nerve jumped in my throat. 'You have

lost someone from your family because of them?'

'My whole family. One way and another ... My father's ship fell victim to them when I was but an unbreeched child, and every man on board was lost.'

The blood was singing in my ears suddenly. A ship out of Falmouth lost to wreckers when Tom was but a young boy ... A connection with Francis ... Joshua's warning came rushing in to haunt me and I heard myself whisper faintly: 'Your father ... he was not the captain...?'

Tom gave me a strange look. 'The bosun,' he said. 'Why?'

'No matter,' I replied faintly. 'Go on.'

'My mother was left with two children to raise alone. Fortunately for us our grandfather gave us a home on his farm and my brother and I did not suffer too much. There were families left without the breadwinner who, through the work of those evil men, had to sell every stick of furniture, everything they possessed, in order to eat. So, in that respect at least, we were the lucky ones. But my mother never got over what had happened. She died when I was only fifteen years old, of a broken heart, I think.' He paused, raising his chin and drawing a deep breath. 'My brother, Roger, was two years older than me. He knew that wrecking still went on and he vowed to bring the murdering swine to justice. He was determined to avenge our father's death and the death of so many others down the years. As soon as he was old enough he became a riding officer.'

'You mentioned him before,' I said, a lump coming to my throat as I remembered Tom's cold, hard tone when he had spoken of his brother, and how I had thought it meant they were at loggerheads. How I had misjudged him!

'Roger was, I may say, one of the few not in the pay of the smugglers,' Tom went on. 'For a while he had a certain amount of success. He was responsible for the recovery of a goodly quantity of contraband and the arrest of those who ran the goods in and out. But they were small fry compared to the gang he wanted – the gang responsible for the wreckings – and he would not rest until he saw them safely behind bars. It was the death of him. One dark night as he rode his patrol he was ambushed and his body thrown down a mineshaft.'

He paused. In the moonlight I could see the grief and anger written all over his face, and this time there was no mistaking it. I said nothing, waiting until he was composed enough to continue.

'Just before he died, Roger had confided in me that he was close to his objective. He would not tell me much – he said it was better I did not know. I think he was afraid I might go rushing in with all the impetuosity of youth and blow his investigation wide open as well as placing my own life and his in danger. All he would say was that it was a ruthless and well-organised gang, which was headed by a prominent figure in the community – someone who scarcely needed the extra profits that wrecking could bring, but did it anyway for the sheer evil pleasure that comes from having power over life and death. And then, before he could gather his evidence and present it to the authorities, he was killed.'

Tom's hands were balled into fists.

'He was killed because he got too close to the truth, I'm convinced of it,' he said. 'Murdered in cold blood to save the skins of the wreckers.'

'I am so sorry...' I murmured.

He scarcely seemed to hear me. 'I vowed to take up the fight,' he went on. 'I discovered that Francis Trevelyan was a smuggler on the grand scale and it seemed to me that he fitted the bill. I insinuated myself into his organisation in the hope of discovering if I was right, and finding evidence to prove it. So far, however, I have to confess I have been unable to do so. And with winter drawing in, the wreckers will begin their evil work again and more men will die needlessly.'

'What makes you think the leader of the

wreckers still has this bell you are seeking?' I asked.

'Roger told me he had talked to a man who used to be one of their number but who has since repented of his wicked ways. The bell was amongst the items stripped from one of the ships they wrecked, and the leader had taken it as a grisly keepsake. It is of little value unless melted down and cannot be sold because it bears the name of the ship – the leader wanted it only for his own satisfaction.'

'And did he not tell you the name of this leader?'

'No – as I explained, he was afraid I might take matters into my own hands. But he did lead me to believe the ringleader kept the bell on display, or at least somewhere accessible where he could take pleasure in looking at it. That's why I am afraid I have been barking up the wrong tree all these months. If the bell is not at Morwennan House, then I must be looking in the wrong place.'

'Oh, Tom...' I was icy cold now, and it had nothing to do with the sparkling frost and the biting night air. This cold came from inside me, chilling my blood and my bones.

'So there you have it, Charity,' Tom said urgently. 'That is the reason I asked for your help – and continue to ask for it. What I plan to do is this. I intend to seek out the man to whom Roger spoke, the man who knows the identity of this fiend, so that at least I know for sure if I am right in targetting Francis as the ringleader. It will mean I shall be away for a few days at the very least, for I have to follow the same trail that Roger followed and that may not be easy.'

'Wouldn't it have been better if you had done that in the first place?' I suggested.

'With hindsight, yes,' Tom agreed. 'But I was so sure it was Francis's gang who were responsible, Francis who kept the bell to gloat over. Now ... well, I am not so sure. But will you continue to search for me, Charity?'

'I will, but I'm sure there's no ship's bell at Morwennan House,' I said – and oh, how I wanted to believe that! It was an insupportable thought that there should be even more evil under that roof than I had already discovered. And yet ... my thoughts went to the poor mariners who had died, and would die unless the perpetrators of this wickedness were caught and brought to justice. Mariners like my own father – and Tom's. And their dependents and loved ones whose lives had been changed for ever, as mine and Julia's had been.

'But I will keep on looking,' I vowed. 'I'll search for secret hidey-holes – I'll leave no stone unturned.'

Tom looked a little startled by my sudden zeal.

'You are not the only one to suffer at the

hands of wreckers,' I said. 'I have only recently learned of it, but my family too was torn apart by their wickedness. It's the reason I was raised as an orphan on the parish. So you can count on me to do everything I can to help you.'

'Oh, Charity...' His hands tightened on mine. 'But you must take care. Remember these are ruthless people we are dealing with. They dispose of anyone who is a threat to them without a second thought – and enjoy it. I don't like the thought of placing you in danger. I would never have asked for your help if I had not been desperate, and now ... You must promise me to take the greatest care. It may be, of course, that you are right and the bell is not at Morwennan, in which case I dare say you are safe enough. But should Francis be the man I am seeking then you could be in great danger. Should you find the bell, say nothing to anyone until I return.'

I nodded. And then, for no reason I could think of, but driven perhaps by some deep instinctive suspicion, I heard myself ask: 'You say the ship's name was inscribed upon the bell. What was it?'

And Tom replied, just as I had somehow known he would: 'The *Guinevere*.'

Twenty-One

I did not tell him. I don't know why, I simply could not. Perhaps it would have opened the floodgates on too much that I was not yet ready to share with him, though he had shared so much with me. And I needed first to have time to think through the implications of this revelation which had stunned me even though in some inexplicable way I had known it already.

If Tom was right, Francis was behind the wrecking that had taken the life of my father – and Tom's – and made me a virtual orphan. That was the terrible thing I could not bring myself to face. Surely – oh surely! – Tom must have come to the wrong conclusion! Even he was now beginning to doubt what he had once been so sure of – and with reason. In all the time I had been at Morwennan I had never seen anything to lead me to believe his gang of smugglers were also wreckers.

I could only hope and pray that when Tom found the informant his brother Roger had spoken of he would learn that the evil ringleader he was so determined to bring to justice was someone other than Francis Trevelyan. Not only because I found the prospect so unbearable but also because it would make my own sworn task to rescue Julia the more perilous for both of us.

But still I did not tell him. It was as if I had lost my tongue. As we walked back to Morwennan House I was in a daze. I think I might have stumbled and fallen more than once on the rough path had it not been for Tom's arm steadying me.

The sea was calm as velvet, black velvet broken only by swirls of creamy lace where it broke against the shore, the air so still that the haze of my own breath seemed to hang in front of my face like fine mist, yet inside I was once again thrown into turmoil. When I saw the lights at the windows of Morwennan House and its square solid outline broken only by its chimney pots silhouetted against the dark sky, I felt a sense of rising panic and the same familiar claustrophobia, only sharper, more choking than ever before. Oh, it truly was a house of evil! Yet I hoped with all my heart that Tom was wrong and the evil stopped with the things I had already discovered for myself.

At the door, in the deep shadow cast by the trees and out of sight of the windows, he took me in his arms. My heart fluttered like a trapped bird and I buried my face in his chest. The fabric of his cloak was a little rough, but comforting against my cheek, and suddenly, for all my fears, for all my turmoil, I felt a fierce stab of joy. I still did not know for certain whether Tom wanted me for myself or for what information I could glean for him that would help him in his obsessive quest. But at least I knew that he was no smuggler, not one of *them*. And I knew too that what Joshua had intimated was not true. He was not my brother or half-brother. For the moment it was enough.

I sighed, nestling against him, one good person in this evil world. He took my face and raised it, oh so gently, looking at me with an expression I had never seen on a man's face before. It was tenderness and desire and concern and pride all rolled into one. And with another leap of my heart I recognised it as love.

'Oh, Charity,' he said softly, so very softly, and all the same things I had seen in his face were there in his voice. 'I wish I did not have to leave you here. I want to take you with me – keep you safe.'

'But you can't,' I said. 'And in any case, I could not go with you.'

I almost told him, then, the reason I could not leave. I almost told him about Julia, locked in her attic room. The words were there, clamouring to be spoken.

But then he kissed me.

His lips were gentle at first on mine, then harder, and he wrapped his cloak around us both so that I could feel the beating of his heart next to mine. His hands moved to my hips, holding the full length of me close against him and there was a sweet sharp ache somewhere in the deepest part of me, an unbearable urgent longing in the secret places between my thighs. I felt the muscles in my legs and buttocks tighten as I strained towards him, the unfamiliar desire exhilarating and frightening me both at the same time. And all the while he kissed me. My lips parted beneath the pressure of his and his tongue slid inside my mouth. I had not dreamed of being kissed in such a way, not even realised that such a kiss existed, but oh! the pleasure of it, tasting his tongue as it circled mine.

Closer I pressed to him and closer, inhibtions forgotten as surely as all my troubles and fears. This was a stolen interlude, a wonderful glimpse of a forbidden world where love and longing and sensuality all mingled to induce a state of euphoria that made everything else unimportant. There was nothing beyond Tom's arms and body and mouth. We were locked together in our own private world within the shelter of his cloak.

Then quite suddenly he released me and I felt bereft.

'It's time I went, Charity,' he said roughly. 'If I stay here with you a moment longer I shall forget that you are a lady – and I, so I like to think, am a gentleman!'

Colour flooded to my cheeks then for I realised I had certainly not been behaving like a lady. Nor had I wanted to! Oh, what must he think of me, to return his kisses so shamelessly, to press my body against his so that every line of it must have been as apparent to him as his had been to me! And to have gloried in it like some common slut...

'I have really let myself down, haven't I?' I said in an agony of confusion.

'Oh, Charity!' He laughed. 'You are wonderful. Don't ever change. Except...' He took a long curl which had escaped my hair pins, twisting it between his fingers. 'Except that I shall teach you how to enjoy such things and feel no shame. We'll soar together, you and I, when this is all over.'

When this is all over. His words drew me back to reality, the world of uncertainty and danger and impossible problems and responsibilities that weighed me down like a collar of stones, the world I had escaped for just a few short minutes when my body and his had been all that mattered. I wanted to weep with despair as well as loss.

When this is all over. A promise for the future, yes. But when would it end – and how? What would I have to endure first, and what would the outcome be?

Tom touched my cheek lightly.

'Take care, my love.'

I nodded, aware that he too was in danger. 'And you.'

He kissed me again, very lightly this time, with none of the passion, only tenderness, then he released me and was gone.

I watched him walk away, a tall, strong figure in the moonlight, and felt my heart was going with him. Then I opened the door, which was on the latch, and went into the house.

And so the waiting began again, the waiting now not just for word from Joshua, but from Tom too. It seemed to me I could not remember a time when my life had been calm and ordinary; now it was so full of emotional turmoil normality had ceased to exist for me.

I thought of Tom often, my whole body coming alive as I remembered the kisses we had shared and the wonderful unfamiliar sensations I had experienced. And I longed for him too with my whole being. But overlaying all this was my anxiety for him and for Julia and Charlotte, and a powerful dread of what was yet to come. So many shocks had I had in the last weeks that I felt as if I were primed and tensed ready for the next one, which might be around any corner.

And it came, just when I was least expecting it.

It was mid-afternoon, a cold dark day. Though fires had been lit in each of the living rooms since morning, sitting to work on some grammar with Charlotte I had grown cold. I hoped I was not about to come down with a chill, and I decided to go to my room and fetch an extra wrap.

Leaving Charlotte hard at work I went upstairs. My room was at the very end of the landing; as I passed Francis's door, which was ajar, I heard a moan, and then another.

I stopped, alarmed. Had Francis been taken ill? He had seemed his usual self earlier, but who knew? He had obviously retired, for I would not have expected him to be anywhere but in his study at this time of day, and it sounded as if he was in pain. Might he be suffering an attack of some kind?

Anxious to discover what was wrong I pushed the door a little wider and peeped cautiously round. Then I froze in shock. Francis was indeed lying on his bed but he was not alone. Selena was with him. They were rolling together like a pair of lovers.

For a moment I simply could not believe what I was seeing, then I took a quick involuntary step backwards and my elbow caught the planter which stood in a small alcove beside the door, causing it to rock violently on its spindle legs. The sound was enough to alert Francis, lost though he might have been in his obnoxious activity.

'What was that?' I heard him say sharply.

And Selena's answering voice, a little alarmed: 'Someone is there!'

The bed creaked; I knew someone was coming to investigate. Panic filled me. I couldn't let them know I had seen them – I would die from the shame of it. But I could not possibly get all the way down the staircase in time, and the haven of my own room was too far away along the landing. There was only one place of escape that I could reach before Francis threw the door wide and saw me there outside. Selena's room, directly opposite Francis's, and only a step from where I stood.

Without a moment's hesitation, without stopping to think what I was doing, I dived into it, looking around me wildly for some place of concealment in case they should investigate further. In the bare room there was only one hiding place that I could readily see – behind the ornate Chinese screen.

I ran to it, slipping out of sight behind it. I was shaking and my cheeks were hot. I pressed my hands to them, eyes tight shut, straining my ears to hear what was going on outside.

'There's no one there,' I heard Francis say. I took a deep steadying breath in an effort to compose myself. In a couple of moments he would go back into his room, hopefully close the door, and I would be able to creep out and escape back downstairs. But oh! the shame of what I had witnessed! Francis and Selena – oh, it was beyond belief...!

I removed my hands from my face and opened my eyes. And saw it. Right beside me, there behind the screen.

A ship's bell.

My knees turned weak. A mist rose before my eyes. The blood drummed in my ears. I thought for a moment I was going to faint clean away and the fear of it momentarily wiped everything else from my mind.

If I should faint now I would undoubtedly be discovered. Such a thing would place not only me at risk, but Julia too. Desperately I focused every bit of my attention on willing myself to master the weakness that threatened to overcome me.

And I won. Little by little the faintness passed and, though my knees still trembled and I felt nauseous and ill, the immediate danger of collapsing into a tumbled heap and perhaps bringing the screen crashing down with me had passed.

I had to get out of Selena's room without being observed, to the safety of my own room or the parlour. But first I had to satisfy myself that this was indeed the bell Tom had been seeking.

Steeling myself I looked at it again. *Guinevere*. The name was clear in the brass, which still shone as brightly as it must have done when it was new, confirming what in my heart I already knew.

I hesitated a moment, then bent to touch it with fingers that trembled. This was the bell from my father's ship. A direct link to the heritage that had so long been denied me. Had he touched it too? He would have taken pride in it, I felt certain.

I crept to the doorway and peeped out, my heart pumping. There was no one on the landing. I slipped out and hurried to my own room, where I collected the wrap I had come upstairs to fetch in the first place, for I knew Charlotte would think it odd if I returned without it and, should I meet Francis or Selena, it would provide the reason for me wandering about upstairs in the middle of the day. It might, of course, tell them that it was I who had been outside their door as they rolled together on Francis's bed, but that scarcely mattered to me any more. Disgusting though their antics were, yet they were as nothing compared with the discovery I had made. The discovery that, according to Tom, proved Francis's involvement in the evil that had stolen the life of my father and so many other poor souls.

One thing I could not understand. The perpetrator of the wrecking had kept the bell to gloat over, Tom had said. And certainly, judging by its perfect condition, it had been regularly polished, as if it were some precious artefact in an art connoisseur's collection. So why had it been, not in Francis's room, but in Selena's?

Charlotte looked up as I re-entered the parlour.

'I've finished all my sums, Charity. I did them quickly, didn't I?'

Quickly? It seemed a lifetime since I had left her there and gone upstairs; in fact it had only been a few minutes, not even long enough for Charlotte to wonder what was keeping me.

'Very good,' I said absently.

'Aren't you going to look at them?' she asked, looking puzzled.

'Yes ... yes, of course...'

Somehow, until I had word from either Joshua or Tom, I had to keep up a pretence of normality. But oh, it was not going to be easy!

'Julia, I know it's painful for you, but I want you to try to tell me about the night you lost me,' I said, sitting down at her feet and taking her hands in mine.

Selena and Francis were both out, Mrs

Durbin had unlocked the attic door for me and was keeping an eye on Charlotte. I had just a little while in which to try and discover the truth behind the evil – and the tragedy – of Morwennan House.

At first, when I had found the bell from the *Guinevere*, it had seemed conclusive proof that Francis was indeed the man behind the gang of wreckers; now I was not so sure. There were too many unanswered questions, too many areas of uncertainty. Maybe my tortured mind was resisting the terrible possibility that I was employed by my father's murderer, but it had occurred to me to wonder if there might be some other reason for the bell being here, kept lovingly polished all these years. Could it be that some other gang had been responsible for the wrecking but Francis had somehow managed to gain possession of the bell as a link to the days when Julia was young and healthy and strong? Or that he had revenged himself on the gang who had all but destroyed her and taken the bell as a trophy of war? It all seemed far-fetched, but then, so was everything else in this dreadful puzzle.

There were too many questions without answers and I felt I needed to have them before Tom returned and I delivered Francis into his hands.

How, for instance, had Francis come to rescue Julia and bring her back to

Morwennan? How had I managed to survive a bitterly cold night, wet through, on an exposed beach? What had occurred in the years that followed? And why, most importantly of all, had Francis told the world that Julia had died when Charlotte was born and incarcerated her in the attic?

None of it made the slightest sense and I had made up my mind to try to make one more attempt to learn at least something of what had happened from Julia herself. Her mental state had improved so much since I had been visiting her, and she had come to trust me. I very much hoped that she might feel able to confront the events of that terrible night.

But my heart sank as I saw the familiar blank look in her eyes.

'Please, Mama,' I said, using the name that had been so difficult to get used to in the beginning, but which now afforded me so much pleasure. 'Please try to remember.'

'But I can't,' she whispered.

'You can,' I urged her.

'No. There was a storm – I remember that. I was very ill and very frightened. And then ... We foundered. The sea...' Her eyes were wide, her voice trembled. 'The sea was terrible ... so cold. And there were men on the beach. I thought they were going to save us but instead they threw rocks. They tried to drive us back...'

She broke off. Steeling myself to ignore her obvious distress I pressed her: 'And then? What happened then?'

'I don't know. Truly, Nancy, I don't know. I don't remember anything until I woke up here, back at Morwennan. And you had gone ... You had gone!'

A little ray of hope sparked within me.

'You remember waking up here?'

'Oh yes, I'll never forget that. I thought I must have died and gone to hell...'

'So tell me what happened when you woke up,' I said gently. 'Tell me what happened afterwards.'

And: 'Very well,' she said.

Twenty-Two

Julia

The nightmares came first. In a fevered state Julia felt an overwhelming sense of loss, heard the shouts and the roar of the sea, knew she was battling against some terrible fate, screamed, sobbed, writhed, her head twisting back and forth on the pillow, then drifted back into blessed unconsciousness ... The only reality had been something too terrible to bear; she took refuge in a place where nothing and no one could reach her. Then, gradually, as her fever-wracked body healed, the refuge became more distant, more inaccessible. There was no longer any escape from the overwhelming despair. It weighed her down and weak tears poured down her cheeks from beneath closed eyelids.

She opened her eyes, recognised what looked strangely like her old room at Morwennan and frowned, puzzled. It was another illusion, there was no other explanation. She stared blankly at that familiar ceiling, moved her head slightly on the pillow to take in the walls and became aware of someone sitting beside her bed. She could not see them, they were outside her line of vision, yet a familiar scent, a recognisable presence pervaded her senses. Her stomach clenched. Julia turned her head a little more and saw what in her heart she already knew.

The person was Selena.

She sat in the comfortable wicker chair, her embroidery in her lap. She seemed to tower over the bed like some evil spirit.

'So,' she said, her lip curling. 'You are awake.'

'I don't understand...' Julia murmured weakly.

'You were found half drowned,' Selena said coldly. 'Francis had you brought home.'

Frantic, Julia tried to raise herself on the pillows.

'Nancy! Where's Nancy? And John? I must find them! I must go to them!'

Selena set aside her embroidery and stood up, looking down at Julia with eyes as hard as the lumps of rock that had taken the lives of John and his crew.

'They are dead,' she said baldly. 'Everyone perished in the shipwreck but you. God alone knows how you came to survive, but you did, and Francis, more fool he, has decided to take you back.' She moved to the door, a stiff figure in violet silk. 'I'll fetch him. He'll want to see you, no doubt.'

'Julia! Thank God! Oh my dear...'

Francis threw himself on to his knees at her bedside. Tears were streaming down his cheeks. It was as if she had never left him, as if she had suffered some terrible illness or accident whilst still living with him as his wife and the last years had never happened at all.

Julia found herself wondering if Francis and Selena, like the tortured nightmares, were all part of some delusion. She stared at him with dull, puzzled eyes.

'Oh, I thought I had found you only to lose you again! You have been ill, my dear, so ill...'

'What happened?' she whispered. 'What am I doing here?'

'The ship you were on was lured on to the rocks by wreckers.' His face was ravaged, his hands trembled.

So it was true. All the horrible nightmares were not figments of her imagination but memories. Julia struggled to cope with the enormity of it.

And what of Nancy and John? Selena had said they were dead. But Nancy had been in her arms. If she herself was alive then surely ... surely...

'My baby!' she cried, struggling to sit up. 'I

have to find my baby!'

Francis's face changed, his features distorted by a look that was part fury, part pain.

'You have no baby, Julia. He died, don't you remember?'

'No! My little girl! Nancy...'

'You have no little girl,' he repeated, his tone hard. Then he reached for her hands, covering them with kisses. 'You are home now, my love. I'll take care of you, never fear. Selena wanted me to leave you to your fate, but for once I wouldn't let her have her way. You are my wife, Julia, and I'll keep you safe. Safe with me to the end of your days.'

She shook her head, hysteria rising in a flood tide.

'No – no, you don't understand...'

'Oh, I do, my love.' He stroked her hair, easing her back on to the pillows. 'I understand very well. You are home now. That is all that matters.'

The grief overwhelmed her and the blackness, the same grief and blackness she had experienced after the birth – and death – of her little son, only a thousand times worse.

John, her only love, was lost to her, and little Nancy too, both drowned on that terrible night when the wreckers had wreaked their evil under a storm-torn sky.

She was trapped, trapped here for ever at Morwennan with Francis, who loved her so obsessively. Yet that scarcely mattered. Without John and Nancy, nothing mattered any more.

There can be no denying it, Francis treated her well, as indeed he always had, but for that first unforgivable episode when he had taken her in the carriage on the day they became man and wife, and on the rare occasions when his frustration with her continued rejection of him tried his patience beyond its limits.

His obsession for her was such that it was almost, but not quite, enough for him that she was his, more utterly and completely now than she had ever been; her total dependence on him almost, but not quite, satisfied him. It was as if he had caged some rare and beautiful bird of paradise. He could look at her and enjoy the looking, he could display her proudly to his friends, he could stroke her feathers, listen to the soft musical lilt of her voice, buy her treats that he thought might please her. He had passed the point now of expecting her ever to return his love or even respond to his uxorial advances. A pattern was set in those early days when Julia was still fragile as a butterfly's wing. She had her own room and he had his and he made no attempt to force himself on her.

It was as if, so long as he imposed restraint upon his physical desires for her, he could convince himself that the lack of normal marital relations was his doing and not hers, that it was his sacrifice for her good. To have had her turn from him, or lie weeping silently in his embrace, would have been to expose the whole charade to the light of day, and would have served as nothing but a bitter reminder that she found him repulsive. As it was, he could pretend that she was his adored wife, too sick in body and mind to be put through the rigours of the act of love.

And so Francis satisfied his needs with the loose women who plied their trade around the harbours and in the bars of the less reputable inns, and resumed his intimacy with Selena as he had during the years of Julia's absence. But never once did he take a mistress, nor want to. The loose women meant nothing to him, his relationship with Selena was so long-standing that he saw it merely as an extension of their fondness for one another as siblings. But to take a mistress – that would have been something quite different. It would diminish Julia in the eyes of his friends and associates, who would surely know about it – it would diminish her in *his* eyes. Julia belonged on a pedestal, a fragile treasure to be looked up to and idolised. And that was where he kept her.

For her part Julia found that her dependence on him slowly gave birth to something close to affection. She had no one else – her father had lost the farm and moved to Launceston, Aunt Prudence had died suddenly the year after the wrecking. Not that Francis had ever allowed Julia to visit her – he would never forgive Prudence for her part in Julia's desertion and did not want to be reminded of it. Julia loathed Selena, and Francis discouraged her from making friends. Besides himself the only person who was close to her was Mrs Durbin and it was not enough. Gradually she began to turn to Francis for companionship, gradually, as she came to realise he was making no demands on her, she grew almost fond of him without even acknowledging to herself what she was feeling.

The years passed and, though Julia's grief never left her, it subsided to a dull ache, just as her grief for her baby son had done. No human being can live for ever in that state of agony, and Julia was no exception. Had she known that little Nancy was growing up in a rectory not more than half a day's drive away she would never, of course, have allowed what had occurred to recede into the past, she would have been filled with fierce determination never to rest until she found Nancy. But she did not know. She believed the little girl had drowned along with John in the boiling surf.

Though as the years went by they came less often, Julia still experienced times when the grief overcame her. Sometimes there was an identifiable cause, such as the anniversary of Nancy's birth, sometimes it washed over her for no reason at all. She would weep then, her arms wrapped around herself, doubled up with the agony of loss, the longing for her child and for John. She would weep with the sobs wracking her frail body and the scalding tears drenching her face until she could weep no more, but still the pain remained.

One such night Mrs Durbin, bringing her a bedtime posset, found her crouched in a corner of her room, head bent low, arms around her knees like a mad woman. She ran to Julia, distressed.

'Oh, my lamb, don't! Oh, sweeting, you'll make yourself ill! Whatever is it?'

'My baby,' Julia sobbed. 'I want my baby!'

Mrs Durbin took Julia in her arms, shushing her as one would shush a child until at last Julia's sobs subsided.

'You mustn't upset yourself like this,' Mrs Durbin counselled. 'You must try to be grateful for what you have. A good husband, a nice home...'

'I want my baby!' Julia whispered.

'Oh I know, I know...' Mrs Durbin had no children of her own but she had in her time longed for them, and she could, in some way, share Julia's pain. 'You know what I think? I think you should have another child. You're young enough yet. Mr Francis would be delighted, wouldn't he? And you would have something to take your mind off your loss.'

Julia shook her head, the tears welling again.

'No! No other baby could ever take Nancy's place.'

'That's what you thought when you lost the little lad now isn't it?' Mrs Durbin reminded her. 'And then Nancy came along and you loved her just the same. You forgot...'

'I did not!' Julia cried fiercely. 'I did not forget my son! And I don't want to forget Nancy!'

'Well of course you don't. And you never will. That's not what I was going to say. You don't forget those you have loved. You just forget to be quite so sad.'

Julia made no reply. But Mrs Durbin's words remained with her and when she was calm enough to gather her thoughts the seed the older woman had planted began to take root and grow.

Perhaps there was something in what she said. It would be good to hold a child in her arms again. Julia closed her eyes, remembering the sweet scent of soft baby skin, the gossamer feel of fine baby hair against her cheek.

Before long Julia found she could think of nothing else. At last she went to her husband.

'Francis ... do you think we might try to have a baby?'

He stared at her, unable to believe his ears. She laid her hand on his sleeve, looking up at him with pleading eyes.

'Oh, Francis, I want a baby so much!'

He took her face between his hands and bent to kiss her forehead with great tenderness, though all he wanted was to sweep her into his arms and ravage her there and then.

'Oh, my dear,' he said against her hair. 'I never thought I'd hear those words from you.'

'Then ... then you don't mind?'

'There is nothing,' he said, 'that I could want more.'

That night, for the first time in twelve years, Francis and Julia slept in the same bed. That night, for the first time in their entire marriage, she gave herself to him willingly.

This time Julia conceived less easily. Older, no longer the vibrantly healthy girl she had been, her body resisted what she longed for with her whole heart and soul. Then, when she had almost given up hope, the miracle happened.

As she watched her body swell with the longed-for child, Julia was filled with joy and hope for the future and Francis was equally delighted at the prospect of being a father. If, before, he had treated Julia like a fine piece of Dresden china, now he cosseted her even more. Nothing was too good for his wife and his unborn child.

At last, it seemed, the tortured couple were about to achieve some sort of normal family life.

It was not to last. Selena – bitterly jealous, usurped once again – was to make sure of that. She stalked the house like an angry tigress waiting for her opportunity to take revenge on the woman she had always considered her rival.

It came on a foggy November night some three weeks before the date Julia had calculated her baby was due.

All day a cold drizzle had fallen; by four in the afternoon it was almost dark already and the mist that had threatened all day began to close in.

Julia had been in her room resting. She crossed to the window to pull the drapes and was alarmed to see a motley crew of rough-looking men gathered in the garden beside the gate that led to the cliff path. They looked, she thought, like a band of ruffians with their unkempt hair and shaggy beards, their whole demeanour oddly threatening and somehow made the more sinister as the glow of their lantern lights spread around them like fiery halos in the swirling mist and darkness. One was a huge gorilla of a man, another a hunchback, certainly none of them had she ever seen at Morwennan before.

Julia's heart began to pound. They were up to no good, she felt sure. Leaving the drapes half-drawn she ran downstairs in search of Francis.

The front door was ajar; she heard voices and ran to pull it fully open. Francis was there, and a man who looked every bit as unsavoury as the ones she had seen in the garden. She stopped in her tracks, startled and afraid.

'Francis...'

He turned to her impatiently. 'What is it?'

'There are men in the garden...' Her eyes were on Francis's visitor; burly and un-shaven, he was regarding her with belligerent suspicion. Her voice faltered. This man was, she felt sure, one of them.

'It's all right,' Francis said shortly. 'Go inside.'

'But...'

'Go inside, I tell you!' She had never heard his tone so sharp, so authoritative, and she had no choice but to obey.

Selena was in the parlour, a piece of the

eternal embroidery in her lap. She looked up as Julia entered, her eyes cold as steel.

'What's going on?' Julia burst out. 'There are men in the garden – awful-looking men – and one of them is at the door talking to Francis. He means no good, I'm sure of it. What are we to do?'

Selena raised an eyebrow, but her needle still flashed in and out of the linen she was working on.

'We do nothing, Julia.'

'But ... we could all be murdered!' Julia gasped. 'You haven't seen them, Selena! They are evil! Why, the one at the door could have a pistol trained on Francis at this very moment – or a knife in his ribs. He spoke to me so sharply, telling me to come indoors. Something is very wrong, I know it is!'

'Calm yourself, for the love of God,' Selena said coldly. '*We* are in no danger, I assure you.'

'But...' Julia broke off. How could Selena be so sure? *We* are in no danger. Why had she laid emphasis on the 'we'? 'I don't understand,' she faltered.

'No, you do not.' Selena smiled, the unpleasant smile that pulled the corners of her mouth downward. 'Francis was anxious to protect you. But I think it is time you knew the truth.'

Julia stared at her, a feeling of dread creeping through her.

'Truth? What truth? What are you talking about, Selena?'

Selena laid her embroidery on the small table at her side with great care. Her eyes never left Julia's and Julia realised she was actually enjoying this, relishing what was to come.

'You know, of course, how Francis makes the money that buys you all this.' With a sweep of her hand she indicated the comfortably furnished room with all its treasures, the drinks table laden with crystal decanters full of fine spirits, and finally Julia's own silk gown and hand-made slippers. 'You know he is a smuggler on the grand scale, overseeing the entire operation from the negotiations with the free trade captains to the dispersal of the contraband inland by a series of storage and distribution points. He is even part owner of a two-hundred-ton lugger, the *Yellow Rose*.' She paused.

'Yes, of course I know that,' Julia said impatiently. 'I've never liked it, but...'

'But you are prepared to accept the benefits it brings,' Selena said smoothly.

'I suppose so – yes. But...'

'And if I were to tell you that some of Francis's profits come from other sources? Sources that cost him nothing? How would you feel about your fine silks and laces then?'

'Selena, you are talking in riddles!' Julia

said sharply, but there was a small uncertain quaver in her voice. 'How can it cost him nothing when the captain and the ship's crew have to be paid?'

The corners of Selena's mouth turned down still further as her smile broadened.

'Dead men ask no wages, Julia.'

'Dead men?' Julia was a small frozen statue now as she began to realise the full horror of what Selena was saying. 'Selena ... you don't mean ... you can't mean...'

'Wrecking. But of course, my dear,' Selena replied calmly. 'If a ship is driven on to the rocks no money has to change hands. The whole cargo can be salvaged free and gratis. Why, everything of value on board falls into the hands of those waiting on the shore. It can be a most profitable exercise – and I am afraid to say that many of the men who do such things take great pleasure in it, too. They are a drunken, lawless lot on the whole – a breed apart from those who assist Francis with his regular free trade. Gypsies, sailors, poachers – the one thing they have in common is greed and a bloodlust. Not the most savoury of characters – as you observed tonight.'

'The men in the garden,' Julia whispered. Her lips felt stiff. 'They are ... wreckers.'

Selena nodded. 'I am afraid so, yes. It looks like being a perfect night for such activity and they are anxious to make it a busy and profitable one. But they need someone to lead them – someone with a cooler head than they, and the means to help them dispose of their spoils.'

'Francis.'

Selena merely smiled again.

'But how could he?' Julia cried. 'It's murder – cold blooded murder! How could he be involved with something so terrible? Especially after what happened to me! He knows it was wreckers that caused the death of John and my little girl! He knows I almost lost my life too!'

'Oh yes, he knows that very well,' Selena said silkily. 'Very well indeed.'

'Then how could he...' Julia broke off. There was something in Selena's tone that told her there was a great deal more that she had not said ... yet. The first awful suspicion began to dawn on her, too horrible to assimilate all at once. 'Selena – you are not saying ... No! No, I won't believe it!'

'How do you think you came to be saved, Julia?' Selena asked. 'It was a bad night, that one. They did not know that part of the coast well enough and they reckoned without the shallows. The crew were reaching land. They could not allow that. They had to die, all of them. And you would have died too if you had not been recognised. But you *were* recognised and the order was given to let you live. Francis brought you home unconscious

– you know nothing of who it was that carried you out of the water to dry land. We could not be sure, of course, that you had been unconscious from the outset. That is why you found me at your bedside, my dear, when you became lucid. We needed to know how much you remembered.'

Julia was white now, as white as she had been that night when she had been lifted, half-drowned, out of the icy sea. The enormity of what Celia was telling her was overwhelming, her mind still rebelled against it. And yet ... and yet ... without doubt it had the ring of truth, and it explained so much.

She had on occasion wondered that the cold-hearted Selena who hated her so had sat willingly beside her sickbed. For a time she had almost been prepared to revise her opinion of her sister-in-law on the strength of it. Now, in a flash, she understood why the duty of care had not been assigned to a nurse, who might learn something Selena and Francis wanted kept secret.

She had wondered too, many times, how it was that she had survived whilst John and little Nancy had perished. Now she understood that also. Francis had been there on the shore that terrible night. It was Francis who had carried her from the waves and brought her home.

And by the same token it was Francis who had caused the deaths of her lover and

390

her child.

Julia began to scream.

Dimly she was aware of Selena rising, gripping her flailing arms, shouting at her to be quiet, slapping her sharply across the cheek. Dimly she was aware of Francis, alerted by the commotion, entering the room.

'Murderer!' she screamed, beating at him with her hands. 'Murderer!'

Francis, stronger than Selena, restrained her, holding her fast until the first hysteria passed.

'Julia, my dear, whatever...?'

She glared at him, her eyes full of passion and a hatred such as he had never seen in them before.

'She knows,' Selena said bluntly.

'Yes, I know!' Julia cried. 'It was you who killed John and my little Nancy. You, Francis! You!'

'Julia, no...!'

'You won't get away with it!' she sobbed. 'I'll see to it that you don't. I'll go to the authorities. I'll tell them everything. You'll hang for this, Francis Trevelyan!'

'On your word?' Selena interceded smugly. 'Oh, I think not.'

Julia ignored her.

'And if you don't hang, Francis, at least I'll make sure you never have your child,' she threw at him. 'I'll take him away where you'll never see him. And if you prevent me, then

I'll kill him. I'll kill your child, God help me, as you killed mine.'

Francis too was now deathly pale. 'You would not...'

'Oh, I would.' Her hands went to her stomach, covering the precious mound. 'I would do anything, Francis, rather than have him grow up with you for a father!'

'Julia...'

Her eyes were wild. 'I'd tear him from my belly now if I could...' She broke off, gasping, as the first pain, sharp and searing, gripped her. Her knees buckled; Francis gripped her by the elbows, supporting her.

'Dear God, Selena, look what you've done now! It's coming! The baby is coming before its time.'

Selena said nothing. But Julia saw a smug satisfied smile twist the older woman's mouth before the pain, the hysteria, the whole terrible enormity of what she had learned overcame her, the room swam, and she collapsed in a dead faint in Francis's arms.

As she went through labour she heard them talking.

'I am very afraid, Mrs Durbin, that Julia is not going to survive.' Selena's voice, cold and hard.

'Of course she will! She's doing well, the lamb. It won't be long...'

'She is not going to survive.' Selena again. What could she mean? Did she intend to kill her, Julia wondered helplessly. Then she heard Selena say: 'That is what you will tell the outside world, Mrs Durbin.'

'But why ... why?'

'The pregnancy has driven her mad, I fear. Not only is she making all manner of wild accusations against Mr Francis, she is also threatening to harm the child. We can't have that. They are to be separated at birth. A wet nurse must be found in the village and Julia will be confined to her room. We cannot allow her to be alone with the child for a moment.'

'But Miss Selena...'

'It's best all round. Mr Francis is in agreement. If you value your position here you will do as you are told. And if you care for Julia, too. Do you understand?'

'Oh, Miss Selena, I don't know! I never heard of such a thing...'

'Well, hear it now. Julia is going to die in childbirth. Francis and I will raise the baby. And you will help us – or find yourself new employers – not easy for the two of you together at your ages and without references...'

Julia tried to protest and could not. The pains were too strong, the birth too imminent.

Half an hour later the child was born – a

little girl who seemed none the worse for arriving in the world more than two weeks before her time, and into such a troubled atmosphere. The moment the cord was cut Selena took her from Mrs Durbin, wrapped her in a length of linen and went with her to the door.

'What was it you and Francis decided to call the baby if it was a girl?' she asked coldly.

'Charlotte,' Julia muttered weakly.

'Charlotte. Well, Julia, take a good look at her, for you won't be seeing her again – unless we are unable to find a wet nurse and you have to feed her yourself for a while. But if you do, be assured I shall be there all the time to ensure you do not harm her.'

'I wouldn't – you know that!' Julia whispered. 'What I said, I said in the heat of the moment! I could never harm my child!'

Selena ignored her as if she had not spoken.

'I am afraid, Julia, that you are very sick. We must treat you accordingly.'

Then, the baby in her arms, she marched from the room.

Francis was a powerful man.

Few people knew that the coffin bearing Julia's name was empty but for a few rocks when it was carried to the family tomb in the churchyard a week later, and those who did were either too loyal or too frightened to breathe a word.

Francis walked behind the cortège, and those villagers who stood, cap in hand, to watch it pass by attributed his ravaged appearance to grief. Not one guessed it had been brought about by his agony at what had to be done.

Selena walked beside him, head held high, and her black veil hid the smile of triumph she could not keep from her lips.

She had won. Julia had gone for ever. Though in fact she was incarcerated in her room, to the outside world – and to Selena – she was as dead as if her remains were indeed within the coffin.

As the parson intoned the words of committal and the damp earth thudded on to the heavy oak lid Selena continued to smile.

She had won, just as she had known she would in the end. Once again Francis was under her control. Once again she was mistress of Morwennan House.

It was all she had ever wanted.

Twenty-Three

When Julia had finished telling me her story I knew I had no choice. I knew now just how deep was the evil by which I was surrounded. And I knew that I had to act. I could not wait any longer for Tom and Joshua. Joshua, bless his heart, was a dreamer, not a man of action. For all his good intentions it might be weeks – months – before he pursued some course of action on my behalf – if ever he did so at all. And Tom ... Tom had been gone for more than a week. Had he been betrayed? Had someone in the gang learned that he was not what he purported to be, but a spy who would prove their undoing? If so, then there was every chance that he would meet the same fate as his brother and end up at the bottom of a mineshaft or thrown from the cliffs into the raging sea below.

The thought was a terrible one; it made me want to cry out with pain and grief and fear for all of us, but I told myself I must not think of that now. I must assume the worst and make plans of my own to rescue Julia and get Charlotte away from the corruption and evil of Morwennan.

I thought and thought and in the end I decided I would go to the one person within reach whom I could trust.

I would go to Jeremiah.

I laid my plans with care. I set about persuading Francis to agree to Charlotte and myself visiting her grandparents again.

This scheme, as I saw it, had two advantages.

Firstly it would get Charlotte away from Morwennan. I imagined that Jem would go straight to the authorities – in his position he had far more contacts than I could ever hope to have – and I did not want Charlotte in the house when it was raided by the military.

Secondly, I could reach Jem much more readily from Penallack. It was that much nearer to Jem than Morwennan, and there was a good chance I could walk it in a few hours if I set myself a brisk pace.

'I think it would be good for Charlotte to visit her cousins,' I said, and to my enormous relief, Francis agreed.

The trip was planned for a few days hence. I found myself still hoping Tom might return before it was time for us to leave, but he did not. I managed to see Julia and explain I had to go away again for a little while and charged Mrs Durbin to take especially good care of her whilst I was away. Then, with a feeling of purposefulness and expectation, I packed my things and Charlotte's and we set off in the gig.

As we breasted the hill, leaving the threatening shadow of the trees behind, I found myself wondering if I would ever set foot in Morwennan House again. Perhaps the military would rescue Julia when they arrested Francis and the next time I saw her would be in quite different circumstances.

As before, the Trevelyans made me exceedingly welcome and I could not help but feel guilty when I thought of how I meant to trick and use them. But desperate situations call for desperate measures.

We spent a pleasant evening playing loo for counters, but when it was time for bed I mentioned that I was feeling very tired and unwell. That was all part of my plan. I did not want to arouse suspicion next day by affecting some sudden illness.

'I do hope I am not getting one of my sick headaches,' I said with an apologetic little laugh. 'I thought I had grown out of them and I certainly hoped so, for when they come upon me they lay me low all day.'

'At least if that happens you will know that Charlotte is being taken care of,' Anne Trevelyan said, playing right into my hands and making me feel more guilty than ever. 'You can stay in your room and rest, my dear.'

I smiled with an effort. 'I hope it won't come to that.'

That night I slept so badly I was truly in danger of getting a headache. As I lay watching the sky gradually lighten I wished I could have been on my way already, but I had decided that the best course for a good start was to wait until daylight, and until I had established with the household that I would have to remain in my room all day. There was more risk of my being seen leaving, of course, but I thought I could manage it if I was careful and chose my time well.

When Charlotte came into my room shortly after eight to see if I was awake, I play-acted in a manner that would not have shamed the troupe of travelling players Tom had taken me to see.

'Oh, Charlotte, I am so sorry,' I moaned, covering my eyes with my kerchief. 'Will you be happy playing with your cousins today without me?'

'I'll be riding Moonlight!' she replied promptly. 'I wouldn't have time to spend with you anyway!' And then, ashamed of her frankness, she asked solicitously: 'Is there anything I can get for you, Charity?'

'Maybe just a posset...'

I needed an adult member of the household to see me, needed to tell them I would prefer not to be disturbed again.

Anne brought me the posset herself, a

measure of her concern for me. I thanked her, asked her to draw the curtains because the light was hurting my eyes, and promised that if I needed anything I would ring the bell, but that it was unlikely I would do anything other than doze fitfully all day. Then, when I was alone again, I got up and dressed myself in a warm gown and boots, arranged the pillows to look like a huddled figure under the blankets in case anyone should look into my room during the day and waited impatiently for my opportunity.

It came when the family were at breakfast. I slipped down the back stairs, out through the deserted kitchen, and, heart beating very fast with the fear of being seen, into the grove of trees at the rear of the house. How I was going to get back in unnoticed I did not know, but I could not worry about that now. With any luck, if Jem acted quickly, the whole nightmare would be over by nightfall. All I had to do now was make my way across country.

The walk took a good deal longer than I had expected. The lanes were rutted and mired deeply for winter; by the time I had covered a few miles my legs were aching, my boots caked with mud, and the hem of my gown filthy. But I hurried on, barely stopping to draw breath.

I had no real idea how long the walk had taken me when I saw the first shacks that marked the outskirts of town. I only knew that my feet, covered in blisters, felt as if they were on fire, and there was an empty protesting hole where my stomach should have been. But I pressed on unrelenting into the town, looking for the buildings where Jem had his office.

A gig was coming towards me along the road, a fine gig drawn by a matched pair of chestnuts and driven by a young man who sat tall and straight in his seat. I stared in utter disbelief, thinking that exhaustion must be causing me to hallucinate. It couldn't be, surely...

But as the gig approached I grew even more certain that I was not mistaken and I saw that the driver was staring at me too, as if he were unable to believe the evidence of his own eyes, and reining the horses to a halt.

'Charity!'

I felt a great wave of gratitude that fate seemed to be favouring me and I ran towards him. I had come in search of Jem, and I had found him with no effort at all.

'Charity – what on earth are you doing here?' he asked, sounding staggered. 'And the state of you! What have you been doing?'

'Oh, Jem!' Weak tears of relief were pricking my eyelids. 'Oh, Jem, I need your help desperately! Oh, please – you *will* help me, won't you?'

He looked with something like distaste at my face, grimy and damp with sweat, and my muddy clothes and boots. Then he shook his head and grinned at me.

'You'd better climb up,' he said.

I told him everything, the words tumbling out one on the other as we sat there side by side in the gig. Occasionally he interrupted me with a question but mostly he sat in silence, letting me talk, his face growing darker with every word I uttered. Then, without a word, he flicked the reins.

'Where are we going?' I asked.

'Firstly, to get you something to eat. If you have had nothing all day, and you've walked all the way from Penallack, you must be famished.'

'Oh, thank you!' I said, thinking how I had misjudged Jem all these years. But then of course he was no longer a rather self-obsessed boy but a man – and a well set-up one, judging by the cut of his clothes, the breeding of his horses and the fine gig he was driving. As Joshua had said, for someone who had started out as a mere clerk, Jem had done very well for himself.

'No need to thank me,' Jem said wryly. 'It's for my benefit too that we should get some food inside you. I don't want you swooning from hunger. I know the landlord of an inn not far from here. He'll provide you with sustenance.'

'I don't want to tarry too long,' I said anxiously. 'Time is of the essence. I could be missed at any moment and the alarm raised.'

'We'll waste no time, never fear,' Jem said grimly. 'I'm as anxious as you to bring this matter to a conclusion.'

I nodded, grateful that at last I had someone strong and resourceful on whose shoulders I could lay all my anxieties. Then I sat back in my seat, watching how skilfully he handled the reins and how the horses leaped to do his bidding. The hedges raced past, the clop of the hooves and the swish of the wheels mesmerised me. I was very tired. After a few minutes I closed my eyes and I think I might even have dozed a little.

The gig jolting to a halt brought me fully awake again. We had pulled on to the forecourt of an inn, a low grey building with a creaking inn sign which read the *Tinners' Arms*. I frowned. We seemed to have come a good way, for there were no other houses or indeed buildings of any kind in sight.

Before I could ask any questions, however, Jem had leaped down from the gig and tossed the reins round a hitching post.

'Wait there. I won't be long.'

I stared at the inn feeling oddly uncomfortable. It was as if, in my doze, I had had a bad dream I could no longer remember, but the aura of it had spilled into wakefulness, imbuing this place with an atmosphere I did not care for.

I did not like it, though I could not say why, except that in its own way it had something of the same air of menace as Morwennan House.

I looked at the small dark windows, at the door so low that Jem had to dip his head to go through it, and at the inn sign creaking mournfully in the cold wind, and I shuddered unaccountably. It did not look like a place of merriment, and indeed, so far from civilisation, I could not imagine who would make up its clientele. But it was on the road, so perhaps the coaches stopped here to change the horses and obtain refreshment for the passengers, though I could see no signs of that either.

With some relief I saw Jem emerge from the doorway with something in his hand. The landlord followed him out – a short, squat man with a greasy apron tied around his muscular frame. I did not like the look of him either. Jem stood talking to him for a few minutes and I felt the landlord's eyes on me. Uncomfortable, I turned away.

Jem returned to the gig and handed me a pasty and a flagon of ale.

'Eat this, Charity.'

Then he unhooked the reins, climbed up into the gig, and clicked the horses. We moved off, and I knew the landlord was watching us go.

'What a strange place,' I said, my mouth full of pasty.

'Yes, but the food is good,' Jem said.

It was – or certainly it tasted so to me, famished as I was. The pastry, though not as light as Mrs Durbin's or Mama Mary's, was fresh enough, and there were good big chunks of meat amongst the potato and swede turnip that filled it right to its thickly crimped edges.

'Is it a coaching inn?' I asked.

'I suppose so,' Jem said non-committally.

I finished my pasty in silence, content to leave things in Jem's hands, and washed it down with some of the ale. I think I might have drowsed a little again, for when I next became fully aware it seemed to me there was something familiar about the landscape, grey and barren as it was in the fading afternoon light.

'Where are we?' I asked, puzzled and a little uneasy.

'Don't you know?' Jem replied.

'But it looks like ... Where are we going, Jem?'

He flicked the reins; the horses raced faster.

'Why, to Morwennan, of course!' he replied.

My heart gave a great frightened leap.

'To Morwennan?' I repeated stupidly.

'Certainly. To Morwennan. From what you tell me there is no time to lose.'

He flicked the reins again; the horses galloped even faster.

'But Jem – we can't go there alone!' I cried in alarm. 'First we need to summon assistance! I thought you would go to the authorities – call in the military! It's far too dangerous for us to go alone! We shall achieve nothing!'

'Oh, stop worrying, Charity! Leave everything to me.' There was a faint smile on Jem's face; I rather thought that he was enjoying this.

I was reminded of the boy who used to lead our expeditions, especially the ones to places where Dr John and Mama Mary had forbidden us to go. But, for some reason I could not explain, the memory was of no comfort to me.

'But Jem – I'll be missed at Penallack!' I said. 'The alarm will be raised. For all I know I've been missed already.'

He cast a quick narrow look at me.

'They know nothing of this at Penallack, do they?'

'Oh no! I'm sure they don't.'

'Then they will just think you have run away,' he said. 'With some young man. This Tom, perhaps.'

'Perhaps so...' I bit on my lip. Charlotte

was going to be so upset. 'But Charlotte knows that Tom is out of the district.'

Jem glanced at me again. Perhaps it was the wind in his face that made his eyes look so narrowed...

'Where is it he's gone, did you say?'

'I don't know. He wouldn't tell me. All I know is that it's to see someone who used to be part of the gang before he fell out with them and became an honest man. Someone who told Tom's brother Roger about the existence of the bell, and its significance.'

'Jud Falconer,' Jem said, almost to himself.

I scarcely heard him. I was too fearful for Tom's safety.

'Oh, Jem, I'm so worried about him! You don't think, do you, that some terrible fate has befallen him, such as happened to his brother? These people are so dangerous. They'll stop at nothing. Life to them is cheap.'

'He knew the risks, no doubt,' Jem said grimly. 'He embarked on his crusade with his eyes wide open.'

'Yes – yes, he did. But if something has happened to him ... Oh Jem, I don't think I could bear it!'

'You know the risks too,' Jem went on. 'Are you telling me, Charity, that you want to change your mind – walk away from all this, go back to Penwyn and forget it ever happened?'

'I couldn't do that!' I cried passionately. 'My mother is a prisoner at Morwennan and the man responsible for my father's death is her gaoler! I couldn't walk away from that, much less forget it!'

'Well then,' he said. 'You will just have to face up to the consequences.'

'I know.' I gnawed on a fingernail, terrified at the thought of what lay ahead, but resolute as ever.

We were very close now to Morwennan. Jem slowed the horses to turn into the steep decline under the trees.

'What are you going to do?' I asked, my voice shaking with nervousness. 'What are you going to say?'

Jem made no reply. He pulled the horses up outside the coach house. For the first time it occurred to me that he had seemed to know the road to Morwennan very well. Not once had he asked me for directions. And stopping here too, at exactly the point where the Morwennan carriages always stopped – it was almost as if he was familiar with it, as if he had been here before...

The door of the house was open; Francis stood there. He must have seen our approach from his study window. His face was like a thundercloud.

'What are you doing here?' he said.

I thought he was speaking to me. Then, with a sense of shock, I realised it was Jem he was addressing.

Jem's hand was beneath my elbow, holding it firmly, propelling me towards the house. 'She knows,' he said, and there was a hard edge to his voice. 'She knows everything.'

Twenty-Four

For a brief horrified moment I simply could not take it in. My mouth dropped open, I glanced at Jem, shocked and confused, and saw for the first time the ruthlessness written all over his handsome face. I tried to speak; no words would come.

'She knows everything,' he said again. 'I thought it best to bring her here so that we can decide how to deal with the situation.

Francis looked at me as if he were disappointed in me. 'Oh, Charity, Charity...' And to Jem he said: 'You had better come inside. You did the right thing, Jeremiah.'

I understood then. My numbed brain grasped what it had been so reluctant to accept. I had not been mistaken when I had thought I had seen him with Francis on the day of the fair. Jem was one of them. I had gone to him for help and run straight into the hands of my enemy.

All the blood seemed to drain from my body; I thought I might swoon. But Jem's hand was beneath my elbow, propelling me into the house, and somehow my legs were still working.

The heavy door slammed shut after us like the door of a prison cell. Francis called out Selena's name; she appeared in the parlour doorway, looking more than ever like a bird of prey with her hooked nose like a powerful beak and her beady eyes sharp on me.

'Charity? Why are you here? I thought you were at Penallack with Charlotte. And Jeremiah too ... What *is* going on?'

'We have a problem,' Francis said. 'Charity knows our secrets.'

'All of them,' Jem said. 'She came to me for assistance. She wanted to go to the authorities, I'm afraid.'

'But Jem had the presence of mind to bring her straight here,' Francis said. 'We have to talk about what's best to do.'

And: 'Let us go into the parlour,' Selena said, for all the world as if she were greeting visitors socially.

We did as she bid. Jem pushed me down on to the chaise and sat himself down beside me, legs comfortably outstretched now that he had relieved himself of responsibility. I inched away from him; I could not bear to touch him, this honorary brother who had betrayed me. Francis took his own comfortable chair. Only Selena remained standing and I realised with a little shock that it was she who was taking charge of the proceedings.

411

'So, Charity,' she said, fixing me with that beady stare. 'What is all this about?'

Terrified though I was, I was determined not to be cowed.

'You know very well!' I said with all the dignity I could muster. 'I know that Julia, my mother, is not dead, but incarcerated in the attic. I found her there and I have been visiting and talking with her. I know too that this house is the headquarters of a gang of smugglers – and worse.' I drew a deep breath. 'Not only smugglers – but wreckers too. The very wreckers who caused the death of my father and all his crew twenty years ago.'

Selena looked at me steadily. 'Julia told you this? She cannot be believed, I'm afraid. She is quite mad.'

'She is not mad!' I flashed. 'She is as sane as you or I – surprisingly so, after her years of solitary confinement! But in any case, she was only confirming what I already knew. I found the bell, you see. In your room. The bell from the *Guinevere*.'

Francis half-rose. 'You fool, Selena! I told you it was a mistake to keep that damned bell! But you wanted to gloat over it, did you not? You wanted it to remind you of your victory over Julia!'

'Oh be quiet!' Selena said, her voice low but so icy it could have cut glass. 'Don't talk to me of mistakes. You were guilty of the biggest one, falling in love with the stupid woman in the first place, marrying her against her will and remaining besotted with her ever since. You should have left her to die on that beach, and Charity too. Then we would have none of this trouble.'

'I know your opinions only too well, Selena,' Francis snapped back. 'If it had been you there that night instead of me you'd have done just that, no doubt. You'd have delighted in making damned sure they died, both of them. Just as you have delighted in planning the wreckings down the years. You have a cruel streak, Selena.'

I was angry suddenly, so angry that momentarily I forgot my fear. And they, for their part, seemed to have momentarily forgotten I was there, accusing one another, quarrelling as they so often did, the deep-rooted resentment, hatred even, that they seemed to bear one another, in spite of that unspeakable bond between them, blinding them to all else. Oh, but their relationship was incestuous in more ways than one – Selena's jealousy of Francis's obsession with Julia, Francis oddly dependent on his sister – it was there, laid bare. And they had no conscience, either of them, no shred of remorse for the lives they had wrecked, the misery they had caused.

And Selena was in this as deep as Francis – deeper, perhaps. The wreckings you have planned down the years, he had said, and I could well believe he was speaking the truth. Selena was the one with the brains here. Selena was the one who dictated, Francis the figurehead for the benefit of the gang, but her lapdog none the less.

'You admit it then,' I said. 'You admit to wrecking.'

But so intent were they upon their quarrel they seemed not to hear me.

'I would have made sure they both died, certainly. I'd have held that damned woman under the water myself until she drowned,' Selena said. Her hands were working in the folds of her gown as if even now she could carry out the evil task. 'As for the child ... how could you bring yourself to save the child she bore by another man? For that's what you did, Francis, is it not? You had to bring your precious Julia home with you, and you couldn't bring yourself to leave her child to die. You arranged for her to be brought up as a foundling, didn't you? And you never had the courage to tell me.'

'It's true I couldn't see Julia's child left to die,' Francis admitted. 'It was weak of me, I dare say. But I could not stand to have to look on the evidence of her infidelity either. I could not contemplate raising another man's child. So ... I did the best I could for her.'

'I knew it!' Selena cried triumphantly. 'I

414

knew the moment I set eyes on Charity that she was the child Julia kept weeping for until she made me sick with her pathetic behaviour. I knew it could be no coincidence.'

'And so you brought her here to torment me,' Francis said heavily. 'You simply could not resist letting me know that you had learned what I did out of compassion all those years ago and taunting me with it. Well, that only goes to prove that I am not the only one who lets my emotions rule my head. If I had left Charity to die that night, none of this would have happened, I grant you. But neither would it have happened if you hadn't brought her here for your own damned amusement.'

I was shaking now, shocked by the revelation that Francis had known all along of my existence, had even, for all I knew, placed me with the Palfreys. Was there some long-standing connection between them? Was that how Jem had come to be involved with Francis and Selena's gang? Surely, oh surely, my own dear Joshua was not mixed up in this too? Was that the reason he had been so slow to assist me? I could hardly believe it, and yet my whole world had shifted around me once more and there was nothing but quicksand beneath my feet.

'Did you know of this?' I asked Jem.

He ignored me, instead addressing Francis and Selena. 'This is getting us nowhere. For the love of God, you two, put your differences to one side and quarrel about them later if you must. We have more important things to worry about just now. Tom Stanton for one.'

'Tom Stanton?' Selena said sharply. 'What about Tom Stanton?'

'You made a mistake with him.' Jem said to Francis. 'He is the brother of Roger Stanton, the riding officer you were forced to dispose of some little while back, and no friend to you, I'm afraid. Even now he is away seeking that old turncoat Jud Falconer with the intention of finding proof to set the law on you – and destroying our most profitable organisation.'

Francis was on his feet. 'The devil he is! Why in God's name did I trust him?'

'Because you are a fool, Francis,' Selena said tartly. 'You are right, Jeremiah, if Tom is abroad trying to put a case together against us there's no time to waste. He must be found – and dealt with without delay.'

'I've already set things in motion,' Jem said. 'I warned the landlord of the *Tinners' Arms* to be on the lookout for him, and he will organise search parties in his district.'

I drew a quick sharp breath. The *Tinners' Arms*, where we had stopped for my pasty! Jem had pretended it was out of concern for me; in fact he had been mustering the troops. I had had a bad feeling about that place – and I had been right. Would that my intuition had warned me about Jem! But then, I conceded, it had – and I had taken no notice. I had wanted someone to trust so badly that I had ignored Tom's advice to confide in no one. Now I had made things a thousand times worse, and placed not only my life in danger, but Tom's too. Even now he was being sought by the evil landlord and his cronies, and when they caught up with him there was little doubt that he would meet the same fate as his brother before him.

'So, the roads to the north are covered,' Selena said. 'We must alert those to the south and west and have the word spread along the chain. Make ready to leave at once, Francis. Tom must be caught before he gets what proof he needs and goes to the authorities with it.'

'I'll take the fastest horse I have.' Francis took a step towards the door, then looked back at Jem. 'Will you come with me, Jeremiah?'

'Better not,' Jem drawled. 'My horses are tired. And besides...' He nodded in my direction.

'Oh yes, what are we going to do about Charity?' Francis asked.

'I'm afraid Charity will have to be dealt with, and I think you are the one who should deal with her, Francis – even if you do it twenty years too late. We'll keep her safe for you, don't worry.' Selena smiled coldly. 'My, you are going to be busy! When you have taken care of Tom, then you can take care of Charity. And Julia too. It's high time she was disposed of – and if you cannot bring yourself to do it, even now, then I will. Charlotte is growing up – she will soon begin asking awkward questions.'

'You are unbelievable!' I cried, but once again they ignored me as if I was no more than a minor inconvenience.

'Off you go now,' Selena instructed Francis, 'and do take care not to disturb Mrs Durbin. I had thought these long afternoon naps of hers were getting to be a nuisance. Today, though, I must say it is quite convenient.'

Francis made a hasty departure and Selena, Jem and I were left alone.

'So, little Charity,' Selena said with a curl of her lip. 'How are we going to ensure you do not make any more mischief until Francis returns?'

'She's a spirited little thing,' Jem said. 'She always was. I very much fear she may try to run away again and raise the alarm.'

'I agree. And after all we have tried to do to make her feel at home here, too!' Selena mocked me. 'Well, there's nothing for it, I'm afraid. You seemed to want to seek out the company of your mother, Charity. Perhaps we should oblige you. I think we should lock you with her in the attic. Just until we can put a more permanent solution into operation, that is.'

'Pity,' Jem said, eyeing me speculatively.

I returned his gaze furiously. 'How could you do this, Jem? How can you be involved with something so terrible?'

He shrugged. 'Perhaps the riches to be made are an inducement.'

'But it's against everything you were brought up to honour!' I cried. 'What would your papa and mama say if they knew?'

'They don't know though, do they?' he returned smoothly. 'And once you have been dealt with there's no danger they ever will.'

'You are wrong there!' I declared. 'I've already taken Joshua into my confidence. If I disappear he is certain to begin asking questions...'

The moment the words were out I could have bitten off my tongue. A steely glimmer came into Jem's eyes.

'Oh dear. You don't mean poor pious Joshua has to be dealt with too!'

'You wouldn't!' I cried, horrified. 'Not your own brother!'

'I'm afraid you know very little about me, Charity,' Jem said amiably. 'I've grown too used to my comfortable lifestyle since I threw in my lot with Francis. I don't think I would let anything – or anyone – rob me of it now.'

419

'How did you come to get involved with them?' I asked before I could stop myself.

'Oh, a lawyer's clerk makes very little real money,' Jem said lightly. 'I was looking to improve my prospects and the Merlyns at Penwyn Hall pointed me in Francis's direction.'

'The Merlyns!' I exclaimed. The very friends Selena had been staying with when she employed me. 'So you knew, even when I came here...'

'That they were smugglers, yes. And I knew Francis was the one who arranged for you to be fostered by my parents. Papa told me one day, though of course neither he nor I knew the reason behind it. He believed Francis had found you on the beach the morning after the wrecking when he was searching for survivors, all in the name of humanity.'

'Jem, you are evil. As evil as they are!' I said spiritedly. 'Be sure your sins will find you out.'

'You sound exactly like Papa,' he said languidly. 'I am growing tired of you berating me, Charity. I think, Selena, that it is time we locked her in the attic where she has no one to castigate but her poor mad mama.'

He pulled me to my feet, twisted my arms behind me and forced me out into the hallway. I fought, kicked and screamed, and the commotion brought Mrs Durbin to the kitchen door.

'Lawks, whatever is going on?' The colour was high in her cheeks, her mouth working.

'Unlock the door, Mrs Durbin,' Selena commanded.

'But...'

'The door! Charity is going to join Miss Julia for a while. And I'll thank you to keep silent about it.'

Mrs Durbin looked flustered and unhappy but she did as she was bid. Too many years of obedience had conditioned her; she would not argue with the woman who was her mistress, whatever her personal feelings.

Jem pushed me into the darkness. The door slammed shut behind me and the key turned in the lock.

'Nancy! Oh, it is so good to see you! I have missed you so much!'

Julia's face lit up when she saw me. I did not know what to say. How could I tell her this was no ordinary visit? That all my efforts to save her from her prison had ended in disaster, with me making things a thousand times worse, and we were both now in mortal danger.

I did not know what to say and I did not know what to do. Indeed, what could I do? I was now as much of a prisoner as she was, at the mercy of the Trevelyans. The best I could hope for was that when Mrs Durbin came to bring us food – if she came! – I could persuade her to help us. If only she would leave the door unlocked, I could try to make my escape and go for help. Perhaps she would even raise the alarm herself. But my hopes were faint indeed. Mrs Durbin, though not a bad woman, was too afraid for her home and the livelihood of herself and her husband to go against Francis and Selena, and I could offer her nothing in the way of inducement.

As for Tom ... I could not see that Tom could come to my rescue either. Jem had put it abroad that he was a threat to the organisation and he would be dealt with the moment he showed his face – if he was not dead already.

My stomach clenched at the thought. I tried to close my mind to it and could not. If Tom were dead then I could scarcely care what happened to me. But I must care – for Julia's sake, and Charlotte's too. Hopeless as it seemed, I must remain strong and resourceful. I must try to find a way out of this nightmare for the three of us.

It was almost dark already in the attic. With trembling hands I lit the lamps and began searching around for something with which I could defend myself and Julia. I would find no weapon, I knew, but there must be something...

My eye fell on the heavy pottery jug on her washstand. Brought crashing down on the back of an unsuspecting head it would cause quite a nasty injury. If I were to hide behind the door I might just be able to pull it off. The trouble was that Francis, Jem and even Selena were all considerably taller than me. If I was to have a chance of braining any one of them I needed to be taller...

I fetched Julia's dressing stool and set it behind the door, then stood the jug beside it.

'What are you doing, Nancy?' Julia asked, puzzled.

I did not answer her directly. Rather, I set the spare easy chair facing hers with its back to the door so that, at first glance, it would not be apparent to anyone entering the room that no one was sitting in it.

'If you hear footsteps on the stairs, Mama, I want you to stay seated in your chair as if you were talking to someone sitting opposite you,' I said.

'But you *will* be...'

'No,' I said. 'I won't be. But I don't want whoever comes in at the door to know that. It's a game,' I added quickly, seeing her puzzled frown. 'Just a game. But if I play it right, I hope to be able to take you away from here once and for all.'

'Oh, Nancy, I don't know...' She looked doubtful.

'Don't worry about it,' I said. 'Just do as I say.'

Of course, it might be Mrs Durbin who

came, I thought. If it were, I would not need to stand on the stool. She was much shorter than I. I did not relish the idea of cracking poor Mrs Durbin's skull, but I would do it all the same. I could not trust her to help me and desperate situations called for desperate measures.

Then, keeping my ears strained for the first sound that would indicate someone was coming, I settled down to wait. How long it would be I did not know. But when someone did come I would be ready.

Perhaps an hour passed before I heard the click of the downstairs door being opened. Instantly I was on my feet.

'Remember – just behave normally,' I whispered to Julia.

The tread on the stairs was heavy – much too heavy for it to be Mrs Durbin. I did not have time to wonder whether I was relieved or not that it was not her. My heart was beating so hard against my ribs that I felt sure it would give me away. I climbed up on to the stool, the jug raised between my hands, tensed and waiting.

The footsteps came closer along the corridor. Suppose they *both* came – Jem *and* Selena – I thought in sudden panic. I had only one missile, only one chance...

A figure came around the door. I just had time to register that it was Selena before I brought the jug crashing down on to her head.

And it worked! It worked better than I had dared to hope. The jug shattered over Selena's crown and she never even saw it – or me. With a little gasp that was almost a moan she folded up like a pack of cards and collapsed in a heap on the floor. Julia gave a little cry and shrank startled into her chair.

'Not a word!' I cautioned her sharply.

I checked on Selena. She was out cold.

'I am going for help,' I said urgently to Julia. 'Wait here. I may be some time.'

As quickly and as quietly as I could, I made my way along the passageway and down the stairs. The door at the foot was ajar. Cautiously I peeped round. There was no one in the hall. I slipped out, scarcely daring to breathe. The key was in the lock; though all my instincts were to make a run for the front door, I took a moment to turn it and push the bunch of keys into my pocket. If Selena should regain consciousness I did not want her raising the alarm. Then and only then did I dash across the hall.

I had almost reached the front door when a thunderous knock at it brought me up short. Oh dear lord, there was someone there! And I had almost run straight into them! Now my escape route was cut off and, worse, the knocking would have alerted Jem.

I hesitated there in the middle of the hall, caught like a rabbit in the light of a poacher's torch. Then the front door burst open.

To my utter amazement I saw Joshua standing there.

Twenty-Five

He was dishevelled. His eyes were wild. He looked as if he had ridden long and hard.

'Joshua!' I gasped.

'Charity! You're safe...'

A movement behind me – Jem emerging from the parlour. I heard it and at the same moment I saw Joshua's face change, relief turning to horror.

To my utter amazement he thrust his hand into his pocket and pulled out a pistol, levelling it at Jem.

'Stay where you are!' he cried in a trembling voice.

'Joshua!' Jem said. He sounded startled but, to his credit, quite in command of himself. 'What on earth are you doing?'

He started across the hall; Joshua's finger closed on the trigger. He was shaking so much I braced myself for it to go off.

'Stay where you are, Jem, or I'll shoot! I mean it!'

Jem stopped short again, raising his hands placatingly.

'Have you gone mad, Joshua?'

Joshua's face was pale above his clerical collar, high spots of colour staining his cherubic cheeks. 'I know all about you, Jem, and what you have been up to since you left home. Thanks to Charity, I've learned the truth.'

'I don't know what you're talking about,' Jem blustered, still trying to placate the brother who faced him with uncharacteristic hatred and determination in his blue eyes.

'Don't play the innocent, Jem,' he said, his voice harder now than I had ever heard it. 'You payroll Francis Trevelyan's smuggling gang, don't you? Your clerical work is just a cover. I could hardly believe it when I first learned of it – my own brother, the very person I had told Charity to go to if she needed assistance – mixed up with these evil people. Well, you won't get away with it.'

'Joshua...' Jem had turned white now; to have gentle God-fearing Joshua waving a gun at him and facing him with his misdeeds must be quite a shock to him, I realised. And it was all because of me.

'I never expected to find you here, though,' Joshua went on. 'I came to warn Charity and take her away from this terrible place before I go to the authorities. And thank God I did! Get out, Charity, whilst I cover you.'

'Joshua – I can't!' I cried. 'Not without my mother!'

'Joshua, can't we talk about this?' Jem

pleaded.

'The time for talking is long past,' Joshua said. 'Fetch your mother, Charity. We'll take her with us.' He waved the gun, indicating the parlour doorway. 'Into that room, Jem, if you please, and don't try to stop us.'

'Very well...' Jem was, I think, on the point of doing as Joshua said, when there was a sudden scream from the kitchen doorway.

'Lawks, whatever...?' It was Mrs Durbin, alerted by the sound of angry voices.

Momentarily distracted, Joshua half turned towards her and Jem took his chance. He lunged at his brother, knocking the gun from his hand and sending it skidding across the floor. Then, next moment, the two brothers were fighting, just as they had all those years ago on the cliff path after Jem had locked me in the fishing hut. Only this time it was no boyish scrap. This time it was in deadly earnest.

All around the hall they went, trading punches, and through the door into the parlour. First one had the upper hand, then the other, but with a sick fear in my stomach I had no doubt who would be the eventual winner. Jem was stronger than Joshua and fitter. He did not lead the sedentary life of a priest – and he was meaner of nature. In the last resort Joshua would be no match for him.

With a small sob I scrambled beneath the

hall table to retrieve Joshua's gun. Never in my life before had I held a firearm in my hands, nor ever wanted to. But now, with determination born of desperation I hooked my finger over the trigger. I would pull it if I had to. My life and Julia's – and now Joshua's too – depended on it.

But for the moment there was nothing I could do. The two men were too close together, their positions changing too fast as first one, then the other, gave and received blows. I couldn't risk a shot. It would be all too easy to hit my beloved Joshua instead of Jem...

A chair overturned with a crash, taking Joshua with it. I screamed as he thudded down, convinced he must be badly hurt, or at least winded, but as Jem closed in, Joshua's legs jackknifed and his booted feet caught Jem full in the stomach. Jem staggered back like a drunken man and I screamed again as he cannoned into the small table that stood between chaise and window. It went over, taking with it the lighted lamp that stood on it.

Joshua was scrambling to his feet now, hurt, but determined to fight on. Jem too was rolling over with the grace of a tiger, ready for him. But suddenly I could see nothing but the flaming oil lamp close – so terribly close! – to the floor-length curtains. I made a dive to try to pull them out of reach of the flames and Jem, quick-witted and dangerous as ever, saw his chance to regain possession of the gun.

He made a grab for me, his fingers closing around my wrist in an iron grip. In total panic I screamed and twisted wildly. And the gun went off.

To my horror I saw the surprised expression on Jem's face, heard the gasping intake of his breath. Then the grip of his fingers on my wrist eased, his knees sagged, and he went down, collapsing almost gracefully to the floor. Blood was spreading scarlet on his waistcoat, trickling on to the Indian rug, bubbling in a fine froth on his lips.

I stood motionless, frozen with shock and the awful dawning realisation of what I had done.

I had killed a man. Not just any man, but one who had been raised as my brother. I drew a quick, shallow breath. To my own ears it sounded like a sob.

But there was no time now for either grief or guilt or even relief. For Jem had prevented me pulling the curtains out of reach of the blazing lamp. They had caught fire and the flames were racing up them in a fierce orange onslaught towards the ceiling. A chair was burning too. In no time at all the room would be an inferno.

Joshua too had realised the danger. He took one long anguished look at his brother, lying there dead at his feet, and grabbed my hand.

'Come on, Charity! We have to get out! The whole house will go up!'

'My mother!' I cried. 'I can't go without my mother!'

'Fetch her then,' Joshua instructed me. 'I'll try to douse the flames, but I fear it is too late...'

A frightened Mrs Durbin was in the doorway.

'Help me!' I cried. 'Help me rescue Julia!'

She stood with her hands pressed to her apple cheeks as if mesmerised by the flames.

'Come on!' I cried again, and rushed to the attic door.

I did not stop to see if she followed me but I rather thought she would not. All this was too much for her.

Selena still lay unconscious. Julia stood beside her, holding her skirts up around her ankles as if they would be contaminated if they so much as brushed against her sister in-law, yet oddly fascinated by the motionless woman at her feet.

'Julia,' I said, trying to sound calm. 'It's time to go.'

Her eyes widened with apprehension. 'Go? Go where?'

'We have to leave this house,' I told her. 'Come with me now.'

'No – oh no, I can't!'

'Yes,' I said urgently. 'Yes, you can.'

'No!' She shrank back, drawing into herself. 'No – I don't want to! I'm frightened!'

'Julia – you must!' I took her arm. I knew the fire must be gaining strength below – already I could smell the smoke and hear the roar of the flames. 'Come on – you'll be with me.'

And still she hung back. I felt the beginnings of panic. There was no way I could force her bodily from the house – frail she might be, but I knew instinctively she would fight me every inch of the way. And by the time I got her to the foot of the stairs it would be too late. Our escape route would be cut off. Julia would die in the house where she had been incarcerated all these years. And I would die with her.

'Please, Julia!' I begged her in desperation. 'Take my hand now.'

'Come along now, Miss Julia. Come along now, my sweeting. There's nothing to be afraid of. You trust me, don't you?'

At the sound of her voice I turned to see Mrs Durbin in the doorway. I had not expected to be able to count on her, but now she came bustling in, talking to Julia as she always did – as if she were a child. To all intents and purposes she was perfectly composed now, though her face was very flushed.

'Come on, my lamb,' she urged. And to my immense relief, Julia responded. She went to the old woman obediently, taking her outstretched hand.

Gently Mrs Durbin led her past Selena's prone form. I saw her mouth tighten a shade as she glanced at her but she said nothing. My hands flew to my throat as a great wave of guilt almost choked me. Selena would almost certainly perish and it would be my fault, just as Jem's death lay at my door. I couldn't simply leave her here – no, no matter what she had done.

I bent over her, taking her by the shoulders and shaking.

'Selena! Can you hear me? Selena!'

She made no move. Could I drag her down the stairs, I wondered? I peeked out of the door – Mrs Durbin and Julia were at the foot now. As they opened the door to the hall a fresh cloud of acrid smoke wafted up. I would try. I had to try...

A hand fastened round my ankle. Selena had regained consciousness and hidden it from me until she saw her chance. I screamed in shock and tried to wriggle free, but she held me fast.

'Let me go! We have to get out! The house is on fire!' I cried.

'Oh no, Charity. You are going nowhere.' Her voice was thick, groggy, but very determined. 'Julia's gone, hasn't she? Well – you

434

can stay in her place.'

'Selena – are you mad? The house is on fire!' I cried again.

She only laughed – the wild, deranged laugh of a woman whose whole life has been a monument to greed and jealousy and hatred.

Then I found a strength I had not known I possessed. Somehow, I managed to kick Selena full in the face. She gasped and cried out – and I was free. Without a backward glance I dashed down the stairs. Joshua was at the foot, looking up and anxiously calling my name. I almost fell into his arms.

'Come, Charity, quickly!'

The hall was full of thick black smoke, already a beam or two had caught light; the parlour was certainly an inferno, and flames billowed from the doorway like a glimpse of the gateway to hell.

'Julia...?' I asked. The smoke was stinging my eyes, burning my throat.

'Mrs Durbin has got her out. Come on.'

We made a dash for the door, coughing and spluttering as we took the fresh air into our lungs. Julia and Mrs Durbin were standing on the path, watching for us anxiously. Julia held out her hands to me and when I could get my breath again I took them. Together, we started up the gully.

Behind us, Morwennan House burned.

★ ★ ★

It was not, of course, over. In many ways it was just beginning.

Joshua took us to Penwyn and I must confess Dr John and Mama Mary were wonderful. I suppose ministering to parishioners all their lives had prepared them for dealing with every eventuality; certainly I saw for myself with the eyes of an observer rather than a member of the family just why they were loved and respected by Dr John's flock.

Julia was confused and frightened – they treated her with tenderness, kindness and consideration. Mrs Durbin had become belligerent and tearful by turns – they appeased and comforted her. I, though I tried to hide it, was in deep shock – they offered me the kind of common-sense, practical support that I had once taken for coldness and now recognised as solid goodness. And all this with their eldest son lying dead and their illusions about him shattered. They were, I think, saintly in their response to what had happened, and the support they provided; I can only think that the God they lived their lives for moved in them in those terrible dark days.

Joshua too was a credit to his calling, though I would have expected nothing less of him. It was he who, together with Dr John, went to the authorities with the whole sorry tale, and then drove to Penallack, where he sought an audience with Squire Trevelyan in order that the news could be broken gently to Charlotte.

I was, of course, worried about her, especially when I learned that Francis had been arrested, though I tried to tell myself that her grandfather and her uncle and aunt would do their very best for her, and that the company of her young cousins would be good for her at this time.

I worried how I would introduce her to Julia, and how she would accept the fact that her mother was not dead at all but alive, and decided it would be best if she were told that Julia had been very ill and it was for her own good that Francis had kept her away from all human company. Not that it was my decision, of course, it was for the Trevelyans to take the lead in the matter. But I felt sure Julia would go along with such an interpretation of events; why, she almost believed it herself.

I worried about Julia, and how I would gradually reintroduce her to the world; I worried about finding a home for us, for we could not impose upon Dr John and Mama Mary for ever.

And most of all I worried about Tom. My anxiety for him never left me, permeated all else, so that even when all the other problems were occupying my mind I was aware of that other, enormous cloud hanging over

437

me. And the worst thing of all was not knowing for certain what had become of him, whether he was alive or dead.

In the end I talked to Joshua about it, even though I knew he would be hurt by my concern for Tom, because I had to talk to someone or go quite mad.

'I think he must be dead,' I said, biting my lips in an effort to hold back the tears. 'Francis is in custody, the smuggling ring has been broken up, there's no reason any more for him to still be off chasing evidence. I think they must have caught up with him and killed him before they were rounded up themselves.'

Joshua considered.

'They were dangerous men, certainly, and Tom pursued them at his peril. But ... would he know where to find you, Charity?'

'It shouldn't be difficult,' I said. 'The Trevelyans know where I am, the authorities know where I am, half Morwennan village must know where I am. I'm sure Tom could find me...' I hesitated and then added softly: 'If he wanted to.'

That, of course, was the other thing that was causing me heartache. If Tom was not dead then he had made no effort to find me. He had been using me all along, and though at least his motives were honourable and not, as I had feared, the result of a falling-out between thieves, yet he had been using me all the same, and discarded me now that he no longer had need of me.

And that, in some ways, hurt even more than thinking Tom was dead. For at least if he were dead I had the illusion of his love to cling to.

Either way he was lost to me and the pain of it was almost more than I could bear.

'Oh, Charity, I don't know what to say to you,' Joshua murmured, looking wretched. 'Only that I will always be here for you...'

'I know you will, dear Joshua,' I replied. 'You risked your life for me and I will never forget that. But...'

'I know.' He smiled slightly. 'I am not Tom.'

'No. Because you are Joshua. My dearest brother,' I told him.

And knew it was no consolation to either of us.

The days dragged by, my hope died, and I tried to lose myself in caring for Julia and helping her to readjust to the world.

One day word came from Penallack. Grandfather Trevelyan had prepared Charlotte; she would like to meet her mother.

Again Joshua rose to the occasion and drove us in the gig to Penallack. How he had managed to get so much time off from his curate's duties at St Agnes, I did not know; I could only suppose he had pleaded extenuating circumstances.

Strangely Julia did not seem in the least

nervous at the prospect of meeting Charlotte; I think I was more nervous than she. And in the event her confidence proved to be justified. Charlotte took to her mother with an innocent acceptance that amazed me; her delight reminded me of a child at Christmas, and the rapport between them was instant and wonderful to see.

It would be far more difficult for me to explain to her that I was her sister, I thought, but for the moment there was no need for that. For the moment I was simply Charity, her governess, who was looking after her mama, and that was as it should be.

When we had all shared a meal I suggested Charlotte should take Julia to the paddock and introduce her to Moonlight.

'Your mama loves horses too, is that not right, Julia?' I said.

'Oh, yes!' Julia's face lit up. 'I had a horse of my own once, long ago. Rascal. I used to ride him at a gallop until we were both exhausted.'

'You *galloped*!' Charlotte exclaimed, clearly impressed, and Joshua and I exchanged a smile.

Out in the paddock, Charlotte showed off by putting Moonlight over the little jumps her grandfather had erected for her and Julia watched proudly.

'We have one or two horses you could ride when you feel fit enough, m'dear,' Samuel

Trevelyan offered. Julia flushed with pleasure, then frowned.

'I'd love to, but it's been so long since I was in the saddle. I'm not sure if I could handle a horse any more.'

'Why, Rapunzel is as gentle as a lamb!' Samuel assured her. 'And in any case, you would get your touch back in no time. It's not something you ever forget.'

Then he stiffened suddenly, looking past us over the expanse of moorland, shading his eyes against the low, bright winter sun.

'Who can this be? I'm not expecting any more visitors today...'

We all turned to look. A horse and rider were approaching at a fast canter. I stared and stared, the first flutter of almost disbelieving hope swelling to equally disbelieving certainty.

It couldn't be. Not here at Penallack. And yet ... It was!

'Tom!' I cried. 'Oh, Tom!'

And began to run towards him.

He was out of the saddle, slipping to the ground, taking me in his arms. Heedless of the others, he held me close, groaning against my ear.

'Charity! You're safe. Thank God!' He put me away then, looking down at me. 'But what are you doing here?'

'What are you?' I countered.

'Looking for you. I hoped the squire might know of your whereabouts and it seems I was right.'

I nodded, reluctant to let go of his hands, yet knowing that for the moment I must.

'Tom,' I said, indicating Julia, 'this is...'

Before I could finish, Charlotte was off Moonlight's back and running over to throw herself eagerly at him.

'Tom! Tom – you'll never guess who this is! This is my mama!'

He explained to me later what had happened – how close he had come to meeting the fate I had feared.

He had sought out the turncoat from the gang, who had confirmed to him that Francis – or rather Selena – was indeed the one who kept the bell of the *Guinevere* to gloat over, though he did not of course know the reason why, and Tom had set out for home.

But as he galloped over the wild and windswept moors he was set upon.

The men who took him were part of the distribution chain, but well down the pecking order. Though one of their number at least had been all for murdering Tom there and then, the others countermanded this. They knew Tom as a close associate of Francis's and thought it more politic to leave it to him to make the decision concerning Tom's fate. They sent word that a traitor had been caught and waited for a reply from Francis.

It was then, whilst Tom was still their prisoner, that events at Morwennan had gathered pace and Francis had been arrested. The men who held Tom scattered in fear of their own freedom and Tom was able to make his escape. He was unsure of the exact facts or circumstances, for he had heard only fragments of his captors' conversation, but he was desperate to get back to Morwennan to ensure I was safe.

He had, however, contracted a fever in the freezing cold and damp of the shanty in which he had been kept. And as he battled along the open moorland roads, exhaustion, sickness and hunger had overtaken him. He had collapsed in a ditch and might have died there had it not been for a passing tinker who took him to his hovel and nursed him back to health.

The moment he was fit enough Tom had set out again – only to find Morwennan House reduced to ash and rubble that still, he said, seemed to smoke when the mist hung over the valley.

He heard in the village that Selena had perished in the fire, along with someone else – and naturally his fears were that it was me, especially when mention was made of a connection with the rector of Penwyn. Yet more versions of the tale had it that the mystery victim was a man. Tom had clung on to the last shreds of hope and visited Francis in gaol in an effort to learn the truth.

'He is a broken man,' Tom told me. 'After all he has done I should not, I know, feel sympathy for him, but strangely enough I do. He was, I think, a victim too, in his own way. A victim of his emotions, and certainly a victim of his sister's power-crazed madness.'

I nodded. I tended to agree.

'He told me Charlotte was with her grandfather,' Tom went on. 'That was when I realised I might find you there too. And he begged me to tell Charlotte how he loves her and that, whatever occurs, they will one day be together again.'

My lips tightened. My hope was that Charlotte would be with her mother. But I could not deny Francis loved Charlotte dearly and had never been anything but a good father to her.

'There is one thing more,' Tom said. 'The bell certainly was at Morwennan.'

'I know,' I said. 'I found it – in Selena's room. But it was destroyed, I suppose, in the fire.'

'A brass bell?' Tom smiled. 'Oh no. Not destroyed. It's a little out of shape, perhaps, but it is still unmistakeably a bell. And inscribed with the name *Guinevere*.'

I stared at him. 'How do you know?'

'Because I found it in the ruins,' Tom said.

'I no longer need it for evidence, of course, but I thought ... I thought perhaps you would like to have it.'

'Me!' I said, surprised, 'Oh, I don't want it! Not after Selena...'

'It was the bell from your father's ship,' Tom pointed out. 'It is perhaps the only thing of his you will ever have.'

It was true. How thoughtful Tom was!

'Yes, I see,' I said. 'Thank you, Tom.'

And hoped that maybe in time I would be able to look at it and not feel the fear I had felt that afternoon when I had first set eyes on it behind the screen in Selena's room, not feel that she had somehow contaminated it with her evil, poring over it.

I must try to put all that had occurred behind me. For Julia's sake, I must make sure that my life was not wasted as hers had been.

And with Tom beside me I felt sure it would not be.

I am an old woman now, and looking back I can truly say my life has been a happy one.

Tom and I were wed, and he took both Julia and me home to Falmouth, where he bought a house for us in Flushing, not so far from the one where Julia and John had been so happy during their short time together. Gradually Julia regained her health and strength and I saw glimpses of the gay and lively girl she had once been.

Charlotte remained with her grandfather, her aunt and uncle and cousins, which is perhaps as it should be, since stability was what she most needed in her young life, and when Francis finished his prison sentence he was able to spend time with her. But she visited us frequently and always looked forward to seeing us. She grew up to be a charming and spirited young lady, and eventually she married well and had a family of her own.

Samuel Trevelyan offered the faithful Durbins a cottage on his estate; they accepted, and lived there in contented retirement to the end of their days; Joshua married a sweet wife, and is the much-loved rector of a prosperous parish on the north coast.

It is a long while now since I went to Morwennan; the last I heard, the house had been rebuilt. However luxurious the new owners have made it, I should not like to live there, for I believe the evil must have been absorbed into the very ground, and certainly the trees still cast a dark shadow over the whole valley.

And the bell of the *Guinevere* holds pride of place in our drawing room. Tom was right – eventually I came to treasure it as the one thing left to me of my father's.

And more than that, it is a symbol that good can come from evil, a reminder of how in the end a seemingly cruel Fate brought happiness and contentment into all our lives.

I am an old woman now. I have seen many changes in my lifetime. But, as long as I live, I will never forget. Morwennan will live with me for ever.

The
Royal
Navy
Handbook

The Definitive MoD Guide

CONWAY MARITIME PRESS

The front cover main image shows HMS *Ocean* with helicopter squadrons embarked.
Frontispiece is a computer-generated image of the Future Aircraft Carrier.

This handbook has been produced by the Defence Procurement Agency, an Executive Agency of the Ministry of Defence, in conjunction with the Directorate of Corporate Communications (Royal Navy).

Whilst every care has been taken in the compilation of this publication to ensure its accuracy, the editor, his team and the publisher cannot accept any responsibility for loss occasioned by any person acting or refraining from action as a result of use of any material in this publication. The Views expressed are not necessarily those of the MOD. In carrying advertising the MOD is not endorsing the products or services offered. Neither is it responsible for the delivery of the service in question.

Editorial enquiries to: DPA Press Office,
Maple 1c 2120 MoD Abbey Wood Bristol BS34 8JH
tel 0117 9130636/0385 email: DPASecPO@dpa.mod.uk and DPASecPO2@dpa.mod.uk

Advertising enquiries to: McMillan-Scott plc 10 Savoy Street London WC2E 7HR
tel 020 7878 2316

© Crown copyright, 2003.

Published in 2003 by Conway Maritime Press,
a division of Chrysalis Books plc
The Chrysalis Building
Bramley Road
London W10 6SP
www.conwaymaritime.com

ISBN 0-85177-952-2

Design and layout by Steve Dent

Printed by Pensord Press, Tram Road, Pontllanfraith, Blackwood, Gwent, NP12 2YA

Contents

A naval task group centred on HMS *Illustrious*

The Royal Navy Handbook

by the Secretary of State for Defence the Rt Hon Geoffrey Hoon MP

This book is a new departure for the Ministry of Defence and builds on the very wide range of information that we already publish about the status and operations of the Armed Forces.

It focuses in particular on the order of battle of the Royal Navy and the large and comprehensive current and future equipment programme that supports the fighting fleet, much of it at the leading edge of existing technology. This book is a new way of providing this information, in greater detail than before.

I have referred to the Royal Navy, but in the current military environment of joint operations, both Army and Royal Air Force aircraft fly from Royal Navy ships. Other RAF aircraft, such as our highly effective Nimrods, fly from shore bases but are key to anti-submarine and maritime patrol operations.

This book reflects that ever-increasing interoperability between the Armed Forces.

It also gives a wealth of detail on the MoD's future naval construction programme, which is the largest for many years. Classes of aircraft carriers, large destroyers, nuclear-powered attack submarines, assault landing ships and support vessels are already in the programme. Further ahead we are considering plans for additional types of new and advanced warships and future support at sea to the fighting fleet.

The main armament of our new aircraft carriers will be provided by a Short Take Off and Vertical Landing (STOVL) variant of the US F35 combat aircraft. This means our Armed Forces can continue to build on their knowledge and experience, built up over decades, of the immense versatility and unique combat capabilities that STOVL aircraft bring to military operations.

Defence is constantly changing and the appalling events of 11 September 2001 made it clear we needed to look afresh at the ways we deal with international terrorism and other unconventional threats.

The outcome is a 'New Chapter' to our 1998 Strategic Defence Review, and a clear strategy for the UK to react to future conflict quickly and make better use of intelligence and information that is the key to our success.

The men and women who serve in the Royal Navy now and in the future – and the civilian workforces that support them – will be continuing traditions stretching back over 800 years. The pages of this book show that the Royal Navy remains one of the most powerful in the world. Under plans laid in the Strategic Defence Review its military power will increase to make it even more effective as it carries out its many duties supporting the interests of Britain and her allies worldwide.

Geoffrey Hoon

May 2003

by Admiral Sir Alan West KCB DSC ADC
1st Sea Lord and Chief of Naval Staff

The Royal Navy is as busy and relevant today as at any time in its long history. All around the world, every day of the year, our ships, aircraft and people are hard at work, defending the UK's interests and acting as a force for good.

In these days of cheap and easy air travel, it is easy to forget that our country is an island nation. It relies on international trade for much of its wealth, and over 90 percent by volume of that trade is still transported by sea.

The ocean is our national frontier and our shipping route to the world, including our Commonwealth partners and UK Overseas Territories. Furthermore, the great majority of the world's countries have a coastline and two thirds of all people live within 100 miles of the sea.

Therefore, a strong and versatile navy is an important asset for a country like the UK with global trade and territorial interests, and a significant player on the international geopolitical scene through such organisations as the United Nations, European Union and NATO.

Remembering that the High Seas give universal right of access and start at only 12 miles from land, a capable navy can exert worldwide influence without running the diplomatic gauntlet of host nation support. As a consequence of the 1998 Strategic Defence Review the UK armed forces have been progressively changed from their entrenched Cold War state to their current form.

For the Royal Navy, this has meant an increased emphasis on flexibility of assets and rapid deployability. Amphibious capability in particular has been modernised and enhanced markedly, reflecting the growing requirement to conduct operations close to shore rather than open-ocean fleet actions.

This shift of emphasis has magnified the value of 'jointery' as land, sea and air forces are likely to be operating in close proximity and with shared objectives.

The structure of today's Royal Navy is one of four fighting arms: surface ships, submarines, naval air and the Royal Marines. The whole is a unique combination of land, sea and air capabilities merged into a single, flexible force.

It is equally comfortable operating alone, in joint operations with the Army and RAF, or in multinational forces with NATO allies or *ad hoc* coalition partners.

This inter-operability places great emphasis on command and control, the ability to communicate and co-ordinate. Successful joint operations depend on the continuous rapid transfer of enormous amounts of data, so mutual compatibility of equipment across service and national boundaries is of vital importance. As it stands today, the Royal Navy has about 130 ships and about 300 aircraft.

Commitment to modernisation is manifest in the biggest military shipbuilding programme in Europe, including Type 45 destroyers, Albion class amphibious assault ships, Astute class nuclear submarines and Wave class tankers.

The replacement aircraft carrier project moves on apace, in tandem with the develop-

ment of the Joint Strike Fighter, due in service in 2012.

Trained manpower numbers 37,000 with an enviable reputation for resilience and adaptability, and training which sets the standards for the world.

The fleet operates from three naval bases, two air stations, six Royal Marines bases and a number of training and headquarters establishments.

In addition, the Royal Naval and Royal Marines Reserves provide a vital bank of trained manpower for operations and exercises, as well as small specialist cadres in such fields as media relations.

In parallel with recent material changes, the organisation of the fleet has been completely revised in the last year.

The 'Fleet First' organisation has rationalised the management of the fleet, stripping out redundant management layers and moving the majority of command and support staff from London to Portsmouth.

At the same time the 'Topmast' project has radically overhauled the way that the fleet's manpower is organised, making better and more efficient use of people whilst allowing them greater opportunities to develop their careers and more effectively addressing their domestic and family needs.

Women are fully integrated into all branches of the Royal Navy except for the Submarine Service and the Royal Marines, where there are compelling and fully justified reasons to remain all-male.

On any day of the year, the Royal Navy will typically be involved in some or all of the following tasks:

- conflict and peacekeeping – as in the Gulf, Afghanistan and Sierra Leone;
- UN sanctions enforcement – as in the Arabian Gulf;
- humanitarian relief – as in Caribbean hurricanes and Mozambique;
- anti-drugs patrols in the Caribbean and elsewhere;
- hydrographic surveys and production of Admiralty charts;
- patrolling our fishing grounds and oilfields;
- helping the community – as in the Foot-and-Mouth crisis.

In addition to everything else, every day of the year the Royal Navy provides the nation's continuous nuclear deterrent with Vanguard class submarines and their Trident missiles. Most of all, the Royal Navy has the diversity and balance of forces to react to almost any crisis around the world, as in the Gulf. In these volatile times, it is almost impossible to predict where the next crisis will erupt, so forces are constantly at high readiness to swing into action and demonstrate time and time again that…

…the team works.

Admiral Sir Alan West KCB DSC ADC
1st Sea Lord and Chief of Naval Staff

A computer-generated image of a Type 45 Destroyer – six ships of a planned class of up to 12 are already on order

The Royal Navy Handbook

Technical information in this book is presented wherever possible in metric, rather than Imperial figures, except for the speed and range of ships and aircraft, for which knots and nautical miles continue to be used internationally.

All Royal Navy vessels have been designed using metric measurements for nearly 30 years and metric is the standard form of measurement used throughout British industry and the MoD.

Measurements are all taken at the maximum dimensions. Thus, length quoted in technical information is given as length overall, beam is maximum beam and draught is maximum draught.

Displacement of warships and auxiliaries is given only at maximum deep load according to the most recent information, or a class average of this figure, since this represents the true displacement of a ship.

The displacement of submarines is given at maximum deep load when dived. Displacements of Marine Services vessels are given in Gross Registered Tonnage.

Machinery power output is usually given in megawatts rather than the earlier measurements, which included brake and shaft horsepower.

The calibre of weapons and their range is again given using metric measurements. For example, the 4.5in Mk8 gun is given as 114mm.

In some cases, particularly with older equipment, power outputs have been given using Imperial figures, but these cases are the exception.

This book has drawn heavily on the resources of many in the Ministry of Defence, principally the integrated project teams across the Defence Procurement Agency (DPA) and the Defence Logistics Organisation (DLO) that are procuring new equipment or supporting it in service. Significant help has also come from Directorate Capability Resources and Scrutiny in the MoD Central Equipment Capability organisation and, of course, Directorate Corporate Communications (Navy), led by Cdre Tony Rix RN and the Royal Navy. ■

Ralph Dunn
Editor
Head of Media Relations
Defence Procurement Agency

Web links

This handbook represents the present and future planned order of battle of the Royal Navy, and elements of its sister services, the Army and the Royal Air Force, that have a direct contribution to maritime combat, in May 2003.

The latest news covering decisions and developments on major equipment programmes and on MoD policy issues can always be found on the MoD website at **www.mod.uk**, on the RN website at **www.royalnavy.mod.uk**, at the DPA web site at **www.dpa.mod.uk** or at the DLO website which forms part of the main MoD website and can be found under **www.mod.uk/dlo**.

STRATEGIC FORCES

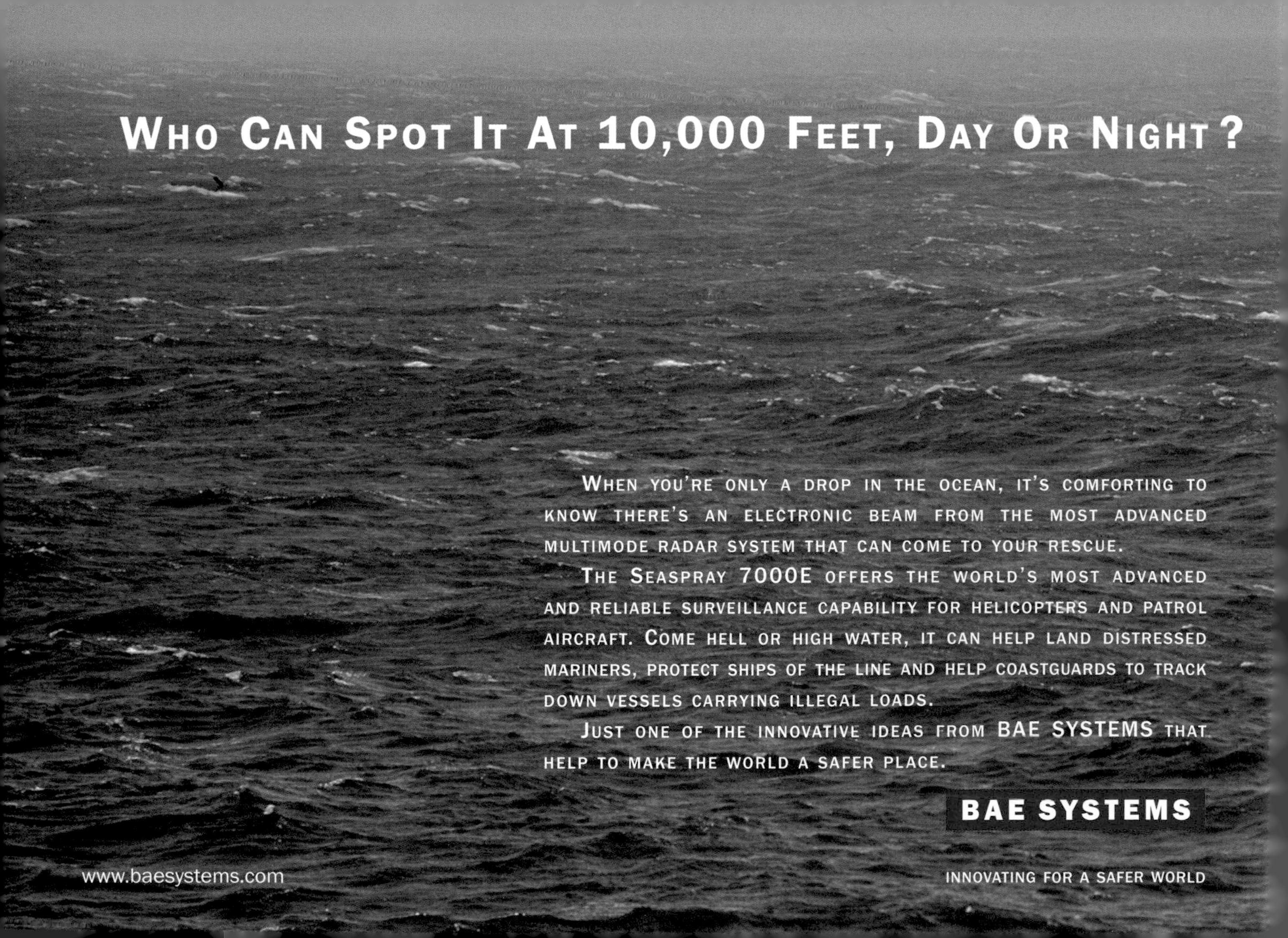
WHO CAN SPOT IT AT 10,000 FEET, DAY OR NIGHT?
WHEN YOU'RE ONLY A DROP IN THE OCEAN, IT'S COMFORTING TO KNOW THERE'S AN ELECTRONIC BEAM FROM THE MOST ADVANCED MULTIMODE RADAR SYSTEM THAT CAN COME TO YOUR RESCUE.
THE SEASPRAY 7000E OFFERS THE WORLD'S MOST ADVANCED AND RELIABLE SURVEILLANCE CAPABILITY FOR HELICOPTERS AND PATROL AIRCRAFT. COME HELL OR HIGH WATER, IT CAN HELP LAND DISTRESSED MARINERS, PROTECT SHIPS OF THE LINE AND HELP COASTGUARDS TO TRACK DOWN VESSELS CARRYING ILLEGAL LOADS.
JUST ONE OF THE INNOVATIVE IDEAS FROM BAE SYSTEMS THAT HELP TO MAKE THE WORLD A SAFER PLACE.
BAE SYSTEMS
www.baesystems.com
INNOVATING FOR A SAFER WORLD

Strategic Forces

The Royal Navy has been responsible for the UK's strategic deterrent since 1967, when HMS *Resolution*, the first of four nuclear-powered Polaris missile submarines, went to sea.

Up to then, the deterrent had been provided by the RAF's V-bomber force, equipped with free-fall nuclear bombs.

Resolution class submarines provided the UK nuclear deterrent with long range accurately targeted missiles carried by less vulnerable submarines. Nuclear power gave these submarines the ability to conduct dived deterrent patrols lasting for several months.

The submarine's effectively unlimited endurance and the long range of the missiles ensured that these boats could be positioned anywhere within vast areas of ocean and still be able to strike rapidly at targets should war have occurred.

These boats, then the largest submarines built in the UK and operated by the RN, served into the 1990s, providing unbroken deterrent patrols for more than 25 years.

Their Polaris missile system was upgraded during the 1980s under Project Chevaline in order to maintain its effectiveness against predicted countermeasures by the then Warsaw Pact.

A new UK-designed space flight vehicle was built and equipped with two warheads and a range of very advanced and still classified UK-developed decoy systems.

Resolution class boats were succeeded in service from 1994 by the even larger Vanguard class submarines, equipped with Trident II D5 missiles.

These boats, displacing nearly 16,000 tonnes when dived, are the largest submarines operated by any nation other than the USA and Russia. Their construction and entry into service was carried out on schedule and at below original costings throughout the programme. However, the entry into service of this class coincided with the end of the Cold War, the collapse of the Warsaw Pact and the break up of the former USSR.

The 1998 Strategic Defence Review set out a new operating regime for these submarines, which reflected the new strategic environment under which the Vanguard class would operate at reduced readiness states and would routinely be at several days' notice to fire, rather than the few minutes required in the Cold War.

Fewer than 200 operationally available nuclear warheads are now maintained for the 58 missiles used by the boats, and while continuous deterrence at sea is maintained, only one boat will ever be on deterrent patrol at any one time.

Submarines on patrol now carry a maximum of 48 warheads, half the previous figure and the same number of warheads carried by HMS *Resolution* when she entered service. The D5 missiles are de-targeted, which means they are not aimed at any country in peacetime. The

A Trident II D5 missile in flight

necessary targeting information would quickly be added if required in a crisis.

Trident submarines on patrol also now carry out a variety of secondary tasks, without compromising their security. These include hydrographic data collection, equipment trials, and exercises with other vessels.

While the primary role of the Vanguard class remains that of nuclear deterrence, they are equipped with a comprehensive range of sensors, decoys and a powerful torpedo armament for use in self-defence. ■

Strategic Missile Submarines (SSBN) Vanguard class

Dimensions
Length: 149.9m
Beam: 12.8m
Draught: 12m
Tonnes (dived): 15,980

Machinery
1 PWR2; steam turbines;
Shafts: 1
Speed: 20 knots +
Range: unlimited

Complement: 135
(single crew)

Weapons systems
Missile launchers:
16 Trident II D5
Weapons tubes: 4 x 533mm
Weapons:
Spearfish torpedoes
Decoys: SCAD
Command: SMCS

Sensors
Masts: Optronics masts and
others for radar and ESM
Sonars: Integrated S2054
bow and towed arrays
Comms: Satcoms,
HF and data links

These are the largest submarines in service in any navy except those of the USA and Russian Federation and are approaching twice the size of the vessels they replaced in services, the Resolution class.

Their construction and commissioning remained exactly on schedule throughout a long and complex programme involving industries on both sides of the Atlantic.

In order to maintain a high level of availability each boat is allocated two full crews, known as Port and Starboard. Initial construction plans for this class were for smaller submarines carrying the earlier Trident C4 weapon, but in the early 1980s the decision was taken to install the then-new D5 variant to maintain commonality with the US Navy. This necessitated a much larger submarine which in turn has allowed for greatly improved accommodation spaces on board.

The Vanguard class was the first to be equipped with the more powerful Pressurised Water Reactor 2 (PWR2), which succeeded PWR1, used in previous UK-designed nuclear submarines.

HMS *Vanguard* will be the first submarine to be fitted with the new Core H, which will provide enough fuel for the rest of the submarine's life, ending costly refuellings.

The rest of the class will receive Core H on refit in the newly constructed D154 refuelling and defuelling facility at Devonport. The new core is being installed in HMS *Vanguard* during a long overhaul period (scheduled refuel) which started in the D154 facility in 2002. ■

	No	Builder	Laid Down	Launched	ISD
Vanguard	S28	Vickers SEL	1986	1992	1993
Victorious	S29	Vickers SEL	1987	1993	1995
Vigilant	S30	Vickers SEL	1991	1995	1996
Vengeance	S31	Vickers SEL	1993	1998	2000

See also:
◪ **Strategic Forces**   **page 15**
◪ **Faslane Naval Base**   **page 194**
◪ **Devonport Naval Base**   **page 196**

Vanguard class
Port profile

HMS *Vanguard*

COMBAT FORCES

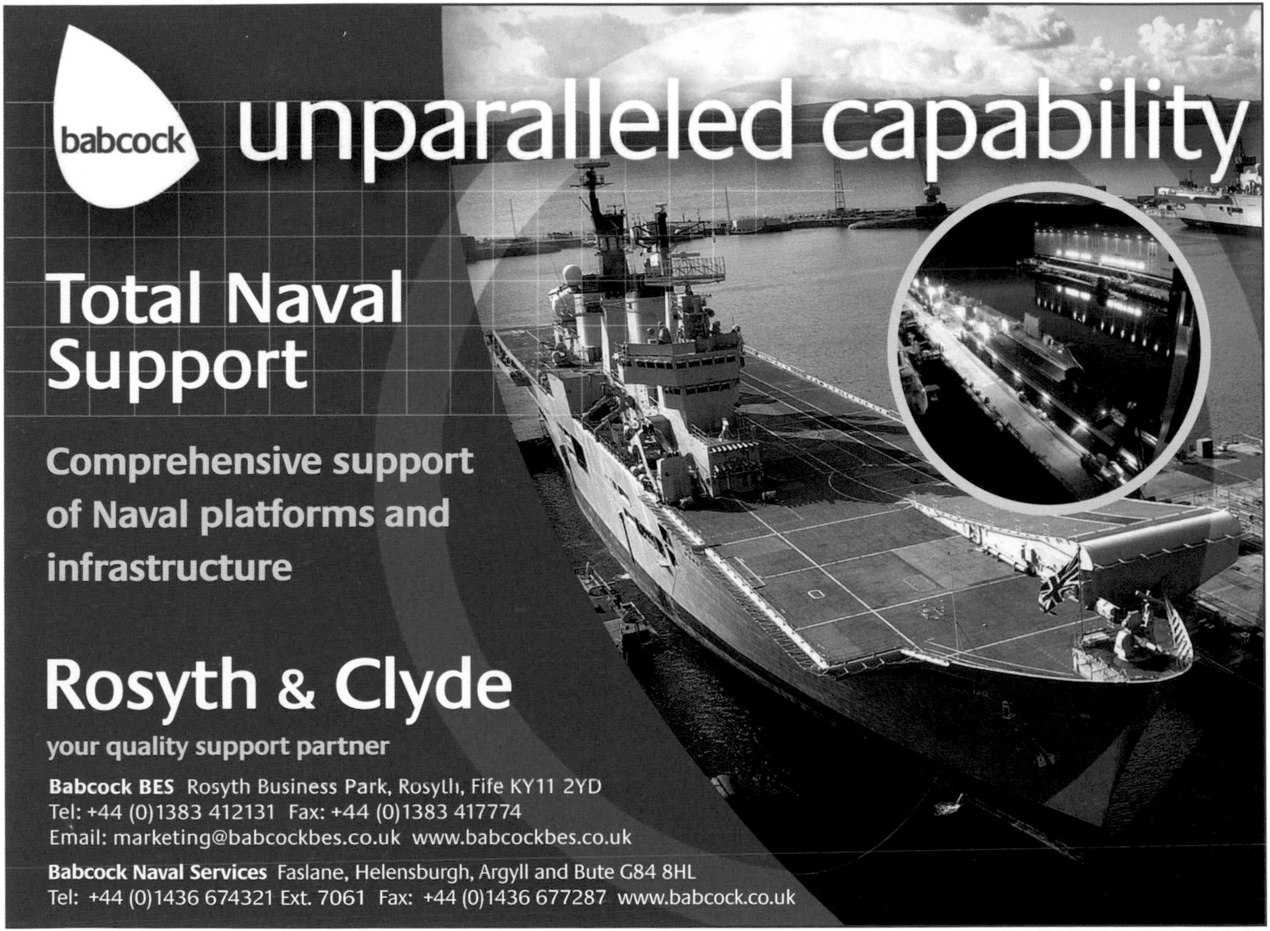
babcock
unparalleled capability
Total Naval Support
Comprehensive support of Naval platforms and infrastructure
Rosyth & Clyde
your quality support partner
Babcock BES Rosyth Business Park, Rosyth, Fife KY11 2YD
Tel: +44 (0)1383 412131 Fax: +44 (0)1383 417774
Email: marketing@babcockbes.co.uk www.babcockbes.co.uk
Babcock Naval Services Faslane, Helensburgh, Argyll and Bute G84 8HL
Tel: +44 (0)1436 674321 Ext. 7061 Fax: +44 (0)1436 677287 www.babcock.co.uk

Combat Forces

This section focuses on the quintessentially nautical fighting arms of the Royal Navy: surface ships, submarines – and aircraft. It also focuses on rapid deployment forces and the Royal Marines Commandos – which have achieved much greater prominence since the 1998 Strategic Defence Review – and the large and powerful contribution made to maritime warfare by Royal Air Force and Army air power.

Today's fleet is constituted with flexibility and rapid deployability in mind. The fleet numbers around 130 ships and submarines, of which around 80 may be termed general purpose combat forces.

Exact numbers are hard to define, since the current active shipbuilding and disposal programmes alter them almost weekly. In manpower terms, this is the biggest section of the Navy, with well over half of the total 37,000 personnel being employed in association with surface ships. The submarine service accounts for around 8,000 personnel. A restructuring of the way manpower is allocated to ships means that personnel are drafted to a specific flotilla for significant periods, contributing to the stability of their domestic lives.

The Fleet was re-organised in 2002 into three flotillas, one based at each of the three naval bases at Portsmouth, Devonport and Faslane.

Aircraft carriers are the largest ships in the fleet. Their innate versatility, powerful command facilities, their embarked carrier air

HMS *Ark Royal* transits the Suez Canal on deployment to the Gulf in 2003

groups which provide them with their main armament, and their power projection role make them the key to modern expeditionary operations. With air groups tailored to the job in hand, they can deploy rapidly around the world to the locality of crises, operating their aircraft with no requirement for airfields and infrastructure ashore.

Destroyers and frigates are, as always, the workhorses of the fleet, the former being optimised for air defence and the latter for surface and subsurface warfare. They are equally at home in large task groups or on independent operations which may include sanctions enforcement, humanitarian relief or anti-drug patrols.

Attack submarines are an essential part of UK naval force. Their stealth and speed allows them to arrive early and undetected in theatre, where they are excellent intelligence gatherers. In combat, they are sophisticated and deadly hunters of enemy ships and submarines, and the recent introduction of the submarine-launched Tomahawk Land Attack Missile has given submariners another significant string to their bow.

With its long range and precise accuracy, Tomahawk is able to hit a target while causing minimal collateral damage. It is fast becoming the weapon of choice in the early stages of an operation.

Smaller fighting ships include our world-leading mine countermeasures (MCM) ships. Sophisticated and cheap mines are readily available the world over, and the neutralisation of their threat is a skilled and painstaking business. The threat from mines is likely to appear early and remain long after actual hostilities have ended, so MCM forces are often among the first in and last out.

Offshore patrol vessels play an important role in home waters by enforcing fishery laws and providing a presence in UK oil and gas fields, to protect these valuable natural resources. ■

Future Aircraft Carrier (CVF)

	No	Builder	Laid Down	Launched	ISD
Unnamed	R	....	....	....	2012
Unnamed	R	....	....	....	2015

Dimensions
Length: up to 290m
Beam: up to 75m
Draught: up to 10m +
Tonnes: around 60,000

Machinery
Integrated full electric propulsion using gas turbines and/or diesels; Electric motors.
Speed: 25 knots +
Range: about 10,000 nautical miles

Complement: to be decided

Weapons systems
Self defence: to be decided
Aircraft: Up to 48: typically a mix of F35 (STOVL), Merlin & MASC

Aircraft weapons
A wide range of advanced missiles and precision guided bombs

● Dimensions based on current MoD planning assumptions, to be finalised.

The 1998 Strategic Defence Review (SDR) concluded that the Invincible class aircraft carriers, which were designed for Cold War anti-submarine operations, needed to be succeeded by a new generation of aircraft carriers.

SDR endorsed a programme to build two significantly larger aircraft carriers, with the first to be delivered in 2012 and the second in 2015.

This programme is now well under way. The main role for the two new carriers will be to deploy air power in support of joint operations and to be able to exert influence during a crisis independent of access to air bases on land.

Defence Procurement Minister Lord Bach announced in late 2002 that this class would be designed to a new adaptable concept so that the ships would have the maximum flexibility to meet the UK's defence needs throughout their service lives of up to 50 years.

They are to operate the STOVL variant of the Lockheed Martin F35 – the same version that the US Marine Corps will operate – in the strike and air defence roles. They will also be able to operate Merlin anti-submarine helicopters, and aircraft procured under the associated Maritime Airborne Surveillance and Control project, which will provide airborne radar cover for the carriers and ships in company.

However, they will also be capable of modification to operate further generations of aircraft, whether or not these are STOVL aircraft. Lord Bach said: "This adaptable carrier will essentially be fitted for, but not with, catapults and arrester gear and given

A Future Aircraft Carrier overflown by an F35

Port side view of the CVF design selected by the MoD

a ramp for STOVL operations.

"This option is expected to support aircraft performance comparable to operation from a STOVL-specific carrier design.

"We think it represents an innovative and sensible way to secure the best return from our investment in the carriers and as such represents good long term value for money.

"They will operate STOVL F35 aircraft, but it is highly desirable that they could be modified to fly a further generation of aircraft, even beyond the F35, whether or not these are STOVL. That is why we have decided that they will be built to an innovative and adaptable plan."   >>

Future Aircraft Carrier (CVF)

Other benefits of the larger conventional design selected by the MoD include the potential for F35 combat aircraft to make 'rolling' landings, rather than landing vertically. This means the aircraft could land at heavier all-up weights, conferring significant operational flexibility.

When announcing the decision on the design of the new ships and the selection of STOVL aircraft to fly from them, the Minister stressed that the

The larger design will allow F35 aircraft to make rolling landings

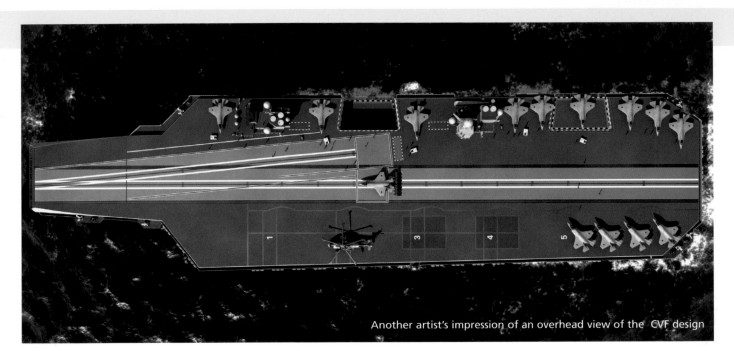
Another artist's impression of an overhead view of the CVF design

CVF programme was of the highest importance to the Government. These two carriers will, on current MoD planning assumptions, be the largest warships built in Britain or anywhere outside the USA and Russia.

The ships themselves are expected to remain in service for much longer than the F35 aircraft – hence the adoption of the adaptable design. Total cost of the two ships is expected to be no more than about £2.8 billion. They will be designed and built in Britain.

A Defence Procurement Agency project team has, since SDR, taken the programme through an initial assessment phase, to a second assessment phase involving rival teams led by BAE Systems and Thales Naval UK.

In 2003 the MoD announced that the carriers would be designed and built by an alliance between the MoD and industry, bringing together the UK's best design capability and project management expertise. Subject to final negotiations, BAE Systems will be the preferred prime contractor, with Thales UK performing a major role as key supplier. The project will develop the carrier design put forward by Thales UK. Orders for the ships are due to be placed in 2004. ∎

Aircraft Carriers (CVS)

	No	Builder	Laid Down	Launched	ISD
Invincible	R05	Vickers SEL	1973	1977	1980
Illustrious	R06	Swan Hunter	1976	1978	1982
Ark Royal	R07	Swan Hunter	1978	1981	1985

Dimensions
Length: 209.1m
Beam: 33.5m
Draught: 7m
Tonnes: 22,000

Machinery
COGAG; 2 shafts
Gas turbines x 4:   72mw
Speed: 28 knots
Generators: 12mw

Complement:
Ship: 685 + 386 aircrew
Military lift:
                up to 600 troops
Command: ADAWS 20
Comms: SCOT, HF, Inmarsat,
                       datalink

Weapons systems
Guns: 2 x 20mm
CIWS: 3 x Goalkeeper or
                       Phalanx
Decoys: 8 x Seagnat
Aircraft:
            up to 24 FA2, GR7,
  Merlin, Sea King ASAC 7

Aircraft weapons
            AMRAAM & AIM9L
  SRAAM, LGB & Sting Ray

Sensors
Radar: 1 x 1022 search,
  1 x 996 search, 1 x 1008
          nav, 2 x 1007 nav
ESM: UAT
Sonar: 2016/2050

These are the largest warships ordered for the Royal Navy since the Second World War and the last aircraft carriers to be designed by the MoD. The role that these ships fulfil has evolved almost out of recognition over the past 20 years. They were originally designed to carry large numbers of anti-submarine helicopters and to be protected from air attack by the Sea Dart GWS30 weapons system.

GWS30 has now been removed and the flight deck plating carried forward over the formerly open foc'sle, increasing the area available for parking aircraft on deck. The former Sea Dart missile magazine has also been reconstructed to support RAF Harrier GR7 strike aircraft. Air defence is provided by Sea Harrier FA2s and fleet air defence destroyers.

HMS *Ark Royal*, the last ship of the class, incorporated many improvements on build and the other two have been progressively uprated over the years during major overhauls. All three ships now have 12 degree angled ski-ramps to allow greater operational payloads to be flown off.

These versatile ships now deploy regularly with RAF GR7s aboard, as part of a mixed air group that can be tailored to operational needs. Air groups include Sea Harrier FA2s, Harrier GR7s, Sea King ASAC7 and additional ASW Sea Kings or Merlins.

Force command systems have been extensively upgraded and further upgrades continue with refit periods for HMS *Invincible* in 2002 and HMS *Illustrious* in 2004. HMS *Illustrious* served in the Landing Platform Helicopter role in 2002 in support of operations in Afghanistan and HMS *Ark Royal* served in this role in the Gulf in 2003. All are based in Portsmouth. ■

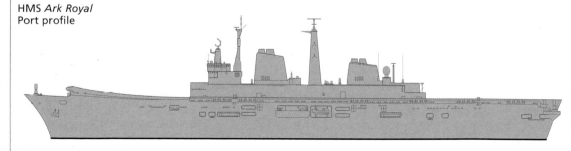

HMS *Ark Royal*
Port profile

HMS *Ark Royal*

Dimensions
Length: 97m
Beam: 11.27m
Tonnes (dived): 7,800

Machinery
1 PWR2; steam turbines
Shafts: 1
Speed: 25 knots +
Range: unlimited

Complement: 98
Military lift: Special Forces

Command: ACMS

Weapons systems
Weapons tubes: 6 x 533mm
Weapons:
Spearfish torpedo
Tomahawk cruise missiles

Sensors
Masts: Non-hull
penetrating array with
optronics and ESM
Sonars: Integrated S2076
bow, flank &
towed arrays
Comms: Satcoms, HF and
data link

This class of advanced attack submarines was developed from the preceding Trafalgar class and was designed for considerably reduced through-life cost, combined with greatly increased military capabilities.

The Astute class will receive the newly-designed reactor Core H on build, which will provide enough fuel for the submarine's full 25-year service life – ending the need for costly and complex reactor refuellings.

The boats are the largest attack submarines ordered for the Royal Navy and, with six weapons tubes and greatly increased weapons stowage, carry much more firepower than earlier classes. They will be equipped with the Tomahawk cruise missiles and the Spearfish heavyweight torpedo.

Improved technology means crew numbers have been further reduced to 84 with accommodation available for 98. For the first time in an attack boat, all crew members will have their own bunks.

A range of non-hull penetrating masts replace traditional periscopes. Targets are viewed through optronic arrays via video monitors, with imagery recorded for analysis, reducing the time masts have to be raised above water.

	No	Builder	Laid Down	Launched	ISD
Astute	S20	BAE Systems	2001	....	2008
Ambush	S21	BAE Systems	....	....	....
Artful	S22	BAE Systems	....	....	....

The first three of the class are under construction at the BAE Systems shipyard at Barrow-in-Furness. Delays in the construction of these submarines means the final delivery schedules of the second and third boats remain subject to confirmation. Ministers have stated that up to three further boats of the class may be ordered, but no decision has yet been taken.

This class will be based at Faslane, alongside new training facilities. ■

An image of an Astute class nuclear attack submarine, dived

A computer generated graphic of HMS *Astute*

Dimensions
Length:	85.4m
Beam:	9.8m
Draught:	9.5m
Tonnes (dived):	5,200

Machinery
1 PWR1; steam turbines
Shafts:	1
Speed:	20 knots +
Range:	unlimited
Complement:	130
Military lift:	Special Forces
Command:	SMCS

Weapons systems
Weapons tubes: 5 x 533mm
Weapons:
Spearfish torpedoes;
Tomahawk cruise missiles
Sub-Harpoon
Decoy: SCAD

Sensors
Masts:	Masts carrying advanced optronics, ESM & radar
Sonars:	2020/2074 2046 towed (2076 upgrade boats)
Comms:	Satcoms, HF

The design of the Trafalgar class was an outgrowth of that of the preceding Swiftsure class, with a slightly lengthened hull and changed internal layout

The seven-boat class introduced into service a new range of powerful sonars. HMS *Trafalgar* was trials submarine for the potent and advanced Spearfish torpedo.

These submarines are equipped with the PWR1 reactor which needs refuelling on average twice during a submarine's service life, giving these boats unparalleled freedom to operate worldwide.

During major refits and reactor refuellings the opportunity is being taken to upgrade equipment on these boats to include the sophisticated SMCS command system, the Spearfish torpedo, the Tomahawk cruise missile and improved sonars.

Submarines of this class have deployed operationally with Tomahawk missiles. Their weapons systems mean they are equally capable of dealing with hostile surface ships or submarines. They can also undertake covert surveillance tasks.

Under the Swiftsure and Trafalgar Class Final Phase Update the four newest boats of the class will be equipped with the integrated Sonar 2076 suite and brought, in terms of equipment, to the initial build standard of the successor Astute class.

Early boats of this class will be succeeded in service by the Astute class. All are based at Devonport. ∎

	No	Builder	Laid Down	Launched	ISD
Trafalgar	S107	Vickers SEL	1979	1981	1983
Turbulent	S87	Vickers SEL	1980	1982	1984
Tireless	S88	Vickers SEL	1981	1984	1985
Torbay	S90	Vickers SEL	1982	1985	1987
Trenchant	S91	Vickers SEL	1984	1986	1989
Talent	S92	Vickers SEL	1986	1988	1990
Triumph	S93	Vickers SEL	1987	1991	1991

See also:
▨ **Swiftsure class**   **page 32**
▨ **Trafalgar class update**   **page 180**

Trafalgar class submarine
Port profile

HMS *Turbulent*

Dimensions
Length:	82.9m
Beam:	9.8m
Draught:	8.5m
Tonnes (dived):	4,900

Machinery
1 PWR1; steam turbines
Shafts:	1
Speed:	20 knots +
Range:	unlimited
Complement:	116
Military lift:	Special forces
Command:	DCB/DCG or SMCS

Weapons systems
Weapons tubes: 5 x 533mm
Weapons:
Spearfish torpedoes
Tomahawk cruise missiles
Sub-Harpoon
Decoys: SCAD

Sensors
Masts:	Optronics, radars and ESM
ESM:	UAP
Sonars:	2074, 2072 2046 towed
Comms:	Satcoms, HF and data links

The Swiftsure class was the third class of nuclear-powered attack submarine to serve in the Royal Navy, following HMS *Dreadnought* and the five-boat Valiant class.

HMS *Swiftsure*, the name ship of the class, taken out of service in 1992, introduced a new hull design with improved hydrodynamic characteristics, improved internal layout and a range of new sonars. These boats are equipped with PWR1 reactor which needs periodic refuelling. This is now done with the advanced Core Z.

Regular equipment upgrades have maintained and enhanced the effectiveness of these submarines. Updates have included sonars, quieting measures, and in some of the class the new Submarine Command System (SMCS).

Weapon system updates to this class have included Sub-Harpoon anti-ship missiles, Tomahawk cruise missiles and Spearfish torpedoes, in succession to the Tigerfish torpedo.

HMS *Splendid* was trials submarine for Tomahawk and was quickly deployed after completion of successful test firings off the USA to take part in missile strikes during the allied campaign to liberate Kosovo in 1999.

These submarines normally operate a cycle of three months to six months duration submerged patrols broken by a port visit.

All of the class are based at Faslane. They will be succeeded in service by the early boats of the Astute class, now in build at Barrow-in-Furness. ■

	No	Builder	Laid Down	Launched	ISD
Sovereign	S108	Vickers SEL	1970	1973	1974
Superb	S109	Vickers SEL	1973	1974	1976
Sceptre	S104	Vickers SEL	1973	1976	1978
Spartan	S105	Vickers SEL	1976	1978	1979
Splendid	S106	Vickers SEL	1977	1979	1981

See also:

▨ **Spearfish**	**page 178**
▨ **Swiftsure class update**	**page 180**
▨ **HMNB Faslane**	**page 194**

Swiftsure class submarine
Port profile

HMS *Superb* off Gibraltar

Type 45 Destroyers (DDG)

	No	Builder	Laid Down	Launched	ISD
Daring	D32	BAE Systems	2003	2005	2007
Dauntless	D33	BAE Systems	2004	2006	2009
Diamond	D34	BAE Systems	2004	2007	2009
Dragon	D35	BAE Systems	2005	2007	2010
Defender	D36	BAE Systems	2006	2008	2010
Duncan	D37	BAE Systems	2006	2008	2011

Dimensions
Length:	152.4m
Beam:	21.2m
Draught:	5.0m
Tonnes:	7,350

Machinery:
Integrated electric
WR21 turb x 2:	40mw
Electric mtrs x 2:	40mw
Generators:	2 x 2mw
Shafts:	2
Speed:	29 knots
Range @ 18kts:	7,000nm

Complement: 187 (max 235)
Military lift: up to 60 troops

Command: CMS 26 stations

Weapons systems
Missiles:	48 x Aster 15/30
Guns:	114mm Mk8 Mod1
	2 x 30mm
CIWS:	2 x Phalanx 1b
Decoys:	4 x Seagnat
Aircraft:	1 Merlin or Lynx

Aircraft weapons
Missiles:	Sea Skua
Torpedoes:	Sting Ray

Sensors
Radar:	Sampson MFR
	S1850 LRR
	Navigation set
ESM:	To be decided
Sonar:	MFS 7000
Comms:	Sat, HF, Datalink

These ships are the largest and most powerful destroyers ever ordered for the Royal Navy and the largest general purpose surface warships – excluding carriers and amphibious ships – ordered since the Second World War. Up to 12 ships are planned and they are designed around the sophisticated and powerful joint UK/French/Italian Principal Anti-Air Missile System (PAAMS).

This system will set new standards for UK air defence when it enters service on HMS *Daring* in 2007. Key to PAAMS is the Sampson Multi-Function Radar, which tracks targets and directs missiles towards them. It is backed up by the S1850 Long Range Radar used for area search out to 400km. Other key elements are the 26 workstation Combat Management System, where operators will control engagements, the Sylver missile launcher silo and Aster 15 short range and Aster 30 long range missiles. PAAMS will defend the Type 45 and ships in company from salvo attacks by the most sophisticated anti-ship missiles from any direction and at supersonic speeds.

The design uses advanced stealth techniques to cut radar reflectivity. The ships will also have a powerful general purpose capability and can carry up to 60 Royal Marines Commandos and their equipment. They also have a large margin to accommodate the installation of new equipment during their 25-year service lives, if it is required. Space and weight has been reserved for anti-ship missiles and either cruise missiles or a 155mm gun. ∎

Type 45 Destroyer
Starboard profile

T45

Type 45 Destroyer

Type 42 Destroyers (DDG)

Batch 1 & 2

Dimensions
Length:	124.6m
Beam:	14.3m
Draught:	4.8m
Tonnes:	4,820

Machinery
COGOG gas turbines
Cruise x 2:	8mw
Max speed x 2:	36mw
Shafts:	2
Speed:	30 knots
Generators:	4 x 1mw

Complement: 287 (max 312)
Military lift: up to 10
Command: ADAWS 12/20

Weapons systems
Missiles:	Sea Dart
Guns:	1 x 114mm
	2 x 20mm
CIWS:	2 x Phalanx
Decoy systems:	Seagnat
Helicopters:	1 x Lynx Mk3/8
Air weapons:	
	Sting Ray torpedo
	Sea Skua ASM

Sensors
Radar:	1 x 1022 search
	1 x 996 search
	2 x 909i
	1 x 1007&1008 nav
ESM:	UAA2 or UAT
Sonar:	2016/2050
Comms:	SCOT1c, HF,
	datalinks, Inmarsat

This class of destroyers was designed around the powerful GWS30 Sea Dart weapons system to provide the fleet with medium range air defence.

The radars, Action Data Automation Weapons System (ADAWS) and the missile in these ships have all undergone significant modernisation to maintain their effectiveness. Early ships completed with the Type 996 search radar and the Type 992 target indicator radar. Batch 2 vessels were equipped with the current Type 1022 search radar.

The missile, which can range beyond 80km, is accelerated to Mach 2 by a rocket booster and is then sustained in flight by a liquid-fuelled ramjet.

Of the first batch of six ships two,

	No	Builder	Laid Down	Launched	ISD
Cardiff	D108	Vickers SEL	1972	1974	1979
Newcastle	D87	Swan Hunter	1973	1975	1978
Glasgow	D88	Swan Hunter	1974	1976	1979
Exeter	D89	Swan Hunter	1976	1978	1980
Southampton	D90	Vosper Thornycroft	1976	1979	1981
Nottingham	D91	Vosper Thornycroft	1978	1980	1983
Liverpool	D92	Cammell Laird	1978	1980	1982

HMS *Sheffield* and HMS *Coventry*, were lost in the 1982 Falklands conflict and one, HMS *Birmingham*, was taken out of service in 1999.

The first two batches share the same hull design and are listed together here. These ships will be the first to be succeeded in service from 2007 by the Type 45. They were the first UK class of all-gas-turbine warships.

This class succeeded the lone Type 82 Sea Dart-armed destroyer HMS *Bristol*. ∎

See also:
▨ **Type 45**	**page 34**
▨ **Type 42 Batch 3**	**page 38**
▨ **Lynx Mk3/8**	**page 62**

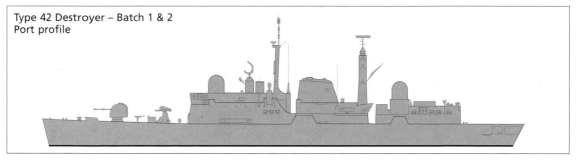

Type 42 Destroyer – Batch 1 & 2
Port profile

HMS *Liverpool* on close escort duty with HMS *Ocean* in the Gulf during operations in Iraq in 2003

Type 42 Destroyers (DDG)

Batch 3

	No	Builder	Laid Down	Launched	ISD
Manchester	D95	Vickers SEL	1979	1980	1982
Gloucester	D96	Vosper Thornycroft	1979	1982	1985
Edinburgh	D97	Cammell Laird	1980	1983	1985
York	D98	Swan Hunter	1980	1982	1985

Dimensions
Length:	141m
Beam:	15.2m
Draught:	4.5m
Tonnes:	5,200

Machinery
COGOG gas turbines
Cruise x 2:	8mw
Max speed x 2:	36mw
Shafts:	2
Speed:	30 knots
Generators:	4 x 1mw

Complement: 287 (max 312)
Military lift: up to 10 troops
Command: ADAWS 20

Weapons systems
Missiles:	Sea Dart
Guns:	1 x 114mm
	2 x 20mm
CIWS:	2 x Phalanx
Decoy systems:	Seagnat
Helicopters:	1 x Lynx Mk3/8
Air weapons:	
	Sting Ray
	Sea Skua

Sensors
Radar:	1 x 1022 search
	1 x 996 search
	2 x 909i
	1 x 1007&1008 nav
ESM:	UAT
Sonar:	2016/2050
Comms:	SCOT1c, HF, data-link, Inmarsat

This final batch of the Type 42 was considerably lengthened and the beam increased to give improved sea-keeping and accommodation and create a margin for the addition of new equipment.

Their main armament, as with the earlier ships of the type, is the powerful GWS30 Sea Dart weapons system and, with their sister ships, they provide the fleet and ships in company with medium range air defence.

Most recently Sea Dart proved its potency when HMS *Gloucester* shot down an anti-ship missile in the 1991 Gulf War. GWS30 is composed of air search and target identifying radars, the ADAWS combat management suite, two Type 909 target illuminating radars, a twin arm missile launcher fed from a below-decks magazine and the Mach 2+ Sea Dart missile itself. The radars, ADAWS and the missile have all undergone significant modernisation to maintain their effectiveness.

Structural improvements include a strengthening beam fitted at main deck level to the outside of the hull of these four ships to maintain hull stiffness in a seaway.

Initial completion of the batch was delayed to incorporate new damage control arrangements and weapons, including the Phalanx CIWS, after the Falklands conflict.

These ships are planned to be succeeded in service by the new Type 45 destroyers, with the last of this batch due out of service around the middle of the next decade. ■

See also:
▪ **Type 45**	**page 34**
▪ **Type 42 Batch 1 & 2**	**page 38**
▪ **Lynx Mk3/8**	**page 62**
▪ **Sea Dart Mod 3**	**page 170**
▪ **Sting Ray Mod 1**	**page 178**

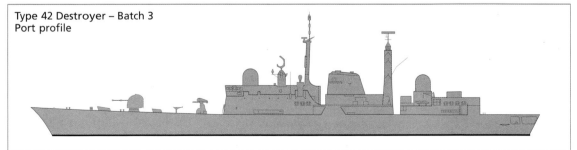

Type 42 Destroyer – Batch 3
Port profile

HMS *Edinburgh* in the Gulf during operations in 2003

Future Surface Combatant (FSC)

The Future Surface Combatant (FSC) is planned as a class of up to 20 ships that will succeed Type 22 and Type 23 frigates when they start to leave service at the end of their lives around the middle of the next decade. Studies into the ship and its capabilities are under way at the Defence Procurement Agency (DPA).

FSC has developed from early sets of studies into a successor class to the Type 23 frigates. At that stage the project was named Future Escort and was biased towards anti-submarine warfare. The 1998 Strategic Defence Review and the changed strategic environment it reflected led to a major recasting of the military requirements underlying the project.

The bias towards anti-submarine operations reflected in the Future Escort project was replaced with a requirement for a wide capability against surface, air and underwater threats when operating alone or in company with other ships.

The MoD's statement of need for the class said: "FSC will deliver fighting power from the sea worldwide, countering the diverse and less predictable threats of the future through adaptable responses within a network-enabled environment. It will contribute to the protection of the UK homeland and deployed forces by providing specialist capabilities in maritime interdiction and force protection, and will support land operations through littoral manoeuvre and precision attack. As a single class or wider contribution of agile maritime platforms, operating either alone or as part of a Task Group, the FSC will provide an enduring contribution to national and multinational joint operations."

MoD's outline requirements cover the ability to defend a maritime force against surface and submarine attack and influence the land battle by attacking enemy troop formations. FSC will also be able to deliver on shore and re-embark land forces used for early-entry operations.

Conceptual studies cover a large monohull frigate, a possible variant of the Type 45 destroyer design, a combination of larger and smaller vessels and other variations, including use of a trimaran hull form. The emphasis will be on versatility through the life of the ships, the ability to undertake multiple roles and the space and weight to easily accommodate new systems and equipment. ∎

An early DPA image of a trimaran-hulled concept of FSC

An early DPA image of how a mono-hulled Future Surface Combatant could look

Type 23 Frigates (FFG)

Dimensions
Length:	133m
Beam:	16.1m
Draught:	5m
Tonnes:	4,900

Machinery
CODLAG,
Gas turbines x 2:	25mw
Generators x 4:	5.2mw
Electric motors x 2:	3mw
Shafts:	2
Speed:	28 knots

Complement:	185

Command:	DNA1
Comms:	SCOT1c, HF & data link

Weapons systems
Missiles:	32 x Sea Wolf
	8 x Harpoon
Guns:	1 x 114mm
	2 x 30mm
Decoys:	4 x Sea Gnat
	Outfit DLF3
Torpedoes:	4 x tubes for Sting Ray
Aircraft:	1 x Lynx or Merlin
Air weapons:	Sting Ray
	Sea Skua

Sensors
Radars:	1 x 996 search
	2 x 911
	1 x 1007 & 1008 navigation
ESM:	UAT
Sonar:	2050
	2031Z in first ten

The Type 23 is the largest class of frigate constructed for the Royal Navy since the 26 ships of the Leander class.

Like the Leanders, the Type 23 Duke class provides the backbone of the Royal Navy's anti-submarine frigate force, and will do so for many years to come.

They were designed to carry out anti-submarine operations in the rough waters of the north Atlantic, using their towed array sonar to locate targets.

The Type 23 frigates were the first 'stealthy' ships to enter service in the Royal Navy, with superstructure and hull angled off the vertical to reduce radar reflectivity.

The ships are also equipped with a new Combined Diesel Electric And Gas (CODLAG) propulsion system that allows them to cruise slowly and extremely quietly, using electric motors, while hunting submarines.

After the Falklands conflict, Harpoon anti-ship missiles and a 114mm gun were added to the design to give the class a powerful suite of weapons that fits them for wide service as general purpose frigates .

With the end of the Cold War the frigates have progressively taken on new worldwide roles in more temperate waters. For the future an extensive series of equipment upgrade is in prospect for these ships. Most noticeably they are to exchange their 114mm Mk8 guns for the Mod 1 version, which has a new multi-faceted turret to reduce radar reflectivity.

The ships are also to receive modifications to their Sea Wolf GWS26 system, which will include new production missiles and updated guidance systems, to maintain system >>

	No	Builder	Laid Down	Launched	ISD
Norfolk	F230	Yarrow Shipbuilders	1985	1987	1990
Marlborough	F233	Swan Hunter	1987	1989	1991
Lancaster	F229	Yarrow Shipbuilders	1987	1990	1992
Argyll	F231	Yarrow Shipbuilders	1987	1989	1991
Iron Duke	F234	Yarrow Shipbuilders	1988	1991	1993
Monmouth	F235	Yarrow Shipbuilders	1989	1991	1993
Montrose	F236	Yarrow Shipbuilders	1989	1992	1994
Westminster	F237	Swan Hunter	1991	1992	1994
Northumberland	F238	Swan Hunter	1991	1992	1994
Richmond	F239	Swan Hunter	1992	1993	1995
Somerset	F82	Yarrow Shipbuilders	1992	1994	1996
Grafton	F80	Yarrow Shipbuilders	1993	1994	1997
Sutherland	F81	Yarrow Shipbuilders	1993	1996	1997
Kent	F78	Yarrow Shipbuilders	1997	1998	2000
Portland	F79	Yarrow Shipbuilders	1997	1999	2001
St Albans	F83	Yarrow Shipbuilders	1999	2000	2002

Type 23 Frigate HMS *Marlborough*

Type 23 Frigates (FFG)

An aerial view of HMS *Lancaster*

effectiveness.

They are also to receive the new and powerful towed Sonar 2087, which will be fitted into the space vacated by the existing towed Sonar 2031Z, which equips the first ten ships of the class.

Sonar 2087 will equip the ships to find the much quieter modern submarines that may operate in inshore waters in the future.

Further studies are in hand into ways of extending the life of these large and capable vessels and further enhancing their military capabilities.

See also:

▧ **Merlin**   **page 60**
▧ **Lynx Mk3/8**   **page 62**
▧ **Sea Wolf**   **page 170**
▧ **Sonar 2087**   **page 176**
▧ **Sting Ray Mod 1**   **page 178**

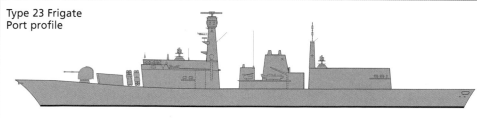

Type 23 Frigate
Port profile

HMS *Portland*

Type 22 Frigates (FFG)

Dimensions
Length:	148.1m
Beam:	14.8m
Draught:	5.5m
Tonnes:	5,300

Machinery
COGAG gas turbines,
2 shafts

Cruise x 2:	8mw
Max speed x 2:	25mw
Speed:	30 knots
Generators:	4 x 1mw

Complement:

Ship:	250 (max 301)
Command:	CACS5

Weapons systems
Missiles:	Sea Wolf
	8 x Harpoon
Guns:	1 x 114mm
	2 x 20mm
CIWS:	1 x Goalkeeper
Decoy systems:	4 x Seagnat
Helicopters:	
	Lynx or Sea King
Air weapons:	Sting Ray
	Sea Skua

Sensors
Radar:	1 x 967/8 search
	1 x 1007 nav
	2 x 911
ESM:	UAT
Sonar:	2050
Comms:	SCOT1c & HF

	No	Builder	Laid Down	Launched	ISD
Cornwall	F99	Yarrow Shipbuilders	1983	1985	1988
Cumberland	F85	Yarrow Shipbuilders	1984	1986	1989
Campbeltown	F86	Cammell Laird	1985	1987	1989
Chatham	F87	Swan Hunter	1986	1988	1990

These four ships were the third and final batch of the highly successful Type 22 Broadsword class frigates.

The first four ships of the Type 22 were built with a shorter hull. The following six were given a much longer hull to accommodate towed array sonar and other new equipment.

The four final ships, all taking 'C' class names, were ordered to replace frigates and destroyers lost in the 1982 Falklands conflict. They were a developed version of the six Batch 2 Type 22 frigates, complete with a range of upgraded and new equipment.

Most obvious is the addition of a 114mm gun on the foredeck and the addition of a Goalkeeper CIWS and eight Harpoon anti-ship missiles behind the bridge.

These ships were also equipped with the new fuel-efficient Spey engine, which gives improved range. When completed they were the best equipped and armed frigates to serve in the Royal Navy for many years.

Significant upgrades are planned to maintain their effectiveness. They will receive updated Sea Wolf missiles and guidance radars but will retain the existing hand-loaded six-barrelled launchers fore and aft, served from ready-use magazines behind the launchers, replenished from magazines deep in the ship. They are also to be equipped with the updated 114mm Mk8 Mod1 shore bombardment gun. All have command facilities and are based at Devonport. ■

See also:
⊿ **Sea King Mk5**	**page 70**
⊿ **Sea Wolf**	**page 170**
⊿ **Devonport**	**page 196**

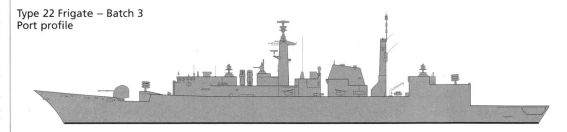

Type 22 Frigate – Batch 3
Port profile

HMS *Chatham*

Mine Countermeasures Vessels (MCMV) Hunt class

Dimensions
Length:	60m
Beam:	10.5m
Draught:	2.2m
Tonnes:	750

Machinery
Diesels x 3:	1.5mw
Generators x 3:	0.6mw
Shafts:	2
Speed:	15 knots
Bow thruster:	1

Weapons systems
Guns:	1 x 30mm
Decoy systems:	Oufit DLK

Mine warfare systems
Two PAP 104/5 remote controlled submersibles and towed sweeps, plus mine clearance divers

Sensors
Radar:	1 x 1007
ESM:	UAR
Sonar:	193M

Command
CMS:	CAAIS

Complement:
Ship:	45

These large mine countermeasures vessels can both hunt mines, using their advanced sonar, and sweep them using influence sweeps.

They were the first class of ships in the world to be constructed of fibre reinforced plastic, to reduce vulnerability to magnetic influence mines.

Two of the class, *Bicester* and *Berkeley*, were sold to Greece after being declared surplus following the Strategic Defence Review.

Ships of this class will receive the new minehunting sonar 2193 on refit and a new Nautis M command system.

This very advanced system will be able to detect and classify mines that can evade detection by current systems. It is able to see a bowling ball-sized target out to 1,000m. ■

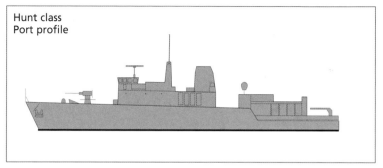

Hunt class
Port profile

HMS *Quorn*

	No	Builder	Launched	ISD
Brecon	M29	Vosper Thornycroft	1978	1980
Ledbury	M30	Vosper Thornycroft	1979	1981
Cattistock	M31	Vosper Thornycroft	1981	1982
Cottesmore	M32	Yarrow Shipbuilders	1982	1983
Brocklesby	M33	Vosper Thornycroft	1982	1982
Middleton	M34	Vosper Thornycroft	1983	1984
Dulverton	M35	Vosper Thornycroft	1982	1983
Chiddingfold	M37	Vosper Thornycroft	1983	1984
Atherstone	M38	Vosper Thornycroft	1986	1986
Hurworth	M39	Vosper Thornycroft	1984	1985
Quorn	M41	Vosper Thornycroft	1988	1989

HMS *Quorn*

Dimensions
Length:	52.5m
Beam:	10.9m
Draught:	2.3m
Tonnes:	600

Machinery
Diesels x 3:	1mw
Generators x 3:	0.75mw
Shafts:	2
Speed:	13 knots
Bow thruster:	2

Weapons systems
Guns:	1 x 30mm
Decoy systems:	Oufit DLK

Mine warfare systems
Two PAP 104/5 remote controlled submersibles and towed sweeps, plus mine clearance divers

Sensors
Radar:	1 x 1007
ESM:	UAR
Sonar:	2093 VDS

Command
CMS:	Nautis M

Complement:
Ship:	34 (max 40)

This class was originally named the Single Role Mine Hunter and was planned to complement the capabilities of the preceding Hunt class and to be cheaper to build.

One ship was ordered in 1984, four more in 1987 and the final seven in 1994.

One of the class, HMS *Cromer*, was declared surplus as part of the Strategic Defence Review and is now used as a training ship for Britannia Royal Naval College, Dartmouth.

These highly manoeuvrable vessels are considered among the best mine-hunters in the world.

They have been deployed overseas on exercises and in support of operations, most recently in the Gulf.

Three ships of this type were sold to the Royal Saudi Arabian Navy. ∎

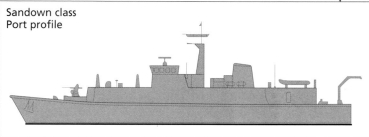

Sandown class
Port profile

	No	Builder	Launched	ISD
Sandown	M101	Vosper Thornycroft	1988	1989
Inverness	M102	Vosper Thornycroft	1990	1991
Cromer	M103	Vosper Thornycroft	1990	1992
Walney	M104	Vosper Thornycroft	1991	1992
Bridport	M105	Vosper Thornycroft	1992	1993
Penzance	M106	Vosper Thornycroft	1997	1998
Pembroke	M107	Vosper Thornycroft	1997	1998
Grimsby	M108	Vosper Thornycroft	1998	1999
Bangor	M109	Vosper Thornycroft	1999	1999
Ramsey	M110	Vosper Thornycroft	1999	2000
Blyth	M111	Vosper Thornycroft	2000	2001
Shoreham	M112	Vosper Thornycroft	2001	2001

HMS *Sandown*

Offshore Patrol Vessels (OPV) River class

Dimensions
Length:	79.5m
Beam:	13.6m
Draught:	3.8m
Tonnes:	1,677

Machinery
Diesels x 2:	4mw
Shafts:	1
Speed:	16.5 knots
Range @ 12kts:	7,800nm

Weapons systems
Guns:	1 x 20mm

Sensors
Navigation radar

Complement:
Ship:	30 (plus RM boarding party)
Boats:	2 x Pacific 22

This class, known under the project name of Future Offshore Patrol Vessel (FOPV) and now as the River class, is being procured under a novel leasing arrangement from the shipbuilder.

The ships, which are larger and more effective than the Island class vessels they will replace, are being leased for five years, pending decisions on the future requirements for Offshore Patrol Vessels.

Each of the vessels is expected to spend twice as many days at sea than Island class vessels. so the three new ships will be able to carry out the same tasks as the five Island class. The Royal Navy will draw each ship's company of 30 from a pool of about 45 personnel. This method of personnel rotation is already in use on the survey vessel HMS *Scott*.

The class will all be in service by 2004. ■

	No	Builder	Laid Down	Launched	ISD
Tyne	P281	Vosper Thornycroft	2001	2002	2003
Severn	P282	Vosper Thornycroft	2002	2002	2003
Mersey	P283	Vosper Thornycroft	2002	2002	2004

HMS *Tyne* running trials

Offshore Patrol Vessels (OPV) Island class

	No	Builder	ISD
Anglesey	P277	Hall Russell Aberdeen	1979
Guernsey	P297	Hall Russell Aberdeen	1977
Lindisfarne	P300	Hall Russell Aberdeen	1978

This class of ships was ordered in the mid 1970s to form part of the Royal Navy's Fishery Protection Squadron.

Originally the Island class was composed of seven ships, of which four have been sold abroad.

The armament and equipment have been updated during their service lives, most recently by the substitution of the original 40mm Bofors gun by a modern 20mm cannon.

These vessels are now supported by Vosper Thornycroft UK under a contractor logistic support plan

All of the class will be taken out of service as the new River class ships, which are under construction at VT UK's Woolston shipyard, Southampton enter service. ■

Dimensions
Length:	59.5m
Beam:	11m
Draught:	4.5m
Tonnes:	1,260

Machinery
Diesels x 2:	4.2mw
Shafts:	1
Speed:	16.5 knots

Weapons systems
Guns:	1 x 20mm

Sensors:
navigation radar
Complement:
Ship: 36 (plus RM boarding party)

Boats: 2 x Avon Sea Riders

HMS *Anglesey*

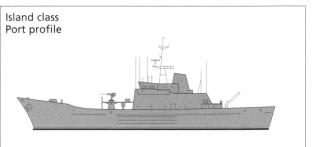
Island class
Port profile

Dimensions
Length:	81m
Beam:	11.5m
Draught:	3.6m
Tonnes:	1,427

Machinery
Diesels x 2:	4.2mw
Shafts:	2
Speed:	20 knots

Weapons
Guns:	1 x 30mm

Sensors
Radar:	994
	1006 nav

Complement: 45 (+ 25 RM)

Boats: 2 x Avon Sea Riders

These ships were originally begun as a private venture by the shipyard concerned.

They were subsequently taken over by the MoD during construction and have served very successfully in the Royal Navy since.

They are dual role designed ships with the ability to carry out fishery protection and offshore patrols, and the added flexibility of being able to operate helicopters as big as the Sea King from the large flight deck.

One of the class has generally been on long term patrol duties off the Falkland Islands, while the other forms part of the Fishery Protection Squadron.

The squadron's duties include regular surveillance patrols of the UK's offshore gas and oilfield installations.

These vessels are expected to remain in service until late this decade.

See also:

Combat forces	page 18
Sea King	page 64

HMS *Dumbarton Castle*

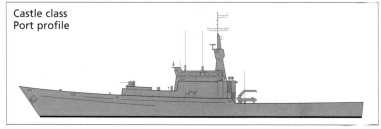
Castle class
Port profile

	No	Builder	ISD
Leeds Castle	P258	Hall Russell Aberdeen	1981
Dumbarton Castle	P265	Hall Russell Aberdeen	1982

Royal Navy Maritime Airpower

Maritime air power is by its very nature tri-service, with Army, Navy and Air Force each lending support to each other. Nimrod aircraft, for example, are key RAF assets but their role in anti-submarine warfare is clearly a maritime one.

The Fleet Air Arm provides the Royal Navy with a multi-role aviation combat capability able to operate autonomously at short notice in all environments, day and night, over the sea and land. It has some 6,200 people operating approximately 200 combat aircraft and more than 50 support/training aircraft.

There are two Naval Air Stations. HMS *Heron* at Yeovilton in Somerset is the base for the Sea Harrier FA2 and helicopters which support 3 Commando Brigade RM; the Sea King Mk4, Lynx Mk7 and Gazelle. It is also the parent air station for all maritime Lynx (Mks 3 & 8) and the Royal Navy's Historic Flight. HMS *Seahawk* at Culdrose in Cornwall supports the new Merlin anti-submarine helicopter, the Sea King Mk7 ASAC, 771 SAR Squadron and the Jetstream aircraft of 750 Naval Air Squadron. There remains a search and rescue unit at Prestwick Airport in Ayrshire. Specialist air engineering training is now undertaken at HMS *Sultan* at Gosport in Hampshire.

Additionally there are a small number of Lynx attack helicopters and Gazelle reconnaissance/training aircraft which work with 3 Commando Brigade.

This emphasis on pooling the expertise of

Sea Skua-armed Lynx Mk8 on a destroyer's flight deck

the three Services more closely to produce an integrated fighting force, thereby maximising the UK's military punch, was a significant focus of the 1998 Strategic Defence Review.

One key initiative that emerged from the SDR was an historic agreement between the Chief of the Naval Staff and the Chief of the Air Staff to establish a joint RN/RAF fixed wing force, Joint Force 2000 – now known as Joint Force Harrier – to operate from both land and aircraft carriers. This brought together the Sea Harrier FA2 and RAF Harrier GR7 into joint operating packages. While the FA2 will be withdrawn from service between 2004 and 2006, the Joint Force will continue to be complemented by RN and RAF pilots. In future the RN and RAF both plan to operate a single, common aircraft from land and sea – the Future Joint Combat Aircraft – the Lockheed Martin F35.

Another initiative was the Joint Helicopter Command (JHC), established in October 1999, to bring all battlefield helicopters from each of the three services under one command organisation. Its headquarters are located alongside the Army's Land Command HQ at Wilton in Wiltshire.

Amongst his tri-service assets, the Commander JHC has operational command of the Royal Navy's Commando Helicopter Force (CHF) based at RNAS Yeovilton in Somerset. This force, comprising a deployable HQ and four Naval Air Squadrons (845, 846, 847 and 848) provides armed action, tactical mobility and aviation combat support to 3 Commando Brigade Royal Marines. Army Apache attack helicopters (also part of the JHC) will provide the armed attack capability to 3 Commando Brigade from about 2005 as existing anti-tank missile armed Lynx are phased out.

The CHF HQ is responsible for operational planning and co-ordination for the squadrons and, during operations, will be closely integrated with the Amphibious Task Group Commander and 3 Commando Brigade HQ.

CHF personnel (aircrew, maintainers and support staff) number 900 men and women of the Royal Navy and Royal Marines. They are trained to be equally at home operating from ships such as HMS *Ocean* and the soon-to-arrive *Albion* and *Bulwark*, or ashore in dispersed sites, from where they are able to provide a rapid response to the brigade's requirements. ■

Dimensions
Length: 15.37m
Width: 10.65m
Weight: 27 tonnes

Machinery
Power:
          1x 39,000lb turbofan
Vertical lift: 1 x 20,000lb
  thrust shaft driven fan &
  19,000lb main engine
                        thrust
Radius of action:
              about 500nm
Speed: supersonic

Weapons systems
  A wide range of internally
    and externally carried
      ordnance will be
        accommodated

Aircrew: F35: one

Defence Procurement Minister Lord Bach announced in late 2002 that the Royal Navy and Royal Air Force would operate the Short Take Off and Vertical Landing (STOVL) variant of the F35 Joint Strike Fighter (JSF) under a UK procurement programme named Future Joint Combat Aircraft (FJCA).

The F35 will be able to operate in all weathers, day and night, conducting stealthy offensive air support and supporting long range air interdiction, as well as anti-surface warfare, tactical reconnaissance and air defence of the fleet.

The MoD intends to buy up to 150 of these aircraft, the world's most advanced stealthy 'jump-jets', in a programme that could be worth up to £10 billion. The FJCA will succeed the aircraft in service with the Joint Force Harrier which operate from both aircraft carriers and land bases.

STOVL JSF meets fully the UK's military needs and builds on Britain's unique and valuable knowledge of STOVL aircraft acquired during nearly four decades of operations with Harriers on land and at sea.

One of the key deciding factors for the MoD in selecting the F35 was the flexibility conferred by STOVL capabilities, among which are the ability to operate from carriers at sea in conditions so severe that no other carrier-borne fixed wing aircraft are able to take off or land.

The UK has been a fully collaborative partner on the US-led JSF programme since 1996. Early investment amounted to £200 million and the MoD's interest was specifically targeted on a Short Take Off and Vertical Landing (STOVL) aircraft as a direct successor to both RN Sea Harrier FA2 and RAF Harrier GR7 aircraft.

In 2001 the MoD committed itself to nearly £2 billion of further expenditure on the development of the programme, of which some £600 million covered the integration of UK-specific weapons and communications equipment into the JSF.

In late 2001 the US authorities selected the Lockheed Martin F35 as the successful candidate in a competition with Boeing for the JSF programme, and awarded the company an Engineering and Manufacturing Development contract.

Production of aircraft for the UK is planned to start in 2008 with the first deliveries due in 2010 and entry into service in 2012 – a date that will coincide with the arrival of the first of the Navy's new aircraft carriers. ■

STOVL JSF prototype Lockheed Martin F35

The Future Joint Combat Aircraft – the Lockheed Martin F35

Sea Harrier FA2 800 Sqn, 801 Sqn, 899 Sqn

Dimensions
Length: 14m
Width: 8m
Weight: 11.5 tonnes

Machinery
Power: 1x21,500lb turbofan
Speed: 600 knots

Aircrew
Single seater (FA2)
Two seater (T8)

Weapons systems
Missiles: up to 4 x
AMRAAM
Sidewinder SRAAM
Bombs: or up to 5 x 500lb
or 1,000lb conventional or
laser-guided bombs

Squadron
Aircraft: 7 x FA2
(899 Sqn: 9 x FA2 & 4 x T8)
Aircrew: 10

Support crew: 110

This air defence aircraft flown by Royal Navy personnel combines the abilities of a maritime fighter with reconnaissance and strike capabilities.

The current FA2 is a heavily updated version of the original FRS1 model that fought with such distinction in the 1982 Falklands conflict.

The key to the aircraft's success is its ability to combine a powerful air defence capability, with reconnaissance and ground attack roles in one small STOVL airframe.

STOVL ability is the key to the FA2's operations from the current generation of Invincible class aircraft carriers, using a ski-jump for take off and landing vertically at the end of a mission.

The current fleet of nearly 50 FA2s is composed of some new-build and some modified FRS1 aircraft.

FRS1 aircraft were procured to provide air defence for the fleet during Cold War anti-submarine operations in the North Atlantic, but after they had demonstrated their unique multi-role flexibility in the 1982 Falklands campaign, embarked squadron strengths were increased and the aircraft became a key element of the UK's ability to project power around the globe.

During the Falklands conflict 29 aircraft flew more than 2,000 sorties, destroying 22 enemy aircraft and conducting ground strikes, with no losses in air-to-air combat. Key improvements to the FA2 were the addition of a powerful Blue Vixen radar to enhance the capabilities of the AMRAAM medium range air defence missile, and new avionics. As well as serving in the Balkans and Iraq it was used extensively over Sierra Leone in 2000.

The 1998 SDR established the Joint Force Harrier (JFH), with both RN Sea Harriers and RAF GR7s now forming a single Group, No 3, headquartered at RAF Strike Command in High Wycombe.

Squadrons normally embark on carriers with up to seven FA2 aircraft, with a similar number of RAF-manned GR7 aircraft. It was announced in 2002 that JFH is to migrate to an all-Harrier GR force maximising investment in one aircraft type until its planned replacement by the Joint Combat Aircraft, the Lockheed Martin F35. FA2 squadrons will progressively disband between 2004 and 2006.

Four front line squadrons of Harrier GR7s will be operated with aircraft modified to GR9 standard. Two squadrons will be predominantly RN manned. All aircraft will retain air defence capability using Sidewinder SRAAMs. ■

See also:

◩ Invincible class   page 26
◩ Harrier GR7   page 74

Sea Harrier FA2
Starboard profile

A Royal Navy Sea Harrier FA2

Merlin HM Mk1   700M Sqn, 814 Sqn, 820 Sqn, 824 Sqn

Dimensions
Length:	22.81m
Rotor diameter:	18.59m
Weight:	14.6 tonnes

Machinery
Power:	3 x 2,200shp gas turbines
Speed:	167 knots

Aircrew
Merlin HM Mk1:	three

Weapons systems
ASW: up to four Sting Ray torpedoes or depth charges

Sensors
Radar:	Blue Kestrel
Dipping Sonar:	Flash
Sonobuoys:	AQS903
ESM:	Orange Reaper

Squadron
Aircraft:	6-8 HM Mk1 (OEU: 2 HM Mk1)
Aircrew:	up to 58 (OEU: 12)
Support crew:	up to 112 (OEU: 25)

The powerful and sophisticated Merlin HM Mk1 is a replacement for the long-serving anti-submarine Sea King HAS Mk6.

It is the first Royal Naval derivative of the EH101 helicopter, designed and produced under a collaborative programme by UK's GKN Westland Helicopters Ltd and Italy's helicopter manufacturer, Agusta. The manufacture of the Merlin HM weapon system ultimately took place under the Prime Contractorship of Lockheed Martin ASIC.

Normally flown by a crew of three (a pilot, an observer and an aircrewman), Merlin is designed to operate from both large and small ships' flight decks, in severe weather and high sea states, by day and night.

Merlin was originally conceived as a key part of the Type 23 frigate weapon system, where it would have prosecuted contacts picked up by the frigate's towed array sonars.

Merlin is configured both structurally and in terms of mission system and cockpit design to meet the demands of the harsh maritime environment. It can go further, faster and with a greater weapon and sensor load than the Sea King and has been dubbed 'the flying frigate'. Merlin represents a £4.6 billion investment by the MoD and the programme runs to 44 aircraft.

The aircraft is now embarked on the carrier HMS *Ark Royal* and will soon equip Type 23 frigates. Aircraft operating from frigates are attached as single aircraft flights to 824 Squadron.

As numbers of embarked individual flights rise they will eventually come under the control of a newly formed squadron.

The last squadron equipped with Sea King Mk6, 820 Squadron, handed back its aircraft and reformed with six Merlin helicopters early in 2003.

All anti-submarine Merlins serving in Royal Navy squadrons, including the Operational Evaluation Unit, are based at HMS *Seahawk*, at Culdrose in Cornwall. ■

See also:
▨ **Invincible class**   **page 26**
▨ **Type 23 Frigate**   **page 42**
▨ **Naval shore establishments page 191**

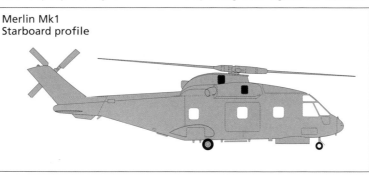

Merlin Mk1
Starboard profile

Merlins landing on a flight deck

A Merlin HM Mk1 helicopter

Lynx HMA Mk3/8 702 Sqn, 815 Sqn

Dimensions
Rotor diameter: 12.8m
Length: 12.06m
Weight: 4.7 tonnes

Machinery
Power: 2 x 900hp turbines
Speed: 180 knots

Weapon systems
Surface attack: Sea Skua anti-ship missile; machine gun pods

Anti-submarine: Sting Ray torpedo; depth charges;

Aircrew: two

The Lynx is primarily an anti-ship and anti-submarine helicopter designed to operate from the frigates and destroyers of the Fleet.

This fast and capable aircraft is being updated to the Mk8 standard, which is now in service with the Fleet.

The aircraft is being fitted with a very advanced Central Tactical System and Passive Identification Device in addition to the equipment currently fitted.

The Lynx forms an integral part of a warship's detection and weapon system and can project the influence of a ship over great distances with the key element of surprise.

Each independent flight, embarked on Type 42 destroyers or on frigates, comprises a pilot, an observer and a team of seven maintainers. They deploy from their headquarters at RNAS Yeovilton to join their particular ship whenever it sails.

A Lynx Mk8 in the foreground, with a Mk3 beyond

The Lynx Mk8 carries the Sea Skua anti-ship missile, which proved highly effective during the Gulf war and in the Falklands conflict.

In addition to the Sea Skua the Lynx has the Sting Ray torpedo and depth charges for anti-submarine warfare.

The aircraft may also be fitted with a heavy machine gun. ■

Lynx Mk8
Starboard profile

See also:
▨ **Type 42 Destroyers**   page 34
▨ **Type 23 Frigates**   page 42
▨ **Sting Ray torpedo**   page 178

Surface Combatant Maritime Rotorcraft

Royal Navy frigates and destroyers could be equipped with a new and considerably updated version of the long-serving and highly effective naval Lynx helicopter, under plans announced by Defence Procurement Minister Lord Bach in 2002.

The Surface Combatant Maritime Rotorcraft (SCMR) project is intended to provide an organic maritime attack helicopter on assigned frigates and destroyers, to deliver an attack/surveillance capability in the open ocean and littoral in support of maritime, joint or combined operations. Roles include targeting, anti-surface and anti-submarine weapon delivery, and battle damage assessment. In addition it will provide key elements of frigates' and destroyers' constabulary, Search and Rescue (SAR) and humanitarian support capabilities.

The programme is in its Assessment Phase. During the Concept Phase of this project a number of options were considered for this capability, including UAVs, and numerous other helicopter types.

Concept studies have shown that the Agusta Westland Future Lynx has the best potential to fulfil the capability requirement to provide the Royal Navy with battle-winning helicopters.

A new airframe should allow for a service life of at least 25 years and a new engine will provide improved performance, in particular in hot and high climatic conditions. SCMR is closely linked with the planned Battlefield Light

An AgustaWestland Super Lynx prototype aircraft

Utility Helicopter (BLUH), which is required to support land operations.

The Future Lynx proposal is a strong contender for both BLUH and SCMR and a common programme could realise significant procurement savings. An assessment phase contract for BLUH was let in December 2001. ■

Sea King ASAC Mk7 849 Sqn

Dimensions
Length: 22.2m
Rotor diameter: 18.9m
Weight: 9.8 tonnes

Machinery
Power: 2 x 1,600shp
                              turbines
Speed: 125 knots

Aircrew
Sea King Mk7:   three

Sensors
Radar: Cerberus
Comms: Link 16 Joint
            Tactical Information
            Distribution System

Squadron
Aircraft: 13 x Mk7
Aircrew: 45
Support crew: 100

This squadron provides Royal Navy carrier task groups with essential long range warning and intelligence on threats from hostile missiles and aircraft.

The Airborne Surveillance and Control (ASAC) Mk7 helicopters have been overhauled and equipped with some of the most modern radar and sensor systems available.

Flying high above the carrier group, they give the fleet added protection against enemy low-flying aircraft and sea-skimming missiles.

A new pulse doppler radar, the Cerberus, has been fitted in the inflatable dome that is suspended beneath the aircraft's fuselage when airborne.

It has the ability to detect targets overland as well as over water and has an integrated 'identification friend or foe' system (IFF), which will help the ever-increasing commitment to coastal operations with which the squadron finds itself tasked.

A high-speed datalink automatically transmits radar information to friendly ships and aircraft, thus negating the need for time-consuming voice reports.

This system, which represents the cutting edge of technology, dramatically enhances the performance of

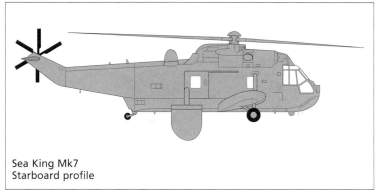

Sea King Mk7
Starboard profile

this already impressive platform.

The Squadron has three flights, Headquarters (HQ) Flight, A Flight and B Flight. The Headquarters, based at RNAS Culdrose, provides support to the frontline flights and is a training facility for observer aircrew. It operates three aircraft. The A and B Flights are embarked in aircraft carriers, each operating three Mk7 Sea Kings.

Between 1992 and 1996 both flights were involved in providing support to the ships involved in NATO operations in the Former Yugoslavia and particularly in Operation Sharp Guard, blockading the coast of Montenegro.

These aircraft are projected to be succeeded in service under the Maritime Airborne Surveillance and Control (MASC) project, which is run by the DPA's Future Aircraft Carrier project team. MASC is examining a range of options for meeting the airborne surveillance requirements needed in the future. A wide range of potential solutions to MASC are under study, among them a force of Merlin helicopters equipped for the role. ■

See also:

◪Future aircraft carrier   page 22
◪Merlin   page 60
◪Naval shore establishments page 191

Sea King Mk7
ASAC helicopters
with distinctive
Cerberus radar

Support Amphibious and Battlefield Rotorcraft

Within the next 15 years or so, several key RN and RAF helicopter types are due to go out of service.

These include the RN's Commando Sea King HC4s and the RAF's SAR Sea King Mk3/3As and Puma HC1 Support Helicopters.

Support, Amphibious and Battlefield Rotorcraft (SABR) is the DPA project that is undertaking initial studies to identify, develop and procure sufficient systems to provide a Battlefield Support capability and to meet the separate SAR requirement. Evolving Littoral Manoeuvre (LiTM) and new Air Manoeuvre (AM) doctrine will influence the Battlefield Support requirement.

In the amphibious arena, SABR will be required to deploy 3 Commando Brigade (3 Cdo Bde) Royal Marine forces in support of LiTM, and be optimised for sustained operations at sea. SABR will also contribute to 16 Air Assault Brigade (16 AAB) AM, in particular the tactical deployment and subsequent support of elements of an Infantry Battle Group.

Full account of the existing RAF Chinook and Merlin support rotorcraft will be taken to ensure that the balance of Battlefield Support capability is provided in the most cost-effective manner. The RAF also provides a 24-hour military and civil SAR service around the UK, over land and sea, from six bases. This service is complemented by Royal Navy and HM Coastguard helicopters at a further six bases.

Support Helicopters are playing an increasingly prominent role in UK operations, and they will represent a substantial part of our commitment to Rapid Reaction Forces. Recently they have demonstrated their inherent flexibility by aiding disaster relief efforts worldwide.

Drivers to the early studies are:
- contribute to the move of the 'F' echelon of 16 AAB, in a single wave (up to 750 men and associated equipment);
- the ability to embark on and operate from amphibious warfare ships;
- deploy the Light Mobile Artillery Weapon System (LIMAWS) in support of 3 Cdo Bde and 16 AAB;
- contribute to the support of the Attack Helicopter in the field;
- freedom to operate in locations in which 16 AAB and 3 Cdo Bde forces are expected to function. ■

Initial studies, subject to formal MoD approval, have investigated the numbers of aircraft required to fully provide the combined SABR Battlefield Support and SAR capability.

This analysis will be further refined during the SABR Assessment Phase. Final decisions are not expected to be taken for some years.

A number of different candidate aircraft types are under study to meet the requirement. These include variants of Chinook, Merlin, Sikorsky CH53, Sikorsky S92, Sikorsky Black Hawk and the Eurocopter NH 90.

Battlefield Support rotorcraft must be able to be based for long periods in field conditions, to survive and operate on the modern, digitized battlefield and be optimised for the key tasks of tactical troop movement, mobility of combat support and re-supply of equipment.

For the Battlefield Support programme, MoD will prepare and conduct a competition between candidate aircraft suppliers. In Service Date is expected on current assumptions to be about 2011. ■

A Sea King HC Mk4 takes off from the deck of a Royal Navy aircraft carrier

Sea King HC Mk4 845 Sqn, 846 Sqn, 848 Sqn

Dimensions
Length: 22.2m
Rotor diameter: 18.9m
Weight: 9.7 tonnes

Machinery
Power: 2 x 1,600shp turbines
Speed: 100 knots

Aircrew
Sea King Mk4: two

Military lift
Troops: 27 fully equipped
Cargo: or up to 3 tonnes under slung

Weapons systems
Self defence: fitted for self-defence machine gun armament

Sensors
DAS: comprehensive defensive aids suite to include directed infra-red countermeasures & NVG-compatible flightdeck

Squadron
Aircraft: 10 x Mk4
Aircrew: 48
Support crew: 147

These three squadrons of Mk4 Sea Kings have provided the backbone of the dedicated airborne lift for 3 Commando Brigade Royal Marines for many years. All three squadrons now form part of the Joint Helicopter Command and are often joined on amphibious operations by RAF helicopters, principally the Chinook.

The Mk4 is a troop-carrying version of the Sea King helicopter. It came into service during the late 1970s, succeeding the long-serving Wessex helicopter.

The Mk4 is still a capable aircraft which proved its abilities in the 1982 Falklands conflict, the 1991 Gulf War, during extended service in the Balkans, in Sierra Leone, and most recently supporting the Royal Marines on operations in the Gulf in 2003.

It can carry up to 27 fully-equipped Commandos, or combat equipment such as a 105mm light gun and ammunition, or a Land Rover.

The aircraft is equipped to fly at low level in extreme conditions day or night, anywhere in the world and in any climate. It carries a complex array of navigational and communications equipment. The two front line squadrons, 845 and 846, regularly deploy on board RN and RFA vessels, including HMS *Ocean*. They can also fly from new Dutch amphibious ships, which have operated closely with their RN counterparts for many years.

Under current amphibious warfare doctrine these aircraft deploy ashore with the Royal Marines to self-contained secure bases. The squadrons have a wealth of experience operating in temperate climate and in the extreme cold of north Norway, where temperatures can drop as low as minus 30°C.

The Commando Helicopter Training Squadron, 848 NAS, instructs up to 60 aircrew and 150 maintainers annually. It is also ready to deploy operationally. The aircraft is planned to be succeeded in service under the SABR programme. ∎

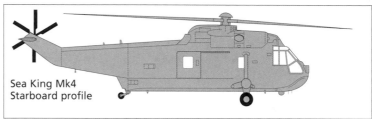
Sea King Mk4
Starboard profile

A Sea King Mk4 helicopter in SFOR markings

An 845 Sqn Sea King Mk4 picks up Royal Marines on operations at Umm Qasr in Iraq

Dimensions

Length:	22.2m
Rotor diameter:	20m
Weight:	9.8 tonnes

Machinery

Power:	2 x 1,600shp turbines
Speed:	125 knots

Aircrew

Mk5:	five

Sensors

Radar:	Sea Searcher

Squadron

771 Sqn	6 x Mk5; 2 x Mk6
Gannet SAR Flt:	3 x Mk5
771 Sqn	48 & 17 RNR
771 Sqn	140

The Sea King Mk5 is equipped as a dedicated Search And Rescue helicopter, with distinctive red fuselage markings.

It carries out rescue missions from HMS *Seahawk*, RNAS Culdrose, to a range of 250 nautical miles out into the south western approaches to the UK.

With the decommissioning of 810 Squadron in 2001, 771 Squadron assumed the responsibility for Advanced and Operational Flying Training for Anti-Submarine Warfare (ASW) Pilots and Observers, as well as the residual Sea King Mk5/6 Pilot, Observer and Aircrewman Conversion and Refresher Courses. This role has concluded but two Mk6 Sea King individual ship's flights for Type 22 frigates remain parented by 771 Sqn at Culdrose.

The SAR Flight operating from HMS *Gannet* at Prestwick has three aircraft and is attached to 771 Squadron. ■

See also:

◄ **Type 22 Frigate** page 46
► **Naval shore establishments** page 191

Aircrewman on the winch

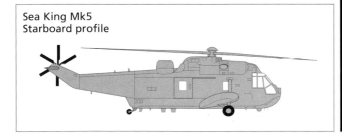

Sea King Mk5
Starboard profile

A Sea King Mk5 in the hover during a rescue exercise

Jetstream T2 750 Sqn

Machinery
Power: 2 x Turbomeca Astazou 16D turboprop
Speed: 214 knots
Ceiling: 25,000 feet

Passengers
T2: 6
T3: 16

Squadron
750 Sqn RNAS Culdrose
'Heron' flt RNAS Yeovilton

750 Squadron is based at RNAS Culdrose. It provides basic training for the Fleet Air Arm's Observers (airborne warfare officers) who will fly in Sea King, Merlin and Lynx helicopters.

When fully qualified, they will control and co-ordinate ships, aircraft and weapon systems across the spectrum of maritime warfare. The Jetstream provides these young men and women with an introduction to aviation and teaches them the basic skills on which they will build during further phases of training. Each aircraft has two training consoles at which students practise navigation and basic tactical skills, normally operating over water and far from base.

The aircraft is powered by two Turbomeca Astazou 16D turboprop engines, giving a maximum speed of 214 knots at sea level and a service ceiling of 25,000 feet. It can carry six passengers, has an endurance of four hours and a range of 1,000 miles.

This makes it a useful personnel carrier and the squadron has an occasional operational role in this field. In particular, 750 Squadron had a busy period in 1994 when it was employed in ferrying medical supplies into Albania. The T3 variant of the Jetstream equips the squadron's detached 'Heron' Flight based at RNAS Yeovilton. This aircraft is virtually identical to the T2 except that it has no radar and no dedicated training facilities, being configured for passenger transport with 16 seats.

The flight's four aircraft provide the Royal Navy with a very useful and cost-effective VIP and general transport capability. ■

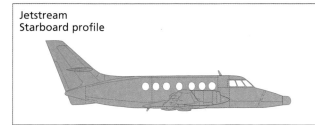

Jetstream
Starboard profile

A Jetstream T2 in flight over the Cornish coast

RAF Maritime Airpower

Royal Air Force aircraft and personnel make a central contribution to maritime operations, both through shore-based Nimrod maritime patrol aircraft and through the increasing operation of strike aircraft and helicopters from RN carriers and RN and RFA amphibious warfare ships.

In the following pages RAF aircraft that already operate from RN ships, or may do so in the future, are listed because they form an essential part of the UK's overall maritime warfare capability.

Also listed is the shore-based Nimrod MR2 and its eventual successor, the powerful and more advanced Nimrod MRA4.

Joint operations across the traditional single-service boundaries are now the norm, and nowhere is this more evident than with air operations.

For the future the RAF-crewed and operated Harrier GR7 force is to be modified to a new advanced GR9 standard, which will then be jointly crewed and operated by a mix of RN and RAF personnel.

This force will be available for operations from land bases and from ships and will mirror the eventual operational pattern that is proposed for the Lockheed Martin F35, when it enters service in 2012 in succession to the Harrier force.

The Chinook helicopter, which can operate from many RN and future RFA amphibious warfare vessels, and was used successfully to transport men of 45 Commando Royal Marines on operations in Afghanistan in 2002, is also listed here.

Also listed is the new Merlin HC Mk3 support helicopter, which has been designed to be able to operate from RN and RFA vessels. ■

Royal Marine Commandos board an RAF Chinook in Afghanistan

Harrier GR7/9 1(F) Sqn, 3(F) Sqn, IV(AC) Sqn, 20 (Reserve) Sqn

Dimensions
Length: 14.12m
Width: 9.24m
Weight: 11 tonnes

Machinery
Power: 1x 86.7kn turbofan
Speed: 600 knots

Squadron
Aircraft: 12 x GR7 & 1 x T10
(20Sqn):   9 x GR7 & 5 x T10
Aircrew: 16
Support crew: 140

Weapons systems
Bombs: up to 7 x BL755 or
               7 x 540lb or
         4 x Paveway II LGB or
         2 x Paveway III LGB
Missiles:
         up to 4 AIM9L SRAAM
             4 Maverick ASM
Rockets: 4 x CRV-7 pods

Sensors
         1 x TIALD pod, FLIR
         1 x Recce pod

Aircrew
Single seater (GR7/9)
Two seater (T10/12)

This Royal Air Force aircraft is the latest in the long line of Harrier 'jump-jets' originating from the 1960s.

The second-generation GR5 and GR7 versions replaced the original Harrier GR3s in the late 1980s and early 1990s in the offensive support role. The GR7 is, in essence, a licence-built American-designed AV-8B Harrier II fitted with RAF-specific navigation and defensive systems as well as other changes including additional underwing outrigger pylons for Sidewinder ASRAAMs.

Constructed of composite materials, and with a bigger more efficient wing, the improved design of the Harrier II allows the aircraft to carry twice the load of a GR3 over the same distance or the same load twice the distance. Some are being fitted with a more powerful engine and will be designated GR7a or GR9a.

First flight of the Harrier GR7 was in 1989, and deliveries to RAF squadrons began in 1990. A total of 96 aircraft were ordered, including 62 interim GR5s which were later modified to GR7 standard.

Modifications included forward-looking infra-red (FLIR) equipment which, when used in conjunction with the pilot's night vision goggles, provides a night-time, low-level capability.

The Harrier remains a highly versatile aircraft and can easily be deployed to remote forward operating locations. Although optimised for low-level close-support operations at sub-sonic speeds, the Harrier is also ideally suited to medium level operations where it uses its highly accurate angle rate bombing system (ARBS). It is also equipped with the Thermal Imaging and Laser Designator (TIALD) pod which equips it to mark targets for guided bombs.

Following the successful deployment of RAF GR3 aircraft from RN carriers during the 1982 Falklands conflict and the invaluable role they played as ground attack aircraft, embarkation of RAF Harriers aboard Invincible class ships became more and more frequent, eventually resulting in the creation of Joint Force Harrier in 2000.

It was announced in 2002 that the MoD would move to an all-GR7 force by 2007 and that GR7 would be upgraded to a new GR9 standard. This will ensure that a credible expeditionary offensive capability is maintained until the aircraft leaves service around 2015. It will be fitted to carry the Brimstone anti-armour weapon and precision guided bombs. ■

A Harrier GR7 strike aircraft

An RAF Harrier GR7

Dimensions
Length: 38.65m
Width: 35.06m
Weight: 87.2 tonnes

Machinery
Power:
    4 x 12,140lb turbofan
Speed: 500 knots

Aircrew
Nimrod MR2:   13

Weapons systems
ASW: up to 9 Sting Ray
            torpedoes
Air defence:
    Sidewinder SRAAM
Anti-ship: Harpoon

Sensors
Radar: Searchwater
Sonobuoys: Full suite

Squadron
Aircraft: 6 x MR2
(42 Sqn: 3 x MR2)
Aircrew: 120 (42 Sqn 50)
Support crew:
    320 (whole fleet)

The Nimrod aircraft is a military derivative of the world's very first jet airliner, the de Havilland Comet, and is the only jet-powered maritime patrol aircraft.

The aircraft has three distinct roles to fulfil in the Royal Air Force. In its anti-ship and anti-submarine roles it is concerned with the detection, localisation and identification of surface and subsurface vessels.

In the SAR mode its role is to detect and pinpoint those in distress and to guide the much slower and shorter-range rescue helicopters straight to the casualty or incident.

The Nimrod MR2 carries a crew of 13 and is fitted with radar, magnetic and acoustic detection equipment.

Nimrod aircraft served in the 1982 Falklands campaign and the Gulf War of 1991, where they undertook maritime surveillance of the Arabian Gulf.

The aircraft has a powerful radar mounted in the nose for the detection and classification of surface vessels. The fuselage tailcone extends well beyond the fin and rudder to house a magnetic anomaly detector (MAD) unit. A suite of sonobuoys are carried, which are dropped from the aircraft to localise hostile submarines.

The submarines can then be

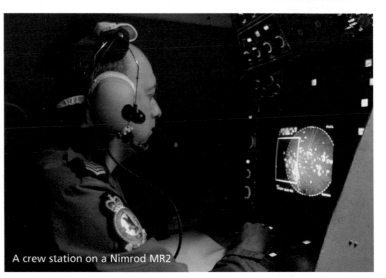

A crew station on a Nimrod MR2

attacked with Sting Ray torpedoes, dropped from the Nimrod's capacious weapons bay. The aircraft is also equipped to carry Sidewinder air-to-air missiles and Harpoon anti-ship missiles.

The Nimrod is unique in that it can fly rapidly to an operational area on four engines and then shut down two of them for economy. An in-flight refuelling probe projects from the fuselage above the cockpit for flights of extended endurance. Despite being based on an old airliner, the Nimrod has the low wing loading and low aspect ratio wings necessary for tight manoeuvring only 70 metres or so above the sea when finding a submarine or during SAR operations.

The entire fleet of the type is based at RAF Kinloss in Scotland. ■

See also:
▣ **Nimrod MRA4**   **page 78**
▣ **Sting Ray torpedo**   **page 178**

A Nimrod MR2 at RAF Kinloss

Nimrod MRA4

Dimensions
Length: 38.63m
Width: 38.71m
Weight: 104 tonnes

Machinery
Power: 4 x 69kn turbofans
Range: 6,000nm +
Speed: 500 knots

Aircrew
Nimrod MRA4:   10

Although based on the long-serving Nimrod MR Mk2, this aircraft will be almost completely new and when it enters service will bring powerful new capabilities to maritime battlespace.

The Nimrod MRA4 will replace the existing force of Nimrod MR2 aircraft, for which wartime roles include Anti-Submarine Warfare (ASW), Anti-Surface Warfare and SAR.

The requirement for this project was endorsed and an initial data gathering phase authorised in November 1992.

British Aerospace was selected as the prime contractor in July 1996 to supply a complete package of 21 mission-equipped Nimrod MRA4 aircraft, together with a training system and initial logistic support.

A fixed-price £2.8 billion contract was awarded in December 1996, under which existing MR2 aircraft fuselage and empennage structure would be re-lifed and reassembled, with redesigned wings and new-technology fuel-efficient BR710 turbofan engines.

Although some of the MR2 systems are retained, the majority of the air vehicle systems are replaced, including the flight deck.

The mission system, which is the heart of the weapon system, is entirely new and is extremely sophisticated. Crew numbers have reduced from 13 to ten.

Nimrod MRA4 will be able to monitor more sonobuoys than the MR2, giving it a much greater search area in which to locate submarines. Its advanced on-board sensors will improve its capabilities against conventional submarines when 'snorting', and enhance performance in coastal waters.

It carries a greatly improved communications suite, will have a dramatically improved time on station, enabling operations at greater ranges from its airbase and will be able to operate autonomously worldwide. Technical and resourcing difficulties encountered during 1998 led to a re-baselining of the programme. However, the delay will enable certain enhancements in capability to be included.

With all these changes, the MRA4 essentially amounts to a new and very powerful aircraft.

In late 1999 the Air Vehicle Critical Design Review was held. Actions from that review were closed in early 2000, effectively signifying completion of the weapon system design.

Detailed design and manufacture proceeded during 2000, with the first new wing completing manufacture at BAE Systems Chadderton and being delivered to BAE Systems Woodford.

By early 2002 it had been recognised that the submarine threat had not grown by as much as had been anticipated. This, coupled with the greater availability and capability of the Nimrod MRA4 aircraft, led to a reassessment of the requirement, and consequently the number of aircraft ordered was reduced in early 2002 from 21 to 18.

Industrial problems have delayed the In Service Date of this aircraft, which will now be achieved by 2009. ■

See also:
◁ RAF Maritime Air Power   page 73
◁ Nimrod MR Mk2   page 76

A BAE Systems artist's impression of the Nimrod MRA4 in flight

Chinook Mk2 7 Sqn, 18 Sqn, 27 Sqn, 78 Sqn

Dimensions
Length: 15.54m
Rotor diameter: 18.29m
Weight: 22 tonnes

Machinery
Power:
            2 x 3,750shp turbines
Speed: 160 knots

Aircrew
Chinook Mk2:   two to four

Military lift
Troops: 44 fully equipped
Cargo: or up to 10 tonnes
                        payload

Weapons systems
Self defence: fitted for self-
        defence machine gun
                    armament

Sensors
DAS: comprehensive
        defensive aids suite to
    include directed infra-red
            countermeasures &
                          NVG-
        compatible flightdeck

Squadron
Aircraft: 10-15 x Mk2
Aircrew: 100
Support crew: 200

The Chinook is one of the most easily identified helicopters in the world. It is the only tandem-rotor design in service with the RAF.

This large twin-engined medium-lift helicopter normally operates with a crew of four.

Mounting the engines externally above the fuselage gives the aircraft a large spacious cabin capable of accommodating up to 44 fully-equipped troops, or up to ten tonnes of cargo or small vehicles internally or externally on one of three mounting points.

The large cabin has a rear loading ramp door, which makes it a straight-forward task to load and unload the aircraft in a very short time. This large load-carrying ability makes the Chinook an ideal battlefield support aircraft, and it is able to operate from the LPH (HMS *Ocean*) as well as air-craft carriers.

The rotors counter-rotate and this means that no tail rotor is required to counteract the torque of the powerful engines. This counter-rotation means the blades must be synchronised to prevent them striking each other.

The Chinook first caught the public's attention in the UK for the role it played in ferrying troops into combat during the 1982 Falklands conflict.

The original design dates back to the early 1960s and first took to the air in September 1961. The aircraft ordered for the RAF in the late 1970s, known as Chinook HC1s, were equivalent to the US Boeing Vertol CH-47C then available. The subject of many updates, they are currently known as Chinook HC2s, having been fitted with NVG-compatible flight decks amongst many other improvements.

Recently delivered new build aircraft will be known as HC2As. ∎

A Chinook over the deck of HMS Ocean

See also:
◁ **RAF Maritime Air Power**   page 73
▷ **Royal Marines**   page 109

An RAF Chinook Mk2 helicopter

Merlin HC Mk3 *28 Sqn*

Dimensions
Length: 22.81m
Rotor diameter: 18.59m
Weight: 14.6 tonnes

Machinery
Power: 3 x 2,312shp
gas turbines
Speed: 167 knots

Aircrew
Merlin HM Mk1: two

Military lift
Troops: 24 fully equipped
Cargo: up to four tonnes
underslung

Weapons systems
fitted for self-defence
machine gun armament

Sensors
DAS: comprehensive
defensive aids suite to
include directed infra-red
countermeasures
FLIR: Forward looking infra-
red and NVG-compatible
flightdeck

Squadron
Aircraft: 8 x Mk3
(to increase to 18 x Mk3 in
2003)
Aircrew: 60
Support crew: 170

The Merlin HC Mk3 is the first of a new generation of medium support helicopters for the Royal Air Force, which are also capable of operation from Royal Navy vessels.

Twenty two of the aircraft have entered RAF service, under a £750 million programme, with 28 (AC) Squadron at RAF Benson, Oxfordshire.

Based on the military utility version of the Anglo-Italian EH101, Merlin Mk3 is designed to operate by day and night, in hot, cold and icing conditions undertaking a wide variety of missions, including troop transport, small vehicle and/or cargo carrying capability.

It will support ground forces in a wide range of operational scenarios, including combat search and rescue, in national, NATO and UN operations. A range of special-to-role and portable support equipment is also available to further tailor the aircraft for operations.

Merlin Mk3 fills a capability gap between the Puma and the Chinook. The programme to procure the aircraft was announced by the Secretary of State in early 1995 and the contract was placed later that year with Westland Helicopters.

The aircraft is designed to carry 24 troops in crash-attenuating seating, fitted with active noise reduction (ANR) headphones. The seats can be folded away and a range of cargo or small vehicles loaded via a rear ramp or side door. A cargo winch and roller conveyor for palletised freight are integrated. Underslung loads can be carried.

A first for the RAF helicopter fleet is the fitting of an air-to-air refuelling probe which will greatly increase the aircraft's range and reduced deployment times.

The Merlin is equipped with active vibration damping control, which means the level of noise and vibration inside the cabin is no greater than in a turboprop aircraft. As a result, crew fatigue is much reduced, and airframe life is increased. ∎

Merlin HC Mk3 in service with 28 Sqn

See also:
▧ **Merlin Mk1** page 60
▧ **RAF Maritime Air Power** page 73

An RAF Merlin HC Mk3 helicopter

MBDA has prime contractorship of some of the world's most advanced missile systems.

MBDA provides capability to the Royal Navy with long range air defence (Sea Dart), short range anti-missile systems (VL Seawolf) and anti-surface missiles (Sea Skua). MBDA's Advanced Anti-Air Missiles System, PAAMS, will equip Type 45 destroyers and will have the capability to integrate Self Defence, Local Area Defence and Fleet Area Defence.

Aster PAAMS

Army Aviation support

Army helicopters and personnel have been involved in operations from RN carriers and RN and RFA amphibious warfare ships for decades.

The Army is a key component of the UK's amphibious operations. Soldiers from the Royal Artillery, Royal Engineers, Royal Signals, Royal Logistics Corps, the Intelligence Corps and Army Air Corps form an integral part of 3 Commando Brigade. All of them have passed the tough all-arms Commando Course, and they wear their regimental cap badges on the coveted green beret.

The Commando Brigade's Lynx and Gazelle helicopters are Army aircraft, operated by Royal Navy, Royal Marines and Army personnel. The Lynx Mk 7 will be succeeded in the amphibious anti-armour role by the Army's new Apache attack helicopter, which will be able to operate from RN vessels.

Lynx Mk7 anti-armour aircraft and Gazelle reconnaissance aircraft that have operated with 3 Commando Brigade Royal Marines for many years, are Army aircraft, manned by a mixture of RN, RM and Army personnel. The Lynx is planned to be succeeded in the amphibious warfare anti-armour role by a squadron of the Army's new attack helicopter, the Apache, which will be capable of deploying to RN vessels.

This powerful helicopter could, depending on operations, be part of the versatile mix of aircraft that can fly from the next generation of large aircraft carriers, exemplifying joint operations across traditional single-service boundaries. ∎

Lynx Mk7, an Army aircraft operating with 3 Cdo Brigade RM

Army Apache attack helicopter

Apache Attack Helicopter

Dimensions
Length: 17.76m
Rotor diameter: 14.63m
Weight: 7.7 tonnes

Machinery
Power: 2 x 2,200shp turbines
Speed: 140 knots

Aircrew
Apache AH: two

Weapons systems
Missiles: up to 16 Hellfire missiles or 76 x CRV-7 rockets
Guns: 1 x 30mm cannon & 1,160 rnds of ammo

Sensors
Radar: Longow MMW radar
Optics: surveillance & target acquisition TV (mag x 127); thermal imaging (mag x 36); direct view (mag x 18)

Defensive aids: RWR, LWR, MWS
Chaff and Flares

Subject to a Service Level Agreement with the Royal Navy, one Army attack squadron will be double-earmarked to provide support to amphibious operations.

Ship Helicopter Operating Limit trials have begun on board HMS *Ocean*. The Apache attack helicopter will replace the Lynx anti-tank helicopter used by UK armed forces. Sixty-seven Apaches are being procured for the British Army.

Fitted with the Longbow mast-mounted millimetric-wave fire control radar and 16 Hellfire 'fire-and-forget' missiles, the Apache will provide a major enhancement in operational capability. The aircraft can fire CRV-7 unguided rockets and also carries a powerful 30mm cannon slung under the nose.

Based on the Boeing (formerly McDonnell Douglas) AH-64D Apache Longbow which entered service with the US Army in 1998, the aircraft, being built to UK specifications by AgustaWestland, has an all-weather day and night capability, and is widely considered to be the most significant weapons system to enter service with the British Army since the tank in 1916.

The formidable surveillance and tar-

Apache attack helicopter firing a salvo of CRV-7 rockets

get acquisition (STA) capability of the sensor suite, together with other improvements in weapon systems and avionics, means that the Apache will represent a significant increase in capability when compared to the Lynx Mk7 now in service with the British Army and the Royal Marines.

It will be a fully digitized platform which, when linked to other STA and weapon systems, will be capable of providing both the catalyst and the driving force to revolutionise the future battlefield. The aircraft has entered service, and training for the operational conversion of three Army Lynx regiments is under way. ■

See also:
Army Aviation support page 85
Lynx Mk7 page 88
HMS *Ocean* page 92
Royal Marines page 109

An Apache Attack Helicopter displays its chain gun and CRV-7 rocket pods

Lynx AH Mk7 847 Sqn

Dimensions
Rotor diameter: 12.8m
Length: 12.06m
Weight: 4.7 tonnes

Machinery
Power: 2 x 900hp turbines
Speed: 145 knots

Weapons systems
Anti-armour: Eight TOW wire-guided anti-tank missiles
Machine guns

Aircrew: three

A second variant of the Lynx, in service with the British Army, is the AH Mk7, which flies in support of the Royal Marines Commandos as an anti-tank aircraft. The attack/utility version is operated in support of the Royal Marines in conjunction with the Commando Sea King. It fires the TOW anti-armour missile and gives land force commanders an autonomous and flexible response against tanks and armoured personnel carriers during amphibious operations.

The aircraft shares the same airframe and machinery as the Mk8 but instead of wheels for deck landing the aircraft is equipped with skids.

Targets are acquired via a powerful roof mounted sight, which helps to reduce exposure of the aircraft when engaging a target.

These aircraft can embark on the Landing Platform Helicopter HMS *Ocean* to work alongside other tactical helicopters that operate ashore with the landing force.

In British Army service Lynx Mk7 is being superseded by the Apache attack helicopter, for which shipborne operating trials have begun. ■

See also:
▨ **HMS** *Ocean*   page 92

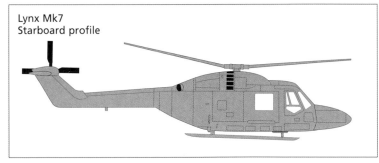

Lynx Mk7
Starboard profile

Gazelle AH Mk1 847 Sqn

Based at RNAS Yeovilton, where it combines with the Lynx attack aircraft to form 847 squadron in support of the Royal Marines, the nimble Gazelle is used primarily in the reconnaissance and communications role.

These aircraft would transfer from Royal Navy amphibious warfare and auxiliary ships to support 3 Commando Brigade ashore, operating from secure bases.

Being small, light and difficult to spot, the 847 Squadron Gazelle provides a useful reconnaissance asset for the Brigade Commander.

It is also used to fulfil a number of other tasks, including casualty evacuation, fighter aircraft control, the direction and control of artillery fire and the limited movement of men and material around the battlefield. ■

Dimensions
Rotor diameter:	10.5m
Length:	12m
Weight:	1.9 tonnes

Machinery
Power:	1 x 44kn turbine
Speed:	120 knots

Weapon systems
Self defence:	crew personal weapons
Aircrew:	one or two

A Gazelle AH Mk1 in the hover

Gazelle Mk1
Starboard profile

See also:

▧ **3 Commando**   **page 110**

HMS *Ocean* (foreground) pictured with RFA *Fort George*

The Royal Navy Handbook

Rapid Deployment Forces

The end of the Cold War and subsequent re-appraisal of the UK's ability to deploy forces to the world's trouble spots, carried out in the Strategic Defence Review, has led to a step change in the profile of the Royal Navy's amphibious and rapid deployment capabilities, matched by a major increase in spending on new ships and equipment.

The elderly amphibious assault ships HMS *Fearless* and HMS *Intrepid*, both dating back to the mid-1960s, are being replaced from 2003 by the much larger, more versatile and more powerful vessels HMS *Albion* and HMS *Bulwark*. These two ships will complement the newly-acquired assault helicopter carrier HMS *Ocean*, which entered service in 1998, and will be supported by the four large Bay class landing ships now on order for the Royal Fleet Auxiliary.

The Bay class have been designed and are being constructed according to the latest commercial practice and will be the first major MoD vessels of war to have no rudders, instead using fully steerable propulsors. They replace a class of much smaller vessels procured during the 1960s which are at the end of their lives.

Together, the introduction of these three classes of ship means that by 2006, all the UK's primary amphibious shipping will have been completely modernised, bringing a significant increase in capacity and capability. These ships contain numerous improvements over their predecessors and together represent an investment in new amphibious shipping totalling about £1.2 billion.

Key improvements include wide assault routes so that troops can move quickly during disembarkation carrying full equipment; the ability to support helicopter operations up to and including the Chinook; uniform top speed of 18 knots enabling the ships to combine tactically; greater range; better seakeeping; and lower through-life costs.

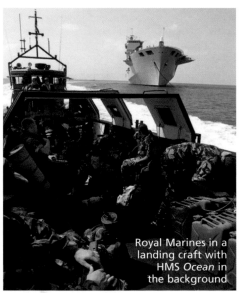

Royal Marines in a landing craft with HMS *Ocean* in the background

New landing craft, the large Mk10 and the smaller Mk5, are also being introduced into service. Both bring with them considerable improvements in range, payload and speed of embarkation and disembarkation over the vessels they are succeeding in service.

The Royal Marines Commandos, which in 2002 spearheaded UK operations in mountainous regions of Afghanistan and also operated in a peacekeeping role in Sierra Leone, will gain new world-wide capabilities through these new classes of ships. The Corps itself is also receiving new fighting equipment in the form of its first protected vehicle, the Viking, and a range of new small arms. It has also reorganised its fighting arms to better deploy its new combat power.

Complementing these amphibious warfare vessels, which are designed to land troops and vehicles straight into combat, is a six-ship new strategic sealift service which will for the first time give the Ministry of Defence the ability to move thousands of armoured and unarmoured vehicles and large quantities of stores straight to a port in a theatre of operations. The strategic sealift service is being procured under novel methods introduced as part of the MoD's Smart Acquisition programme.

The Ministry will only pay for using the number of ships it needs at any particular time – normally four. All six of these specially constructed, fast and capable vessels, will be available in a crisis. ∎

Landing Platform Helicopter (LPH) *Ocean*

Dimensions
Length:	203.4m
Beam:	35m
Draught:	6.5m
Tonnes:	20,700

Machinery
Diesel motors x 2:	13.5mw
Shafts:	2
Speed:	18 knots
Generators:	8mw
Bow thruster:	450kw

Complement
Ship:	285
Air group:	180
Maximum:	1,275
Command:	ADAWS 20

Weapons systems
Guns:	4 x 20mm
CIWS:	3 x Phalanx
Decoys:	8 x Seagnat

Aircraft: 12 x Sea King Mk4
6 x Lynx

Sensors
Radars:	1 x 996 search
	2 x 1007 nav
	1 x 1008 nav
ESM:	UAT
Comms:	SCOT1d & HF

Military lift
Troops:	830
LCVP Mk5:	4
Vehicles:	Up to 40 trucks and artillery

This is the first Royal Navy ship designed from the keel up as an amphibious warfare helicopter carrier and the first major warship to be built following a design and build competition between rival shipbuilding companies.

HMS *Ocean* demonstrated that large warships could be constructed quickly and cheaply and that size alone did not equal cost. Her total cost, at about £150 million, was little more than that of a frigate.

Her hull is based on an Invincible class aircraft carrier up to the waterline. Above water significant changes were made to include accommodation for more than 800 Royal Marines Commandos and their personal weapons and equipment, and a large hangar to accommodate 12 Sea King HC Mk4 helicopters.

At the after end of the hangar a garage, accessible from the flightdeck by ramps through the ship's stern and starboard quarter and from the after aircraft lift, can accommodate the vehicles and artillery needed to support a landing force.

Fully-equipped troops can move quickly to their assault stations using wide uncluttered passageways,

A landing craft speeds past HMS *Ocean*

speeding disembarkation. HMS *Ocean* is designed to operate away from land, using her aircraft to move troops to their objectives and supply them on operations. She is also equipped with four fast troop landing craft for use when close inshore. The ship has proved a considerable success and has been much in demand since commissioning on disaster relief and active operations, most recently in support of the UK Forces in Afghanistan and the Gulf. ∎

	No	Builder	Laid Down	Launched	ISD
Ocean	L12	VSEL/Kvaerner Govan	1994	1995	1998

HMS *Ocean*
Port profile

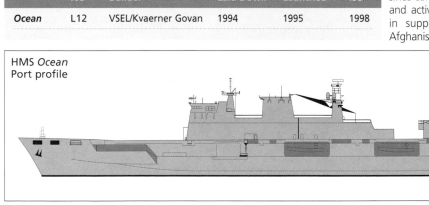

Port quarter view of HMS *Ocean* under way

Landing Platform Dock (LPD) *Albion & Bulwark*

Dimensions
Length:	176m
Beam:	28.9m
Draught:	7.1m
Tonnes:	18,500

Machinery
Integrated electric propulsion
Diesels x 2:	13mw
Electric motors x 2:	12mw
Shafts:	2
Speed:	18 knots
Auxiliary generator:	3mw
Bow thruster:	108kw
Complement:	325

Command
CMS: ADAWS 2000 & CSS

Weapons systems
Guns:	2 x Goalkeeper
	2 x 20mm
Decoy systems:	Seagnat

Military lift:
Troops:	up to 710
Landing craft:	4 x LCU Mk10
	4 x LCVP Mk5
Vehicles:	Up to 60: mix of up to 6 tanks or 30 Viking ATVP
Helicopters:	can operate up to 3 Sea King Mk4

Sensors
Radar:	1 x 996 search
	2 x 1007 nav
ESM:	UAT
Comms:	Satcoms and digital Integrated Comms System

These two ships will succeed the now-retired HMS *Fearless* into service and in doing so provide a range of new and improved capabilities for UK amphibious operations.

Albion and *Bulwark* are nearly half as large again as the previous ships and carry four of the new, large and powerful Roll-on/Roll-off design LCU Mk10 landing craft in a stern dock.

This is accessed from a spacious vehicle deck which can carry twice as many vehicles as HMS *Fearless*.

Troops can move down wide assault routes to the large Chinook-capable flight deck, or to disembarkation stations for four davit-mounted new LCVP Mk5 troop landing craft.

These improvements double the speed at which men and vehicles can be disembarked, thereby dramatically speeding the build-up of troops ashore during the critical early phases of landing operations.

The ships will carry the biggest and most sophisticated force command system and operations room afloat in the RN.

It will have 72 workstations and will be used by the staffs of Commander Land Forces and Commander Amphibious Task Group to plan and

HMS *Albion* entering Plymouth

	No	Builder	Laid Down	Launched	ISD
Albion	L14	BAE Systems (Marine)	1998	2001	2003
Bulwark	L15	BAE Systems (Marine)	1999	2001	2004

HMS *Albion* passing Plymouth Hoe on her way to her operational base at Devonport for the first time

Landing Platform Dock (LPD)

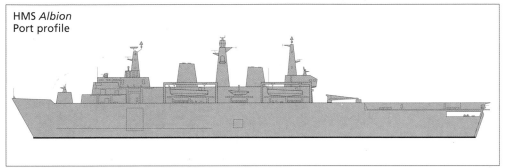

HMS *Albion*
Port profile

HMS *Bulwark* goes down the ways in November 2001

execute complex joint and maritime operations.

This sophisticated Command Support System, backed by a powerful digital Integrated Communications System, which links the ship to shore, other ships and UK headquarters, will give British forces the ability to process and work with more and better operational information, and will give UK troops significant advantages.

The general arrangement of the two ships includes a large command and control area on Number 1 Deck and above – in the ship's superstructure – with some accommodation.

Main accommodation for the ship's company and embarked military forces, along with the galley and some office space, is on 2 Deck.

The vehicle storage areas are on 3 and 4 Decks forward, with the large floodable well dock extending between 3 and 6 Deck aft.

Machinery spaces and stores are located on 5 Deck and below, forward. Munitions and stores are moved around from magazines and stores areas using a system of overhead rails and gantries, significantly speeding the disembarkation of stores.

Vehicles drive on to the capacious vehicle deck from the dockside through a large door in the hull forward. This greatly speeds vehicle embarkation and means vehicles can drive aft onto LCU Mk10 landing craft in the fully enclosed floodable dock to be taken ashore.

Vehicles can also be driven from the storage decks up to the large flight deck to be lifted ashore slung beneath helicopters.

The electric propulsion system used aboard the two ships has led to a major reduction in the number of marine engineering personnel needed aboard. Combined with a high level of automation and new technology, crew numbers have been brought down to 325 from more than 550 on board the previous class. ■

See also:

◪ **Sea King Mk4**   page 68
◪ **Chinook**   page 80
◪ **LCVP Mk5**   page 108
◪ **LCU Mk10**   page 106

An impressive aerial view of HMS *Albion* while on sea trials

Landing Ship Dock (Auxiliary) RFA (LSD(A)) Bay class

Dimensions
Length:	176m
Beam:	26.4m
Draught:	5.8m
Tonnes:	16,160

Machinery
Diesel motors x 2:	12mw
Propulsors:	2
Speed:	18 knots
Range @ 15kts:	8,000nm
Complement:	59 (RFA)

Weapons systems
Guns:	Fitted for self-defence gun and decoy systems
Aircraft:	Chinook-capable

Military lift
Troops:	356
Landing Craft:	One LCU Mk10 or 2 LCVP Mk5
Mexeflotes:	2 powered rafts
Vehicles:	Up to 150 trucks or 24 Challenger 2 tanks

Sensors
Radar:	Navigation set
ESM:	Suite
Comms:	Military package

These large and capable ships will replace four of the five RFA Landing Ships Logistic (LSL), most of which came into service nearly 40 years ago.

The genesis of the Bay class ships was MoD concern over the high cost of giving the two oldest LSL vessels a major reconstruction to give them a further 15 years of life. Studies showed that new and more potent ships would be a more cost-effective solution.

The Alternative Landing Ship Logistic programme was started by the MoD in 1997, and after a competition between several companies an order for the design and build of an initial two ships was awarded to Swan Hunter (Tyneside) in late 2000, with an order for a further two going to BAE Systems Marine at Govan in late 2001.

The design is an enlarged adaptation of the adaptable and versatile Dutch Rotterdam class ships, with increased vehicle stowage. Vehicles can drive on to the spacious stowage deck from a side ramp. A lift connects the vehicle deck with the upper deck where more vehicles and ISO containers can be stored. Offload is via the Chinook-capable flight deck, mexe-flote rafts carried on the ships' sides or landing craft through the stern dock. The large flight deck can also operate two Sea King-sized helicopters. The ships have been designed to accept a range of upgrades, which could include the addition of an aircraft shelter, enlarged flight deck with a second spot and increased troop accommodation to 500. Self-defence equipment can be fitted for deployments. ■

	No	Builder	Laid Down	Launched	ISD
Largs Bay	L3006	Swan Hunter	2001	2003	2004
Lyme Bay	L3007	Swan Hunter	2002	2004	2005
Mounts Bay	L3008	BAE Systems	2002	2003	2005
Cardigan Bay	L3009	BAE Systems	2002	2004	2005

A computer-generated bow view of a Bay class ship

See also:

◪ Chinook	page 80
◪ LCU Mk10	page 106
◪ LCVP Mk5	page 108

A computer-generated image of one of the Bay class showing the large flight deck and the entry to the stern dock

Landing Ship Logistic RFA (LSL)

Dimensions
Length:	140.5m
Beam:	19.5m
Draught:	4.5m
Tonnes:	8,750

Machinery
Diesel motors x 2:	9.8mw
Shafts:	2
Range @ 15kts:	13,000nm
Complement:	49 (RFA)

Command
CMS:	CANE

Weapons systems
Guns:	Fitted for self-defence gun and decoy systems
Aircraft:	1 Sea King Mk4 or Lynx

Military lift:
Troops:	343
Mexeflotes:	2 powered rafts
Vehicles:	Mix of up to 50 vehicles, including Challenger 2 tanks

Sensors
Radar:	1 x 1007 nav
	2 x Bridgemaster
Comms:	Military package

This ship was ordered in 1984 as a replacement for the vessel of the same name sunk as a war grave after suffering severe damage during the Falklands conflict.

RFA *Sir Galahad* has many improvements over her predecessor including a large bow visor as opposed to bow doors, for discharging men and equipment onto a beach.

She has more spacious and improved vehicle stowage, and carries a wide range of stores that would be used to support UK amphibious forces on operations.

RFA *Sir Galahad* is designed to carry out the traditional function of running onto a beach to discharge troops and vehicles. But she can also disembark her cargo offshore using her bow and stern ramps to feed men and vehicles onto large, powered, Mexeflote rafts.

These can be hung on either side of the ship's hull and carried to the theatre of operations. Equipment can also be loaded onto the Mexeflotes using the ship's onboard cranes.

She is equipped with three cranes: two forward with a capacity of greater than eight tonnes and one forward of the bridge that can lift up to 25 tonnes.

RFA *Sir Galahad* is also equipped with a large flight deck which can operate a Sea King Mk4 helicopter.

When on operational deployments this ship can be fitted with an array of defensive equipment, including launchers for decoy systems and self-defence gun armament, including 20mm cannon and general purpose machine guns. She was used to deliver humanitarian aid to Iraq in 2003.

Along with other Landing Ships Logistic, RFA *Sir Galahad* is based at Marchwood Military Port, Southampton.

She is to be replaced by the Bay class landing ships. ■

	No	Builder	Laid Down	Launched	ISD
Sir Galahad	L3005	Swan Hunter	1985	1986	1988

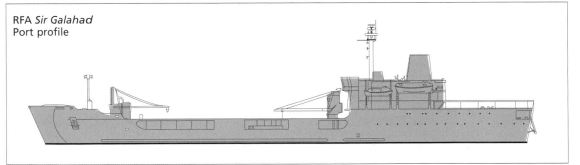

RFA *Sir Galahad*
Port profile

RFA *Sir Galahad*

Landing Ship Logistic RFA (LSL)

Dimensions
Length:	125.6m
	(SLEP ships: 137m)
Beam:	18.2m
Draught:	4m
Tonnes:	5,700
	(SLEP ships: 6,700)

Machinery
Diesel motors x 2:	7mw
Propulsors:	2
Speed:	17 knots
Complement:	51
	(SLEP ships: 49)

Weapons systems
Guns:	Fitted for self-defence gun and decoy systems
Aircraft:	1 Sea King Mk4 (Sir Tristram only) or Lynx

Military lift:
Troops:	340
Mexeflotes:	2 powered rafts
Vehicles:	Mix of up to 50 vehicles, inc tanks

Sensors
Radar:	2 x Bridgemaster (SLEP ships 1 x 1007)
Comms:	Military package

This class was ordered in the early 1960s, originally for service with the Ministry of Transport.

They have served all over the world supporting UK forces in conflicts, such as the Falklands, the Gulf and Afghanistan, and in humanitarian and peacekeeping operations, such as in Sierra Leone.

One of the class, RFA *Sir Tristram*, was badly damaged in the Falklands conflict and was subsequently reconstructed to an enhanced standard, with a new mid-body hull section added to the ship.

This reconstruction was taken as the starting point for a projected Ship Life Extension Programme (SLEP) for the other three remaining ships of the class.

RFA *Sir Bedivere* was the first to undergo reconstruction at Rosyth between 1994 and 1998. She re-

RFA *Sir Bedivere* in the Gulf with HMS *Ledbury* alongside

engined and underwent significant reconstruction.

Additional work needed on the ship, due to her age, was uncovered during the project and costs increased. No further ships under-

went the SLEP which was abandoned in favour of the new Bay class landing ship project.

These ships can disembark cargo over a beach, through their bow doors, or offshore in good conditions using bow and stern ramps to feed men and vehicles to large powered Mexeflote rafts.

Equipment can also be loaded onto the Mexeflotes using the ship's on-board cranes. Three of the class will be replaced by the Bay class, while no decision has yet been taken on RFA *Sir Bedivere*. *Sir Geraint* was listed for disposal in 2003. ∎

	No	Builder	ISD
Sir Bedivere	L3004	Hawthorn Leslie	1967
Sir Geraint	L3027	Alex Stephen	1967
Sir Percivale	L3036	Hawthorn Leslie	1968
Sir Tristram	L3035	Hawthorn Leslie	1967

RFA *Sir Geraint* with a light load

Strategic Sealift (RORO)

	Builder	Laid Down	Launched	ISD
Hartland Point	Harland and Wolff	2001	2002	2002
Anvil Point	Harland and Wolff	2002	2003	2003
Hurst Point	Flensburger	2002	2002	2002
Eddystone	Flensburger	2002	2002	2002
Longstone	Flensburger	2002	2002	2003
Beachy Head	Flensburger	2002	2002	2003

Dimensions
Length: 193m
Beam: 26m
Draught: 7.6m
Tonnes: 23,000

Machinery
Diesel motors x 2:
7.2/12.3mw
Propellers: 2
Speed: 18/21 knots
Range @ 18kts: 10,000nm
Range @ 21kts: 8,000nm
Complement: 18

Military lift:
Vehicles: Up 8,000 tonnes of vehicles on three decks. Typical mix of about 220 vehicles including Challenger 2 tanks, tracked combat vehicles including Warrior, FV432, Challenger Armoured Repair and Recovery Vehicle, Sabre, Spartan, AS90 self-propelled howitzer and a range of supporting vehicles

Aircraft: Up to four helicopters, including Chinook, Merlin or Lynx, can be carried

This class of large transport ships is being procured under a novel Private Finance Initiative, through which MoD is buying a 22-year sealift service from AWSR Shipping Ltd.

The service covers the provision of the number of ships that the MoD requires for exercises and operations and is expected to cost some £950 million during the life of the project. When not in use by the MoD, AWSR can use the ships for commercial purposes.

The first three ships have a top speed of 18 knots, while the last three have more powerful engines and a 21 knot top speed, with a slight concomitant decrease in range.

The vessels are capacious and fast. Together, the class can lift a mix of several thousand armoured and unarmoured vehicles and supporting stores and equipment.

The troops to operate the equipment are transported to the theatre of operations separately since these ships are not equipped with accommodation spaces for troops. The vessels are equipped with large ramps that can be lowered on to the dockside for the rapid loading and discharge of vehicles in ports that do not have dedicated Roll-on/Roll-off (RORO) berths. The small British crews are provided by AWSR and are eligible to be sponsored reserves, which means they can be called up to become part of the Armed Forces in a crisis. Typically, four of the vessels may be in use by the MoD at any one time with all coming into use during major exercises or during a crisis. AWSR started supplying a sealift service to MoD in 2002 with the full service available in 2003. ■

One of the Hartland Point class at sea

MV *Hartland Point* showing her large stern ramp

LCU Mk10 1001-1010

Dimensions
Length:	29.8m
Beam:	7.4m
Draught:	1.7m
Tonnes:	240

Machinery
2 diesels:	8.5 knots

Military Lift
1 MBT or 4 vehicles or 120 troops

Complement:	7

These ten landing craft will operate from HM Ships *Albion* and *Bulwark*, and from the new Bay class ships.

A trials pair were delivered in 1999 after being ordered from Ailsa Troon yard in 1998. Extra flexibility is achieved through bow and stern ramps, which mean the LCUs can be loaded from either end.

This dramatically speeds the disembarkation of vehicles from the landing ships. ■

An LCU Mk10 on beaching trials

LCU Mk9S 701, 705, 709

Dimensions
Length:	27.5m
Beam:	6.8m
Draught:	1.6m
Tonnes:	175

Machinery
2 diesels:	8 knots

Military Lift
4 Viking or LandRover & trailers or 120 troops

Complement:	7

Most of this class of large landing craft have left service with the vessels from which they operated, HMS *Fearless* and HMS *Intrepid*.

They are being succeeded in service by the LCU Mk10.

Three of the four Mk9s that are still in service are fitted with Schottel propulsors.

They are operated by the Royal Marines. ■

An LCU Mk9 during amphibious warfare exercises

Landing Craft Vehicles & Personnel (LCVP)

Griffon 2000 TDX(M) C21-24

A Royal Marines hovercraft patrols waterways around Basra in Iraq

These aluminium-hulled hover-craft, known as Landing Craft Air Cushion (Light), were ordered in 1993 and have a range of 300 miles at 25 knots.

Two can be carried on board the Landing Platform Helicopter HMS *Ocean*.

These hovercraft can cross a beach and travel inland to discharge men and equipment. ■

Dimensions
Length:	12m
Beam:	5m
Tonnes:	6.7

Machinery
1 diesel:	33 knots

Military Lift
	2 tonnes or 16 troops & eqpt

Complement:	2

Weapons GPMG:	1

LCVP Mk4 8031, 8401, 8403-8, 8410-20, 8621, 8622

These landing craft came into service in 1986. They are operated by the Royal Marines.

Others, operated by the British Army, serve in the Falkland Islands and the UK.

They were built by McTay and Souter.

Some were operated from the landing ship HMS *Fearless* and others are used by independent Royal Marines formations. ■

LCVP Mk4 on exercises

Dimensions
Length:	13.4m
Beam:	3.3m
Draught:	0.7m
Tonnes:	16

Machinery
2 diesels:	15 knots

Military Lift
	5.5 tonnes or 35 troops with Arctic equipment

Complement:	3

LCVP Mk5 9473 9673-9676 9707 9708 (plus 16)

Dimensions
Length:	15m
Beam:	4m
Draught:	1.5m
Tonnes:	25

Machinery
2 diesels:	20 knots

Military Lift
8 tonnes stores or
35 troops & 2 tonnes stores

Complement: 3

These fast landing craft operate from HMS *Ocean* and will equip HMS *Albion* and HMS *Bulwark*.

The original contract for one LCVP was placed with Vosper Thornycroft UK in 1995. A further four were ordered in 1996, another two in 1998 and a further 16 were ordered in 2001.

These vessels can go further, faster and carry a greater load than the Mk4s. Between them, four can carry a full RM Company. ■

An LCVP Mk5 pictured on operations off Sierra Leone

Rigid Raiding Craft (RRC)/Inflatable Raiding Craft (IRC)

Dimensions (RRC)
Length:	7.4m
Tonnes:	2.2
Speed:	30 knots +

Military Lift
8 troops

The Royal Marines Commandos operate large numbers of rigid Rigid Raiding Craft (RRC) and Inflatable Raiding Craft (IRC) for use in amphibious operations and riverine operations of all types from the Arctic to the tropics.

These craft are embarked on amphibious warfare vessels, such as HMS *Ocean* and LPDs, and can be carried as underslung loads by Sea King Mk4 helicopters. ■

Royal Marines raiding craft on exercise in Africa

Royal Marines Commando Forces

The Royal Navy's own amphibious infantry are the Royal Marines, acknowledged as one of the world's elite fighting forces.

3 Commando Brigade is on permanent operational readiness and is a core component of the UK's Joint Rapid Reaction Force.

When combined with the Royal Navy's amphibious ships, 3 Commando Brigade is a highly mobile, self-sustained and versatile force with a strategic power projection capability which is unique among the British armed

forces.

The brigade can deploy anywhere in the world, at short notice, either to mount an amphibious assault or else to be poised offshore in a strategic demonstration of military force in order to deter an aggressor's hostile intent. Capable of operating ashore as a light brigade in any terrain or climate, their particular is in expertise in mountain and cold weather operations.

The brigade comprises three commando units, combat support and combat service support units. In transition to war it would be enhanced by Royal Marine Reservists as well as Territorial Army units.

The commando units each number around 700 men and are based in Taunton (40 Commando), Plymouth (42 Commando) and Arbroath (45 Commando). These units are the equivalent of light infantry battalions and each can deploy either independently or as an operational group with combat support units.

The latter bring additional capability which can be deployed to tie down or fix enemy forces while the commando units manoeuvre to strike them. This comes from units such as 29 Commando Regiment Royal Artillery.

Offloading an amphibious force and its equipment quickly and efficiently is a key operational step. Some landing craft will be based on the amphibious ships but extra support is afforded by 539 Assault Squadron Royal Marines, and airlift support is provided by the

Royal Marines exercise with newly-issued Light Machine Guns

Joint Helicopter Command.

The Commando Logistic Regiment provides the organised control, distribution and availability of material which has a direct bearing on a commander's ability to achieve his objective. In this, it is a key enabling component of the Brigade.

At the top of everything, the brigade staff and the Command Support Group are responsible for command, control and communications, all vital functions in the complex world of amphibious operations. ■

Commando unit structure

Men:	690
Fully mobilised:	750

Companies

Close coy:	2
Stand-off coy:	2
Logistics coy:	1
Command coy:	1

Vehicles

All Terrain Vehicle:	61
LandRover:	27

Commando unit firepower

24x Milan anti-tank missile launchers (range 2km)
9x 81mm mortars (range 5.6km)
9x 51mm mortars (range 1km)
100x 94mm anti-tank weapons (four per section)
13x sustained fire 7.62mm GPMG
14x 12.7mm Browning MG
12x 0.338 Long Range Rifle
16x Snipers armed with L96 7.62mm rifle

40 Commando, 42 Commando, 45 Commando

The three Commando units that form the cutting edge of 3 Commando Brigade are Taunton-based 40 Commando; Plymouth-based 42 Commando and Arbroath-based 45 Commando.

They are the sea-based equivalent of an elite light infantry battalion, highly mobile, independent and heavily armed, able to deploy and redeploy quickly using their own helicopter force and able to operate and manoeuvre independently, with added artillery and engineer support or as part of a larger formation.

The Commando units are undergoing reorganisation to a new 'Commando 21' standard so that they are better able to exploit the increased firepower and manoeuvrability brought by new equipment.

Instead of the traditional formation structure of three rifle companies, one headquarters and one support company, each unit is being recast with four combat companies, with little change to overall manpower.

The new Command company will take responsibility for overall battlefield command, communications, intelligence, surveillance and reconnaissance.

The Command company will also contain all unit level manoeuvre support troops, who would be used to reinforce in attack or defence. This force is armed with Browning heavy machine guns, General Purpose Machine Guns (GPMGs), Milan guided missiles, long range rifles and has

Men of 45 Commando on operations in Afghanistan in 2002

assault engineers attached.

The Logistics company manages all administrative and logistic activity and is composed of two identical 'A' echelons which each hold one day's combat supplies for the entire commando. 'B' echelon is smaller and can be based on ship.

The new Close companies are manoeuvre forces, with enhanced support. Each of its three troops has a manoeuvre support section of five men equipped with GPMGs, long range rifles and 51mm mortars.

The Stand-Off companies are optimised for manoeuvre support. Each has two direct fire troops, equipped with heavy and medium machine guns and anti-tank guided weapons and one close combat troop equipped as in one of the Close companies.

Each of the Commando units are being equipped with around 30 tracked All Terrain Vehicles (Protected). These 'Viking' vehicles will enable the Commandos to manoeuvre under direct fire. ■

See also:

▨ **Royal Marines Commandos page 109**
▨ **'Viking' page 172**

Men of 42 Commando aboard an 845 Sqn Sea King during operations in southern Iraq

Commando unit structure

Men: 570
fully mobilised: 705

Gun batteries:
7 (Sphinx) Cdo Battery
8 (Alma) Cdo Battery
79 (Kirkee) Cdo Battery
Others:
23 (Gibraltar 1779-83)
Cdo HQ Battery
148 (Meiktila) Cdo
Forward Observation
Battery

Commando unit firepower:
Gun Batteries
3 x 6 105mm Light Guns
1 x 6 105mm Light Guns
(Territorial Army)

Vehicles Pinzgauers

This affiliated Army regiment, based in the Citadel of Plymouth, is the close support Artillery Regiment that operates with 3 Commando Brigade Royal Marines.

It directly supports the force with three batteries of 105mm light guns – each battery has six guns and reinforces each of the commando units. A further six guns are available from a Territorial Army Commando Battery.

The light gun has a range of more than 17 kilometres and is capable of firing a shell every ten seconds. It can be airlifted by Sea King Mk4 and is ready for action within minutes of deployment. The Pinzgauer is the prime mover for the light gun, and the BV206D is regularly used as a limber vehicle.

The gun is manned by a crew of six, and can be used in the direct fire anti-armour role as a well as for indirect fire. The gun's fire is directed by Forward Observation Officers (FOOs), also from 29 Commando, who deploy well forward with the rifle companies.

Accuracy is enhanced by laser range finders and the MSTAR mobile battlefield radar unit, carried by FOOs. MSTAR assists them in detecting the fall of shot in relation to the target, and enables them to make rapid

Sea King HC4 lifts a 105mm light gun

adjustments to fire.

Part of 29 Commando is the Poole-based 148 Commando Battery, whose role is to direct naval gunfire support. Most of the RN's frigates and destroyers have a 114mm gun mounted on the bow. With its automatic loading mechanism each can provide a substantial weight of fire to support operations in the littoral area.

Comprising predominantly gunners and specialist radio operators from the Royal Navy, the Battery deploys observers to spot and make adjustments to the fire provided by ships of the naval task force.

The Regiment is equipped with BATES (Battlefield Artillery Target Engagement System) and its lightweight counterpart LACS (Lightweight Artillery Computer System). These two systems allow the unit to computerise fire control orders and send information as data messages. This dramatically speeds up the process of calling for and adjusting fire missions.

When 3 Commando Brigade is operating with a larger formation, such as 3 (UK) Division, 29 Commando groups itself with the remainder of the Division's artillery into an Offensive Support Group (OSG).

Although in this case the regiment no longer directly supports the Brigade, the Brigade has access to reinforcing fire from up to four regiments of Artillery from the OSG. ■

See also:

◩ **Royal Marines Commandos page 109**
◩ **3 Commando Brigade page 110**

An RAF Chinook helicopter moves guns of 29 Cdo Regt in Afghanistan

Commando Logistic Regiment

Commando unit structure
Men: 700
fully mobilised: 1,000

Units
Headquarters Sqn
Landing Force Support Pty
Equipment Support Sqn
Logistic Support Sqn
Medical Sqn

Vehicles
All Terrain Vehicles:
Land Rovers

The regiment is unique in that it is able to provide essential supplies for front-line Commando units for the initial 30 days of any operation by the transfer of stores from ship to shore – making it totally self-sufficient.

It can support any sized force from a company group to a brigade anywhere in the world. Marines, sailors and soldiers form the Regiment, which is organised into five squadrons.

The role of Headquarters Squadron (HQ Sqn) is to co-ordinate the command and control function of logistic distribution, relaying stores information by computer from ship to shore and collating field requirements from forward units and assessing their priority of order for delivery or recovery.

The Landing Force Support Party would be landed immediately after the ground troops during the initial stage of an amphibious operation, to provide control of beach and landing support areas.

The Equipment Support Squadron provides the second line repair and recovery services for all the equipment used by 3 Commando Brigade. The repair of equipment can range from a rifle through to the replacement of entire engine systems. The ES Squadron ensures that vehicles are repaired as close to the front line as possible, in order that they can be returned to the battle quickly and efficiently. The squadron is primarily manned by Royal Marines, but also contains some Army personnel, from trades such as vehicle mechanics, armourers and metalsmiths.

The Logistic Support Squadron comprises a headquarters and three Troops made up from a combination of Royal Marines and the Army's Royal Logistic Corps (RLC) personnel. The squadron provides 3 Commando Brigade with second line logistic support that includes transport, stores and bulk fuel.

The Medical Squadron comprises a headquarters, two medical troops and a support troop. Each medical troop provides a 50-bed dressing station, akin to a cottage hospital. They can operate independently or join together to make a 100-bed facility.

The dressing stations can be erected and dismantled within three hours and are capable of treating 500 battle casualties each before requiring re-supply, at a rate of 100 per day. They are versatile and rapidly deployed, as they can also be broken down to make 25-bedded units when a smaller operational footprint is required. ■

See also:
■ **Royal Marines Commandos page 109**
■ **3 Commando Brigade page 110**

Soldiers of the Cdo Logistic Regt at work during deployment in Afghanistan

Fleet Protection Group Royal Marines

The Fleet Protection Group Royal Marines (FPGRM) is headquartered at HM Naval Base Clyde on the west coast of Scotland – home to the four Vanguard class missile submarines that make up the UK's strategic nuclear deterrent force.

The Unit was formed in January 1980 as Comacchio Company, but in 1983 it increased in size and became Comacchio Group.

It is now reformed as the newly-evolved FPGRM. The core task for FPGRM remains, as it has been since the formation of Comacchio Group, to provide military support for the protection of the nuclear deterrent at Faslane and Coulport and other important establishments.

FPGRM has more than 430 men organised into three rifle squadrons, O, P and R, and one headquarters squadron.

Its personnel routinely deploy worldwide with the Fleet Standby Rifle Troop (FSRT), and as members of specially trained boarding teams in support of the Royal Navy, RFA and the Royal Air Force.

FSRT tasks are a relatively new focus for the FPGRM. Tasks have ranged from force protection in the Gulf and Sierra Leone to conducting non-compliant boarding operations in order to enforce UN resolutions in the Gulf. The Group also provides security for Northwood HQ in London. ■

See also:

▷ Naval shore establishments page 191
▷ Faslane   page 194

Men of FPG on operations in the northern Arabian Gulf

Men of 539 at sea in a raiding craft

539 Assault Squadron Royal Marines provides organic landing craft and raiding craft capabilities for 3 Commando Brigade Royal Marines.

This squadron has been based at RM Turnchapel in Plymouth since 1993, from where it deploys boat groups for operations and exercises worldwide.

The squadron was formed in 1984 as a result of lessons learnt during the Falklands conflict.

The squadron's number has a significant history – it was derived from the most distinguished Landing Craft Flotilla to take part in the D-Day Landings of 6 June 1944. ■

This squadron, based at Chivenor in Devon, provides engineer support for most Brigade deployments and operations. It consists of a headquarters, three field troops, a reconnaissance troop, a support troop and a workshop. Its tasks centre on mobility, counter-mobility and survivability – from preparing beach landing sites to clearing explosive ordnance. Further support is provided by 131 Independent Commando Squadron RE, 2 Troop of 33 Engineer Regiment (Explosive Ordnance Disposal) and elements of Specialist Team Royal Engineers (Bulk Petroleum). ■

59 Ind Commando Sqn RE

A 59 Cdo soldier with suspected Talebani / Al Qaeda munitions

UK Landing Force Command Support Group

The Headquarters and Signals Squadron, about 450 men strong, is the Brigade Commander's command and control unit, both in the UK and on operations. It is bigger than the equivalent unit in the Army, because of the additional six sub-units which in the Army are found at divisional level. The group is based in Plymouth. Its sub units are:

Brigade Patrol Troop

This consists of six four-man teams working ahead of the main force in a reconnaissance role, reporting directly back to Brigade Headquarters. They may be to the flank or rear or up to 60 kilometres ahead of the main body of the Brigade.

Y Troop

This specialist electronic warfare troop is equipped with the latest equipment to intercept and analyse radio traffic, gathering high-level intelligence on the enemy. Its Radio Reconnaissance Teams, which can deploy as pre-assault forces with the reconnaissance forces, conduct electronic support measures consisting of intercept and direction-finding tasks and then relay the information gained directly back for collation.

Comms Squadron

Communications Squadron is

Reconnaissance forces in the snow

manned by Royal Marine Signallers and provides secure communications for the Brigade. It also provides satellite communications from anywhere in the world to a rear link command or seaborne Headquarters.

Air Defence Troop

This troop is responsible for point air defence – the defence of small sites such as commando HQs or specific vehicles. It is armed with the High Velocity Missile system which can either be shoulder-launched or fired from a ground-mounted firing post.

RM Police Troop

RMP troop co-ordinates vehicle movements out of the beachhead, marks the main supply routes and provides convoy escorts. In addition to general police duties it provides close protection for the Brigade Commander.

Tactical Air Control Parties

These small four man teams are responsible for co-ordinating and directing close air support aircraft during combat.

Logistics Squadron

This Squadron is responsible for logistical support to both Brigade Headquarters and UKLF CSG. ■

Reserve and Training Forces

Reserve forces are integral parts of the Royal Navy, comprising around 4,800 men and women who train in peacetime to enable the Royal Navy to meet its operational commitments in time of stretch, tension and war.

The concept of reserves goes back many hundreds of years, and was formalised with the foundation in 1859 of the Royal Naval Reserve (RNR) which drew from the ranks of the merchant marine community. This was followed in 1903 by the formation of the Royal Naval Volunteer Reserve (RNVR) which drew its membership from all walks of life. During the Second World War, over 500,000 reservists served with distinction alongside their regular Royal Navy counterparts.

Today, the reserve forces comprise the Royal Naval Reserve, the Royal Marines Reserve, and the University Royal Naval Units. Each of these provides excellent training opportunities and experience, while their ultimate objective is to provide a pool of trained manpower to supplement the regular forces in times of need.

The Royal Marines Reserve (RMR) is a volunteer force of 970 officers and other ranks. The primary role of the RMR is to reinforce the Royal Marines Commandos world-wide. In particular, it is designed to provide an infrastructure for force generation and reconstitution in times of national emergency.

University Royal Naval Units (URNUs) are a sub-division of the RNR and provide dedicated

The Royal Marines Reserve conduct training with regular units

reserve training for university undergraduates. There are currently 14 units around the country, many of which extend their membership to more than one university in the area. ■

Royal Naval Reserve

Today's Royal Naval Reserve (RNR) comprises around 3,850 men and women and is largely organised into 13 units based at Reserve Training Centres around the country from Greenock to Devonport and from Belfast to London. Several centres now have satellite bases in towns and cities not served by major RNR units, thereby increasing their accessibility to the public.

Reservists train in a variety of naval skills including communications, seamanship and logistics. In addition there are certain specialisations, including Naval Control of Shipping (NCS) and media relations, where the RNR contains the majority of the Royal Navy's expertise. There is a medical branch, comprising medical practitioners and nurses of all specialities, and an air branch, many of whose members are professional aviators and fly with the Fleet Air Arm during their reserve service.

Reservists are required to complete at least 24 days training per year, which will be split between operational role training alongside regular servicemen, and support activity largely focused on evenings and weekends.

The modern role of the reservist is very much to support the front-line, and the RNR forms a valuable pool of trained manpower which is on call to augment the Fleet in times of increased need. Large exercises and operations will usually see a significant uptake of reservists commensurate with the increased overall workload. Elsewhere, reservists will

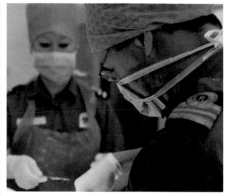

often be used to release regular servicemen for leave when they would otherwise not be spared, and to fill temporary manpower gaps. RNR members are subject to the Reserve Forces Act of 1996 which makes them liable for compulsory call-up in times of national emergency or in support of military operations outside the UK. Although many reservists are former Royal Navy officers and ratings, 75 percent of the RNR is made up of volunteers with no regular experience. Membership brings rewards in the forms of personal development, challenge, adventure and of course financial recompense.

University Royal Naval Units (URNUs) are a sub-division of the RNR and provide dedicated reserve training for university undergraduates. There are currently 14 units around the country, many of which extend their membership to more than one university in the area. Undergraduates join as members of the RNR, holding the rank of Honorary Midshipman, and undergo a programme of training commensurate with a three-year membership, the normal duration of university attendance. Each University unit has an Archer class training vessel assigned, so the majority of training is focused on the seagoing environment. In addition, there are weekly training evenings and the opportunity to partake in the wider spectrum of naval activities and adventurous pursuits. Members are paid at RNR rates and there is no obligation to commit to joining the RN/RNR upon graduation, but URNU training will stand applicants in very good stead. ■

An URNU crew at sea – and a Royal Naval Reserves medic at work

Archer Class (P2000)

Dimensions
Length:	20.8m
Beam:	5.8m
Draught:	1.8m
Tonnes:	54

Machinery
Diesels:	2
Speed:	20 knots
Range @ 15kts:	550nm
Complement:	5 (plus 12)

The 14 Archer class fast training boats of the Inshore Training Squadron provide University Royal Naval Units with their own seagoing training facility. Based in ports close to their respective universities, the vessels can accommodate 12 students, plus a permanent crew of 5. Weekends at sea and longer deployments during vacations give the undergraduates training in naval skills, whilst providing excellent opportunities for personal development.

	No	ISD	URNU
Archer	P264	1985	Aberdeen
Biter	P270	1986	Manchester
Smiter	P272	1986	Glasgow
Pursuer	P273	1988	Sussex
Blazer	P279	1988	Southampton
Dasher	P280	1988	Bristol
Puncher	P291	1988	London
Charger	P292	1988	Liverpool
Ranger	P293	1988	tbd
Trumpeter	P294	1988	tbd
Express	P163	1988	Wales
Example	P165	1985	Northumbria
Explorer	P164	1986	Hull
Exploit	P167	1988	Birmingham
Tracker	P274	1998	Oxford
Raider	P275	1998	Cambridge

HMS *Puncher*

Two more vessels (*Ranger* and *Trumpeter*) are currently employed on patrol duties in Gibraltar. They are likely to be assigned to two new University Royal Naval Units if plans to bring them back to UK are confirmed.

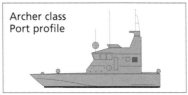

Archer class
Port profile

Royal Marines Reserve

The Royal Marines Reserve (RMR) is a volunteer force of 970 officers and other ranks.

Volunteers join the RMR either straight from civilian life, or after service in the regular force.

Like the RNR, they provide a vital adjunct to their regular counterparts in time of war or emergency and are, naturally, subject to the Reserve Forces Act.

There are five RMR Training Centres: London, Glasgow, Bristol, Merseyside and Newcastle, as well as smaller outlying detachments administered from the main centres.

Volunteers are recruited and undergo their initial training locally. When ready, they are sent to the Commando Training Centre Royal Marines at Lympstone in Devon, where they will undergo the full Commando Course and earn the coveted green beret. The commando tests must be passed in exactly the same way and to the same standards as are demanded of regular Marines.

As with the RNR, members are paid for their service and their annual training commitment is broadly similar. Once fully trained, the reservist has the opportunity to conduct training with regular units, and to qualify in a variety of specialist skills.

The primary role of the RMR is to reinforce the Royal Marines with individuals and sub-units worldwide.

In particular, it is designed to provide an infrastructure for force generation and reconstitution in times of national emergency. In addition, it aims to promote a nationwide link between the Royal Marine and civilian communities. ∎

A Royal Marines exercise – the RMR exists to reinforce and support regular units worldwide

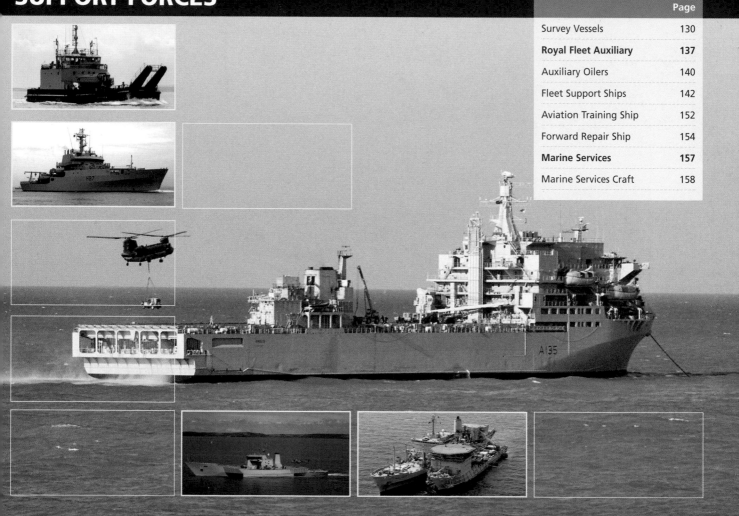

SUPPORT FORCES

RFAs *Fort Austin* (left) and *Diligence* in the Gulf in 2003

The Royal Navy Handbook

Support Forces

Survey vessel HMS *Scott* with Plymouth Hoe in the background

This section covers the supporting forces that are essential to the successful and safe deployment of UK combat forces of the Royal Navy worldwide – principally the civilian-manned Royal Fleet Auxiliary and the Royal Navy-crewed Hydrographic and Meteorological Service.

The Royal Fleet Auxiliary is covered extensively in succeeding pages, with an introductory section which explains the role of the service and its importance to current and future operations. This Support Forces section also covers dedicated training forces, including aircraft and training craft.

The Hydrographic and Meteorological branch has been surveying the world's oceans for hundreds of years; its first purpose-built surveying ship, HMS *Investigator*, was commissioned in 1812. Down the years, little has changed fundamentally in the requirement for oceanographic surveying.

The current generation of hydrographic surveying ships is employed in gathering data in support of the safe deployment of ships from the UK and the maximisation of access in coastal areas.

The ships gather a wide cross-section of hydrographic and other environmental data to support British forces operating worldwide, as well as promoting safety of navigation in waters where the UK is responsible for nautical charting. Depending on the nature of operations, data may be passed to the operational commander or to the United Kingdom Hydrographic Office in Taunton.

The hydrographic flotilla has been the subject of a major revision in recent years. The ageing Bulldog class ocean survey vessels will be phased out by 2003 to be replaced by the state-of-the art Echo class. These ocean-going vessels, like HMS *Scott*, will use a crew rotation system to maximise the employment of the ships. Although much of their time will be spent gathering data in support of long-term projects world-wide, they will also remain at a high state of readiness to react to developing crises when they may be required to provide specialist support to military operations.

Specialist ships are of limited use without suitably trained personnel, and a cadre of hydrographic specialists within the Royal Navy has been in existence since 1817.

The Hydrographic Branch is probably best known for its world-wide Admiralty surveys which provide the raw data for the charts used and respected by mariners everywhere, but the branch has also played a front-line role in most conflicts since the beginning of the 19th century. In response to the increasingly complex and dynamic nature of modern military operations, a new Hydrographic and Meterological (HM) specialisation was formed in 1997, combining the Royal Navy's hydrographic, meteorological and oceanographic experts into a single cadre.

Hydrographic and Meterological personnel serve throughout the fleet, gathering and analysing environmental data from the seabed to the troposphere, and advise on its exploitation for tactical advantage. ■

Survey Vessels Echo class

	No	Builder	Launched	ISD
Echo	H87	Appledore	2002	2003
Enterprise	H88	Appledore	2002	2004

Dimensions
Length:	90.6m
Beam:	16.8m
Draught:	5.25m
Tonnes:	3,500

Machinery
Diesel electric:	4.8mw
Azimuth thrusters:	2
Speed:	15 knots
Range @ 12kts:	9,000nm

Complement: 46 with space for 81

Weapons systems
Guns: Fitted for 2 x 30mm guns plus 2 x 7.62mm GPMGs

Survey equipment
Kongsberg Simrad Integrated Survey System; KS Multi Beam and Single Beam Echo Sounders; Geo-acoustics Side Scan Sonar and Sub Bottom Profiler

HMS *Echo* and her sister ship HMS *Enterprise* are specialist warships, known as Multi-Role Hydrographic and Oceanographic Survey Vessels, which represent a major enhancement of the capabilities of the Royal Navy's Survey Squadron.

Design and build is taking place under a £130 million prime contract by Vosper Thornycroft (UK) Ltd for the Royal Navy under subcontract to Appledore Shipbuilders Ltd in Bideford, Devon. The prime contract also covers the support of the ships throughout their expected 25-year service life with the Royal Navy.

HMS *Echo* is due to enter service in 2003 with HMS *Enterprise* due to follow in early 2004.

The 3,500 tonne HMS *Echo* is equipped with the latest integrated survey systems as well as advanced navigation and communication systems. Both ships have all-electric propulsion systems incorporating 360 degree podded thrusters – a first for the Royal Navy.

Both ships will be available for operations for more than 334 days each year – a 50 percent improvement over older existing vessels. Their considerably improved seakeeping qualities mean they will be able to carry out survey work for 90 percent of the year in the rough waters of the UK's Western Approaches. Existing vessels only carry out survey work in these waters for about 13 percent of the year. The two vessels will work with the fleet in worldwide front-line operational roles, including supporting mine warfare and amphibious operations as well as undertaking specialist surveying tasks necessary to the long-term effectiveness of the Royal Navy. ■

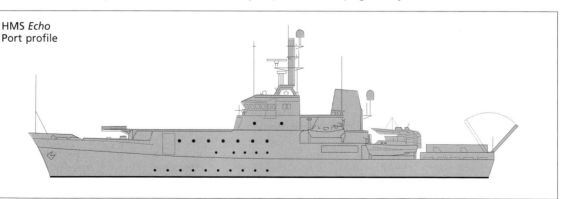

HMS *Echo*
Port profile

No	Builder		ISD
Endurance A171	Ulstein Halton Norway		1991

Dimensions

Length:	91m
Beam:	17.9m
Draught:	6.6m
Tonnes:	6,000

Machinery

Diesel:	6mw
Shafts:	1
Bow & stern thrusters:	1
Speed:	14 knots

Complement: 112 & 14 RM

Weapons systems

Guns:	None
Aircraft:	2 x Lynx

Sensors

Radar:	Type R84 &
	M34 ARG
	Type 1006 nav

Survey equipment

2 boats equipped for inshore survey

This large, modern and capable vessel was constructed as a Class One Ice Breaker in Norway in 1990 under the name MV *Polar Circle*.

The MoD chartered her in 1991 before she was bought outright and commissioned as HMS *Polar Circle* on 21 November that year.

She was renamed HMS *Endurance* after earlier vessels of the name in the Royal Navy and, ultimately, the ship that carried the great explorer Sir Ernest Shackleton on his expedition to the South Pole in 1914-15.

She is based at Portsmouth, as was her immediate predecessor of the same name, and has the distinctive red hull of a Royal Navy Antarctic Patrol Ship.

Her mission is to patrol and survey the Antarctic and South Atlantic, maintaining a UK presence and supporting the international community of Antarctica. This involves close links with the Foreign Office, United Kingdom Hydrographic Office and the British Antarctic Survey.

She deploys annually to the Antarctic, her operating area for seven months of the year. *Endurance* is capable of hydrographic survey in both the deep-water oceans and the inshore waters of Antarctica. To assist with the inshore surveys she carries two survey motor boats, which can operate independently from each other and from the ship.

The ship also carries two Lynx helicopters which can be used for a variety of purposes, including re-supplying boat camps, and transporting British Antarctic Scientists and survey teams. *Endurance*'s unique design and strength enable her to break through the pack ice, so that she is able to reach otherwise inaccessible regions. The ship embarks a Royal Marine detachment, all of whom are trained in survival techniques in arctic conditions. In addition to their other roles, the Marines are employed as escorts to the surveyors for cold weather support. ■

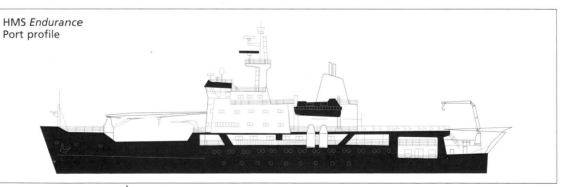

HMS *Endurance*
Port profile

HMS *Endurance* on patrol

Survey Vessel

	No	Builder	Launched	ISD
Scott	H131	Appledore	1996	1997

Dimensions

Length:	131.5m
Beam:	21.5m
Draught:	9m
Tonnes:	13,500

Machinery

Diesels x 2:	8mw
Shafts:	1
Bow thruster:	1
Speed:	17.5 knots
Complement:	63

HMS *Scott* has been designed to commercial standards and provides the Royal Navy with a deep bathymetric capability off the continental shelf.

The ship is fitted with a modern multi-beam sonar suite which will permit mapping of the ocean floor worldwide.

The ship is fully lean-manned with a complement of only 63, made possible by moving toward commercial manning practices such as the use of fixed fire-fighting equipment and extensive machinery and safety surveillance technology. ■

See also:

◪ **Support Forces**   **page 126**

HMS *Scott*

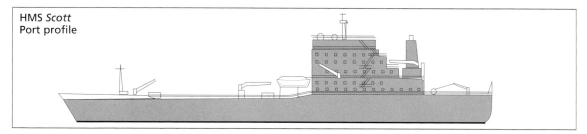

HMS *Scott*
Port profile

Survey Vessel

	No	Builder	ISD
Roebuck	H130	Brooke Marine, Lowestoft	1986

Designed for hydrographic surveys to full modern standards on the UK continental shelf, HMS *Roebuck* is fitted with a range of advanced marine survey equipment, including various Global Positioning Systems for integrated navigation and surveying.

The ship also carries one 9m survey motorboat. *Roebuck* has functioned as a support ship for Mine Countermeasures Vessels providing support during long deployments.

This ship was due to pay off on completion of the Echo class but studies are in hand concerning a possible extension to HMS *Roebuck*'s life. ■

See also:

▨ MCM vessels .... **page 48**
▨ Echo class .... **page 130**

Dimensions
Length:	63.9m
Beam:	13m
Draught:	4m
Tonnes:	1,200

Machinery
Diesels x 4:	2mw
Speed:	14 knots
Complement:	46

HMS *Roebuck*

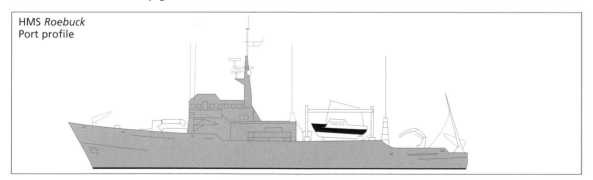
HMS *Roebuck*
Port profile

Survey Vessels

Dimensions

Length:	16m
Beam:	4.55m
Draught:	1.6m
Tonnes:	26

Machinery

Diesels x 2:	0.5mw
Speed:	16 knots

Survey suite

Echo-Sounder; Singlebeam Echo-Sounder

Complement: 8

	No	Builder	Launched
Gleaner	H86	Emsworth	1983

HMS *Gleaner* is one of the most advanced survey vessels in the Royal Navy, using multibeam echo sounders to survey inshore areas around the UK.

Instead of collecting just a line of soundings that traditional methods allow, she can gather swaths of soundings across the seabed and produce accurate and detailed pictures of the sea floor. *Gleaner* was designed to conduct inshore surveys along the south coast.

However, since then she has conducted surveys all around the British coastline, and has also ventured abroad as far as Paris and The Netherlands. ■

HMS *Gleaner*

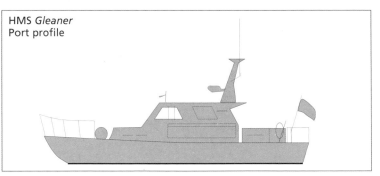
HMS *Gleaner*
Port profile

Royal Fleet Auxiliary

The Royal Fleet Auxiliary is a civilian-manned flotilla which supports the Royal Navy at sea. Its tankers and stores ships supply the fleet with the fuel, ammunition, food and equipment needed to maintain deployment.

Replenishment at sea (RAS) is a routine operation for the RFA, but demands the highest standards of seamanship as ships sail together in close proximity linked together, day or night and in all weather.

RFA tankers are stationed permanently in the Arabian Gulf, South Atlantic and West Indies as floating fuel stations. In addition, large task groups will invariably have their own dedicated tankers and stores ships.

Another important RFA task is to provide secure logistic support and amphibious capability for the Royal Marines and Army. Logistic landing ships of the Amphibious Ready Group carry troops, vehicles and equipment, and can land them either directly onto beaches, or by helicopter, landing craft and mexeflote rafts from further offshore. Strategic lift ships transport vehicles and equipment around the world for operations, exercises and routine re-supply freighting.

Two RFA ships have specialist roles. RFA *Argus* provides a training facility for Royal Navy helicopter crews and can also be used as a primary casualty reception ship. The forward repair ship RFA *Diligence* provides battle damage repair and supports mine countermeasures vessels and submarines on overseas deploy-

RFA *Fort George*

ments.

With their ability to carry large amounts of stores and to operate helicopters, RFA vessels are well-suited to provide humanitarian aid. In recent years they have brought relief to communities in crisis around the world, including Bangladesh, Angola, Mozambique and Nicaragua. The West Indies tanker permanently carries stores and equipment for hurricane damage relief.

With 2,300 officers and ratings (all civilians), the RFA is the biggest employer of British-reg-

istered seafarers and is an important player on the British shipping scene.

With the exception of a small number of training and administrative posts ashore, the men and women of the RFA spend their entire careers at sea, like their counterparts in the rest of the Merchant Navy.

Their unique role requires specialist training in such skills as battle damage control, flight-deck operations, and military communications to prepare them for their life alongside the armed forces. ■

Military Afloat Reach and Sustainability

Armed Forces Minister Adam Ingram has announced the launch of a new DPA project team that will address afloat support for the future Navy when existing Royal Fleet Auxiliary tankers and store ships are disposed of.

The thinking behind MARS is that although new warship platforms are important, being able to support them as part of the RN's capability to deploy worldwide is also of central importance.

Mr Ingram said: "We need to determine the best way of supplying and replenishing the modern Navy, following the retirement of our ageing Royal Fleet Auxiliary support vessels. It is vital that we get those crucial capabilities right."

The Military Afloat Reach and Sustainability project team has been established at the Defence Procurement Agency in Abbey Wood to determine the best way to meet those needs.

These could include more new-build, new-design ships, more flexible than the current single-role support shipping, faster, and able to adapt to a number of different roles. The solution is expected to be phased in over the latter half of the decade.

The MARS integrated project team formed at the end of July 2002. RFA vessels that are expected to be succeeded under MARS include ageing Rover class small fleet tankers, some of the larger support tankers and the stores ships RFA *Fort Austin* and RFA *Fort Rosalie*.

The MoD requirement covers the supply of bulk consumables to warships that are under way – principally fuels, water and dry stores.

An early action by the DPA project team was to hold discussions with industry to help develop thinking on ways that the Armed Forces' requirement for future afloat support could be met. ■

RFA *Fort Austin*, due to be succeeded under MARS

A small fleet tanker at sea – studies into successor afloat-support capability vessels are under way

Auxiliary Oiler RFA (AO)

	No	Builder	Launched	ISD
Wave Ruler	A390	BAE Systems	2001	2003
Wave Knight	A389	BAE Systems	2000	2003

Dimensions
Length: 196m
Beam: 27.8m
Draught: 10m
Tonnes: 31,000

Machinery
Generators x 4: 18.8mw
Auxiliary Generator x 1:
1.5mw
AC Synchronous Tandem
Motor: 1
Speed: 18 knots

Complement:
80 plus 22 RN aircrew

Weapons systems
Guns: 2 x 30mm guns, plus
fitted for 4 x GPMG
and 2 x Phalanx CIWS
Aircraft: 1 x Merlin HM Mk1

Sensors
Radar: KH 1007;
I and E/F band commercial

Cargo
Fuel: 16,900 tonnes
Dry stores: 915 tonnes

These new ships are fast fleet tankers capable of replenishment at sea of warships, and with the ability to meet future fuel requirements plus provide a platform for future helicopters.

They are electric ships – which means they are driven by an electric motor, powered by diesel generators – and take advantage of the latest propulsion control technology.

A double-hulled design helps to prevent pollution should the outer hull sustain damage. Their cargo will be mainly Petroleum, Oil & Lubricants (POL) and they replace the O Class ships, Olna and Olwen.

The vessels have been built to commercial standards with military requirements incorporated where necessary. The contract was placed with what was then Vickers Shipbuilding and Engineering Ltd (VSEL), now part of BAE Systems Marine Ltd, in March 1997. Both ships were due to be handed over to MoD by the shipbuilder in 2002. However, due to emergent technical and project management difficulties the ships will now enter service in 2003.

The first RFAs Wave Knight and Wave Ruler were built in 1946, originally merchant ships named as Empire Naseby and Empire Eveshame respectively. They were both converted into Fast Fleet Replenishment Ships, and during their RFA service they operated all around the world, including in the Korean War, and in the first 'Cod War' with Iceland. Wave Ruler also saw service at Christmas Island for the H-bomb testing in 1957. ■

See also:
⧆ Royal Fleet Auxiliary   page 137

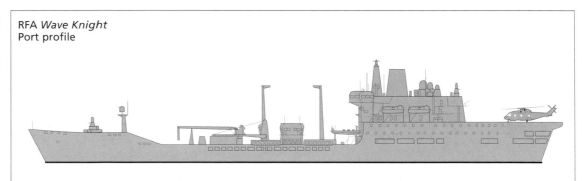

RFA *Wave Knight*
Port profile

RFA *Wave Knight*

Dimensions
Length: 204m
Beam: 30.3m
Draught: 9.8m
Tonnes: 34,000

Machinery
Diesel motors x 2: 19mw
Shafts: 2
Speed: 21 knots

Complement: 134
(of which 95 RFA)
plus 90 RN air group

Cargo
Petrol, Oil & Lubricants:
10,000 tonnes
Dry stores: 3,000m³

Weapons systems
Guns: 2 x 30mm
2 x Phalanx CIWS
Decoys: 4 x Sea Gnat

Aircraft:
Flight deck and hangars to
support up to 5 Sea Kings

Sensors
Radar: 1x 1007 nav
ESM: UAT
Comms: SCOT1d and HF

These two ships combine the functions of fleet oilers and stores ships and a class of up to six of them were planned to support deep ocean submarine hunting operations conducted by Type 23 frigates.

With the end of the Cold War, the focus shifted away from anti-submarine patrols in the Atlantic and no further orders for this class were placed.

RFA *Fort Victoria* and RFA *Fort George* are large and adaptable ships and are equipped with an expansive flight deck, supported by hangars for three Sea King-sized helicopters.

This class can embark and support both anti-submarine helicopters and troop-carrying Sea King Mk4 helicopters, which can transfer large amounts of stores to other ships.

Since they were designed to support anti-submarine operations they have a low acoustic signature and, as with the Type 23 frigates they were designed to support, hulls and superstructures reduce radar reflectivity.

They were designed to carry the same Sea Wolf GWS26 system fitted to the Type 23, but this plan was dropped post-Cold War.

Four dual-purpose replenishment rigs are fitted amidships, enabling transfer of fuel and stores to two ships simultaneously. Both can refuel vessels over the stern. The variety of tasks these vessels can be employed upon is reflected in their complements. The ship's company of 95 RFA officers and ratings is supplemented by 24 civilian Warship Support Agency staff and 15 RN personnel who maintain weapons.

A helicopter squadron is supported by a further 90 RN personnel. ∎

	No	Builder	Laid Down	Launched	ISD
Fort Victoria	A387	Harland and Wolff	1988	1990	1994
Fort George	A388	Swan Hunter	1989	1991	1994

See also:
◩ **Type 23 Frigates** **page 42**
◩ **Sea King Mk4** **page 68**
◩ **Royal Fleet Auxiliary** **page 137**

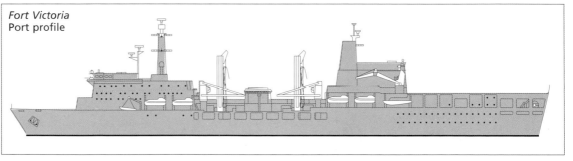

Fort Victoria
Port profile

RFA *Fort George*

Auxiliary Oiler RFA (AO)

	No	Builder	RFA Commission
Oakleaf (ex-*Oktania*)	A111	Udallavert	1986

Dimensions
Length:	173.69m
Beam:	32.23m
Draught:	11.2m
Tonnes:	49,377

Machinery
Diesel motors x 1:	9.3mw
Shafts:	1
Speed:	14 knots
Bow thruster:	1
Stern thruster:	1
Complement:	36

Weapons systems
Guns: Fitted for self-defence gun and decoy systems

Cargo
Petrol, Oil & Lubricants:
22,000 tonnes

Sensors
Radar: 1 x 1226

Communications
Military communications system

This ship, the largest at present in UK naval service, was designed and constructed as a commercial tanker. The ship was taken over by the MoD and underwent a substantial conversion involving a considerable amount of electronics being added both in communications and navigational aids. It also involved the addition of two replenishment rigs and increased accommodation.

This brought her up to RFA standards and equipped her for world-wide naval support operations.

RFA *Oakleaf* does carry some food and stores but her principal cargo is diesel and aviation fuels. She can replenish two ships simultaneously, one on each beam, and can refuel a ship astern. Replenishment At Sea on each beam requires a high degree of seamanship, especially in rough weather and at night. The astern option, which involves trailing the RAS hose over the back of the tanker for the receiving warship, is less efficient but is considered safer in rough weather.

The ship is registered in Barrow-in-Furness. RFA *Oakleaf* is the second ship to bear the name. The first saw service as a liner, and as a dummy battleship, before being used as a tanker. She was torpedoed in 1917. The present ship, formerly Motor Vessel *Oktania* and commissioned in 1981, was acquired from Udallavert of Sweden in 1985 and entered service with the Royal Fleet Auxiliary in 1986. ■

An RAS operation between RFA *Oakleaf* and RFA *Fort Victoria*

RFA *Oakleaf*

Support Tanker RFA (AO)

	No	Builder	Launched	ISD
Brambleleaf	A81	Cammell Laird	1973	1980
Bayleaf	A109	Cammell Laird	1981	1982
Orangeleaf	A110	Cammell Laird	1973	1979

Dimensions
Length: 170.69m
Beam: 25.94m
Draught: 11m
Tonnes: 40,000

Machinery
Diesel motors x 2:   10.4mw
Shafts: 1
Speed: 15 knots

Complement: 56

Weapons systems
Guns: 2 x 20mm;
   4 x 7.62mm machine guns

Cargo
Petrol, Oil & Lubricants:
                22,000 tonnes

Sensors
 Racal Decca 1226 and 1229;
                      I-band

These ships have dual responsibility for the replenishing of warships at sea and for the bulk movement of fuels between Ministry of Defence depots.

All three ships were originally designed as commercial tankers but were taken over by the MoD and converted to RFA service. They can carry some food and stores, but the main cargo for all three is diesel and aviation fuel.

RFA *Brambleleaf* was built as a commercial tanker, *Hudson Deep*, but entered service with the RFA bearing her new name in 1980.

Just two years later she won her Falkland Islands Battle Honours after being diverted to South Georgia from duties in the Middle East, via the Cape of Good Hope.

In late 1997 she had the honour of escorting the Royal Yacht HMY *Britannia* around the ports of Britain on her farewell tour and early in 1998 departed for the Gulf to take up duties as an on-station tanker in support of the Royal Navy's Armilla Patrol.

RFA *Bayleaf* was still in the builder's yard when the Falklands Task Force sailed in 1982, but was rapidly finished and sailed to the South Atlantic where one of her first customers was the Cunard liner *Queen Elizabeth 2*. Since then she has spent much time in the Gulf in support of patrolling Royal Navy warships.

RFA *Orangeleaf* was completed in 1982 and carried out freighting duties before being converted for full service at Tyne Ship Repair Ltd in 1986. She has since seen service with the Royal Navy Task Force during the Gulf War. ◼

See also:
◪ **Royal Fleet Auxiliary**   **page 137**

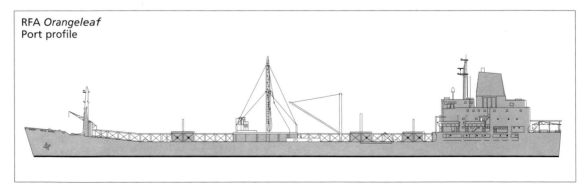

RFA *Orangeleaf*
Port profile

RFA *Brambleleaf* and RFA *Bayleaf*

Small Fleet Tanker RFA (AORL) Rover class

Dimensions
Length:	140.5m
Beam:	19m
Draught:	7.32 m
Tonnes:	11,522

Machinery
Diesel motors x 2:	11.5mw
Bow thruster:	1
Propulsors:	
Speed:	19 knots
Complement:	56

Weapons systems
Guns: 2 x GAMBO 20mm;
  2 x 7.62 mm machine guns

Aircraft: One spot for Sea
  King or Lynx
Sensors
  Litton Marine
  Bridgemaster X2
  Type 1007

Cargo
Petrol, Oil & Lubricants:
  3,000 tonnes

The primary role of this Small Fleet Tanker class is to replenish Royal Navy warships with fuel oil, aviation fuel, lubricants, fresh water and a limited amount of dry cargo and refrigerated stores whilst underway.

The transferring of fuel and stores requires the warship and the RFA ship to steam along side-by-side while the cargo is passed from one ship to the other via hoses and lines rigged between them.

RFA *Grey Rover* was built by Swan Hunter on the Tyne and was accepted into service in the RFA in 1970.

These ships are able to replenish two warships simultaneously, one on each side. They are also fitted with a large flight deck which is served by a large stores lift. This is used when helicopters – usually Sea Kings – are employed as flying cranes, ferrying supplies from ship to ship by air, and is used to speed up the replenishment process or in cases when a ship needs supplies but not fuel.

RFA *Black Rover* and RFA *Gold Rover* were also built by Swan Hunter on the Tyne and were both accepted into service in 1974.

Although not big enough to support a large task group, the Rover class are ideal for supporting individual warships or small groups on deployment. Two of the class are usually found supporting the Royal Navy in the Falklands and West Indies and the third is assigned to the Flag Officer Sea Training at Plymouth. ■

	No	Builder	Launched	ISD
Grey Rover	A269	Swan Hunter	1969	1970
Gold Rover	A271	Swan Hunter	1973	1974
Black Rover	A273	Swan Hunter	1973	1974

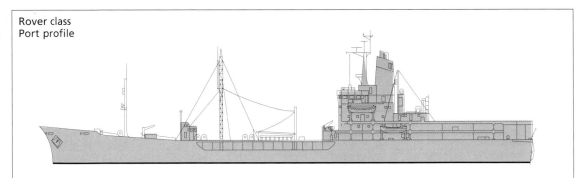

Rover class
Port profile

RFA *Gold Rover*

Dimensions
Length: 185.1m
Beam: 24m
Draught: 9m
Tonnes: 23,384

Machinery
Diesel motor: 17.6mw
Bow thruster: 1
Speed: 21 knots

Complement: 105 RFA and
30 civilian stores staff

Weapons systems
Guns: 2 x 20mm
4 x 7.62mm GPMGs
Aircraft: Hangar space for
4 Sea Kings

Cargo
Dry stores: 13,500m³

Sensors
Kelvin Hughes Type 1007;
I-band
2 x Nucleus2

The role of these ships is to replenish Royal Navy warships with dry stores such as food, spare parts and ammunition while underway.

This complex task is carried out by the RFA and warship steaming along side-by-side and transferring stores along a cable rigged between the two vessels.

Both *Fort Rosalie* and *Fort Austin* are fitted with large flight decks and each ship has hangar space allowing them to operate a number of Sea King helicopters.

This gives the ships an enhanced capacity to resupply by employing the VERTREP process to transfer supplies from ship to ship by helicopter.

It also means that these ships can operate as independent force units with their four helicopters in the anti-submarine or commando role.

The ability to re-arm and re-supply the Royal Navy while underway, coupled to their capacity to carry extra helicopters, makes the Fort class a highly flexible and important part of any naval task group. They have extensive storage areas for stowage of everything from food to weapons.

RFA *Fort Rosalie* was originally named *Fort Grange*, but her name was changed in 2000 to avoid confusion with the tanker/replenishment ship RFA *Fort George*.

Both ships won Battle Honours in the Falklands, saw service in the Gulf War and have operated in the Adriatic in support of UN forces in former Yugoslavia. The Fort class names originate from an earlier class of RFA ships, named after forts in Canada. ■

See also:

◩ **Royal Fleet Auxiliary**   page 137
◩ **Sea King**   page 68

	No	Builder	Launched	ISD
Fort Rosalie	A385	Scotts	1976	1978
Fort Austin	A386	Scotts	1977	1979

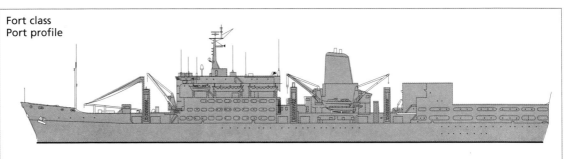

Fort class
Port profile

RFA *Fort Rosalie*

Dimensions

Length:	175.1m
Beam:	30.4m
Draught:	8.1m
Tonnes:	28,081

Machinery

Diesel motors x 2:	17mw
Bow thruster:	1
Shafts:	2
Speed:	18 knots

Complement: 115 plus 137 RN aircrew

Weapons systems

Guns:	2 x 30mm Mk1; 4 x 7.62mm GPMGs
Aircraft:	Five-spot flight deck for helicopters; STOVL capacity

Military lift

Vehicles:	138 x 4 ton vehicles in lieu of aircraft

Sensors

Type 994 MTI; E/F Band. Kelvin Hughes Type 1006; I-band. Racal Decca 994.

	No	Builder	ISD
Argus	A135	Cantiere Navale/Harland & Wolff	1988

RFA *Argus* was built as the container ship *Contender Bezant* by Cantiere Navale in Breda, Italy.

She was acquired for the RFA during the Falklands conflict and converted by Harland and Wolff, of Belfast, before being accepted into service in 1988.

Her primary role is to provide specialist aviation training facilities – which is why more than two thirds of her length is given over to a flight deck to accommodate any of the Royal Navy's helicopters.

RFA *Argus* can also carry and launch VSTOL aircraft such as the Sea Harrier. The vessel is fitted with its own air traffic control centre.

Two enormous lifts built into the flight deck serve four hangar spaces below, on the former vehicle deck.

RFA *Argus*'s flexible design means she is able to fulfill additional roles. As a logistic ship she can be adapted to transport large amounts of equipment very quickly – which was exploited during the deployment of Britain's contribution to the UN Protection Force in the former Yugoslavia.

Argus is also equipped with a hospital complex including two operating theatres and beds for 96 casualties. This was installed when the ship was deployed to the Gulf in 1990.

However, because she does not comply with the Geneva Convention and International Red Cross requirements – she may be fitted with self-defence guns or have operational units embarked – RFA *Argus* is not classified as a hospital ship but as a Primary Casualty Receiving Ship. In 2000 she stood in for the LPD HMS *Fearless* to support Royal Marine operations in Sierra Leone. ■

See also:

▨ **Sea Harrier**   **page 58**
▨ **Royal Fleet Auxiliary**   **page 137**

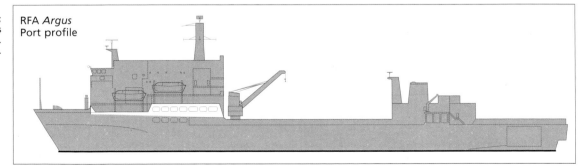

RFA *Argus*
Port profile

RFA *Argus*

Forward Repair Ship RFA (AR)

Dimensions

Length:	112m
Beam:	20.5m
Draught:	6.8m
Tonnes:	10,765

Machinery

Diesel motors x 5:	12.5mw
Azimuth thrusters:	2
Bow thrusters:	2
Shafts:	1
Speed:	12 knots

Weapons systems

Guns:	4 x 20mm
	3 x 7.62mm GPMGs
Complement:	38

This ship was originally built as the MV *Stena Inspector* but was purchased by the MoD and entered service as RFA *Diligence* in 1983.

Her role is to provide forward repair and maintenance facilities to ships and submarines operating away from their home ports.

The ship is fitted with workshops to cater for a wide range of repair and maintenance requirements. She is also equipped to provide auxiliary electrical power, fuel, fresh water, feed water and sullage reception in her forward support role.

One of the key features of her design is the advanced Dynamic Positioning system. This system utilises computer-controlled azimuth and bow thrusters and a variable pitch propeller to allow RFA *Diligence* to maintain a selected static position to within a few metres, in conditions of up to Force Nine – a valuable capability.

Another unusual feature is the helicopter flight deck which is positioned on the roof of the bridge, giving RFA *Diligence* its distinctive appearance.

The ship is normally based in the South Atlantic where her services may be called upon by Royal Navy units operating away from home bases, but she is also often called upon to support RN deployments around the world.

Her usual complement of 38 RFA personnel can be increased to accommodate a naval repair party. ■

See also:

◪ **Royal Fleet Auxiliary**   **page 137**

	No	Builder	Launched	ISD
Diligence	A132	Oesundsvarvet AB Landskrona	1981	1983

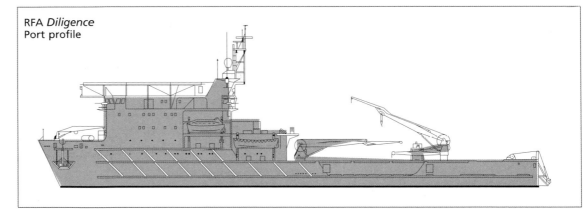

RFA *Diligence*
Port profile

RFA *Diligence* with a Swifsure class submarine alongside

Marine Services

Chief Executive Warship Support Agency (WSA) is tasked by the Defence Logistic Organisation (DLO) with tri-service provision of Marine Services and is responsible for out-of-port and in-port maritime services in support of: Naval Bases, Commander in Chief Fleet, the Meteorological Office, QinetiQ, the RAF and the Army. Tasks include mooring and navigation buoy maintenance, freighting of naval armaments and explosives, maritime support to the QinetiQ underwater research programme and sea-borne services to the fleet.

Maritime services at the Kyle of Lochalsh are provided primarily to support the British Underwater Test and Evaluation Centre (BUTEC) Ranges, and secondarily to fulfil fleet requirements in that area.

In the three main ports at Portsmouth, Devonport and Clyde the service is currently delivered under a Government Owned/Contractor Operated (GOCO) contract with Serco Denholm Ltd.

For Naval Armament Freighting, Mooring Maintenance, the operation of RMAS *Newton* and services at Kyle of Lochalsh, the service is currently delivered by in-house supplier GM Royal Maritime Auxiliary Service (RMAS), from its headquarters at Pembroke Dock

For both RAF training and Range Safety Clearance duties at Army and MoD ranges throughout Britain, services are delivered under a contract with SMIT International. MoD-owned vessels are currently being phased out to be replaced by new tonnage supplied by SMIT.

Marine Services vessels can be seen at work in the UK Naval Bases and are easily identified by their black hulls, buff coloured superstructure and by their flag, which in the case of GM RMAS vessels, is a blue ensign defaced in the fly by a yellow anchor over two wavy lines.

The remaining vessels fly the Other Government Vessels ensign, which is a blue ensign defaced in the fly by a yellow anchor. ■

These Impulse class vessels were specifically designed and built to serve as berthing tugs for the Vanguard class strategic missile submarines based at Faslane.

Currently operated under a GOCO arrangement by Serco Denholm, these vessels were built in 1993 by R Dunston.

They can be used for berthing other submarines and surface ships. ■

Impulse

	No
Impulse	A344
Impetus	A345

Dimensions
Length:	33m
Beam:	10m
Draught:	4m
Tonnes:	400

Machinery
Diesels:	12 knots
Complement:	5

Dimensions

Length:	39m
Beam:	10m
Draught:	4m
Tonnes:	375

Machinery

Diesels:	12 knots

Complement:	5

These twin-unit tractor tugs (TUTTS), built by R Dunston from 1980-86, are berthing tugs in all UK Naval Ports, operated under GOCO by Serco Denholm. They have underwater fendering for work with submarines. ■

Powerful

	No		No		No
Forceful	A221	**Nimble**	A222	**Powerful**	A223
Adept	A224	**Bustler**	A225	**Capable**	A226
Careful	A227	**Faithful**	A228	**Dexterous**	A231

Dimensions

Length:	28.57m
Beam:	7.37m
Draught:	3m
Tonnes:	151

Machinery

Diesels:	10 knots

Complement:	5

The Dog class are general harbour tugs employed in all three Naval bases. All are operated under GOCO by Serco Denholm. *Dalmatian* was built by J S Doig in 1965 and the others by Appledore Shipbuilders from 1967-69. These vessels are the survivors of a class of about 20. ■

Dalmatian

	No		No		No
Dalmatian	A129	**Husky**	A178	**Saluki**	A182
Setter	A189	**Spaniel**	A201	**Sheepdog**	A250

Dimensions

Length:	17m
Beam:	5.2m
Draught:	2.2m
Tonnes:	91

Machinery

Diesels:	7.5 knots
Complement:	4

These Triton class vessels are operated by Serco Denholm under GOCO and used in the Naval Bases to move barges and lighters. All were built by R Dunston between 1972 and 1973. ■

Norah

	No		No		No
Kitty	A170	**Lesley**	A172	**Joani**	A190
Myrtle	A199	**Norah**	A205		

Dimensions

Length:	21.5m
Beam:	6.4m
Draught:	2.8m
Tonnes:	89

Machinery

Diesels:	9 knots
Complement:	4

These Felicity class tugs are operated by Serco Denholm under GOCO and used in Portsmouth and Plymouth on general harbour towage duties. They were all built by R Dunston between 1974 and 1980. Some of the Felicity class vessels have been sold on to industry. ■

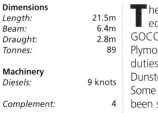

Florence

	No		No
Florence	A149	**Frances**	A147
Genevieve	A150	**Helen**	A198

Marine Services

No	
Kinterbury	A378

Dimensions
Length:	70.6m
Beam:	11.9m
Draught:	4.6m
Tonnes:	1,393

Machinery
2 diesels:	14 knots

Complement:	9

Kinterbury

This ship was constructed by Appledore Shipbuilders in 1981 as a naval armament carrier and used for transporting armaments and general naval stores in the UK and out to Gibraltar. She is occasionally used in support of naval trials.

Kinterbury's sister ship, *Arrochar*, was recently sold on to industry and converted into a trials vessel. ■

Ladybird

Ladybird is an armament carrier and is used to transport small quantities of armament stores in the Devonport area. She is operated by Serco Denholm under GOCO.

Ladybird was constructed in 1973 by Beverley and is the last remaining vessel of a class of about ten sister ships used for moorage, general duties and munition carriage. ■

No	
Ladybird	A253

Dimensions
Length:	33.9m
Beam:	8.5m
Tonnes:	284

Machinery
1 diesel:	11 knots

Complement:	5

No	
Bovisand	A191
Cawsand	A192

Dimensions
Length:	23m
Beam:	11m
Draught:	2m
Tonnes:	225

Machinery
2 diesels:	15 knots
Complement:	4

U sed in support of Flag Officer Sea Training (FOST) at Plymouth, to transfer staff to and from warships and auxiliaries within the Plymouth breakwater area. Based on the Small Waterplane Area Twin Hull principle (SWATH). Operated by Serco Denholm under GOCO.

Both vessels, of the Storm class, were built by FBM Cowes in 1997. ■

Bovisand

Netley

M CA Class IV Passenger Vessel based and operated at Portsmouth, certified to carry 60 passengers, employed on general passenger-carrying services Operated by Serco Denholm on GOCO. Both built by Aluminium Shipbuilders in 2000-2001. ■

Dimensions
Length:	18.3m
Beam:	6.8m
Draught:	1.9m
Tonnes:	77

Machinery
Diesels:	10 knots
Complement:	4

No		No	
Newhaven	A280	*Nutbourne*	A281
Netley	A282	*Padstow*	A286

Marine Services

Dimensions
Length:	27.7m
Beam:	7.3m
Draught:	3.75m
Tonnes:	199

Machinery
Diesels:	10 knots

Complement:	4

MCA Class IIA Passenger vessel operated on the Clyde on general passenger duties. Certificated to carry 60 passengers. Operated by Serco Denholm under GOCO. All built by McTay Marine in 2000 and used as support vessels during naval exercises. ■

Omagh

	No		No		No
Oban	A283	**Oronsay**	A284	**Omagh**	A285

	No
Adamant	A232

Dimensions
Length:	30m
Beam:	8m
Draught	1m
Tonnes:	170

Machinery
2 diesels:	22 knots

Complement:	3

Used on the Clyde for submarine personnel transfers and general passenger duties. Operated by Serco Denholm under GOCO.

Adamant was built in 1992 by FBM (Cowes) and has a unique passenger transport system to allow safe movement of personnel on to and off submarines during exercises in the Clyde. ■

Melton is operated by RMAS at Kyle of Lochalsh under GOCO by Serco Denholm at Plymouth.

It was constructed by Dunston Thorne in 1981 and is the last of a large class of tenders.

Others of the class can be found in private ownership and industry around the UK and overseas. ■

	No
Melton	A83

Dimensions
Length:	24m
Beam:	6m
Draught:	3m
Tonnes:	78

Machinery
Diesels:	10.5 knots

Complement:	4

Newton

Primarily used in the support of Royal Navy training exercises, *Newton* is manned and operated by the Royal Maritime Auxiliary Service. She was constructed in 1976 by the former Scott Lithgow shipyard on the Clyde as a sonar trials resarch vessel.

She has recently been updated during a service life extension period.

RMAS *Newton* can now operate in support of RN activities around the world. ∎

No	
Newton	A367

Dimensions

Length:	99m
Beam:	16m
Draught:	6m
Tonnes:	2,779

Machinery

Diesels:	15 knots

Complement:	26

No	
Oilpress	Y21

Dimensions

Length:	41m
Beam:	9m
Draught:	3m
Tonnes:	362

Machinery

2 diesels:	11 knots

This self-propelled fuel carrier is operated on the Clyde to deliver fuel, operated by Serco Denholm under GOCO.

She was built in 1969 by Appledore Shipbuilders and is the sole survivor of a class of around ten vessels, others of which can be seen operating in private ownership in Malta and the Mediterranean. ∎

This vessel was built as a stern trawler but was converted in 1980 for use as an acoustic research vessel.

She is currently used in support of trials and diving support.

Colonel Templer is based on the Clyde and is operated by Serco Denholm under GOCO. She was constructed by Hall Russell in 1966.

She is also available for use in support of Royal Navy exercises. ∎

No	
Colonel Templer	A229

Dimensions

Length:	56m
Beam:	11m
Draught:	5.6m
Tonnes:	1,300

Machinery

Diesels:	12 knots

Complement:	15
(figure depends on task)	

Marine Services

No	
Warden	A368

Dimensions
Length:	48m
Beam:	10m
Draught:	4m
Tonnes:	626

Machinery
Diesel:	15 knots

Complement:	12

This Trials Vessel is based at Kyle of Lochalsh in support of the British Underwater Test and Evaluation Centre (BUTEC), operated by RMAS.

She was constructed by Richards in 1989 and can be used as a torpedo recovery vessel. ■

Warden

No	
Waterman	A146

Dimensions
Length:	40m
Beam:	8m
Draught:	2m
Tonnes:	263

Machinery
Diesel:	11 knots

Complement:	2

Waterman

Operated on the Clyde by Serco Denholm under GOCO for the delivery of potable fresh and demineralised water, *Waterman* was built in 1978 by R Dunston.

Other ships of this class were bought by private operators in the Mediterranean area when declared surplus by the MoD, and can be seen supplying fresh water to the Greek islands. ■

Tornado

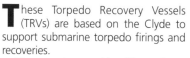

These Torpedo Recovery Vessels (TRVs) are based on the Clyde to support submarine torpedo firings and recoveries.

They are also capable of being fitted to lay and recover mines.

Both were built by Hall Russell. Two sister ships were sold out of MoD service for use in trials and support. ■

	No
Tornado	A140
Tormentor	A142

Dimensions
Length:	47m
Beam:	8m
Draught:	3m
Tonnes:	560

Machinery
2 diesels:	14 knots

Complement:	10

Operated by the RMAS to service navigation buoys and navy moorings around the UK coast. Also used in support of work for the Meteorological Office.

Both of these ships were built by Hall Russell between 1985 and 1986.

One further ship, the former *Salmaster*, was sold out of MoD service. ■

Salmaid

	No
Salmoor	A185
Salmaid	A187

Dimensions
Length:	77m
Beam:	15m
Draught:	4m
Tonnes:	2,200

Machinery
2 diesels:	10 knots

Complement:	18

	No
Moorhen	Y32
Moorfowl	Y33

Dimensions
Length:	32m
Beam:	11m
Draught:	2m
Tonnes:	518

Machinery
2 diesels:	8 knots
Complement:	10

Moorhen

These purpose-built mooring lighters are primarily employed servicing moorings in the dockyard ports, but are capable of coastal passages to service moorings in sheltered anchorages. Operated by the RMAS.

Both these vessels were built by McTay Marine in 1989. A sister ship, *Cameron*, is owned by QinetiQ and used for trials support duties. ■

Dimensions
Length:	99m
Beam:	22.5m
Draught:	3.4m
Tonnes:	1,200

Machinery
Diesels x 2:	4mw
Speed:	20 knots
Complement:	12
	(plus 12 trials staff)

The QinetiQ-owned Research Vessel *Triton* was the world's first large powered trimaran ship. She was built by Vosper Thornycroft and has undertaken extensive trials to assess the advantages of her hull form. Trials data is being fed into the MoD Future Surface Combatant project, which is considering use of a trimaran hull form alongside a range of other alternative concepts. ■

	Laid Down	Launched	ISD
Triton	1999	2000	2000

RV *Triton*

CGI of a Type 45 firing a missile

Future projects

Procurement of new equipment for all three UK Armed Forces, and some overseas armed services, is undertaken for the MoD by the Bristol-based Defence Procurement Agency (DPA).

The DPA has an annual spend on new equipment of about £6 billion and was formed in 1999 from the then Procurement Executive as part of a major Government-led reform of the way MoD bought new fighting equipment and supporting services, under the Smart Acquisition programme.

All procurement activity was concentrated in specialised Integrated Project Teams (IPT), each of which contained the expertise in contracting, finance, military advice and project management skills to ensure the delivery of better new equipment, more quickly and more cheaply than was formerly the case.

The DPA has around 70 IPTs covering around 1,000 equipment projects, ranging in scale from Eurofighter down to new small arms.

The Defence Logistics Organisation (DLO) was formed in April 2000 to oversee all military support activities and to improve support to the UK Armed Forces. It too is built on a structure of IPTs covering the support of defence equipment, ranging from Vanguard class ballistic missile firing submarines to the small tugs and support vessels seen around UK naval bases.

Around one third of DPA IPTs are engaged on new equipment projects to meet the requirements of the Royal Navy and others are working on projects that have maritime applications.

These range from the Future Aircraft Carrier, Type 45 Destroyer and Astute class attack Submarine to a range of other projects, covering new strategic and tactical communications equipment, improved and upgraded torpedoes and missiles, electronic warfare equipment and nuclear reactors needed for submarine propulsion plants. Some projects have an international dimension, such as the Principal Anti-Air Missile System (PAAMS), in which the UK is collaborating with France and Italy to produce the world's most advanced naval air defence system.

Innovative methods of procurement, introduced under the Smart Acquisition programme, have led to radical changes in the way that much British equipment and supporting services are procured. One of the biggest single changes has come with the use of the Private Finance Initiative, under which the MoD pays for a service from a contractor and does not own the equipment.

A typical example is the Roll-on/Roll-off Strategic Sealift service project, procured under the PFI, under which the MoD pays only for the use of up to six contractor-owned transport vessels over 22 years. Vessels not in use by MoD can be hired out to commercial operators. Another example is the Skynet 5 strategic communication service – again a PFI project.

CGI of a Merlin helicopter approaching the flight deck of a Type 45 destroyer

The MoD will pay for the use of satellite communications, using contractor-owned hardware.

In both these cases, under traditional procurement, the MoD would have paid large capital sums for the equipment, much of which would have been used well below capacity in peacetime.

Another change, named incremental acquisition, involves bringing equipment into service quickly but with design margins to accommodate a range of future additional kit.

Project leaders, engineers and their staff at the DPA and DLO work very closely with industry and search constantly for innovative and improved equipment and better methods of bringing equipment into service more quickly. ∎

Sea Dart Mod 3 programme & Sea Wolf Mid Life Update

These two projects are aimed at maintaining the effectiveness of the Royal Navy's two air defence systems; the medium-range Sea Dart system and the short-range Sea Wolf system.

The GWS30 Sea Dart missile system entered service in the mid 1970s on board Royal Navy Type 82 and 42 destroyers and is expected to continue in service with the fleet until the last of the Type 42s is withdrawn around the middle of the next decade.

The system has been upgraded several times and the latest standard, now being introduced, is the Mod 3. This encompasses a new infra-red fuse which equips the missile to deal with sea-skimming missile targets.

The Mod 3 missile is now being delivered to Type 42 destroyers and has successfully completed five customer confidence firings. It can be distinguished from the earlier Mod 2 by a new heat-proof black paint on the forward part of the body.

Target indication to GWS30 is provided by the Type 1022 and the Type 996 radar, which link into a combat management system. This system controls the allocation of targets to two Type 909 target illumination radars and the launch of Sea Dart missiles. The missiles themselves weigh half a tonne and are about four metres long. They are stored in a magazine and are loaded on to a trainable twin arm launcher on the foredeck of Type 42 destroyers.

The missile is propelled to supersonic speed by a rocket booster, which is then jettisoned and the missile flies faster than Mach 2 to the target using a ramjet. The target is illuminated by radar energy from the Type 909 radars and the missile homes onto reflected radar signals until its fuse is activated. ■

The Sea Wolf Mid Life Update (SWMLU) will maintain Sea Wolf system performance against the evolving anti-ship missile threat and is viewed as a key component in the strategy to address the Navy's current anti-air warfare capability gap.

The programme comprises additions and modifications to the baseline systems (GWS25 Mod 3 & GWS26 Mod 1), that will improve survivability against the stressing threats of the future and ensure the continued viability of Sea Wolf-fitted Type 22 and Type 23 frigates.

The update improvements are focused on the tracking and guidance sub-system and include improvements to the I-Band tracking radar, modifications to the operational software, and the addition of an Electro-Optic (EO) tracking and guidance sub-system.

A key feature of the SWMLU package is that all three tracking and guidance sensors (I- and K-Band radars and the EO) will operate synergistically, affording not only higher performance, but also a robust and flexible system capable of effective all-weather operation.

Alenia Marconi Systems is the prime contractor for the £260 million project, with MBDA a subcontractor. In Service Date for the first ship is on successful completion of Naval Weapon sea trials and is scheduled for 2006.

Running in parallel is the Sea Wolf Block 2 missile programme. Under this programme new interchangeable missiles are being manufactured for horizontal launch from Type 22 frigates or vertical launch from Type 23s with an added rocket booster. Deliveries to the fleet are due to start in 2005. ■

See also:

■ **Type 42 Destroyers**   **page 34**
■ **Type 22 Frigates**   **page 46**

A Sea Wolf missile leaves its launcher on a Type 22 frigate (left) and a Sea Dart streaks away from a Type 42 destroyer

Dimensions
Length:	7.5m
Width:	2.1m
Payload:	3.1 tonnes
Battleweight:	10.6 tones
Turning diam:	12m

Machinery
Engine:	Cummins diesel
Capacity:	5900cc

Max power:
183kW (250hp) @ 2,600rpm

Tracks:	moulded rubber with cord, 620 mm wide, 4-track drive

Max road speed:	65 km/h +
Max water speed:	5 km/h
Range on roads:	300 km

Protection
armoured steel, direct fire 7.62mm armour-piercing, anti-personnel mines, nuclear, biological and chemical protection, low radar signature

Crew
Two, plus 10 fully equipped RM

Tactical capability
Very good mobility in difficult terrain. Air portable by C130 Hercules, and CH47 Chinook. Fully amphibious.

All Terrain Vehicle (Protected): Viking

The Viking is the first protected vehicle to be issued to the Royal Marines Commandos in modern times and will open the way for new and radical concepts of operations on the battlefield.

The introduction of the 'go any-where' Viking has been the spur for a major reorganisation of the fighting elements of 3 Commando Brigade.

The vehicle is air portable in a Hercules C130 and can be carried under a Chinook. When the front and rear units are separated other helicop-

Viking operating in marshy conditions

ters can carry them individually. It is fully amphibious and can 'swim' using its tracks.

But its key capability is that it allows the Royal Marines to manoeuvre in a protected vehicle while under small arms fire. This gives commanders a much greater range of options on the battlefield.

The complete contract is for 108 ATV(P)s, upon successful completion of the trials programme in 2002, with series production and deliveries taking place from the manufacturer, Hägglunds Vehicle AB of Sweden, between 2003 and 2005. The contract value is approximately £60 million. Full production is now under way.

The first two ATV(P)s were delivered to RM Barracks Chivenor, for a 12-month trial and evaluation period. During this time the vehicles were tested on land and water in many different locations and climates, including an international defence exercise in Oman in autumn 2001. The vehicles won praise for their performance during the trials.

ATV(P)s will be used by the Royal

Marines in worldwide operations, initially as logistics vehicles for carrying troops and equipment.

They will supplement the 350 or so smaller, unarmoured Bv206 vehicles already in service with the Corps. The ATV(P) has been specially developed and adapted for the Royal Marines, whose special requirements could only be fulfilled by the capabilities of this remarkable vehicle.

The vehicle is available in several variants; the MoD has ordered Troop Carrying Vehicle (TCV), Command Vehicle (CV) and Repair and Recovery Vehicle (RRV) variants.

The vehicle body is constructed from armoured steel, providing endurance and protection against direct 7.62 AP fire and anti-personnel mines. ATV(P) is still mobile even if a track is damaged by such a mine. Smooth contours and edges reduce its radar signature. ∎

See also:
◣ Chinook | page 80
◣ Royal Marine Commandos | page 109
◣ 3 Commando Brigade | page 110

Viking being put through its paces by Royal Marines Commandos

Principal Anti-Air Missile System

The Principal Anti-Air Missile System (PAAMS) is a collaborative programme run by the UK, France and Italy for a new naval air defence system.

In 2002 the UK signed a Memorandum of Understanding with France and Italy that opened the way for the UK to procure a further five shipsets of the Principal Anti-Air Missile System (PAAMS) to add to the one shipset already on order. These six systems will equip the six Type 45 destroyers on order.

The first shipset for the UK is being built under a tri-national contract placed in 1999, which has a value to the UK of about £1 billion.

The key element of the UK version of PAAMS is the Sampson radar. Its height above water is driven by the need to enlarge its radar horizon at sea level to the point at which the system can react to high speed, very low level, incoming anti-ship missiles.

The radar weighs around six tonnes, and, because of its height above water, is a significant driver of the Type 45's ship size.

Tracks from the two radars are fed into a large and sophisticated 26-workstation combined PAAMS Command and Control and ship Combat Management System, which can hold on the system up to 600 potential target tracks. The CMS can control the engagement, simultaneously, of more than ten targets, which alone will represent a huge jump in capability for the Royal Navy.

PAAMS can engage targets automatically, though normally engagements will have naval personnel in the loop. The system will select which sort of missiles – the shorter range Aster 15 or the longer range Aster 30 – will be used. The missile will be launched vertically and will accelerate to a top speed in excess of Mach 4 for Aster 30, and pitch over in the direction of the target. During its flight time the missile will receive a target location update from the Sampson radar and will then switch on its own active radar homing head.

In the final split seconds before it detonates its warhead, the missile will operate its unique 'PIF-PAF' manoeuvring thrusters, which are positioned around the mid-body of the weapon.

These thrusters, akin to those on spacecraft, are powerful enough to move the missile bodily sideways several metres to bring its warhead into lethal range of the target. ■

PAAMS is the world-leading maritime local area air defence system, which will enable Type 45 destroyers to protect merchant vessels, naval and joint expeditionary forces worldwide.

There are five key elements of PAAMS: the Sampson multi-function radar; a long range radar; a sophisticated combat management system; the missile launcher system and Aster 15 and Aster 30 high-speed missiles. The single most important element is the advanced and sophisticated phased array Sampson radar, which is positioned about 30 metres above water and has a range of about 400 kilometres.

The MoD is confident PAAMS will be the best system in the world for destroying all types of anti-ship missiles, whether sea skimming, diving, manoeuvring, stealthy, subsonic or supersonic.

Its capacity for engaging multiple targets simultaneously means that the system cannot be swamped. ■

An Aster 15 missile test firing (left) and a computer-generated image of a Type 45 destroyer

Underwater Battlespace: Sonar 2087

The Royal Navy's anti-submarine warfare capability will be significantly enhanced by the introduction of this advanced new sonar.

Thomson Marconi Sonar Ltd (now renamed Thales Underwater Systems Ltd) was in 2001 named as prime contractor for the demonstration, manufacture and support of Sonar 2087.

A contract worth around £160 million for six shipsets and associated spares has been placed with TMSL.

Defence Under Secretary Moonie said: "These orders will maintain UK industry's capabilities in an important area and could lead to considerable export opportunities."

The refits will be managed by the Defence Logistics Organisation and allocated to Rosyth or Devonport dockyards on a competitive basis. Following trials on the initial ship system, starting in 2002, the in service date is expected to be 2006. Sonar 2087 will be in service for the remainder of the equipped ships' lives.

A key aspect of the Sonar 2087 upgrade is the ability to enhance the equipment as better technology comes along during the lifetime of the equipment. Incremental acquisition upgrades will allow the Royal Navy to retain its detection advantage as the sophistication of the threat increases. Sonar 2087 is a powerful sonar that uses a lower frequency than current systems in order to achieve the required performance.

It will provide Type 23 frigates with the ability to hunt the latest submarines at great distances and localise them beyond the range at which they can launch attacks.

The transmit array is physically large and heavy, in order to put the desired amount of power in the water at these low frequencies, and requires a sophisticated handling system for safe deployment and recovery up to sea state six. Sonar 2087 also incorporates a passive array, as passive sonar detection of submarines remains important.

This array must be stored and handled using the space currently occupied by the Sonar 2031 winch and will feature digital telemetry rather than the current analogue system.

Operation of the active towed body and the passive array should be unimpaired up to normal force transit speed. Sonar 2087 is also a candidate for fitting to the Future Surface Combatant. ■

Sonar 2087 will be the most advanced sonar ever deployed by the Royal Navy. It is a tactical, variable depth, active and passive sonar system which will be retro-fitted to Type 23 frigates during their refit cycle.

It will replace the current passive towed Sonar 2031 and will be integrated with the existing bow-mounted active Sonar 2050.

The two systems will be complementary, with Sonar 2087 giving a long range picture and Sonar 2050 filling in the nearer range.

Submarines remain among the most serious threats to our maritime forces, whether in the open ocean or closer in-shore. The latest generation of submarines – both nuclear powered and conventional – are much quieter and more difficult to detect. This equipment will give the Royal Navy the ability to meet these technological advances and to operate in a wider range of environments, leaving submarines with nowhere to hide.

Six shipsets are on order and the contractor has supplied prices for further batches. ■

See also:
◪ **Future Suface Combatants**   page 40
◪ **Type 23 Frigates**   page 42
◪ **Devonport dockyard**   page 196

In-water trials of early Sonar 2087 equipment

Sting Ray Mod 1 & Spearfish main production order

The Royal Navy and Royal Air Force are to be equipped with the world's most advanced lightweight torpedo system, under a contract announced by the Ministry of Defence in 2003. A £440 million contract for the upgrade of the existing Sting Ray Mod 0 weapon to Mod 1 standard was awarded to BAE Systems. The updated weapon will be significantly more capable and is designed to counter modern submarines in either deep or coastal waters. The Mod 1 has undergone an exhaustive range of tests and trials.

Sting Ray torpedoes are the main anti-submarine weapons carried by Royal Navy surface ships and aircraft and by RAF Nimrod aircraft.

Defence Procurement Minister Lord Bach said when announcing the contract: "The new, more advanced Sting Ray will provide the Royal Navy and Royal Air Force with a world-class anti-submarine capability and will be a key component of our maritime defence force. The programme, which will start delivery in 2006, will ensure that the Sting Ray torpedo remains operational well into the first quarter of the century."

Sting Ray Mod 1 will marry the proven features of the existing Mod 0 platform, which employed largely analogue technology, with an upgraded homing system utilising modern state-of-the-art digital signal processing. The advance in processing functionality will improve target detection, classification and tracking both in benign environments and in the presence of countermeasures.

Complementing the advance in the sonar performance, improvements in shallow water capability have been made possible by enhancements to the propulsion system. These enhancements extend the operational envelope in which the torpedo can be deployed.

It will provide the performance not only to meet current threats, but also to enable future capability enhancements to be rapidly implemented through increased software-based functionality. Provision has been made for software upgrades without the need for hardware modification. These improvements, together with an associated torpedo refurbishment programme, will optimise system integration and improve through-life supportability. A decision will be taken about a new warhead in 2004. The weapon is expected to remain in service until about 2025.■

A Spearfish being struck down on a Royal Navy submarine

Spearfish is the heavyweight torpedo (HWT) replacement for Tigerfish in all classes of Royal Navy submarines, and is a very potent weapon against both submarine and surface ship targets.

The wire-guided torpedo can travel at speeds in excess of 60 knots, is deep diving and has long endurance. It can destroy the most sophisticated targets. Spearfish development was completed in March 1994. Initial production of the weapon proceeded in parallel with final development and an In Service Date (ISD) of March 1994 was achieved with the first batch going to HMS *Vanguard*.

A contract was placed with GEC Marconi (now BAE Systems), Waterlooville, Hampshire, in December 1994 for the delivery of the main production torpedoes and their in-service support for a period of ten years.

Trials in 2002 against a discarded US Navy cruiser demonstrated the ability of a single weapon, fired from the attack submarine HMS *Tireless*, to destroy a large warship. The target's hull was broken in half. ■

A Spearfish torpedo breaking the back of a target hulk

The four most recent Trafalgar class attack submarines are being updated with the world's most advanced sonar system under a £600 million MoD programme.

A good analogy for the performance of the sonar system – Sonar 2076 – is that if the submarine was in Winchester it would be able to track a double decker bus going round Trafalgar Square in central London.

The first boat to be updated, HMS *Torbay*, rejoined the active fleet in 2002 following her re-equipment with the integrated Sonar 2076 – which included new bow, flank and towed arrays – new high-technology combat equipment, and stealth measures that will help maintain her battle-winning edge.

The upgrade will give these boats effectively the same very advanced combat capabilities intended for the much larger Astute class, now in build.

The next of the four submarines in the programme, HMS *Trenchant*, is due to rejoin the fleet later this year with HMS *Talent* and HMS *Triumph* following on.

Defence Procurement Minister Lord Bach said, after spending a day at sea on the submarine during exercises off SouthWest England in 2002: "I have been hugely impressed by the demonstrations of the boat's upgraded capabilities that I have witnessed, allied with the professionalism and efficiency of her crew.

"HMS *Torbay* is an immensely powerful weapon of war and she, along with her three similarly-modified submarines, will be in the vanguard of our underwater warfare capabilities for many years to come."

The programme for all four boats is planned to complete towards the end of the decade and the MoD plans to maintain the effectiveness of these four submarines during the remainder of their service life.

The update is a multi-stage incremental programme. The first stage covers the installation of hardware, particularly the new hull-mounted acoustic sensors that could only be installed during a refit docking. Subsequent stages are largely concerned with software engineering to incrementally implement the advanced processing algorithms that are necessary to exploit the full potential of the new sonar equipment.

The overall prime contractor for the programme is BAE Systems Electronics Ltd Astute Class Project, with Thales Underwater Systems Limited (TUSL) subcontracting.

A key element of the update, Sonar 2076 is a world leader and marks a step change in the RN's underwater combat effectiveness. ■

HMS *Torbay's* fully-integrated Sonar 2076 bow, flank and towed arrays contain some 13,000 sensitive hydrophones, many times the number fitted to unmodified submarines. The processing power contained within Sonar 2076 is about the equivalent of 60,000 PCs.

Fitting this new equipment, involving large flank arrays outside the boat's pressure hull, was a major task. The first three boats of the class, *Trafalgar*, *Turbulent* and *Tireless*, have already been upgraded under an earlier phase of the Swiftsure and Trafalgar Class Update programme. The last four boats of the class, *Torbay*, *Trenchant*, *Talent* and *Triumph*, are being upgraded to a more advanced standard under the Final Phase of the project.

Other Final Phase main components are:
- upgraded Submarine Command System (SMCS)
- new Command Console
- new Tactical Weapon System Highway (TWSH)
- upgraded Rationalised Internal Communications Equipment 10 (RICE 10)
- new Propulsor and new Flexi couplings for seawater services
- upgraded signature reduction measures.
■

HMS *Torbay*, the first submarine equipped under the Final Phase programme, moored in Plymouth Sound

The Skynet 5 programme will equip the UK's Armed Forces with a highly advanced satellite communication system worth around £2 billion, procured under the Private Finance Initiative. The British-based Paradigm consortium was selected as preferred bidder for the Skynet 5 programme. Skynet 5 was then the biggest MoD Private Finance Initiative (PFI) project to come to fruition. A contract was due to be placed in 2002.

Under the PFI, MoD does not buy the satellites, it simply pays for using them and the associated communications facilities over the next 16 years. Spare capacity on the network can be leased to other customers by the contractor.

Paradigm will progressively take over the management of the existing Skynet 4 series satellite constellation in the run up to the launch of Skynet 5 satellites. Skynet 5 will use at least two satellites which will take over orbital locations used by the Skynet 4, as its service life ends.

Satellite communications are important for world-wide operations by British forces and most Royal Navy major warships and submarines have satellite communications facilities and antennae.

The contract award helps maintain UK national capabilities in this high technology arena and it is good for the Armed Forces, because they will be able to concentrate on exploiting the capability offered by modern communications systems, rather than, as now with Skynet 4, actually deploying personnel to run the network.

It will offer genuine interoperability with the UK's allies and puts the UK at the forefront of the world's market-place for military satellite communications.

Paradigm is expected to launch a constellation of purpose-built hardened satellites operating at UHF and X-band (SHF), augmented, as at present, by access to commercial satellite communications resources to provide for surge, growth, diversity, specialist services and to achieve global coverage.

Paradigm will also support terrestrial long line services, providing both the MoD and other customers with a one-stop shop for complete long-haul service provision.

Additional capabilities will be provided through Memoranda of Understanding with other nations.

Skynet 5 will provide different types of communications services, grouped according to the need. Customers may request:

- autonomous bandwidth services (using their own licensed terminals);
- point-to-point services, providing 'bit-pipes';
- switched network services, such as Internet Protocol (IP) and switched voice services (ie. conventional telephony);
- broadband services, such as broadcasts and cell switched services. ∎

Defence Under Secretary Dr Lewis Moonie said when he announced that Paradigm had won the competition: "We are getting a greatly improved service with security and flexibility built in to cope with the growth in military satellite communications requirements we expect over the next few years.

"In addition, the MoD has also managed to reduce the overall cost of Skynet 5 by around £500 million by applying fresh and innovative thinking.

"This project is a clear example of how we are now, using Smart Acquisition principles, getting both better military capability and better value for money."

Services will be managed by an integrated MoD/Paradigm team from within the Defence Communications Services Agency's (DCSA) Global Operations and Security Control Centre (GOSCC), in Wiltshire. ∎

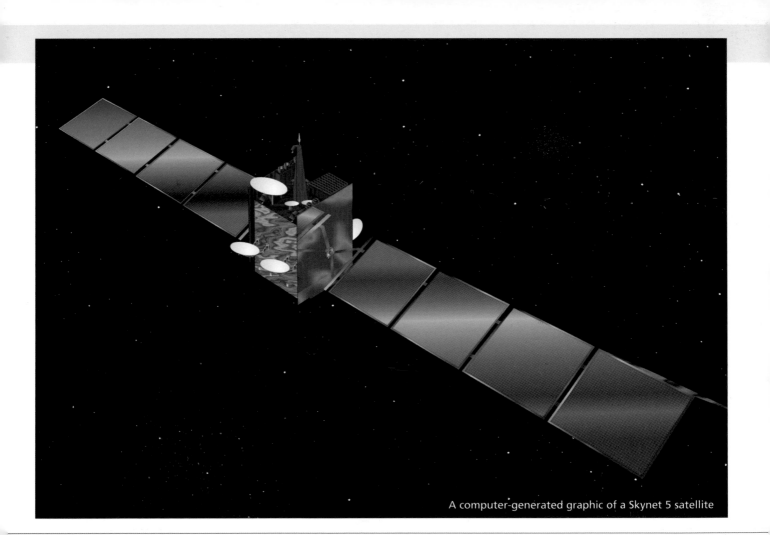

A computer-generated graphic of a Skynet 5 satellite

Bowman and Land Digitization

Bowman is one of the cornerstones of the UK's future land warfare plans and will supply the Armed Forces with one of the key constituents of its future war fighting capability.

The essential aim of UK military doctrine is to destroy the coherence of the enemy. This is done by establishing a tempo of operations which outpaces that of the enemy and this means UK forces must have a quick and efficient flow of information.

Bowman will allow dissemination of far greater volumes of information than ever before, and it will also define the digital battlefield.

The project is key to UK forces establishing the operational speed that will be needed for successful combat and joint operations with allies. Bowman equipment is planned to be fitted to approximately 20,000 military vehicles, 156 ships and 276 aircraft. Around 70,000 trained service personnel will use it. More than 46,500 radios and 26,000 computer terminals will be procured.

It will have interfaces to other communications and infrastructures both nationally and internationally, giving users the ability to communicate and exploit data beyond the boundaries of the Bowman system itself.

The Bowman Supply and Support contract was awarded to General Dynamics United Kingdom Ltd (GD UK) on 13 September 2001.

Bowman continues to make good progress, with MoD and GD UK working effectively to achieve the target in service date of March 2004, when a brigade headquarters and two mechanised battalions, together with artillery and engineer support would be capable of conducting peace support operations.

As a Smart Acquisition initiative, procurement of the Personal Role Radio – a short-range, non-secure, section radio – was separated from the main Bowman project in 1999.

Supplied by Marconi Mobile Ltd, it was accepted into service two months ahead of schedule in 2002, and is being issued to around 45,000 Service personnel. ∎

Bowman will provide tactical, secure voice communications, data messaging, location information and a number of other capabilities for all three Services in support of land and littoral operations, until at least 2026. It will replace the 1970s technology Clansman combat radio.

Significant future milestones on the project include: Operational Field Trials, 2003; conversion of the first unit (an infantry battalion), 2003; full conversion completed, 2007.

The procurement cost of the supply and initial support phase for Bowman is approximately £1.9 billion and the current acquisition cost of the whole project is £2.4 billion. In 2005, 3 Commando Brigade will convert to Bowman.

One of the key requirements of the Bowman system was a need to cut down on the amount of radio transmissions which could be intercepted or jammed. To do this Bowman uses an Automatic Position, Location, Navigation and Reporting (APLNR) system. It is estimated that about 60 percent of the radio traffic on a battlefield is to do with location.

Bowman has a built-in Global Positioning System (GPS) sensor so it always knows where it is and can report its position to headquarters at intervals set by the user.

GPS and APLNR permit commanders to know exactly where their troops and vehicles are – down to the individual soldier. ∎

A Royal Marines Commando using the newly issued Personal Role Radio

UK Co-operative Engagement Capability

UKCEC will be a cornerstone in UK/US maritime interoperability and will significantly improve control of the above water battlespace. Operating with CEC will better allow the Royal Navy to play a full part in any future coalition operations involving the US. The Co-operative Engagement Capability (CEC) has been developed by the US, and the UK is the first and currently the only nation to have been granted access to this very advanced technology.

CEC will also provide significant advantages when working with other NATO navies as, for example, the RN will be able to pass on far higher quality track data over Link 11 and Link 16 communications systems. In due course, it is anticipated that other NATO nations may field this technology and the benefits will be identical to those as for interoperability with the US.

Ships likely to be equipped with UKCEC are Type 23 frigates and Type 45 destroyers. Lockheed Martin Integrated Systems was selected as preferred bidder on the Type 23 element of the MoD programme in 2002, and a contract was due to be placed late in the year for assessment phase work. BAE Systems is contracted for similar work on the Type 45.

Continuous tracking, achieved through CEC distributing and combining data, allows the performance of current sensor and weapon systems to be maximised.

This revolutionary new defence capability brings significant improvements to situational awareness, which, in turn, will lead to much increased survivability and a reduction in the potential for fratricide.The key benefits include:
- a more robust detection and tracking capability against taxing air threats.
- enhanced situational awareness across an expanded battlespace, creating 'decision time' for operational commanders, allowing for earlier engagements of threat tracks and greatly improving self-defence capabilities.
- improved interoperability, primarily at this stage with US forces, but significant interworking benefits are expected when operating with all multinational forces, via datalinks and later as the CEC community expands.
- faster and more reliable automatic identification of tracks leading to a reduced potential for 'Blue on Blue' engagements.

The programme is being managed by the UKCEC project team at the Defence Procurement Agency, and ISD is anticipated for later this decade. ∎

UK Co-operative Engagement Capability (UKCEC) will be a step-change in capability and a significant move into network-centric warfare. It will enhance the Royal Navy's ability to detect, track and engage air targets utilising all available sensors and weapons, significantly enhancing its front line capability.

CEC is a US-designed system that enables ships, aircraft and land-based sensors to be networked with such accuracy and timeliness that command decisions can be made and weapons fired long before an individual platform could have engaged using conventional methods.

It significantly improves the quality of the force picture by eradicating multiple tracks, considerably extends the time for decision-making and provides such high quality data that missiles can engage even when the firing platform has not detected the target on its own sensors.

Non-CEC fitted ships within the force also benefit from a much more precise data-linked picture. ∎

HMS *St Albans* – one of a number of Type 23s expected to be equipped with UKCEC

Underwater Battlespace: Surface Ship Torpedo Defence System

Royal Navy warships and front-line naval auxiliaries are to be equipped with the world's most advanced system for defence against torpedo attack. Named Surface Ship Torpedo Defence (SSTD), it was announced in 2002.

British company Ultra Electronics has been awarded a £60 million contract for the new system, which automatically warns commanders of a torpedo attack and tells them what action to take to counteract the threat.

Defence Procurement Minister Lord Bach said when he made the announcement: "The new emphasis on naval operations close to the shore in support of our troops on land has increased the risk that naval vessels could come under torpedo attack from hostile submarines.

"This system will tell the commanders of our ships when they are under attack and tell them what they can do to negate the threat, by manoeuvring the ship or launching decoys. When it comes into service in 2004 it will be the best available system of its kind and will establish UK industry as a world leader in torpedo defence technology."

The system will enter service in 2004, and incremental enhancements have the potential to sustain SSTD's capability in continuing to address the evolving threat for a considerable period of time.

The UK and US have collaborated on torpedo defence research and development for over a decade, assessing and demonstrating the SSTD technologies. This, coupled with experience of the Submarine Torpedo Countermeasures programme, allows the SSTD project to proceed to manufacture quickly, with only limited demonstration work on maturing technologies.

The emphasis on defensive systems for Surface Fleet assets has, until now, been above water (for example, Goal Keeper and SeaGnat). Against the underwater threat a layered defence is deployed. This includes submarines, maritime patrol aircraft and surface ship sonar.

Operational analysis assesses the torpedo as the principal threat to the RN and RFA fleets which are left vulnerable when deployed in theatre if a torpedo launch cannot be prevented.

The increasing emphasis on rapid response operations, expeditionary warfare and humanitarian relief efforts, coupled to the proliferation of quiet threat submarines and fast inshore attack craft, places surface units at increased threat of torpedo attack – hence the SSTD programme. ■

Sixty-five RN ships and Royal Fleet Auxiliary support ships, ranging from frigates to Invincible class aircraft carriers and auxiliary oilers are to be fitted to receive the Surface Ship Torpedo Defence (SSTD) system by the end of 2005. This work is expected to take between three and four weeks per vessel and will be conducted at Devonport, Portsmouth, Falmouth, Rosyth and Southampton.

Sixteen full sets of SSTD equipment will be procured and will be rotated between ships deploying as Royal Navy operational commitments require. Installing of SSTD equipment into a vessel fitted to receive it will take around 48 hours. SSTD equipment shipsets will be delivered from 2004-2007.

SSTD will replace the existing Sonar 182 system. ■

An Ultra Electronics graphic showing the company's view of how SSTD could develop

The 1998 SDR identified a need for a new Primary Casualty Receiving Ship (PCRS), and the project received its initial approval in 2001.

Following new operational analysis, the requirement has been considerably refined and the minimum afloat bed capacity has been set at 150.

A PCRS has the medical capability of a hospital ship, but differs in the way in which it is deployed. A hospital ship is declared to the International Committee of the Red Cross under the provisions of international law, which restricts its use in military campaigns. In contrast, a PCRS is not subject to these restrictions and is able to operate in the combat area.

An Integrated Project Team in the Defence Procurement Agency is managing the acquisition of the PCRS, which is currently in the Assessment Phase.

Industry has been conducting studies into a variety of technical concepts, including purpose-built vessels and both naval and mercantile conversions. These studies were aimed at reducing project risk.

The medical requirement is likely to include: up to four operating theatres (each with two tables), with commensurate numbers of intensive care, high dependency and general ward beds; a triage area; resuscitation bays; a laboratory; and imaging facilities (x-ray, CT scan, ultrasound).

The host ship is likely to have a large flight deck capable of taking up to two medium helicopters, and it will be capable of operating as part of a maritime task force. It is anticipated that the PCRS will enter service in the second half of the decade. ■

A casualty training exercise taking place on a flight deck at sea

See also:

◧RFA Argus   **page 152**

Shore Establishments and Naval Bases

The Royal Navy has a number of shore establishments around the UK – amongst them HM Naval Bases of Devonport, Clyde and Portsmouth.

These three bases are in partnership with the Warship Support Agency (WSA), which was formed in 2001 by the merger of the majority of the Naval Bases and Supply Agency (NBSA) and the Ships Support Agency (SSA).

The merger removed the rather artificial organisational divide that existed between the SSA's 'decider' and the NBSA's 'provider' functions for delivering maritime material support.

The future of the three Naval bases came into further focus in 2002 with the Base Porting Review. This major review of the basing of all ships and submarines was driven by the increased size, not just of the carriers, but also of many of our other new classes of warships.

This review analysed the Royal Navy's policy for the basing of warships, submarines and Royal Fleet Auxiliary support ships to develop a coherent, long-term investment strategy in waterfront infrastructure to meet the Joint Operational Requirement.

Other shore establishments include HMS *Heron*, located near Yeovil, Somerset, and consisting of 1,000 acres of airfield sites plus ranges and minor estates. The site includes the Royal Naval Air Station (RNAS) Yeovilton, which is home to Royal Navy Sea Harriers, the RN Support Helicopter Force and RN Commando Helicopter Force.

RNAS Yeovilton operates over 100 aircraft in four different categories and is manned by around 1,675 service and 2,000 civilian personnel. HMS *Heron* also has 30 administered outstations, including one in Portugal, and several lodger units.

Training of aircrew and engineers of resident aircraft types is also carried out at Yeovilton. And it is the location for the RN Fighter Controller School, training surface and Airborne Surveillance and Control aircraft controllers.

The principal role of RNAS Culdrose, home of the Fleet Air Arm, is to support the ASW and ASAC helicopter squadrons in meeting the operational requirements of that task group commander. It also provides 24-hour, 365 days-a-year military and civilian SAR for the South West UK region. RNAS Culdrose is also respon-

An aerial view of HMNB Devonport, Plymouth

sible for the Operational and Advanced Flying Training of helicopter pilots, observers and aircrewmen, in subjects as diverse as search and rescue, weather forecasting, aircraft handling and other specialist aviation subjects. ∎

Portsmouth Naval Base has been at the heart of the city since 1194. Today, as many as 14,000 people come to work in the naval base at peak times.

The base is home to almost two-thirds of the Royal Navy's surface ships, including the three aircraft carriers, all Type 42 destroyer and some Type 23 frigate squadrons. Two mine countermeasure squadrons are based there, as well as fishery protection and training units. Finally, HMS *Endurance*, the Antarctic survey ship, is also based at Portsmouth.

The Royal Navy has chosen Portsmouth as the base for two new large aircraft carriers that will replace the existing Invincible class ships, and the port has been confirmed as the base for the new Type 45 destroyers from 2007, of which six are on order of a planned class of up to 12.

The naval base is home to 19 independent organisations, such as the 2nd Sea Lord, The Royal Marine School of Music and the Heritage site.

The primary purpose of the 2nd Sea Lord (and Commander in Chief Naval Home Command) is to provide trained personnel for the Royal Navy. He is the Principal Personnel Officer for the Naval Service and is responsi-

ble for personnel matters on a 'cradle to grave' basis, from recruitment, training, appointments and career management to related matters such as terms and conditions of service, manpower planning, naval discipline, casualties, reserve service, security, welfare, medical and religious issues.

He is based in the Victory Building Headquarters – named after his flagship HMS *Victory*, which was launched in May 1765 and was Admiral Lord Nelson's flagship at the Battle of Trafalgar in 1805.

The heritage area welcomes almost half a million visitors each year, who come to see HMS *Victory* and the other attractions, including the Tudor warship *Mary Rose*, the world's first iron-hulled warship. HMS *Warrior*, built in the 1860s, and the Royal Naval Museum.

Within the integrated naval base is the Royal Naval Supply Depot, which is the Royal Navy's main storage and distribution facility. This provides 80 percent of the non-explosive stores inventory to the surface fleet and 65 percent of the requirements of all naval customers across the UK and ships deployed worldwide.

The naval base hosts a new kind of store which is the largest facility of its kind in Europe. It is an automatic warehouse that is capable of storing items in 396,000 different locations. When fully loaded it can process approximately 2,000 transactions per day. All Operational Ration Packs (ORPs or 'rat packs' for short) used by HM Forces are packed in the Old Pipe Shop in Portsmouth Naval Base.

A glimpse of the future is available at the base in the revolutionary shape of the Research Vessel (RV) *Triton*, currently based there. She is owned by QinetiQ and could point the way towards future development in warship design. ■

HM Naval Base Portsmouth, with the newly-refurbished HMS *Warrior* in the foreground

HM Naval Base Clyde, located some 25 miles north west of Glasgow, is home to the United Kingdom's strategic nuclear deterrent and the headquarters of the Royal Navy in Scotland. The base has two main sites: Faslane on the Gareloch, and Royal Naval Armament Depot Coulport on Loch Long.

The base's primary purpose is to provide home port facilities for the submarines and surface ships of the Faslane Flotilla. These include the four Vanguard class submarines that constitute the strategic nuclear deterrent; five nuclear powered, conventionally armed Swiftsure class submarines; and eight minehunters and patrol vessels. The base is also home to the NATO tri-service Joint Maritime Course, held three times a year, for which it provides both berthing and Command and Control facilities.

The base provides engineering, logistic, and both conventional and strategic weapon support to the Royal Navy. It offers personnel support for approximately 3,000 servicemen and women, 800 service families and some 3,500 civilian staff, split between employees of the MoD and its industrial partner, Babcock Naval Services (BNS).

Lodger units at the base include Flag Officer Sea Training, Captain Faslane Flotilla, Fleet Protection Group Royal Marines, Defence Communication Systems Agency (North), the Northern Diving Group and the MoD Police.

Among new developments is a programme for the improvement of the Shiplift facility, to ensure that it continues to provide excellent docking for current and future submarines and surface vessels undergoing out-of-the-water repairs, inspections and maintenance.

Following confirmation that HMNB Clyde had been chosen as the base port for the new Astute class nuclear attack submarines (the largest and most powerful such submarines ever built for the Royal Navy), a full development programme for infrastructure and support at Faslane is now under way.

Geographically, HM Naval Base Clyde's sphere of influence is much wider than the west coast of Scotland. It is responsible for a number of outstations in various locations across Scotland, including HMS *Caledonia* on the east coast, which provides accommodation and support for naval personnel standing by ships and submarines in refit at Rosyth.

The Faslane site takes its name from Faslane Bay on the Gareloch and it is here that most of the facilities are located. During the Second World War the Navy became a presence in the area, with submarines operating from floating depot ships based in the Holy Loch, Rothesay and Campbeltown. ∎

See also:

HM Naval Base Faslane

Devonport is the largest naval base in Western Europe. It covers over 650 acres, has 15 dry docks, four miles of waterfront, 25 tidal berths and five basins, and 2,500 civilian and service personnel.

It is the base port of one of the largest ships in the Royal Navy, the Commando Helicopter carrier HMS *Ocean* which displaces 20,600 tonnes – and the smallest vessel in service, HMS *Gleaner* – a 25 tonne surveying motor launch.

There are 12 Type 22 and Type 23 frigates, seven Trafalgar class submarines, and five of the six Hydrographic survey vessels.

It has also been confirmed as the base for the two new amphibious assault ships, HM Ships *Albion* and *Bulwark*. These will join HMS *Ocean* to create a centre of amphibious shipping excellence. These base-ported ships and submarines now form the Devonport flotilla.

Devonport has more than 5,000 ship movements annually and it is estimated that the base generates about ten percent of the income for Plymouth and creates business opportunities for 400 local firms.

Five years ago Flag Officer Sea Training (FOST) relocated from

Portland to Plymouth. FOST trains ships from all over the world including regular European and NATO customers, plus training packages for ships from countries including Brazil, France, India, the Sultanate of Oman, Pakistan and Saudi Arabia.

It has mobile teams, particularly in gunnery and nuclear, biological and chemical defence, which means ships do not have to return to Devonport.

There are over 50 lodger units on the naval base estate. One is the Royal Navy Clearance Diving team at Southern Diving Unit (1). This 31-strong unit is responsible for bomb disposal and diving duties all over the South West peninsula – a 1,600 mile patch stretching from Swanage around to Birkenhead and takes in the Channel Islands and Isles of Scilly.

The Naval Base's relations with the community in Plymouth and the wider public has been enhanced further by the development of a Naval Base Visitor Centre. The Naval Base Museum, the Hangman's Cell, and exhibitions on the Royal Navy Field Gun, firefighting, the constabulary and the modern Naval Base itself, have been a huge draw for visitors, who can tour the base on a coach. At a recent naval base open weekend, 4,000 visitors came through the gates to learn about the business activity and heritage on the other side of the wall.

The oldest dock and basin dates back to 1689. But the West Country and the Royal Navy go back even further than that: the ships that defeated the Spanish Armada in 1588 sailed from the mouth of the River Plym.

And the memory of Sir Francis Drake, Mayor of Plymouth as well as great national hero, is kept alive in the name, HMS *Drake*, which was recently extended to cover the the whole of Devonport Naval Base. ∎

HM Naval Base Devonport, Plymouth

HMS *Victory* is the oldest commissioned warship in the world – and the most famous. She is still manned by officers and ratings of the Royal Navy and is now flagship of the 2nd Sea Lord and Commander in Chief Naval Home Command and lies in No 2 Dry Dock at Portsmouth Naval Base.

Her keel was laid down in Chatham on 23 July 1759 and she was launched on 7 May 1765 but was not commissioned until 1778.

HMS *Victory* was flagship of Admiral Lord Nelson when he was Commander-in-Chief of the Mediterranean Fleet. His death onboard as his fleet destroyed a combined Franco-Spanish fleet off Cape Trafalgar in October 1805 earned HMS *Victory* a special place in British history.

She continued her active career until 1812 and was then moored in Portsmouth Harbour for the next 110 years. By 1921 the ship was in a poor state of repair and it was at this point that the Government, supported by the Society for Nautical Research, agreed that HMS *Victory* should be saved as a lasting reminder to the nation of Admiral Lord Nelson, The Battle of Trafalgar, and the Royal Navy's supremacy in the days of sail. She was moved into her present dock on 12 January 1922. ■

HMS *Victory* in Portsmouth Naval Base

See also:

☑ **Portsmouth Naval Base** page 192

The Royal Navy is an Equal Opportunities employer and, as such, encourages people of any racial group, culture or religious belief to apply and enter the service.

The vast majority of branches and specialisations are open to both male and female entrants. There are exciting and rewarding career opportunities available for young people of all academic abilities, qualification levels and vocational interests.

The Director of Naval Recruiting (DNR) at Portsmouth manages all recruiting of personnel into the Royal Navy and Royal Marines (excluding the recruitment of chaplains which is handled by the Chaplain of the Fleet), and in doing so recruits young people into a number of Officer and Rating/Other Rank specialisations.

In attracting potential recruits, emphasis is placed on modern marketing and advertising practices. This is accomplished by multi-media campaigns, the Royal Navy internet site (www.royalnavy.mod.uk) and visits by recruiting specialists to schools, universities, careers fairs, exhibitions and community centres to meet young people and enable them to learn about the wide range of career opportunities.

The counselling of those interested in pursuing a career is the responsibility of a network of Armed Forces Careers Offices and Officer Careers Liaison Centres, maintained nationwide and all staffed by specialist Royal Navy recruiting staff.

The offices provide a focal point for interested potential recruits to meet recruiting staff, learn more about their options and progress their interest. The potential entrant may then make a formal application to join the service.

Rigorous selection procedures are in force, owing to the technical and often physically demanding nature of employment within the Royal Navy and Royal Marines. The various branches and specialisations each have their own entry requirements.

Applicants must undergo psychometric testing, interviews and a medical examination before they can be formally accepted. They will also be subjected to a security check. There are many different regulations for entry, all of which must be administered by expert personnel.

All entrants must have basic standards of literacy and numeracy, and must be physically fit and able to cope with the rigours of training and service in a variety of operational environments. ■

Careers: How to put yourself in the picture

For information on careers in the Royal Navy or Royal Marines, including detailed information on the current regulations, visit the Royal Navy's website at **www.royalnavy.mod.uk** or telephone **08456 075555**. Those who already wish to pursue the idea of a career in the RN or RM should contact their local Armed Forces Careers Office, listed under 'Armed Services' in the Yellow Pages, and ask to speak to a Naval Careers Adviser. ■

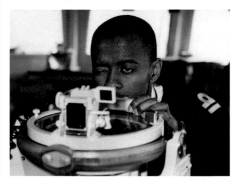

Careers in the Royal Fleet Auxiliary

The Royal Fleet Auxiliary is a civilian organisation, and its way of life aligns more closely with that of the Merchant Navy than the Royal Navy. Entry can be as a rating or an officer, and there are varied career paths available to each:

- The Deck specialisation covers such disciplines as navigation, watchkeeping, replenishment at sea and ship husbandry. Owing to the nature of RFA work, Deck Officers will learn a good deal about maritime operations and warfare.
- Engineering employs both officers and ratings in both the Marine and Systems Engineering specialisations.

The former concentrates on such equipment as the ship's propulsion, the latter on electrical and electronic systems.

- Ratings may specialise in Communications, an area of ever-increasing importance. Modern naval operations necessitate the transfer of enormous amounts of data.
- Underpinning everything else is the Supply specialisation. The officers and ratings are responsible for all the vital onboard administration and manpower issues.

The employment package offered by the RFA is an attractive one, with a competitive salary, pension scheme and a leave entitlement which stands currently at 80 days (officers) and 55 days (ratings) after each four-month sea appointment.

To find out more contact:

The Recruitment Officer
RFA Flotilla, Room F4
Lancelot Building, Postal Point 29
HM Naval Base Portsmouth
PO1 3NH

Tel: 023 9272 6023
e-mail rfarecruit@gtnet.gov.uk
or visit www.rfa.mod.uk

A Sea King Mk4 helicopter lowers stores onto an RFA vessel's flightdeck.

MoD Abbey Wood, near Bristol, is home to the Defence Procurement Agency and Warship Support Agency

Civil Service Careers in the MoD

Whether involved in combat, peacekeeping duties or the provision of humanitarian aid following natural disasters, the Armed Forces depend on the support and expertise of civilian staff.

The MoD looks for special individuals in every role and discipline: people who are eager to gain multiple skills and use them in a truly diverse environment. In return, you'll find tremendous scope for professional and personal development, and training opportunities that are hard to match.

If you want more than just a job and the opportunity of high quality training and development then look at some of our recruitment schemes.

- The Management Recruitment Scheme, for example, is open to everyone with at least 2 A-levels and 5 GCSEs/O-levels or equivalent. These are the support areas within the MoD, and include everything from Finance to Personnel.
- The Engineering and Science Graduate Development Programme is open to recent science and engineering graduates, while the Engineering Sponsorship Schemes offers development whilst at university for engineering students.
- The Civil Service Fast Stream – the MoD takes up to 30 graduates each year from all backgrounds and degree subjects.

Whatever your mode of entry into the MoD, you will find that every single person in the organisation is given comprehensive and wide-ranging training and development, including the opportunity to develop cross-disciplines. The MoD is committed to the Investors in People Standard, which involves full training to meet business objectives.

It is entirely possible to change career direction if you want to whilst still retaining your status and similar conditions of employment – including pension and annual leave allowance.

An example would be engineers moving into personnel or accountancy, and administrators becoming graphic designers or logisticians. For example, just some of the career paths you can choose to move into are: commercial officers; planners; finance and budget; linguists; statisticians; medical staff; management consultants; accountants; surveyors; photographers; vets; trainers; logisticians and commodity managers; human resources; policy and secretariat; and information systems.

The MoD has numerous locations throughout the UK where departments are based, for example the Defence Procurement Agency in Bristol, as well as the MoD Centre in London.

The MoD is an Equal Opportunities employer aiming for the widest possible diversity in its workforce and drawing recruits from every part of the community. However, we particularly welcome applications from ethnic minority people, women and people with disabilities who are currently under-represented in the MoD. Posts within the MOD fall into two categories regarding nationality: Reserved – UK nationals; Non reserved – UK nationals, Irish nationals, Commonwealth citizens, EEA nationals and certain non-EEA family members.

The MoD is part of the Civil Service and appointments must be made on merit on the basis of fair and open competition. These values underpin our recruitment processes.

The Civil Service runs an occupational pension scheme on its employees' behalf. The new pension scheme requires employees to pay small contributions to their pension scheme of 1.5% of their pensionable earnings. There are 25 days annual holiday plus ten days of privilege and public holiday a year. After a certain length of service the level of annual holiday rises to 30 days. For further information please see the MoD recruitment site at www.jobs.mod.uk. ■

Glossary

AAW	Anti-Air Warfare
ADAWS	Action Data Automation Weapons System
ALSL	Alternative Landing Ship Logistic
AH	Attack Helicopter
AIM9L	Sidewinder SRAAM
AMRAAM	Advanced Medium Range Air-to-Air Missile
ARBS	Angle Rate Bombing System
ASAC	Airborne Surveillance and Control
ASM	Air-to-Surface/Anti-Ship Missile
ASRAAM	Advanced Short Range Air-to-Air Missile
ASW	Anti-Submarine Warfare
CACS	Computer Assisted Command System
CAAIS	Computer Assisted Action Information System
CMS	Combat Management System
CIWS	Close-in Weapons System
CFH	Commando Force Helicopter
CGRM	Commandant General Royal Marines
CODLAG	Combined Diesel Electric and Gas
COGAG	Combined Gas and Gas (power-plant)
COGOG	Combined Gas or Gas (powerplant)
CVF	Future Aircraft Carrier
CVS	Aircraft Carrier
DCB	Submarine Command System
DCG	Submarine Command System
DD	Destroyer
DDG	Destroyer (with guided missiles)

DLF3	Decoy System
DLK	Decoy System
DLO	Defence Logistics Organisation
DMT	Dual Mode Tracker
DPA	Defence Procurement Agency
ESM	Electronic Support Measures
EW	Electronic Warfare
FJCA	Future Joint Combat Aircraft
FLIR	Forward Looking Infra Red
FOPV	Future Offshore Patrol Vessel
FFG	Frigate (with guided missiles)
FF	Frigate
GOCO	Government Owned, Contractor Operated
HAS	Helicopter Anti-Submarine
HM	Helicopter Maritime
HC	Helicopter Cargo
HF	High Frequency
ISD	In Service Date
IEP	Integrated Electric Propulsion
IFEP	Integrated Full Electric Propulsion
JFH	Joint Force Harrier
JHC	Joint Helicopter Command
JSF	Joint Strike Fighter
kts	knots (nm/h)
LCU	Landing Craft Utility
LCVP	Landing Craft Vehicle & Personnel
LGB	Laser-Guided Bomb
LPDR	Landing Platform Dock (Replacement)
LPH	Landing Platform Helicopter
LSD(A)	Landing Ship Dock (Auxiliary)
MAD	Magnetic Anomaly Detector

MCM	Mine Counter Measures
MRA	Maritime Reconnaissance & Attack
MR	Maritime Reconnaissance
mw	megawatts
NATO	North Atlantic Treaty Organisation
NAUTIS	Command System
nm	nautical miles
OPV	Offshore Patrol Vessel
PAAMS	Principal Anti-Air Missile System
PWR	Pressurised Water Reactor
RAS	Replenishment at Sea
RA	Royal Artillery
RE	Royal Engineers
RFA	Royal Fleet Auxiliary
RM	Royal Marines
RMAS	Royal Maritime Auxiliary Service
Ro-Ro	Roll-on/Roll-off
SAR	Search And Rescue
SATCOM	Satellite Communications
SDR	Strategic Defence Review
SMCS	Submarine Command System
SCAD	Submarine Acoustic Decoy
SSBN	Nuclear-powered strategic submarine
SSN	Nuclear-powered attack submarine
STOVL	Short Take-Off & Vertical Landing
SQN	Squadron
TIALD	Thermal Imaging and Laser Designation
UAP	Electronic Support Measures
UAR	Electronic Support Measures
UAT	Electronic Support Measures
URNU	University Royal Naval Units
VDS	Variable Depth Sonar

RN, RFA & Marine Services Pennant Numbers

PORTSMOUTH FLOTILLA

Aircraft Carriers
Invincible	R05
Illustrious	R06
Ark Royal	R07

Antarctic Patrol Ship
Endurance	A171

Type 45 Destroyers
Daring*	D32
Dauntless*	D33
Diamond*	D34
Dragon*	D35
Defender*	D36
Duncan*	D37

Type 42 Destroyers
Newcastle	D87
Glasgow	D88
Exeter	D89
Southampton	D90
Nottingham	D91
Liverpool	D92
Manchester	D95
Gloucester	D96
Edinburgh	D97
York	D98
Cardiff	D108

Type 23 Frigates
Kent	F78
Grafton	F80
St Albans	F83
Lancaster	F229
Marlborough	F233
Iron Duke	F234
Westminster	F237
Richmond	F239

1st MCM Squadron
Ledbury	M30
Chiddingfold	M37
Quorn	M41
Grimsby	M108
Bangor	M109
Shoreham	M112

2nd MCM Squadron
Cattistock	M31
Middleton	M34
Hurworth	M39
Sandown	M101
Walney	M104
Pembroke	M107
Ramsey	M110

Fishery Protection Squadron
Dumbarton Castle	P265
Anglesey	P277
Alderney	P278
Tyne	P281
Severn*	P282

Mersey*	P283
Guernsey	P297
Shetland	P298
Lindisfarne	P300

Falkland Islands Patrol Vessel
Leeds Castle	P258

1st Patrol Boat Squadron
Express	P163
Explorer	P164
Example	P165
Exploit	P176
Archer	P264
Biter	P270
Smiter	P272
Pursuer	P273
Tracker	P274
Raider	P275
Blazer	P279
Dasher	P280
Puncher	P291
Charger	P292

ROYAL FLEET AUXILIARY
Brambleleaf	A81
Bayleaf	A109
Orangeleaf	A110
Oakleaf	A111
Diligence	A132
Argus	A135
Grey Rover	A269
Gold Rover	A271

Black Rover	A273
Fort Rosalie	A385
Fort Austin	A386
Fort Victoria	A387
Fort George	A388
Wave Knight	A389
Wave Ruler	A390
Sir Bedivere	L3004
Sir Galahad	L3005
Largs Bay*	L3006
Lyme Bay*	L3007
Mounts Bay*	L3008
Cardigan Bay*	L3009
Sir Geraint	L3027
Sir Percivale	L3036
Sir Tristram	L3505

DEVONPORT FLOTILLA

Helicopter Carrier
Ocean	L12

Assault Ships
Albion*	L14
Bulwark*	L15

Type 22 Frigates
Cumberland	F85
Campbeltown	F86
Chatham	F87
Sheffield	F96
Cornwall	F99

RN, RFA & Marine Services Pennant Numbers

Type 23 Frigates
Portland	F79
Sutherland	F81
Somerset	F82
Norfolk	F230
Argyll	F231
Monmouth	F235
Montrose	F236
Northumberland	F238

Attack Submarines
Turbulent	S87
Tireless	S88
Torbay	S90
Trenchant	S91
Talent	S92
Triumph	S93
Trafalgar	S107

Surveying Squadron
Gleaner	H86
Echo*	H87
Enterprise*	H88
Roebuck	H130
Scott	H131
NP 1008 (Marine Explorer)	
NP 1016 (Confidante)	

FASLANE FLOTILLA

Strategic Submarines
Vanguard	S28
Victorious	S29
Vigilant	S30
Vengeance	S31

Attack Submarines
Astute*	S20
Ambush*	S21
Artful*	S22
Sceptre	S104
Spartan	S105
Splendid	S106
Sovereign	S108
Superb	S109

3rd MCM Squadron
Brecon	M29
Cottesmore	M32
Brocklesby	M33
Dulverton	M35
Atherstone	M38
Inverness	M102
Bridport	M105
Penzance	M106
Blyth	M111

GIBRALTAR SQUADRON
Ranger	P293
Trumpeter	P294

TRAINING SHIP
Bristol (disarmed)	D23

MARINE SERVICES
Melton	A83
Menai	A84
Meon	A87
Dalmatian	A129
Tornado	A140
Tormentor	A142
Waterman	A146
Frances	A147
Florence	A149
Genevieve	A150
Kitty	A170
Lesley	A172
Husky	A178
Saluki	A182
Salmoor	A185
Salmaid	A187
Setter	A189
Joan	A190
Bovisand	A191
Cawsand	A192
Helen	A198
Myrtle	A199
Spaniel	A201
Norah	A205
Forceful	A221
Nimble	A222
Powerful	A223
Adept	A224
Bustler	A225
Capable	A226
Careful	A227
Faithful	A228
Col.Templer	A229
Dexterous	A231
Adamant	A232
Sheepdog	A250
Ladybird	A253
Newhaven	A280
Nutbourne	A281
Netley	A282
Oban	A283
Oransay	A284
Omagh	A285
Padstow	A286
Impulse	A344
Impetus	A345
Newton	A367
Warden	A368
Kinterbury	A378
Oilpress	Y21
Moorhen	Y32
Moorfowl	Y33

Ships of the Royal Fleet Auxiliary do not have home ports and operate across all Naval Bases

* Denotes a ship on order and not yet in service

Index

Index

The Royal Navy Handbook

The Definitive MoD Guide

CONWAY MARITIME PRESS

MINISTRY OF DEFENCE